D0187021

The author of more than fifty books, with over 15 million copies in print, Arthur C. Clarke is one of the most distinguished figures in modern science and science fiction. He is the inventor of the concept of the communications satellite, a past Chairman of the British Interplanetary Society and a member of the Academy of Astronomics.

In 1969, he shared an Oscar nomination with Stanley Kubrick for *2001: A Space Odyssey*, the ground-breaking science fiction film. He has also covered the missions of Apollo 11, 12 and 15 with Walter Cronkite and NASA's Wally Schirra. In 1968 Mr. Clarke was selected to write the epilogue to the astronauts' own account of the Apollo mission, *First on the Moon*.

Berkley books by Arthur C. Clarke

AGAINST THE FALL OF NIGHT
DOLPHIN ISLAND
THE PROMISE OF SPACE
THE SENTINEL

THE PROMISE OF SPACE

ARTHUR C. CLARKE

BERKLEY BOOKS, NEW YORK

This Berkley book contains the complete
text of the original hardcover edition.
It has been completely reset in a typeface
designed for easy reading, and was printed
from new film.

THE PROMISE OF SPACE

A Berkley Book/published by arrangement with
Harper & Row, Publishers

PRINTING HISTORY
Harper & Row edition/April 1968
Berkley edition/January 1985

All rights reserved.
Copyright © 1968 by Arthur C. Clarke.
This book may not be reproduced in whole or in part,
by mimeograph or any other means, without permission.
For information address: Harper & Row, Publishers, Inc.,
10 East 53rd Street, New York, N.Y. 10022.

ISBN: 0-425-07565-6

A BERKLEY BOOK ® TM 757,375
Berkley Books are published by The Berkley Publishing Group,
200 Madison Avenue, New York, New York 10016.
The name "BERKLEY" and the stylized "B" with design
are trademarks belonging to Berkley Publishing Corporation.
PRINTED IN THE UNITED STATES OF AMERICA

CONTENTS

LIST OF FIGURES

ACKNOWLEDGMENTS

It would be quite impossible to thank all those who have helped me, directly or indirectly, during the preparation of this book, but I would like to express my particular gratitude to the following:

Mrs. Esther C. Goddard

James Webb, NASA Administrator; George Mueller, Associate Administrator for Manned Space Flight; Julian Scheer, Director of Public Affairs; Dr. Eugene M. Emme, NASA Historian; Captain Robert Freitag; Jay Holmes

Dr. Wernher von Braun, Director, Marshall Space Flight Center, Huntsville

Dr. Joseph Charyk, President, Communications Satellite Corporation

Dr. Edward Welsh, Executive Secretary, National Aeronautics and Space Council

Frederick C. Durant III, Assistant Director (Astronautics), Smithsonian Institution/National Air and Space Museum

Ellis Levin, Systems Manager, Lunar Orbiter, Boeing

Dr. Harold Rosen, Philip Rubin, Hughes Aircraft Company, Space Systems Division

A. V. Cleaver, O.B.E., Chief Engineer and Manager, Rocket Department, Rolls-Royce, Ltd.

Michael Watson, Manager, International Programs, Advanced Programs Development, Space Division, North American Rockwell Corporation

And especially Bob and Barbara Silverberg, for their work in checking, collecting illustrations, proofreading, and generally coping with the sordid details.

INTRODUCTION

A generation has now arisen that can hardly remember—and can scarcely credit—the days when anyone who talked seriously about space travel was likely to have his sanity questioned. *That* particular battle has been won, but another, equally important, is still in progress. Although there can be no informed person today who doubts the technical feasibility of manned flight to the Moon and planets, there are many who question its value and argue that everything we need to learn about the Solar System can be gathered by robot probes. Others, while agreeing that lunar and interplanetary expeditions will be of great scientific value, think that our current drive into space has been too much motivated by politics to be altogether healthy and believe that it should proceed with more caution, care, and—above all—economy. Professor J. D. Bernal once remarked that wars are run, not by logic, but by "gusts of emotion." There are many who would apply this phrase to the United States space program, at least in its earlier days.

Some of this criticism is valid; some is itself based on emotion—understandably so, in the case of scientists who may see billions going into space when they cannot get thousands for their own pet projects. However, much is based on a total failure to grasp the long-term implications of space flight. After all the lessons that the history of our age has given us, this failure is inexcusable; and to those who continue to make it, it may be disastrous.

Astronautical enthusiasts are fond of quoting Senator Daniel Webster (1782–1852), who once refused to vote a single

cent to the opening up of the West—as it would always be a
howling wilderness, of no use to anyone except savages. (Los
Angelophobes may consider that he had a point.) Unfortunately, there are still plenty of Daniel Websters around, and
before time disposes of their objections, they can do much
harm. Dr. Frederick Seitz, president of the National Academy
of Science, put the matter very well when he said that our
children will wonder what manner of people we were, that we
ever questioned the value of space exploration.

Every revolutionary idea—in science, politics, art or
whatever—seems to evoke three stages of reaction. They may
be summed up by the phrases: (1) "It's completely impossible—don't waste my time"; (2) "It's possible, but it's not worth
doing"; (3) "I said it was a good idea all along." At the moment,
astronautics is still passing through stage 2; I hope that this
book will smooth the transition into stage 3.

It is now thirty years since my earliest articles on space
flight appeared, and twenty since I began work on my first
book, *Interplanetary Flight* (1950). Though intended for a technical series, its sales encouraged my editor, Jim Reynolds, to
talk me into writing a more popular book for a wider audience.
This was *The Exploration of Space* (1951); as was stated in its
preface it was aimed at "all those who are interested in the
'why' and 'how' of astronautics, yet do not wish to go into
too many scientific details. I believe that there is nothing in
this book that the intelligent layman could not follow; he may
encounter unfamiliar ideas, but that will be owing to the very
nature of the subject, and in this respect he will be no worse
off than many specialists." This description is also, I hope,
true of the present work.

Few combinations of words are more hostility-provoking
than the tiresome phrase "I told you so," but perhaps I may be
allowed a few nostalgic flashbacks from *The Exploration of
Space*. One of the photographs, "Automatic Rocket Surveying
Mars," was described as follows:

The little rocket (the last step of a far larger machine) left the Earth
250 days ago and during that time has been coasting freely, like a
comet, along the path that leads to Mars with the least expenditure of
fuel. . . . Under the guidance of a tiny yet extremely complex electronic

brain, the missile is now surveying the planet at close quarters. A camera is photographing the landscape below, and the resulting pictures are being transmitted to the distant Earth along a narrow radio beam. It is unlikely that true television would be possible, with an apparatus as small as this, over such ranges. The best that could be expected is that still-pictures could be transmitted at intervals of a few minutes. . . .

This missile will certainly look peculiar to anyone who imagines that rockets must be sleek, streamlined projectiles with sharply pointed noses. But such refinements are not only unnecessary but actually wasteful on rockets that are launched in airless space. This reconnaissance missile would be carried inside a much larger rocket on its way up through the Earth's atmosphere, its outrigger arms possibly folded together during this stage, and extended when it had entered space.

With the substitution of "hours" for "minutes," this is almost a precise description of Mariner 4, launched thirteen years later. The vehicles even have a striking family resemblance—though it is not likely that "Automatic Rocket Surveying Mars" ever had the slightest influence on the Jet Propulsion Laboratory designers. A given problem must evoke the same kind of solution from any group of engineers, as from Nature herself; witness the superficially identical sharks, dolphins, and ichthyosaurs.

The layout of this Proto-Mariner was evolved by one of the most active members of the British Interplanetary Society, the late R. A. Smith. Ralph Smith's unusual combination of artistic and technical skills did much to popularize astronautics in the 1940's and 1950's; he was responsible for the main illustrations in *The Exploration of Space*. Particularly impressive now, when compared with the Apollo Lunar Module, is his Lunar-type Spaceship, which is still of considerable historic interest. Based on a design study which first appeared in the January, 1939, issue of the *Journal of the British Interplanetary Society*, it may well be one of the earliest attempts to solve, on a fairly realistic basis, the practical problems of landing on an airless world—and taking off again.

In 1952–53, assisted by his colleague H. E. Ross, R. A. Smith prepared a remarkable series of forty-five drawings that showed the possible development of lunar exploration. Earth satellites, orbital rendezvous, extravehicular activities, robot probes, soft-landers, the first Moon bases, and the establishment of self-sufficient lunar colonies were all featured. These illustrations were published in *The Exploration of the Moon* (1954). Going through this volume again today, I find that seventeen of the forty-five events depicted have already occurred, essentially as we described them; plans for the rest are far advanced. Though this is very satisfactory in one respect, it does demonstrate the rapid rate of obsolescence of books on astronautics: they are likely to date even more swiftly than the hardware.

At the end of 1954 I departed for the Great Barrier Reef of Australia and was roughing it on a remote island when news came of the United States' earth-satellite program—the unfortunately named but ultimately successful Project Vanguard. This resulted in another book (again prodded out of me by Jim Reynolds), *The Making of a Moon* (1957). A hasty revision was required when the first new moon turned out to be made in the Soviet Union.

Two years later, I edited and collected all my shorter essays on astronautics, which were published under the title *The Challenge of the Spaceship* (1959). For completeness I should also mention *Going Into Space* (1953), which, as indicated by the title of the British edition (*The Young Traveller in Space*), was intended for the teen-age audience.

Although the explosive development of astronautics over the last decade has made these books very out of date, they have remained stubbornly in print. *The Exploration of Space* was partially revised in 1959, and *Interplanetary Flight* in 1960, but the prolonged and near-fatal flirtation with the Indian Ocean reported in *The Treasure of the Great Reef* (1964) left me neither time nor energy for the complete rewriting that was really required.

Many events have now combined, or conspired, to focus my main interests once more upon space travel. Perhaps foremost was three years' hard labor with Stanley Kubrick on *2001: A Space Odyssey*, which made me start thinking seriously again about probable developments during the rest of this century. Another was a conducted tour of Cape Kennedy, with NASA Administrator James Webb as guide; yet another was being present at Comsat Headquarters the night Early Bird was launched. I could also mention the cumulative impact of seeing the first live television picture from the Moon—meeting Yuri Gagarin and John Glenn—watching Echo slide through the equatorial skies—walking thoughtfully around the sacked and ruined birthplace of the god Apollo, with Leonid Sedov and Wernher von Braun.

These and similar experiences produced a slight crisis of conscience. The result is this book, which I am optimistic enough to hope will not depreciate technologically by more than a few per cent per annum—and so should still be largely valid through the 1970's. It is an entirely new work and replaces all those mentioned above, though I have not hesitated to quote extensively from them where appropriate (as in Chapter 1).

And now, having done my duty, perhaps I may be allowed to get back to the equally important business of science fiction.

Arthur C. Clarke

Colombo, Ceylon
September, 1967

THE PROMISE
OF SPACE

I. BEGINNINGS

I. IMAGINARY VOYAGES

Come, my friends,
'Tis not too late to seek a newer world.
To sail beyond the sunset, and the baths
Of all the western stars.

TENNYSON—Ulysses

The very conception of interplanetary travel was, of course, impossible until it was realized that there were other planets. That discovery was much later than we, with our scientific background, sometimes imagine. Although Mercury, Venus, Mars, Jupiter, and Saturn have been known from the very earliest times, to the ancients they were simply wandering stars. (The word "planet" means, in fact, "wanderer.") As to what those stars might be, that was a question to which every philosopher gave a different reply. The followers of Pythagoras, in the sixth century B.C., made a shrewd guess at the truth when they taught that the Earth was one of the planets. But this doctrine—so obviously opposed to all the evidence of common sense—was never generally accepted and, indeed, at the time there were few arguments which could be brought forward to support it. To the ancients, therefore, the idea of interplanetary travel, in the literal sense, was not merely fantastic: it was meaningless.

However, although the stars and planets were simply dimensionless points of light, the Sun and Moon were obviously in a different class. Anyone could see that they had appreciable size, and the Moon had markings on its face that might well be interpreted as continents and seas. It was not surprising, therefore, that many of the Greek philosophers—and not only the Pythagoreans—believed that the Moon really was a world. They even made estimates of its size and distance, some of which were not far from the truth. Once this had been done, it was natural to speculate about the Moon's nature and to wonder if it had inhabitants. And it was natural—or so, at least, it seems to us—that men should write stories about traveling to that mysterious and romantic world.

In actual fact, only one writer of ancient times took advantage of this now classic theme. He was Lucian of Samosata, who lived in the second century A.D. The hero of Lucian's inaccurately entitled *True History* was taken to the Moon in a waterspout that caught up his ship when he was sailing beyond the Pillars of Hercules—a region where, as was well known in those days, anything was likely to happen.

In a second book, Lucian's hero went to the Moon quite intentionally, by making a pair of wings, after the fashion of Icarus, and taking off from Mount Olympus. For in Lucian's time, as for many centuries to come, it was not realized that there was a fundamental difference between aero- and astronautics. In A.D. 160 it seemed natural enough to imagine that if one could make a workable pair of wings, they could be used to take one to the Moon.

After Lucian, the theme of space travel was neglected for almost fifteen hundred years. When it was again renewed, it was in a very different intellectual climate. The modern era had begun: the Earth was no longer believed to be the center of the universe. And, above all, the telescope had been invented.

It is hard for us to imagine astronomy as it was in the days when all observations had to be made with the naked eye. We now take the telescope for granted, but it is only three and a half centuries since Galileo pointed his first crude instruments at the stars and learned secrets withheld from all other men since history began. No scientist can ever have gathered so rich a harvest in so short a time. Within a few weeks Galileo had seen the mountains and valleys of the Moon, proving that it was indeed a solid world, and had also discovered that the planets, unlike the stars, showed visible disks. He had found that four tiny points of light revolved around Jupiter as the Moon revolves around the Earth, and the inference was obvious that Jupiter was a world with four satellites as against Earth's one, appearing small only because of its immense distance. This was the first direct revelation of the true scale of the universe: astronomers had calculated the distances of the planets before, but now at last man had an instrument with which he could actually see into the depths of space. From this moment the old medieval conception of the universe, with its picture of concentric crystalline spheres carrying the planets between heaven and Earth, was doomed. The frontiers of space receded to an enormous distance: they are receding from us still.

It is hardly surprising that the first serious story of a journey to the Moon appeared within a generation of Galileo's discoveries. It is, however, a little surprising that it was written by the greatest astronomer of the time, indeed, one of the greatest of all time. Johannes Kepler was the first man to discover the exact laws governing the movements of the planets—the same laws which now govern the movements of spacecraft. During the later years of his life Kepler wrote, but did not publish, his *Somnium*. In this book he transported his hero to the Moon by supernatural means, a retrograde step, one might think, for a scientist. But Kepler lived in an age that still believed in magic, and indeed his own mother had been charged with witchcraft. He undoubtedly employed demonic methods of propulsion because he knew of no natural forces that could undertake the task. Kepler, unlike his predecessor Lucian, knew perfectly well that there was no air between the Earth and the Moon, although he thought that the Moon itself might have an atmosphere and inhabitants. His description of the Moon was the first one to be based on the new knowledge revealed by the telescope, and it had a great influence on all future writers (including H. G. Wells, two and a half centuries later).

Kepler's book was published in 1634. Only four years afterward the first English story of a lunar trip appeared— Bishop Godwin's *Man in the Moone*. Godwin's hero, Domingo Gonsales, flew to the Moon on a flimsy raft towed by trained swans. This feat was really quite accidental, for Gonsales had merely been attempting the conquest of the air, not of space. But he did not know that his swans had the habit, hitherto unrecorded by ornithologists, of migrating to the Moon. His involuntary flight to our satellite occupied twelve days, and he had no difficulty with breathing on the way. However, he did notice the disappearance of weight as he left the Earth, and on reaching the Moon discovered that its pull was much weaker, so that one could jump to great heights. This idea is now quite familiar to us, but Godwin was writing fifty years before Newton discovered the law of gravitation.

The idea of lunar voyages was now becoming popular, and in 1640 Bishop Wilkins published a very important book, *A Discourse Concerning a New World*. This was not fiction, but a serious scientific discussion of the Moon, its physical condition, and the possibility that it might have inhabitants. But Wilkins went further than this, for he concluded that there was no reason why men should not one day invent a means of transport—a "flying chariot," as he called it—which could reach the Moon. He even suggested that colonies might be planted there, a proposal which, needless to say, caused some foreign writers to make rude remarks about British imperialism.

During the next two centuries there was a steady trickle of books about space flight. Some were pure fantasy, but others made at least occasional attempts to be scientific. Undoubtedly the most ingenious writer during this period was Cyrano de Bergerac, author of *Voyages to the Moon and Sun* (1656). To Cyrano must go the credit for first using rocket propulsion, even though he certainly had no idea of its advantages. Still more surprising, he anticipated the ramjet. In his last attempt at interplanetary flight, he evolved a flying machine consisting of a large, light box, built of convex lenses to focus sunlight into its interior. The air, being thus heated, would escape from a nozzle and propel the machine skyward.

Although most of the stories of this era were concerned with voyages to the Moon (and sometimes to the Sun, which was also believed to be a habitable world), some writers' imaginations did go a little further afield. Thus Bernard de Fontenelle, in 1686, wrote a widely read book on popular astronomy, *A Plurality of Worlds*, in which he maintained that all the planets were inhabited by beings who had become suitably adapted to their surroundings. And in 1752 the great Voltaire produced *Micromegas*, a work which is remarkably modern in outlook, as it shows man and his planet in the correct astronomical perspective. Micromegas was a giant from the solar system of Sirius who visited Earth with a companion from Saturn. Like so many works of its kind, before and after, *Micromegas* was used chiefly as a vehicle for satire.

By the dawn of the nineteenth century, however, the space-travel story had run into trouble. Too much was known about the difficulties and objections to interplanetary flight, and science had not yet advanced far enough to suggest how they might be overcome. The invention of the balloon in 1783 had diverted attention to atmospheric travel and had also shown conclusively that men could not live unprotected at great altitudes. The Moon and planets had become much less accessible than they had seemed to bishops Godwin and Wilkins.

By the second half of the century, however, the fiction writers had overcome their momentary embarrassment, and stories of space travel had become both more common and more scientific. No doubt the great engineering achievements of the Victorian age had produced a feeling of optimism: so much had already been accomplished that perhaps even the bridging of space was no longer a totally impossible dream.

This attitude is apparent in Jules Verne's famous story *From the Earth to the Moon* (1865). Although much of it is written facetiously—Verne got a good deal of fun out of caricaturing the go-getting Americans who were so anxious to reach the Moon—this work is important because it was the first to be based on sound scientific principles. Verne did not take the easy way out and invent, as so many writers before and since have done, some mysterious method of propulsion or a substance that would defy gravity. He knew that if a body could be projected away from the Earth at a sufficient speed it would reach the Moon; so he simply built an enormous gun and fired his heroes from it in a specially equipped projectile. All the calculations, times, and velocities for the trip were worked out in detail by Verne's brother-in-law, who was a professor of astronomy, and the projectile itself was described in minute detail. One of its most interesting features was the fact that it was fitted with rockets for steering once it had reached space. Verne understood perfectly well—as many people at a much later date did not—that the rocket could function in an airless void, but he never thought of using it for the whole trip.

It is probable that Verne really believed that his spacegun would work, though we know now that the projectile would have been destroyed by air resistance before it left the barrel. On the other hand, Verne can hardly have imagined that his travelers would have survived the initial concussion, which would have given each of them an apparent weight of several thousand tons. No doubt he passed off this minor point with a light laugh for the sake of the story.

Verne never landed his heroes on the Moon, perhaps because he was unable to think of any way in which they could return safely. Instead, they performed a circumnavigation and then came back to earth—landing in the ocean, as the Mercury and Gemini astronauts were to do exactly one century later.

Many writers have pointed out Verne's prescience in siting his spacegun at Tampa, Florida, barely a hundred miles from Cape Kennedy. But he did even better than this, for after discussing the areas of the United States over which the Moon passed in its orbit, he decided that the two most suitable states for the project were Florida and Texas. So, a century ago, he had their legislatures fighting each other for the privilege (and profit) of running a space program. Echoes of this battle still roll around Congress from time to time.

Finally—and this is almost more uncanny—the 1865 American space effort was managed by the Gun Club of *Baltimore*. It was in Baltimore, between 1955 and 1958, that the hardware for the first United States space project (Vanguard) was built by the Martin Company. But I would not for a moment suggest that the following passage from the very first page of *From the Earth to the Moon* could conceivably apply to any space-oriented activities in Baltimore, still less in Washington:

Now when an American has an idea, he directly seeks a second American to share it. If there be three, they elect a president and two secretaries. Given *four*, they name a keeper of records, and the office is ready for work; *five*, they convene a general meeting, and the club is fully constituted. So things were managed in Baltimore....

Verne's novel was an instantaneous success and has remained in print even to this day. It started a minor avalanche of imitations and probably influenced the American writer Edward Everett Hale a few years later. His short story *The Brick Moon*, published in the *Atlantic Monthly* (1869–70), appears to be the first treatment both in fiction and nonfiction of the artificial satellite.

The Reverend Hale (he later became the first, and doubtless the last, science-fiction writer to be chaplain to the U.S. Senate) proposed the construction of his brick moon for reasons that are surprisingly modern; ninety years afterward, the Transit program was to prove their soundness. He pointed out that a small but clearly visible body revolving around the Earth in a close orbit would be invaluable to navigators. Given tables showing the position of such a second moon at any time, one need only take a simple observation of it with a sextant to determine one's longitude. Hale's idea, to put it crudely, was to hoist the Greenwich meridian into the sky so that anyone could see it and so determine his location on the Earth. The artificial moon would fulfill the same role for the observation of longitude that the Pole Star does for latitude.

Though Hale's treatment of his theme was not altogether serious (much of his story is written with the archly elephantine humor that occasionally jars on most modern readers of *Moby Dick*), he had obviously given a great deal of careful thought to the project. He decided that, in order to be visible through a telescope of modest size, his satellite should be 200 feet in diameter. And since a satellite above the Greenwich meridian would be visible over only a part of the globe, there should be a second moon moving in another orbit—say, one passing over New Orleans, the meridian of which is at right angles to that of Greenwich.

So that it could be seen over a large area, the moon would also have to be at a considerable height, and Hale suggested that an altitude of 4,000 miles would be a reasonable figure. If it were too close, he pointed out, it would spend much of its time eclipsed in the shadow of the Earth.

To be of reasonable weight, the moon would have to be hollow, and Hale proposed that brick would be a better constructional material than iron, because it would withstand the heat of the satellite's friction through the atmosphere. This also shows remarkable foresight, since ceramics of various kinds are now widely used as heat-resistant materials for spacecraft.

The problem of getting the brick moon up into its orbit was one which Hale solved in a very original fashion. His heroes, who were altruistically fired with a desire to save the thousands of seamen who perish every year through errors in navigation, built two enormous vertical flywheels. These revolved, their rims nearly touching, in opposite directions, being brought up to speed over a period of months by water power. When the brick moon was finished, it was to be:

gently rolled down a gigantic groove provided for it, till it lighted on the edge of both wheels at the same instant. Of course it would not rest there, not the ten-thousandth part of a second. It would be snapped upward, as a drop of water from a grindstone. Upward and upward; but the heavier wheel would have deflected it a little from the vertical. Upward and northward it would rise, therefore, till it had passed the axis of the world. It would, of course, feel the world's attraction all the time, which would bend its flight gently, but still it would leave the world more and more behind. . . .

The money to build the brick moon was raised by public subscription, and the flywheels were constructed in a remote part of the United States. The moon itself was not a simple shell of masonry, but had its interior divided into thirteen spherical chambers, in contact with each other so that "by the constant repetition of arches, we should with the least weight unite the greatest strength."

However, things did not go quite according to plan. One night, owing to a ground subsidence, the brick moon was accidentally launched—together with all the workmen and engineers who had decided that its spacious chambers made better living quarters than their log cabins. Yet the story has a happy ending for all concerned (except possibly the subscribers to the enterprise). The thirty-seven men, women, and children in the brick moon had survived their unscheduled launching into space, and having large quantities of food (not to mention a few hens) with them, had managed to establish a contented little community. They were able to signal to their friends on Earth by making long and short jumps off the edge of their tiny world, thus producing messages in Morse code that could be read through a telescope. They had no regrets at all for leaving the Earth, and the moral that the author drew was: "Can it be possible that all human sympathies can thrive, and all human powers be exercised, and all human joys increase, if we live with all our might with the thirty or forty people next to us? . . . Can it be possible that our passion for large cities, and large parties, and large theaters, and large churches, develops no faith nor hope nor love which would not find exercise in a little 'world of our own'?"

Hale's story was published in 1869–70; seven years later, at the Naval Observatory in Washington, Dr. Asaph Hall discovered that Mars had two tiny satellites, one of which revolved around the planet more swiftly than Mars turned on its axis. He wrote to Hale, "The smaller of these moons is the veritable Brick Moon." One wishes that both author and astronomer could have known that just eighty years later Earth was to rival Mars in this respect.

The ubiquitous Jules Verne made a passing reference to artificial satellites in one of his lesser works, *The Begum's Fortune*, published in 1879. This novel also contains a prototype of the mad scientist who haunted (one might say infested) so much early science fiction but who is fortunately now almost extinct.

The story concerns the rivalry between two cities, Stahlstadt and Frankville, the nationalities of which should be obvious. Stahlstadt was ruled by the demoniac Professor Schultz, whose main interest seemed to be the invention of diabolical weapons of war. His masterpiece was a giant multiple cannon with the barrels nesting one inside the other—an anticipation, in some respects, of the step, or multistage, rockets of today.

This cannon was intended to destroy Frankville at one blow, but the professor made one of those extraordinary oversights which characterize his species. (I have yet to encounter a mad scientist who was defeated by the hero's brains rather than his own carelessness.) He had made the cannon *too* powerful, and the shell reached such a velocity that it never came down again but continued to circle the Earth.

In the first year of the twentieth century appeared what

still remains the finest of all interplanetary romances, H. G. Wells's *The First Men in the Moon*. Like many of Wells's early novels, it is untouched by time, as it encapsulates forever one moment in history, the last golden afterglow of the Victorian age. On the purely technical side, however, the book marks a retrogression from Verne, whose spacegun was at least plausible and founded on scientific facts. To get his protagonists to the Moon, Wells invented "Cavorite," a substance that could act as a gravity insulator. His heroes had only to climb into a sphere coated with this useful material and they would travel away into space. To steer themselves toward the Moon it was merely necessary to open a shutter in that direction.

This conception of a gravity-insulating or gravity-defying substance did not originate with Wells, and the first person who seems to have employed it was one J. Atterley, whose *Voyage to the Moon* appeared in 1827. Neither Mr. Atterley nor any of his numerous successors ever explain, so far as we are aware, how their antigravitational metals manage to stay on Earth: one would have thought that materials with such a tendency to levitation would long ago have departed into space.

It is not difficult to show that a substance like Wells's "Cavorite" is a physical impossibility, defying fundamental laws of nature. But the idea of antigravity is not in itself absurd, and we shall return to it in Chapter 24.

Wells's book appeared in 1901, and it would be difficult to count, let alone read, the number of works that have since touched upon the subject of interplanetary flight. There are two very obvious reasons for this increase. In the first case, the conquest of the air had acted as a stimulus to imagination; in the second, the foundations of astronautics were being laid by competent scientists, and the result of their work was slowly filtering through to the general public. The researches of Goddard (from 1914 onward) and later of Oberth had focused attention on the rocket, and even before the modern era of large-scale experimental work had proved the accuracy of these men's predictions, the rocket had been accepted as the motive power for spaceships in the majority of stories of interplanetary travel. It can hardly be doubted that these stories—and not merely those few with a carefully scientific basis—have done a great deal to bring closer the achievement of which they told.

When one considers it dispassionately, it is a somewhat extraordinary situation. Even the literature of flight, which provides the closer parallel, is not nearly so extensive or so carefully worked out. The conquest of space must obviously have a fundamental appeal to human emotions for it to be so persistent a theme over such a span of time.

It is sometimes argued, by people who can know very little about either science or science fiction, that the actual achievement of space travel will mean the end of romances about the subject. The reverse is more likely to be the case. True, "first-voyage-to-the-Moon" stories have graduated from fiction to news; but the farther our frontier extends into space, the greater the area of contact with the unknown. When we land on the Moon and *really* learn something about that strange and, it now seems, exciting little world, there will be splendid opportunities for stories about its remote past and its probable future; and the planets, of course, will remain as a playground of the imagination for decades to come. The space-travel tales of the twenty-first century will have the same hard core of realism that makes Wells and Verne so much more satisfying than their unscientific predecessors. The more we really know, the greater is the scope for fiction; only feeble minds are paralyzed by facts.

A little late in the day, scholars are now beginning to study the interactions between science and literature; in her book *Science and Imagination*, for example, Marjorie Hope Nicolson has pointed out the tremendous impact made upon art and general culture by the inventions of the telescope and the microscope. This is a theme to which we shall return in Chapter 30, when the philosophical and cultural effects of astronautics will be discussed.

It is surely only a matter of time before artists, writers, and musicians express their reactions to man's newest conquest of his environment. From the exploration of space has already come such a flood of knowledge as the world has never before seen. But that is not enough, for without feeling and emotion, knowledge alone is no more than a weariness of the soul.

2. FROM FANTASY TO SCIENCE

All men dream; but not equally. Those who dream by night in the dusty recesses of their minds wake in the day to find that it was vanity; but the dreamers of the day are dangerous men, for they may act their dreams with open eyes, to make it possible.

T. E. LAWRENCE—*The Seven Pillars of Wisdom*

There was a time, just before Sputnik I, when Soviet claims to priority in any field of science or invention were treated with amused skepticism. Sometimes this was justified; but in the case of astronautics, there can be no doubt that credit for first working out the scientific principles of space flight goes to Konstantin Tsiolkovsky. His pioneering mathematical papers on the subject were written in the 1880's and were first published in 1903, the very year in which the Wright brothers flew.

Tsiolkovsky was a shy, deaf schoolteacher—although, as in the case of that other inventor Thomas Edison, his deafness was probably far from being a complete disadvantage. He was born in September, 1857, and it is no coincidence that the Soviet Union launched its first satellite within a few days of his centenary.

At the age of fourteen Tsiolkovsky became interested in aviation and conceived the then-daring idea of the all-metal dirigible. This led him on to thoughts of space flight, and to quote his own words: 'There was a moment when it appeared to me that I had solved this problem [at sixteen]. I was so excited that I could not sleep the whole night, and instead spent

14

it wandering through the streets of Moscow and thinking about the great consequences of my discovery. Toward morning, I was convinced of the fallacy of my invention. I still remember that night, and even now, fifty years later, I sometimes dream about rising in my machine toward the stars and feeling the same elation."

The sixteen-year-old Tsiolkovsky's mistake lay in thinking that one could use centrifugal force for propulsion. As we shall see later, this is a common error and crops up, even today, among the perpetual-motion-machine fraternity. He quickly set himself on the right track and realized that the rocket was the only means of providing thrust in the vacuum of space.

By 1898 he had derived the fundamental laws of rocket propulsion (see Chapter 7). He was the first man in history to understand the true scale of the problem involved in escaping from Earth.

Working under great difficulties, with pitifully meager resources, Tsiolkovsky calculated, made models in his little workshop, and wrote numerous popular and technical articles advocating his ideas. Not only were most of these soundly based; they were also so astonishingly ahead of their time that even now we are still catching up with him. To quote from Academician M. E. Tikhonravov's preface to the collected works (Moscow, 1964): "Tsiolkovsky dreamed of sending mankind to the entire solar system; he dreamed of the possibility of a total realization of solar energy; he dreamed of a more comfortable life in a medium without gravity and of cities in interplanetary space."

Besides anticipating and solving in principle almost all the engineering difficulties of space flight, Tsiolkovsky also applied himself to the biological problems. He discussed immersing astronauts in water to reduce the effects of acceleration at takeoff; he designed centrifugal showers so that they could bathe in the absence of gravity; he considered growing plants in cosmic "greenhouses" to purify the air and to provide food; he looked into the design of space suits. Most of these concepts are now so familiar to us that it is hard to realize that someone first had to invent them; that someone was usually Tsiolkovsky.

In his attempt to spread his ideas as widely as possible, Tsiolkovsky wrote several works of science fiction, with such titles as "The Year 2000" and "The Conquest of the Solar System." Most of these were never published (or indeed completed); an exception is the naïve but fascinating novel *Beyond the Planet Earth*, which first appeared in 1918. Many years later, in 1933, Tsiolkovsky became involved in a Soviet motion picture, *Cosmic Voyage*, and made numerous drawings for it, but nothing came of the project. He was perhaps luckier than Hermann Oberth, whose experience five years earlier with the Fritz Lang-UFA movie *The Girl in the Moon* was far from happy.

Tsiolkovsky's work was little known outside his own country until it was discovered by the rest of the world in the 1930's. It is greatly to the credit of the struggling new Soviet state that, after the revolution, he received support and modest acclaim; when he died in 1935, his home town, Kaluga, gave him a lavish state funeral and erected an impressive monument in his honor.

His greatest monument, however, is one that appropriately enough had never been seen by human eyes before it was discovered by Luna 3 on the far side of the Moon. It is the giant crater, one of the most extraordinary of all lunar formations, that now bears his name. This astronomical immortality would, one feels, have left Tsiolkovsky pleased, surprised, and more than a little embarrassed.

The second pioneer, in order of time, was the New England physics professor Robert Hutchings Goddard, born in Worcester, Massachusetts, in 1882. As a boy, Goddard had his imagination fired by the stories of Verne and Wells. In his autobiography, he recalls an incident at the age of seventeen that bears a striking resemblance to Tsiolkovsky's moment of revelation; even the basic error was the same:

On the afternoon of October 19, 1899, I climbed a tall cherry tree at the back of the barn and, armed with a saw and a hatchet, started to trim the dead leaves from the tree. It was one of those quiet, colorful afternoons of sheer beauty which we have in October in New England and, as I looked toward the fields to the east, I imagined how wonderful it would be to make some device which had even the *possibility* of ascending to Mars, and how it would look on a small scale if sent up from the meadow at my feet.

It seemed to me then that a weight, whirling around a horizontal shaft and moving more rapidly above than below, could furnish lift by virtue of the greater centrifugal force at the top of the path. In any event, I was a different boy when I descended the ladder. Life now had a purpose for me. Later in the year, I started making wooden models in which lead weights were to furnish lift by moving back and forth in vertical arcs, or strike against metal pieces as they whirled around horizontal arcs. These naturally gave negative results, and I began to think that there might be something after all to Newton's Laws. . . .

Goddard realized that if he hoped to make any progress, he would have to master physics and mathematics. This he did to such effect that he obtained his Ph.D. at Clark University, Worcester, where he was also to spend all his academic career. By 1909 he had worked out the theory of the multistage (step) rocket, and in a series of more than two hundred patents from 1914 onward he covered almost every conceivable aspect of rocket design, propulsion, and guidance.

Unlike Tsiolkovsky, Goddard had the resources to do a considerable—for that time—amount of experimenting. By 1916 he had demonstrated that his theories were sound and had shown by actual tests that rockets gave a *greater* thrust in vacuum than in air. (There had never been any theoretical doubt of this, but even at a much later date skeptics still refused to believe it.)

Goddard's eyes were clearly focused on the Moon and planets; in his private notebooks he discussed refueling spacecraft from hydrogen and oxygen produced on the Moon, electrical propulsion, atomic power, reconnaissance of the planets by automatic cameras, and similar highly advanced ideas. But he was also a cautious and practical man, and when the time came to draw up a prospectus of his future plans he concentrated on a discussion of atmospheric sounding rockets, which he gave the innocuous title *A Method of Reaching Extreme Altitudes*. Not until the last few paragraphs would the intrepid reader learn that "extreme" could mean "infinite."

This manuscript secured a grant of $5,000 from the Smithsonian Institution, which published it in 1920. Goddard was thus able to increase the scope of his experiments, and on March 16, 1926, he flew the world's first liquid-rocket-propelled vehicle in a field near Auburn, Massachusetts. This flimsy contraption was airborne for just over two seconds, reached an altitude of 40 feet and a speed of 60 mph, and was the direct ancestor of all the giants of today.

In 1929 a successful flight by a somewhat larger rocket, whose peak altitude was no less than 90 feet, caused so much noise that the whole neighborhood was disturbed, and the police were deluged by reports of crashing airplanes. Goddard was forbidden to conduct any more flights at Worcester, but this temporary setback proved to be a blessing in disguise. The resulting publicity came to the attention of Charles Lindbergh, then at the height of his fame. The aviator visited Goddard, discussed his work, and immediately realized its importance. He recommended support for it from the Guggenheim Fund for the Promotion of Aeronautics, which subsequently arranged a grant of $50,000.

Now, for the first time, Goddard was able to devote himself entirely to rocketry. He established a workshop and launching tower near Roswell, New Mexico, not far from the White Sands Proving Ground, where, less than a year after his death, the first Americanized V-2's were to roar into the sky.

At Roswell, with the aid of his wife, Esther, and a handful of assistants, Goddard built, tested, and flew a whole series of increasingly advanced rockets between 1930 and 1941. Although the greatest height reached was only 9,000 feet, they represented an astounding achievement. When one looks at the Goddard exhibit in the National Aerospace Museum, Washington, it is almost impossible to believe that a single man should have attempted to develop such complex systems. Today's rocket designers have thousands of subcontractors who can deliver practically any component straight off the shelf; Goddard had to build almost everything in his own workshop.

Little wonder that to the outside world his progress seemed agonizingly slow and that he was sometimes criticized by other rocket enthusiasts for not publishing or exchanging information. Any such exchange would have been rather a one-way business, and Goddard's reticence was increased by garbled and often facetious press coverage. (Once you have announced that it is possible to reach the Moon, of course, everything you launch is a "failure" if it doesn't get there.) Moreover, his long series of patents proves that he knew exactly what he was doing; after his death Mrs. Goddard (who had acted as his photographer, secretary, and archivist) and the Guggenheim Foundation were jointly awarded $1 million by the Department of Defense for their use—the largest patent settlement on record.

It has often been suggested that Goddard would have made more rapid progress, and history might also have been changed, if he had received more money or technical assistance. Mrs. Goddard does not think that this would have made a great deal of difference; additional funds might have helped, but on the whole, except for two years lost during the Depression, the grants Goddard received were adequate for his scale of operation. She once remarked to me that a *really* large sum of money would have swamped their little team; Dr. Goddard would have spent all his time dealing with accounts, preparing budgets, hiring and firing, answering auditors' queries, testifying before Congress. . . . By avoiding all this, he was a lucky man—and a happy one.

Moreover, like most pioneers, Goddard was a "loner." Though he was witty and cultured and enjoyed social life, in his creative work he was, like Newton, "sailing strange seas of thought—alone."

One well-known American rocketeer who volunteered his assistance did not get very far. I have received piquant accounts, from both surviving principals, of a visit to Roswell by an enthusiastic young aeronautical engineer in 1936. The Goddards, he says, received him cordially, but never once were the dust sheets removed from the large, torpedo-shaped object that lay in full view of his vainly goggling eyes.

After Goddard's death, on August 10, 1945 (he lived just long enough to examine, in a captured V-2, the large-scale realization of his concepts) the range of his vision was slowly appreciated. Today innumerable institutions, awards, banquets, and other functions bear his name. There is the Goddard Space Flight Center near Washington, the Goddard Medal of the American Institute of Aeronautics and Astronautics, the annual Goddard Symposium of the American Astronautical Association, and even Goddard Day (March 16).* At Clark University, where he spent so many years as student, graduate, and pro-

---

*It is ironic to note that the first Goddard Professor of the California Institute of Technology, the brilliant Hsue-Shen Tsien, is now in charge of the *Chinese* rocket program. For an account of the almost incredible events in the McCarthy Era which led to this disaster, see "The Bitter Tea of Dr. Tsien," *Esquire Magazine*, September, 1967.

fessor, a splendid Goddard Memorial Library has been established, thanks to a fund-raising drive sponsored by one of his
greatest admirers, Dr. Wernher von Braun. It was also Dr. von
Braun who started the successful agitation to have a stone
marker placed at the site of the first liquid-fuel rocket launch.

And one day, it can hardly be doubted, Robert Hutchings
Goddard's name will join Tsiolkovsky's on the far side of the
Moon.

While Goddard was preparing his first Smithsonian paper,
a young German-Hungarian student named Hermann Oberth
was also thinking of space travel. Quite independently of his
two precursors, he had covered much the same ground; he had
even fallen into the identical "centrifugal-drive" trap that seems
to lurk in ambush for amateur astronauts. ("Every year," Oberth
has since reported, "I am approached by eight or ten inventors
with what amounts to the same scheme." And not long ago,
the editor of a leading American science-fiction magazine, who
should have known better, gave publicity to a similar proposal.)

It was Jules Verne's Moon novel that set Oberth thinking
about rockets, at first as a means of steering in space. However,
he slowly realized that they could perform the whole mission,
not merely the minor job of course correction. "I should tell a
lie," Oberth has written, "in stating that I was delighted with
this discovery. I was not pleased at all with the enormous fuel
consumption, the hazards of rockets containing solid fuels, the
difficulty of handling liquid fuels, etc."

Realizing that practical experiments were far beyond the
means of a young mathematics teacher, Oberth concentrated
on theoretical studies. By 1923 he had derived the basic equations of rocket flight and had a very clear idea of the speed,
fuel requirements, and general engineering principles of spacecraft capable of traveling beyond the atmosphere.

At his own expense, he published his results in a slim
brochure entitled "The Rocket Into Planetary Space" (1923);
he was quite unaware, then, that Tsiolkovsky had covered much
of the same ground twenty years before. (Later, the two men
exchanged friendly greetings and copies of their publications.)
The scientific establishment, as might be expected, ignored
Oberth's work almost completely. Those few academicians
who deigned to notice it could find no flaws in the calculations,

but that did not deter them from pronouncing them "obviously" absurd.

Despite this, Oberth's views attracted a great deal of attention in the defeated and impoverished Germany of the 1920's; the psychological reasons for this (escapism?) might be worth investigating. His views were widely popularized by a number of young science writers, notably Willy Ley, and in 1929 he expanded them into a formidable volume entitled *Wege zur Raumschiffahrt* (*The Road to Space Travel*).

After a brief discussion of automatic rockets, Oberth quickly got on to the subject of manned vehicles, and in particular, "space stations" in orbit around the Earth. Among their uses he considered meteorological observations, military reconnaissance, the mapping of unexplored places, iceberg warnings (the *Titanic* disaster, which Oberth specifically mentions, was still fresh in mind), and the establishment of communications (by heliograph!) between isolated spots on the Earth.

Perhaps most important of all, Oberth pointed out the enormous value of space stations as refueling bases for interplanetary expeditions. His most imaginative suggestion, however, was the proposal that huge mirrors be constructed in space to reflect sunlight to the Earth. Owing to the weightless conditions that prevail in free orbit, it would be possible to build mirrors literally miles in diameter from quite modest amounts of material. Such reflectors could produce alterations in the intensity of sunlight over large areas of the Earth, thus preventing frosts, controlling winds, and making the polar regions habitable. (Another use was proposed forty years later. In 1966 the U.S. Department of Defense asked five aerospace companies to look into the question of orbital mirrors for tactical military purposes—specifically, for illuminating the jungles of Vietnam at night.)

All this was very exciting, and in 1925 Oberth's ideas led directly to the founding, by a group of young German enthusiasts, of the Verein für Raumschiffahrt (literally, "Society for Spaceship Travel," though it is usually referred to as the German Rocket Society). The vicissitudes of this organization, and Oberth's tragicomic entanglement with the UFA movie company's *The Girl in the Moon*, have been well documented in Willy Ley's standard history, *Rockets, Missiles, and Space Travel*.

Before time ran out, and the Nazis marched in, the VfR had succeeded in launching several types of small liquid-propelled rockets and recovering them by parachute. There was nothing here that Goddard had not already done, but his work was still virtually unknown, whereas the German experiments were conducted in a blaze of publicity. The impecunious rocketeers cannot be blamed for this; it was the only way they could raise money.

Not surprisingly, their work also attracted the attention of the German Army, then looking for weapons that were not banned under the Treaty of Versailles. When that document was drawn up, no one had taken rockets seriously, an error which was to be repeated many times in the decades ahead. As an unfortunate but perhaps inevitable consequence, man's first steps into space were taken under military sponsorship. Not until the Saturn 1's and 5's of the 1960's were any really large rockets developed for purely peaceful objectives; and even here the underlying motivation was not entirely scientific.

Of the three "classical" writers on astronautics, only Hermann Oberth lived to see the full attainment of his dreams. But as he was primarily a theoretician, and not a practical engineer, he had to watch others turn them into reality. Although he eventually joined the Peenemünde staff, the V-2 had already been developed by the time he was able to obtain his security clearance. Then, to make the irony complete, he was set to work on solid-propellant anti-aircraft rockets.

In 1955 he came to the United States to join the Redstone group but was able to stay only a few years before he had to return to Germany in order to claim his teacher's pension. He then went to live in retirement near Nuremberg, but from time to time he emerges in somewhat dubious political company.

I last glimpsed this strange and brilliant man in circumstances that neatly summed up the frustrations of his life. He was one of a crowd of visitors being conducted through the great space center that now bears the name of Robert Hutchings Goddard. None of the young scientists who were acting as guides recognized him; I wondered how many of them even knew his name.

3. "NOTHING TO PUSH AGAINST"

There was a time, not very long ago, when any writer or lecturer on space flight had to devote a good deal of effort to convincing his audience that rockets *could* provide thrust in the vacuum of space, where, obviously, there is "nothing to push against." This infuriating phrase—so true, yet so misleading—is seldom heard now that the capabilities of rockets in space have been amply demonstrated. Nevertheless, most people would probably find it very hard to explain how a rocket does manage to function in a medium where all other forms of propulsion are useless.

It is no answer to say glibly, as do some writers, that the rocket operates by "pure reaction." *Every* form of propulsion does that; it is impossible to conceive, even by the wildest flight of imagination, of one that does not.

A *re*action is simply an opposing thrust or force. When a man walks, the friction between his feet and the ground makes the Earth move backward, ever so slightly. If there were no reaction—if, for example, he were standing on a sheet of completely frictionless ice—there could be no movement.

So it is with automobiles, ships, and aircraft. They all react, through tires, screws, or propellers, on the medium that supports them. This fact was first clearly recognized by Sir Isaac Newton and embodied in his third law of motion—"To every action there is an equal and opposite reaction"—a statement of such deceptive simplicity that it may seem self-evident.

This equality of action and reaction is universally true, but in most of the cases in everyday life we are aware of only the action; the reaction is unobservable. Why this is so is obvious when one considers the case of a man jumping. He imparts an equal reaction to the Earth; but as the mass of the Earth is about 100 sextillion (100,000,000,000,000,000,000,000) times greater than his, the velocity he gives to it is smaller in exactly the same ratio. Only in rather exceptional or dramatic cases is the reaction obvious; the most familiar example is the recoil produced by the firing of a gun. But whether it is obvious or concealed, the reaction is always there, and no movement of any kind is possible without it.

We can best visualize the mode of operation of a rocket by considering what Einstein used to call a "thought experiment," an experiment which no one would actually perform but which illustrates some principle. Imagine a man on a light sled, which also carries a large pile of bricks, and assume that the sled is resting on a sheet of smooth, absolutely frictionless ice.

The man takes one of the bricks and throws it horizontally. Newton's third law (and common sense, which is not *always* wrong) tells us that the action of throwing the brick produces an equal reaction on the sled. But because the sled (plus cargo) weighs much more than the brick, it moves off at a correspondingly smaller velocity. Again, there would be an exact proportionality. If the vehicle's weight was a hundred times that of the brick, it would move at one-*hundredth* of its velocity.

However, this velocity would not be lost, since we have assumed that the ice is completely frictionless. Even if the sled's acquired speed were only a few inches a minute, it would retain this speed indefinitely. (We are also, of course, assuming that there is no air resistance.)

Now the passenger throws away another brick, at exactly the same velocity as before. The speed of the sled at once jumps again, but by a fractionally greater amount this time, for it is now a little lighter owing to the loss of the first brick. And as more and more bricks are thrown overboard, it will continue to gain speed, each time by a slightly greater amount as its mass diminishes.

We can learn several important lessons from this simple analogy; in fact, it teaches almost everything that is necessary to know about rocket propulsion.

First of all, it is obvious that what happens to the bricks after they have left the sled does not matter in the least; all the recoil or thrust is produced during the act of throwing. The

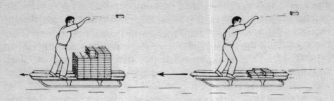

Figure 1. The rocket principle.

bricks could sail on forever or could crash into a wall six inches away—it would make no difference to the sled. The method of propulsion is, therefore, *independent of any external medium*.

As the bricks are used up, so the weight of the vehicle steadily diminishes. (To forestall objections from purists: the words "weight" and "mass" are used interchangeably here, as there is no need to make the distinctions that will be necessary later.) The last bricks will, therefore, produce much greater effect than the first; and the difference can be very large if the mass of the sled has been substantially reduced. If the "empty" weight of the sled is only half that of its full weight, the very last brick will produce twice the gain in speed of the first one. Consequently, not only does the sled's *velocity* increase during the experiment, its *acceleration* does as well.

The analogy with the rocket should now be clear, the main difference between the two cases being that a rocket ejects matter continuously and not in separate lumps, so that it produces a steady thrust instead of a series of jerks. If the man on the sled were pumping water out of a nozzle, the analogy would be exact.

Thus it is possible to have a completely self-contained propulsion system that can operate in a vacuum. Yet, though the logic is impeccable, for a long time even highly qualified engineers and scientists remained unconvinced. They felt in their bones—and some readers may sympathize—that though such arguments were sound for devices that ejected solid masses, like the sled discussed above, they did not apply to a rocket that released a "mere" stream of gas into an infinite vacuum.

In fact, some savants denied that any combustion was possible
in these circumstances; it was for this reason that Goddard went
to the trouble of firing small rockets in vacuum chambers. This
did not stop the *New York Times* from printing an editorial in
1920, in which it expressed hopes that a professor at Clark
College was only *pretending* to be ignorant of elementary physics, if he thought that a rocket could work in a vacuum.* The
writer would doubtless have been surprised to know that one
day the *Times* would receive the National Rocket Club's award
for aerospace reporting—at the Robert H. Goddard Memorial
Dinner.

The critics overlooked the fact that mass is mass, whether
it be in the form of solid lumps or the most tenuous vapor. If
the bricks in our thought experiment were ground into fine sand
before being ejected, it would make no difference to the result.
Similarly if they were volatilized, the final speed of the sled
would be exactly the same as before, provided only that the
ejection speed of the material remained unaltered.

So the answer to the old question, "What does a rocket
push against?" should now be obvious. It pushes against its
own combustion products.

A further and more subtle question is then often asked:
"Just *where* inside the rocket is the thrust developed?" Essentially, a rocket motor—and this is true whether it is solid- or
liquid-fueled—consists of an enclosed space (the combustion
chamber) containing hot, expanding gases which can escape
in only one direction, through a nozzle or orifice.

For simplicity, suppose that the combustion chamber is
spherical (which is actually the case for some high-efficiency
solid rockets) and that there is at first *no* orifice; the chamber
is completely sealed. The combustion products are then unable
to escape, and they produce the same thrust over the entire
interior surface of the sphere. All forces balance out and so
(assuming that the chamber does not burst) there is no movement in any direction.

Now pierce a hole in one side of the chamber. The pressure
exactly opposite this hole will be unbalanced; there will there-

*I have been mean enough to reprint this editorial, despite Mrs. Goddard's
kindhearted protests, in *The Coming of the Space Age* (Des Moines: Meredith, 1967).

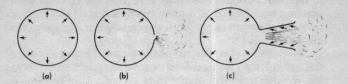

Figure 2. The forces in the rocket engine.

fore be a net force producing movement toward the left. The other forces will still cancel each other, and their only effect will be to exert pressure on the wall of the chamber, which must therefore be built strongly enough to withstand them.

The situation shown in Figure 2 (a) and (b) is that reproduced in the familiar experiment of blowing up a balloon, releasing the neck and letting it jet around the room. This demonstration, though perfectly sound, is not really convincing; a skeptic could always argue that the balloon's gyrations were produced by reaction against the air.

A simple hole like that shown in (b) would result in a highly inefficient performance; most of the escaping gas would expand sideways and do no useful work. Matters can be much improved by the addition of a nozzle (c); when the released gases expand, they press against it as shown, and so provide additional thrust.

Anyone who has followed this argument should now understand that all the thrust of a rocket is generated inside the combustion chamber and nozzle and that any surrounding medium plays no essential part in the process. This is not to say, however, that it has absolutely no effect on the performance of a rocket motor. When any rocket flies inside the atmosphere, the surrounding air actually *hinders* the expansion of the exhaust gases. For this reason the thrust of a rocket increases by 10 per cent or more as it leaves the atmosphere and enters the vacuum of space—the only environment where it can function with full efficiency.

It also follows—and this is perhaps even harder to accept—that a rocket gets no additional thrust at takeoff if the jet impinges on some fixed object, such as the ground or the launching pad. Indeed this must be avoided at all costs, since the reflected stream of hot gases can cause great damage to the vehicle.

Almost all rockets that have been built so far have obtained their thrust from chemical reactions; burning substances have generated hot gases that escape from a nozzle. However, there are endless ways of producing the same effect: *any* power source may be used, from a nuclear reactor to an electric battery. And any material may be used to provide the jet: solids, liquids, gases, electrons, ions, subatomic particles. As long as they have mass and can be aimed in a definite direction, they will give thrust.

Perhaps in the far future there may be spacecraft propelled by the swiftest "jet" that can exist—beams of pure light of unimaginable intensity, created by generators brighter than a billion suns. But they will still be rockets, in the direct line of descent from the crude vehicles which, in our time, first broke through the barrier of the atmosphere.

4. POWER FOR SPACE

By the early 1930's there was plenty of rocket theory but very little practice. Though a few small test vehicles had flown, their performance had not been impressive, especially when set against talk of travel to the Moon and planets. Most people who heard that Goddard's rockets had ascended a few thousand feet probably reacted in the same way as the shortsighted but typical newspaper editor who said of the Wright brothers' first hop off the ground: "57 seconds? If it had been 57 minutes, that *might* have been news."

What the skeptics failed to realize was that, even when the basic theory is completely sound, it requires millions of man-years and billions of dollars to develop a new technology. A man like Goddard could design an entire rocket vehicle, and it might seem to the layman that all that then had to be done was to send the drawings to the workshop. But it is not as easy as that; even the simplest liquid-propellant rocket contains dozens of components, all of which have to function perfectly, and most of which have to be specially built. Apparently straightforward devices such as valves to control the flow of propellants, gyroscopes for steering, pumps for feeding fuel into the combustion chambers, and reliable parachute-ejection mechanisms may demand months of development and dozens of tests. When one considers the mishaps that have plagued programs with virtually unlimited funds and manpower, it seems a miracle that any of the pioneering experimenters ever got their rockets off the ground.

As is well known, rockets fall into two distinct categories, one based on solid, the other on liquid propellants. "Solid" rockets, of which the ordinary back-garden, or Fourth of July, fireworks are the most familiar example, have been in existence for many centuries. Precisely how long is still a matter of debate, but they were certainly recorded in Chinese literature around A.D. 1200.

Although it has been said that the Chinese invented gunpowder and proved their culture by using it only for fireworks, the rocket refutes this, for they employed it with great effort against the Mongols at the siege of K'ai-fung-fu, north of the Yellow River, in 1232. News of the invention reached Europe very quickly, and the rocket was soon in common use both as a firework and as an impressive but usually unreliable weapon. It was not until the end of the eighteenth century, however, that its military application was taken very seriously in the Western world. Then, once again, the demonstration came from the Orient, when the Indian prince Tipu Sahib of Mysore used it against the British at the Battle of Seringapatam (1792). Although Tipu lost (his opponent, Charles Cornwallis, was rather luckier than at Yorktown eleven years earlier), the havoc wrought by his rocket artillery created a great impression. It came to the notice of Colonel William Congreve (not to be confused with the dramatist of the same name) who developed large war rockets with ranges of more than a mile and weights of up to 42 pounds. For a while it seemed that the rocket might replace the gun, as indeed Congreve believed that it would, but the great improvements in artillery soon made it obsolete, except for campaigns against ill-equipped natives.

In the meantime, however, it had found another use, as a launcher of rescue lines to ships stranded offshore. Between 1850 and 1940 the rocket was used almost exclusively for pyrotechnics and lifesaving; if the totals could be added up it might yet turn out that the rocket has saved more lives than it has taken.

No simpler propulsive device than a solid-fueled or powder rocket can be imagined. Even today its simplicity enables it to hold its own in many applications, such as the Polaris and Minuteman missiles, although these involve a fantastic degree of chemical, engineering, aerodynamic, and electronic sophistication. By trial and error, over a period of centuries, the classical design shown in Figure 3 was evolved.

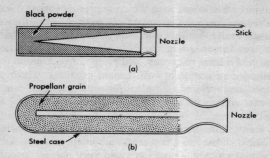

Figure 3. Solid-propellant rockets: (a) firework, (b) modern solid.

The propellant was a slow-burning form of gunpowder
known as black powder, the composition of which is roughly
60 per cent saltpeter (potassium nitrate), 25 per cent charcoal,
and 15 per cent sulfur; note the crude nozzle and the internal-
combustion chamber formed by the conical space in the hard-
packed powder charge. Stability in flight was maintained—if
at all—by the trailing stick.

Cheapness and ease of manufacture were the two merits
of this design; in almost every other respect it was deplorable,
and as a means of carrying substantial payloads any distance
it was useless. One obvious improvement was to remove the
dead weight of the stick and to obtain stability by small fins
or canted exhaust nozzles, which made the rocket spin in flight
like a rifle bullet; but graver defects were not so easily reme-
died. The most serious—for a device which is to be used as
a propulsive engine, not as a missile—is lack of controllability.
Once started, the powder will burn until it is all used up. The
acceleration produced is also extremely high, so that the rocket
reaches maximum speed very quickly and then wastes all its
energy against air resistance.

But a much more fundamental objection to the classical
powder rocket is that its propellants are really very feeble. It
was a long time before this was appreciated, because the spectacular performance of an ascending rocket gives an impression
of great energy.

And yet, pound for pound, such mixtures as ordinary gasoline or kerosene, with the correct proportions of oxygen, give *several times* the energy of gunpowder. True, they do not burn so rapidly, but that is also an advantage, for the last thing wanted is an explosion. On the contrary, what is desired is a controlled release of energy, and preferably a reaction that can be stopped or started at will. Liquid mixtures, which can be pumped and metered, are ideal for providing this. Some typical examples, with their performances, are listed in Table 3, page 58.

One seldom-mentioned advantage of liquid propellants is that some of the most powerful combinations (e.g., kerosene and liquid oxygen—"lox") are also very cheap, costing only a few cents per pound. Since large rockets contain hundreds or even thousands of tons of fuel, this is no trivial matter.

On all counts, therefore—performance, control (including ability to stop and restart), and economy—liquid-propellant mixtures appeared much superior to solid or powder ones. For this reason almost all space-flight discussions from the time of Tsiolkovsky onward were based on liquid propellants—usually alcohol, or a hydrocarbon, or hydrogen, burning with oxygen.

Yet technological progress has a curious way of doubling back on itself. During World War II, after the liquid-propellant rocket had been fully proved, new types of solid propellant were discovered which greatly narrowed the "energy gap." Much more surprising, ways were found of controlling, stopping, and even restarting solid-propellant motors, which have now been built in sizes (20 feet in *diameter*!) beyond all reasonable expectations of a few years ago. Such giant motors are valuable as strap-on boosters to provide additional thrust at takeoff; but it seems unlikely that they will displace the liquid-propellant systems that have dominated space exploration since the 1940's and which will do so at least for several decades to come.

Reduced to their simplest elements, these systems have to comprise the following items:

1. Fuel tank
2. Oxidizer tank
3. Fuel pump

4. Oxidizer pump
5. Pump motor(s)
6. Combustion chamber
7. Guidance system
8. Structure
9. Payload

The first two items had better be defined now to avoid confusion. Together, fuel and oxidizer make up the propellant; the fuel is what burns, the oxidizer is what must be mixed with it to support combustion. The commonest fuel is some variety of kerosene, similar to that burned in jet engines. The most powerful—and the most difficult to handle, because of its extremely low temperature—is liquid hydrogen. The first large rocket (V-2) used alcohol; chemicals like aniline and ammonia may also be used as fuels in special applications.

The oxidizer is usually oxygen itself, in the liquid form; however, chemicals rich in oxygen are sometimes employed (e.g., nitric acid, nitric oxide, hydrogen peroxide). There is even one "oxidizer" that contains no oxygen, the hyperreactive element fluorine, which has been used in some experimental rockets. Like the detergents that wash whiter than white, fluorine is an oxidizer that supports combustion better than oxygen, so well, indeed, that ignition is usually spontaneous.

It is also possible to combine both fuel and oxidizer in a single component, giving what is known as a monopropellant. This considerably simplifies the design of a rocket, since only one tank and one pump are then needed. However, the dangers of such a system are obvious. With separate fuel and oxidizer, nothing can happen until they are mixed in the combustion

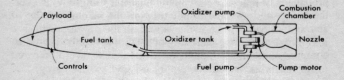

Figure 4. Liquid-propellant rocket.

chamber; barring leaks, the system is fail-safe. But a monopropellant is potentially an explosive and could start reacting in the tank or pipeline before it got to the combustion chamber, with disastrous results. Not surprisingly, therefore, monopropellants have had only limited application.

It will be realized that in the chemical rocket the propellants (i.e., fuel + oxidizer) serve a dual purpose. They are the source of energy of the system, and when ejected after combustion, their momentum provides the thrust. One could, in theory, separate these two functions by burning the propellants but *not* discarding them, and using their energy to eject some other material. This would be an absurdly inefficient procedure in the case of chemical rockets, but as we shall see later, it is precisely what happens in the case of the nuclear rocket, where fuel and propellant fluid are quite separate.

The first time all the items in Figure 4 worked successfully in a really large rocket was on October 3, 1942, when a V-2 missile rose from its launching pad at Peenemünde and plunged into the Baltic 120 miles away. That evening General Walter Dornberger, who directed all German Army rocket development, told his colleagues, "Today the spaceship was born!" It took nineteen years for the baby to become strong enough to carry a man.

The story of German rocket research has been well recorded elsewhere (see Bibliography) and in any case is outside the scope of this book. Sufficient to say that, in 1932, officers from the Ordnance Department witnessed rocket firings by the Verein für Raumschiffahrt but were unfavorably impressed both by the vehicles' performances and the aura of publicity that surrounded them. As von Braun puts it, "I attempted to persuade Colonel Becker that our showmanship was necessary, as a means of relieving our chronic financial stringency. Becker, however, was not slow in pointing out the incompatibility of any and all forms of showmanship with the development of a long-range arm in the Germany of 1932. He finally offered us a degree of financial support provided that we were prepared to do our work in the anonymity assured by the Army...." So, at the ripe age of twenty, Wernher von Braun took charge of liquid-rocket development for the German Army, and ten years later the V-2 made its first flight.

Although it has now been completely dwarfed by its successors, this 14-ton rocket was such an advance on anything
that had gone before that many people (notably Churchill's
opinionated scientific advisor Lord Cherwell) refused to credit
its existence. In almost every department—speed, range, altitude, power—it set new records. Above all, it was the first
manmade object to reach space, for in vertical launchings it
was able to attain heights of more than 100 miles.

In just over 60 seconds of powered ascent the V-2 burned
almost 10 tons of propellants (alcohol and liquid oxygen), which
gave it a speed of 3,800 mph, or more than one mile a second.
This was sufficient for it to continue coasting as a free projectile
for a total distance of 200 miles; after fuel burnout, it was
unguided and traveled on a ballistic trajectory, like a normal
artillery shell, taking 5 minutes for its full flight.

Although it is rather meaningless to talk about the "horsepower" of a rocket—the only parameter which makes much
sense is thrust—the V-2 converted energy at the rate of more
than half a million horsepower; heat equal to that produced by
the electric generating plant for a large city had to be handled
in a volume of a few cubic feet. Cooling was achieved by
allowing the alcohol fuel to circulate through the double wall
of the engine before it entered the combustion chamber. This
idea—regenerative cooling—is now almost universally employed and sounds very simple in theory; but it took thousands
of experiments and hundreds of spectacular explosions, from
the time of Goddard onward, before it was reliably achieved.
If the flow of cooling fluid falters for a fraction of a second,
the ravening heat of the engine will burn a hole almost instantly
through the thin metal of the combustion chamber, which melts
at a temperature thousands of degrees *lower* than the fires it
contains.

The V-2 consumed fuel at a rate more appropriate to a
firefighters' pump than anything that had hitherto been called
an "engine." The total propellant flow was 275 pounds *per
second*; to handle liquids at this rate and to force them into
the combustion chamber against the pressure of the continuous
explosion taking place there, required pumps driven by a 700-
hp motor. By normal engineering practice, this motor would
have absorbed all the rocket's payload; however, as it had to

operate only for one minute, durability was not a problem. The tiny turbine developed for this task was driven by superheated steam produced by the decomposition of hydrogen peroxide. (The violently reactive pure chemical, not the feeble 5 per cent solution sold in drugstores.)

Though the V-2 had four conventional fins, they could affect its flight only in the lower atmosphere, and their main purpose was to keep the missile from tumbling when it approached its target. During powered ascent, most of the control was provided by small rudders or vanes in the jet; since they reacted on the exhaust gases themselves, they were just as effective in space as in the air.

The two sets of rudders (one for lateral, one for vertical control) were programed by an onboard automatic pilot to follow the required flight path. The autopilot used the first application of what is now known as inertial guidance; except for a few experimental models, the V-2 was not radio-controlled, which would have made it liable to outside jamming. Once it had left its launch pad it was on its own; nothing, except a direct hit by another missile, could deflect it from its course.

Inertial guidance is a kind of positional memory; it is the only form of navigation that does not depend upon external landmarks or observations. It allows a man in a moving, completely enclosed box to tell where he is at any time, provided only that he knows where he started from. At first sight this seems impossible, but like many possibilities it looks simple when one knows how it is done.

All movement involves acceleration—a positive acceleration on starting, a negative one on stopping. Acceleration can be readily measured by simple instruments; an ordinary spring balance with a weight on it can be used as an effective "accelerometer."

Imagine such a spring balance, placed on the floor of an elevator cage. When the cage is motionless or is moving at a steady speed, the balance will give its normal reading. But it will read *above* normal (too heavy) when the elevator is starting, *below* normal (too light) when it is stopping. The excess, or deficiency, in weight will be exactly proportional to the acceleration of the cage.

If one timed these changes with a stopwatch and did a few calculations, it would be a straightforward task to calculate the speed acquired by the cage, and hence its position at any moment. This can be done instantaneously by a very simple form of computer. In a highly inaccurate manner, the human brain often performs this same function. When a man enters an elevator, the pressure on his feet tells him whether it is going up or down, and his time sense allows him to estimate when he is approaching the desired floor. And this, in principle, is all there is to inertial guidance.

In practice, needless to say, there are complications. An ascending space vehicle is not like an elevator, constrained to move in a single direction. It invariably travels along a curve, and so is subject to acceleration in all three planes; therefore, it requires not one, but *three* accelerometers to detect its motion and compute its velocity. They also have to be extremely sensitive, yet able to withstand considerable shock and vibration. Reconciling these conflicting requirements has taxed the art of the instrument maker to the utmost.

I do not know who invented inertial guidance, if indeed any single person ever did so. But I can still clearly remember my first encounter with the principle, when it was enunciated by the late J.H. Edwards, an eccentric near-genius who was the technical director of the British Interplanetary Society immediately before World War II. Edwards worked out, and published in the January, 1939, issue of the B.I.S. *Journal*, the mathematics of such an instrument, which he called an "absolute accelerometer." The Society, with wild optimism, even started its construction, and Edwards proposed that we test it on the escalators of the London Underground. (This I should like to have seen.) Little did any of us imagine that far more ambitious tests of such instruments were already in progress on the other side of the North Sea and that many of them would be arriving in London at high velocity within five years.

Luckily for the Allies, Hitler also failed to foresee the future; he did not believe in rockets. He had dreamed that the V-2 would never cross the English-Channel, so did not give it the support that might have changed the progress of the war. For this, both victors and vanquished may well be thankful. The first nuclear chain reaction was achieved in the same month as the first V-2 flight. If southern England had been evacuated as a result of rocket bombardment, the invasion of Europe might never have taken place—and, almost certainly, the atomic bomb would have been used first against Germany, not Japan.

After the collapse of Germany in the spring of 1945, Dr. von Braun and more than a hundred of his top men surrendered to the United States Army—a few jumps ahead of the advancing Russians. Stalin, to his loudly expressed annoyance, secured only a handful of the senior scientists, but several hundred production engineers and technicians were "persuaded" to work in the U.S.S.R. for some years. Perhaps even more valuable to the Russians was the capture of the vast underground V-2 plant at Nordhausen, intact apart from one hundred missiles surreptitiously whisked away by the United States Army a few hours earlier. This operation was quite illegal, since Nordhausen and all its equipment were in the zone already assigned to the U.S.S.R. Many Americans have since wished that the Army had compounded its felony by blowing up the whole plant, instead of leaving it in full working order for its grateful and incredulous allies.

However, since brains are always more valuable than hardware, the United States had much the better bargain; it merely failed to exploit it, for more than five years. By then it was the old story of too little and too late, for the U.S.S.R. had achieved a head start that would take more than a decade to overcome.

Apart from the tremendous increase in size, from the 14 tons of the V-2 to the awesome 3,000 tons of the Saturn 5, the improvements in rocket design during the 1950's and 1960's lay more in increased sophistication and reliability than in major changes of concept. Engines became more efficient as their combustion-chamber pressures were raised from less than 300 to about 1,000 pounds per square inch, with even higher values now in sight. Fuels of greater energy content than alcohol— e.g., kerosene and, finally, liquid hydrogen, the ultimate chemical fuel—were developed. The airshiplike fins of the V-2 shrank and, frequently, vanished altogether from such missiles as Atlas and Titan, which make few concessions to aerodynamics and are virtually flying cylindrical storage tanks. Steering is now effected by pivoting the engine, or engines—just like the outboard motor on a small boat. This is a more complex but more efficient arrangement than the Goddard V-2 solution of rudders in the jet exhaust.

Not so obvious merely by looking at the designs are improvements in materials and constructional techniques, which have steadily reduced the dead, or empty, weight of rocket structures. In the V-2 the propellant tanks were enclosed inside an outer skin; in later rockets the tanks themselves form the main body of the vehicle. The material of which they are built is sometimes so thin that they may have to be pressurized to prevent them from collapsing; they are, in effect, metal balloons, capable of holding a dozen or more times their own weight in fuel and oxidizer.

As a result of all these improvements, the range of single-stage rockets of the V-2 type rose from 200 miles in 1942 to well over 1,000 miles by the 1950's. Though such performances would have permitted scientific, and even manned, flights some hundreds of miles into space, they were not adequate for the task of escaping completely from the Earth. To understand why this was the case, let us now look at the obstacles on the road to the planets.

5. ESCAPE FROM EARTH

Any project for leaving the planet Earth has to take account of two dominant factors—the presence of the atmosphere and the force of gravity. They are not independent; if gravity were weaker, the atmosphere would be less dense, and would also extend farther out into space, since it would not be held so tightly to the surface. Such a situation prevails on Mars, where the gravity is one-third and the air pressure only one-hundredth of ours. On the Moon conditions are even more extreme; the gravity is one-sixth of Earth's, and the atmosphere has leaked away completely. (However, this must not be taken as a general rule; Venus has a slightly weaker gravity than Earth, but her atmosphere, for unknown reasons, is many times more dense.)

To the would-be space traveler, our atmosphere is both a help and a hindrance. On the way out, its resistance cuts back the speed attained by an ascending spacecraft, and extra fuel has to be carried to overcome this loss. The penalty decreases with the increasing size of the vehicle and is relatively unimportant for very large rockets, though it dominates the performance of very small ones.

This is a consequence of the well-known square-cube law. The mass of a body increases as the cube of its dimensions; its surface area, only as the square. Thus larger bodies have proportionately less area, and therefore less air resistance, then smaller ones. If a cannonball and a marble are thrown at the same speed, the cannonball will go much farther. It was this effect which, for more than a thousand years, obscured the true laws of motion.

40

Fortunately the very mode of operation of the rocket minimizes the influence of air resistance. Where the atmosphere is densest, at ground level, the rocket is moving at its lowest speed. When it has gained appreciable velocity, the atmosphere is already thinning rapidly. And by the time the rocket has reached its maximum speed, it is in frictionless space.

On the return from space, the atmosphere is almost wholly beneficial; it acts as a 100-mile-deep cushion, absorbing the enormous velocity of re-entry. None of our past feats and future plans for manned space travel would be possible if we had to do all our braking by rocket power alone. Thanks to heat shield and parachute, the final landing on Earth can be achieved without expenditure of energy.

The question "Where does the atmosphere end?" is one that cannot be answered simply—which is rather unfortunate, since it is now a matter of great legal importance. According to international law, most countries claim jurisidiction over vehicles traveling through their "airspace," whatever that may be. Attempts to define it now run to a good many million words.

The atmosphere, in reality if not in law, has no definite end; it slowly thins out in the near (but not perfect) vacuum of interplanetary space. For every 3 miles of altitude, the air density is approximately halved. Men can live and work without artificial aids at heights of 3 to 4 miles if they are given time to adapt themselves. But 5 miles marks the limit of human endurance for sustained periods; Mount Everest (6 miles high) is already beyond that limit. A man can exist there for some time without breathing gear, but he cannot exert himself.

Signposts are always helpful on any road, and the list on page 42 is an attempt to establish a few on the road to space. Their positions are only approximate and in some cases debatable. As far as an unprotected man is concerned, even 10 miles up is already "space"; at the other extreme, 100 miles is not high enough if one wishes to establish a satellite in a permanent orbit.

The height at which a satellite, moving at orbital speed of 18,000 mph, encounters catastrophically increasing atmospheric drag is almost exactly 100 miles. For many practical purposes, therefore, this may be regarded as the beginning of

TABLE 1
THE EARTH'S ATMOSPHERE

HEIGHT, MILES	TEMPERATURE, DEGREES F.	PRESSURE, ATMOSPHERES	CHARACTERISTICS
0	−100 to +100	1	Sea level
5	0 to −100	4/10	Limit of unaided human life
8	−70	2/10	Limit with oxygen mask
20	−40	1/100	Limit for aircraft
25	0	1/1,000	Limit for balloons
60	−100	1/1,000,000	Ionosphere
70	+100	1/1,000,000,000	Meteors burn up
100	500 to 1,500	1/1,000,000,000,000	Satellites re-enter; "space" begins legally?
600	1,000 to 3,000	10^{-15}	Upper limit of aurora

NOTE: For very high altitudes, the figures shown are merely representitive; they can vary widely. Thus, at 600 miles, the daily temperature variation can be more than 1,000 degrees!

space. Below this altitude, no pure spacecraft is capable of prolonged free orbital flight.

There are a number of ways, not yet widely exploited, in which the atmosphere may be used to assist departure from the Earth. Balloons have been used as platforms to carry small rockets to great altitudes before ignition, and there have been many studies of schemes for using atmospheric oxygen for the early stages of departure. All these involve great engineering complications and in most cases appear to be more trouble than they are worth; but the time may well come when spacecraft receive a considerable part of their initial boost by jet- or ramjet-propelled lower stages, capable of flying back to their launching sites for re-use after each mission.

One of the first facts that scientists discovered when they started making balloon ascents in the eighteenth century was that it becomes rapidly colder as one goes upward. Indeed, this is obvious to anyone who has ever done any mountaineering. At great heights, though the Sun may be shining in the clear sky, it is always extremely cold, and it is possible to get sunburn and frostbite simultaneously.

It is cold at great altitudes, despite the increased strength of the unhindered sunlight, because the air is too thin to absorb much heat; it can thus no longer act as a thermal bath, warming all bodies immersed in it. The temperature recorded by a thermometer (shielded from the Sun, of course) reaches a minimum of -60 degrees F. at an altitude of about 10 miles; then, surprisingly, it starts to climb again. At 30 miles' altitude it has risen to the freezing point; this zone of relative warmth coincides with the existence of a layer of ozone, very tenuous but vital for the protection of life on Earth, as it blocks the Sun's dangerous ultraviolet rays.

Thereafter the temperature falls again to a second low, and about 60 miles up it reaches a new minimum of -100 degrees F. But now we are approaching the ionosphere, where incoming solar radiation produces intense electrical activity. So the temperature starts to rise again, very rapidly. Soon it is hotter than at sea level; 100 miles up (the frontier of space) the temperature reaches the boiling point and continues to rise rapidly to 1,000 degrees or beyond.

These facts, which were discovered in the 1930's, were

gleefully seized upon by some critics of space flight to prove that any vehicle would melt as soon as it left the atmosphere. I will remember one newspaper article that had the sensational title "We Are Prisoners of Fire." Others suggested that shooting rockets into the inferno overhead would cause it to leak downward and burn up the world.

The explanation of this paradox is that at such extreme altitudes, the atmosphere is so thin that the word "temperature" no longer has its conventional meaning. At ground level the molecules of nitrogen and oxygen which compose the air are so tightly jammed together that they travel, on the average, only a few millionths of an inch before they collide with their neighbors. The air thus behaves as a continuous fluid, and a thermometer immersed in it will give a definite reading, just as it would in a bath of water.

One hundred and fifty miles up, however, the situation is entirely different. The molecules have to travel, not millionths of an inch, but something like *one mile* before they encounter each other. Although their individual velocities may be those that correspond to temperatures of thousands of degrees, they are so few and far between that the amount of heat they actually contain is negligible. A thermometer immersed in them would give no meaningful reading at all.

A good analogy of this situation is provided by the common "sparkler" firework. This gives off showers of incandescent sparks so bright that their temperatures appear to be several thousands of degrees. But when they fall on the hand, they produce no sensation whatsoever; they contain so little matter that their heat capacity is negligible. So it is with the air of the ionosphere and beyond.

As far as *outgoing* spacecraft are concerned, therefore, the atmosphere is not very important; it is little more than the scenery along the road. But that road, of course, winds uphill all the way, because of the inescapable influence of gravity. That is the force which has bound us so long to our native planet and which even now taxes our skill and resources to the utmost when we attempt to leave it.

Gravity may be one of those fundamental, irreducible entities which has no "explanation"; it simply *is*. Despite immense efforts, scientists have made little progress in understanding it, and none in modifying or controlling it. In the seventeenth century Sir Isaac Newton discovered the law of gravitation, which makes apples fall and keeps stars in their courses, but his great law was a description, not an explanation. Though it could predict, with amazing accuracy, the movements of bodies under the influence of gravity, it said nothing about the mechanism, if any, of this universal force.

Almost three hundred years later, Einstein's General Theory of Relativity introduced some subtle modifications to the Newtonian picture. It replaced the idea of a force acting between two bodies with that of curved space—a concept that only mathematicians can grasp and which so far has had not the slightest practical application. For the purposes of space travel, it is as if the General Theory had never been formulated; astronauts will always base their calculations on Newton's law. Any deviations from it are so tiny that they will cause about as much concern as does the curvature of the Earth to an architect when he is planning a house.

Let us, therefore, forget all about theories of gravity and consider only its effects. (Later, in Chapter 24, we will see if there is any chance of neutralizing it in the manner beloved by the early science-fiction writers.) Like the air itself, gravity is such a universal phenomenon that we take it for granted and seldom think about it in the ordinary course of events. It may dominate the lives of steeplejacks and mountaineers; we are usually aware of its existence only when we slip, run upstairs in a hurry, or drop a valuable and fragile object.

It was Galileo who demonstrated the surprising fact that all objects fall at the same rate, no matter how much they weigh. For 2,000 years, since the time of Aristotle, most thinkers had taken the common-sense view that the heavier the object, the faster it would fall; no one until Galileo had thought of putting the matter to an exact, quantitative test. He found that the acceleration produced by gravity on *any* unsupported body was 32 feet per second per second (usually written 32 ft./ sec.^{2}).

This means that, starting from rest, a falling object is moving at 32 feet per second (20 mph) after *one* second; 64 feet per second (40 mph) after *two* seconds; 96 feet per second (60 mph) after *three* seconds; and so on. Thus very large velocities can be built up extremely quickly—though near the Earth's surface, air resistance soon comes into play and limits the maximum speed attainable.

The value of 32 feet per second is usually referred to as 1 g, and is almost constant over the whole globe. (It is a fraction of a per cent larger at the poles than at the equator.) However, the acceleration of gravity varies considerably from planet to planet; as is well known, it is much lower on the Moon, where the value is approximately one-sixth of Earth's (i.e., five feet per second per second). On some very tiny moonlets and asteroids, only a few miles in diameter, gravity is so weak that a falling body would scarcely appear to move. But on the giant planet Jupiter, gravity is about 2½ times as great as on Earth; a falling object would gain speed by 50 miles per hour *every* second!

It is a fact of everyday experience that moving upward against the force of gravity involves work, and therefore a source of energy must be available. A climbing man obtains this energy from the food he has eaten; he would be doing well if he climbed one mile on one meal. An ascending rocket must get the energy it needs for its mission from the fuel and oxidizer it carries in its tanks. Mountaineer and rocket thus face similar problems, but they solve them in very different ways.

A climbing man expends energy at a more or less constant rate and moves at a fairly uniform speed. He can also stop at any point and rest, without falling back and losing any of the altitude that he has gained. But a vertically rising rocket cannot do this, since it has no support; during every second of flight, gravity is inexorably deducting 32 feet per second from its speed. For this reason spaceships and mountaineers have to use entirely different strategies to attain their objectives.

Yet the spaceship has one advantage: the force that it is fighting diminishes with increasing altitude, according to the inverse-square law first enunciated by Newton. For the non-mathematically minded, this simply means that if you double your distance from the Earth's center, gravity is reduced to a quarter; increase the distance three times, it is reduced to one-ninth; ten times, to one-hundredth; and so on. Thus for small distances the weakening of gravity is very slight, but at great distances it fades away rapidly. Though it never becomes zero,

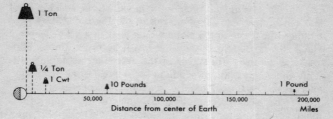

Figure 5. Gravity and distance.

for almost all practical purposes it may be ignored after a few million miles.

Some actual figures may help to make the picture clearer. One hundred miles up—where the closest satellites orbit, just before they re-enter the atmosphere—gravity still has 99 per cent of its sea-level value. The average man, standing on bathroom scales at the summit of a 100-mile-high mountain, would observe that he had lost about two pounds of weight, and would not be aware of the difference. (The astronaut whizzing past him at 18,000 mph at exactly the same altitude, of course, feels no weight at all. The reason for this will be discussed in detail later; for the moment it is necessary only to note that the mountaineer is supported, while the astronaut is in free fall. Anyone who has ever had a chair suddenly jerked away from underneath him will appreciate the distinction.)

At an altitude of 1,000 miles—a quarter of the Earth's radius—gravity is cut to 64 per cent of its sea-level value. To reduce it to one-half, it is necessary to climb to 1,700 miles. These heights are of course very modest in terms of rocket performances, but they show why gravity is a constant, invariant factor in our everyday lives.

Figure 5 expresses the same facts in graphical form, with the Earth drawn to scale. Note that at the Moon's distance of 240,000 miles the force of gravity is almost too small to be indicated; nevertheless, it is still powerful enough to keep the enormous mass of our solitary natural satellite firmly chained in its orbit.

The steady falling off of gravity with distance from the Earth gives us a mental picture, or model, from which a great deal can be learned. Climbing out of the Earth's gravity field is rather like ascending a slope which is at first very steep but which slowly flattens out until at last it becomes almost horizontal. Thus the early stages of the ascent are extremely difficult and require the expenditure of a great deal of energy, whereas the final ones require practically no energy at all.

We can set a precise numerical value to the height of this imaginary gravitational hill, up which we must climb in order to escape from the Earth. When we calculate the *total* amount of work which has to be done to leave our planet completely, we obtain a surprisingly simple and mathematically beautiful result. It turns out that lifting a body right away from the Earth, and out into the depths of space, requires exactly the same amount of work as lifting it *one* Earth radius—4,000 miles—against a constant gravity pull *equal to that at sea level*. So if you desire a mental picture of the energy needed to escape from the Earth, imagine climbing a mountain 4,000 miles high, assuming that there is no falling off in gravity on the way to the top. Alternatively imagine climbing a 4-mile high mountain 1,000 times: it comes to exactly the same thing.

To make this mental image more realistic, and more useful, it is best to turn the mountain upside down—to convert it into a pit or crater. From the gravitational point of view, we dwellers of the Earth's surface are in the position of people at the bottom of a gigantic funnel, 4,000 miles deep. To escape, we have somehow to climb the steeply sloping walls; near the bottom they are almost vertical, but eventually they flatten out into an endless plain. This horizontal plain represents gravitationless space, across which we can travel for immense distances with very little expenditure of energy—once we have reached it.

The above calculation is one case of a completely general law, applying to every body in the universe. To escape from any star, planet, or moon demands as much work as moving vertically through the radius of that body, against a gravity field equal to that at its surface. Let us anticipate a little and see what this implies in the case of our nearest neighbor, the Moon.

We have already said that its surface gravity is one-sixth

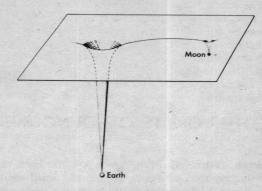

Figure 6. The gravitational fields of Earth and Moon.

the Earth's; its radius is very nearly one-fourth of our planet's. Hence the work required to escape from it is only $\frac{1}{6} \times \frac{1}{4}$, or $\frac{1}{24}$th, of that needed to leave Earth. Any lunarians are thus at the bottom of a gravitational crater a mere 170 miles, not 4,000 miles, deep. This shows how very much easier it is to escape from the Moon than from the Earth.

Figure 6 shows these two imaginary gravitational craters (the Moon's is so small that it has been necessary to exaggerate it). Remember that this picture is only a mathematical model, having no more physical reality than the isobars familiar to millions on the television weather charts or the contour lines on a map. But a study of it can give a very clear impression of the energy requirements for the Earth-Moon journey, and we shall return to it again when we study this in more detail. For implicit in this simple model is the entire theory of flight from world to world; we can use it to visualize the orbits of spaceships and space probes not only around the Earth but also, as we shall see later, around the Sun itself.

6. OTHER ORBITS, OTHER MOONS

During the first decade of the Space Age, the Earth acquired almost a thousand new moons—some very small and temporary, others weighing many tons and with lifetimes comparable to that of our natural Moon. Virtually overnight, what had been one of the most impractical and theoretical fields of mathematics—celestial mechanics—became a branch of engineering affecting the prestige and destiny of nations.

Celestial mechanics is horribly complex: many pure mathematicians would also consider it horribly ugly, despite the grandeur of its subject matter. Even some of its simplest problems have remained unsolved after centuries of effort, though answers can always be obtained to any desired degree of accuracy by brute-force methods using giant electronic computers. These machines have revolutionized the subject; it is not too much to say that space research would be as impossible without them as without the rocket itself.

Luckily, all the important basic ideas in this area can be grasped without any knowledge of mathematics at all, by the use of the model described in the last chapter—the 4,000-mile-deep crater which is the analogue of the Earth's gravitational field. The lower slopes of this model are shown in Figure 7; if we imagine that it is made of some smooth, hard material such as perfectly frictionless glass, we can use it to demonstrate the movements of space vehicles in the neighborhood of the Earth. All that we have to do to reproduce them for any initial conditions of velocity and direction is to see what happens to

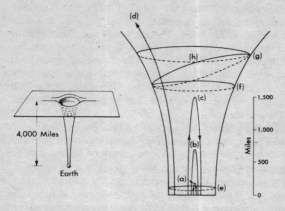

Figure 7. Orbits in the Earth's gravitational crater.

an object when it is projected along the slope, like a marble flicked inside a wineglass.

The case of a vertical launching is the simplest; obviously, the greater the initial speed, the higher the object will rise before gravity reduces its velocity to zero. Then it will fall back, gaining speed, until it returns to the starting point—at its initial velocity.

Although this example may seem rather trivial, we can learn several very important points from it. The first is that velocity can never be lost in space; it can be exchanged for altitude, but it can always be exchanged back again. In general, no matter what path or orbit a body takes around a planet, when it comes back to the same altitude (or distance) it will always be moving at the same speed (though not necessarily in the same direction; in this case the speed has been reversed, but the *energy* is the same).

It is also clear that as the velocity of projection increases, the altitude reached increases *even more rapidly* because of the steadily flattening slope. Figure 7 shows, to scale, the heights reached by bodies launched away from the Earth at speeds of (a) 5,000, (b) 10,000, and (c) 15,000 mph.

It is obvious that as the speed of projection increases still further, there will be a certain critical velocity at which the body will never fall back. Though it will lose most of its initial speed during the ascent, it will still have some velocity left when it reaches the "rim" of the crater, and so it will continue to move on outward forever. The speed that is just sufficient to climb out of a gravitational field is known as the velocity of escape; for the Earth its value is about 25,000 mph, or 7 miles per second.

If a body starts off with more than this critical speed, it will still have something in hand when it leaves the gravitational pit. However, the excess velocity cannot be obtained by simple subtraction, because we are really dealing with *energies*, not merely velocities. A body starting from the bottom of the crater at a speed of 7 miles per second reaches the top at zero velocity; but one beginning at 8 mps emerges at considerably more than the one mps that might be expected. The rather curious results that follow are shown in this table:

INITIAL VELOCITY, mps	FINAL VELOCITY, mps
7	0
8	4
9	5½
10	7

This matter is not very important as far as the present argument is concerned, but in the case of actual missions it has a great effect on fuel requirements and flight times (see Chapter 7).

Now consider the case of a body projected not vertically up the gravitational slope, but horizontally—at right angles to it. If its speed is adjusted properly, it can remain orbiting at a constant altitude, like a motorcyclist in the "Wall of Death" popular in circus sideshows. (Though this analogy is a good one, it is not quite accurate, because friction operates here, and the rider has to keep his engine running to counteract it.)

This is the now-familiar case of a satellite in a circular orbit, at a constant distance from the Earth. It is obvious that the higher the satellite, the more slowly it needs to move to preserve its position. A very close satellite requires an orbital speed of 18,000 mph (5 mps), whereas a distant one like the Moon need move at only about 3,600 mph (1 mps).

It also follows that as altitude or distance increases, the time to complete one orbit increases at an even greater rate, for not only is there more distance to be covered, but the speed in orbit is less. This fact is expressed in Kepler's famous third law—"the square of the time for one revolution increases as the cube of the radius"—which was the clue that led Newton to his law of gravitation.

We have by no means exhausted the possibilities of our model, for let us now consider the case of an object projected along its surface at some arbitrary speed or inclination. If it does not have enough velocity to maintain itself at the height where it enters into the system, it will drop down the slope, but as it does so it will gain speed, like any falling body. When it has reached its lowest point—and its greatest velocity—it will start to rise again, continually retracing the same inclined curve. This, of course, is the analogue of a satellite in an elliptical orbit.

In Figure 8 the elliptical orbit has been drawn so that it touches two circular ones; it can lie anywhere, but this has been done to illustrate another idea—transfer from one orbit to another. It will be realized that at the upper point of contact, an object in the elliptical orbit is moving more slowly than one in the circular orbit here; this is why it falls back to the lower level again. If it is to remain in the higher orbit—make a rendezvous—it must be given an additional impulse.

Conversely, at the lower point of contact the body in the transfer orbit is moving too fast for a rendezvous; it must therefore receive an impulse to slow it down if its orbit is to be "circularized."

Before we leave, for the moment, this highly instructive model, there is just one more case to be considered, that of a body entering the gravitational field from a great distance and at a considerable speed.

This is the exact reverse of the "escape-velocity" case; the object will gain speed as it slides down the wall of the crater. It will gain so much, in fact, that it will whip completely around the bottom of the crater and rise out of it, to disappear once

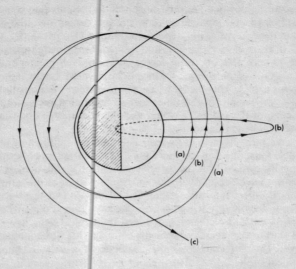

*Figure 8. Orbits around the Earth: (a) circular, (b) elliptical,
(c) parabolic.*

more toward infinity—eventually regaining all its original speed,
though it will be heading in some different direction.

There are fun-fair operators, doubtless unversed in celestial mechanics, who have learned to profit by this example.
They display attractive vases, which can be won by anybody
who can toss a ball into them. It looks easy, because the open-
ings of the vessels are quite wide; but the trick is almost impossible, because any ball that does get into the smooth interior
promptly emerges again with barely diminished speed. The
astronomical analogue, of which there are several examples
every year, is the comet which enters the solar system from
the depths of space, does a hairpin turn around the Sun, and
then heads out once more toward the stars.

A careful study of the perhaps rather unlikely model in
Figure 8 will, therefore, give a very good idea of all the possible
trajectories and orbits of a space probe or satellite moving in
the gravitational field of the Earth. More than that, it may be

generalized for *all* celestial bodies—the Moon, the Sun, or any of the planets. Only the numerical values are different; thus, for the Moon, escape velocity is only 1½ miles per second (compared with 7 mps for Earth). For the Sun, however it is an enormous 400 miles per second; some idea of the forces raging there can be gathered from the fact that solar eruptions frequently exceed this speed, so that matter is continually escaping from the Sun. It must be remembered that Figure 8 is a *model*, not a map; it shows the characteristics of possible orbits, not their actual shapes in space.

It will be seen that there are two possible classes of orbits, closed and open. The closed ones are circles and ellipses; they repeat themselves indefinitely. All real orbits are in fact ellipses; the circle is the theoretical, limiting case of the ellipse with zero eccentricity—a state of perfection which does not exist in nature, though it has been approached by some artificial satellites. Venus has the most perfectly circular orbit, with an eccentricity of 0.0068. A synchronous satellite like Early Bird has an orbital eccentricity of only 0.0005—ten times better.

The open orbits, which never repeat themselves but lead off to infinity, are hyperbolas or parabolas. Like the circle, the parabola is a limiting case which exists only in theory. It is the orbit of a body which has exactly *enough* velocity to escape—not one micron per millennium more or less. So in practice, all escape orbits are really hyperbolas.

The Greek mathematicians, in the fourth century B.C., discovered that all these curves can be obtained by cutting a slice through a cone. If the slice is parallel to the base, the result is a circle; as the section is tilted, the resulting curve becomes first an ellipse, then a parabola, then a hyperbola. So the Greeks called them all "conic sections" and worked out their mathematical properties from a pure sense of aesthetics.

Two thousand years later, Kepler found that the ellipse is the path in which all the planets travel around the Sun. This caused great dismay to the classical scholars, who believed that anything as celestial as a heavenly body must move along the only "perfect" curve, the circle.

One can hardly imagine what they would have thought, could they have known that the time was coming when the conic sections would lead man himself into the heavens.

7. THE PRICE OF SPEED

We have seen in the last chapter that the speed required for even the simplest and easiest space mission—orbiting the Earth—is about 5 miles a second, or 18,000 miles an hour. To escape completely requires 7 miles a second (25,000 mph), but once this critical speed is attained, a whole range of possibilities opens up, as shown by the table on page 58.

Ignoring for the present the rather odd fact that it is twice as difficult (in terms of velocity) to reach the Sun as the nearest star, this shows that a very slight extra speed over the mimimal escape velocity brings the closer planets within range, as has already been demonstrated by the various Mars and Venus probes.

Tsiolkovsky used the phrase "first cosmic speed" for the orbital velocity of 5 mps, and "second cosmic speed" for the escape velocity of 7 mps; these expressions are still employed in contemporary Russian space writings. Even the lower velocity seemed so wildly beyond hope of attainment at a time when airplanes could barely reach 100 mph that one can hardly blame the early critics of astronautics for their skepticism.

And yet Tsiolkovsky and his successors had shown in complete theoretical detail how such speeds might be attained by means of rockets, provided that certain engineering problems could be overcome. It was all a question of getting a sufficiently high exhaust velocity and an efficient enough structure. These were the two vital factors; everything else was secondary.

Let us go back to the brick-carrying sled used in Chap-

56

ter 3 to demonstrate the rocket principle, and consider how its performance—that is, its final velocity after all its "propellant" has been expended—depends on these two parameters.

Common sense, without any mathematical aids, tells us that the final velocity will be directly proportional to the speed of ejection of the bricks. If the bricks are thrown out at 20 mph and the sled reaches a final speed of 1 mph, then it will reach 2 mph if the ejection speed is increased to 40 mph, assuming exactly the same number of bricks are thrown out as before.

Thus the exhaust speed of a rocket is its most important characteristic, for its final speed, at "all burnt," is directionally proportioned to this. Table 3 gives some values for a few representative propellants.

When these figures are compared with the mission requirements shown in Table 2, it will be seen at once that the old-style powder rocket is pitiably inadequate. But even the modern, liquid-propellant rockets have exhaust speeds which are only a fraction of the "first cosmic velocity." To perform any space mission, therefore, we must build rockets capable of traveling *several times as fast as their exhaust speed*.

At first sight, it may seem impossible for a rocket to attain a speed greater than that of the jet that propels it; I have known able mathematicians who intuitively dismissed the idea. But it must be remembered that the jet exhaust always leaves the rocket at the same speed, *whatever* the velocity of the rocket itself may be relative to some arbitrary external point. As long as there is any fuel aboard, the jet will continue to give the same thrust, and the rocket will continue to accelerate.

To return to the analogy of the sled and its load of bricks, each brick gives the same impetus to the vehicle, whether the sled is standing still or moving at 100 miles an hour across the ice. Since the fuel is carried along with the vehicle and shares its speed at any time, the sled's velocity cannot affect its performance.

The fact that rocket exhaust speeds are considerably less than those needed for space missions does not, therefore, make them impossible; it merely makes them difficult. We can see how difficult if we look again at the man on the sled and ask ourselves what amount of propellant he would have to throw off in order for his vehicle to reach "exhaust speed," that is,

TABLE 2
MISSION LAUNCH SPEEDS

	LAUNCH SPEED	
MISSION	MPH	MILES/SEC.
Close Earth orbit	18,000	5
Escape from Earth	25,000	7
Voyage to Mars or Venus	26,000	7
Voyage to Jupiter	32,000	9
Voyage to Pluto	35,000	10
Voyage to nearest star	37,000	10
Voyage to Sun	70,000	20

TABLE 3
ROCKET PROPELLANTS

PROPELLANT	EXHAUST VELOCITY, MPH
Black powder (firework)	700
Modern solid propellant	3,000 to 5,500
Alcohol-oxygen (V-2)	6,200*
Kerosene-oxygen (Atlas, Saturn)	6,500*
Hydrogen-oxygen (Centaur, Saturn)	8,500*
Hydrogen-fluorine	9,000*
Hydrogen (nuclear rocket)	20,000 and up
Ions (electric rocket)	40,000 and up

Sea-level values. Exhaust velocities in vacuum could be 10 to 15 per cent higher.

the speed with which he is throwing out the bricks.

It is easy to see what the *minimum* weight must be. If all the propellant could be ejected simultaneously, in one explosive effort, and if its weight equaled that of the empty sled, then the velocities would also be matched. After the Big Bang, we would have two equal masses moving in opposite directions, with equal speeds [Figure 9 (a)].

In this case, the initial mass of the system (vehicle plus propellant) would be twice that of the empty, or final, mass. It would be said to have a "mass ratio" of 2. Such a ratio presents no engineering difficulties, though it is a good deal higher than usual for surface vehicles; the average automobile has a mass ratio of about 1.03, since only about 3 per cent of its weight is fuel. It is attained by some aircraft, which can carry their own empty weight in fuel.

However, the explosive, or "instant-burning," case we have described is not applicable to the rocket, where combustion takes place over a period of time which may last for several minutes. And certainly the man on the sled would require a considerable time to throw out a mass of bricks more than equal to his own weight!

This alters the situation a good deal, reducing the efficiency of the system. Because all the propellant is *not* ejected at once, work has to be done to accelerate the unused material, up to the moment until it is finally discarded. This means that more propellant has to be carried—and more propellant has to be carried to accelerate *that*, in an infinite but fortunately diminishing series. The very last brick on the sled has to be

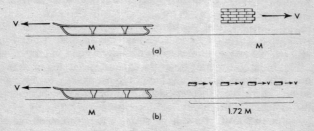

Figure 9. The rocket-velocity law.

carried to the bitter end; when it is finally jettisoned, it has almost reached the velocity of the payload; yet all the work done to accelerate it to that point is a complete waste, though an unavoidable one.

It is straightforward, though tedious, to calculate the additional mass of bricks now needed to bring the vehicle up to "exhaust speed" without using any higher mathematics. (Anyone who likes to try may assume that the propellant mass is split into first 1, then 2, then 4, 8, 16, etc., bricks. As the individual units get smaller and smaller, he will see that the answer converges to a limiting value.) In the case of a real rocket, where there is a continuous flow of material, the calculus has to be used, and it can be easily shown that in order for the vehicle to reach the speed of its exhaust, the mass ratio must be increased from 2 to the somewhat higher value of 2.72. Thus the vehicle has to eject 1.72 times its empty weight of propellant [Figure 9 (b)]. The 0.72 is the penalty we have to pay for carrying along part of the fuel until it is needed; it might be much worse.

The now-primitive V-2, it is interesting to note, had a mass ratio considerably higher than 2.72. Its loaded weight was 28,000 pounds, its empty weight 8,500 pounds, and the ratio of these two figures is 3.3. In theory, therefore, a V-2 could travel faster than its exhaust (5,000 mph); that it actually achieved only 3,600 mph was due to air resistance and gravity losses. It could have attained its theoretical performance in the vacuum of space.

Now let us be more ambitious. What load of bricks has the sled to carry, if its final speed is to equal *twice* that of its "exhaust"?

It turns out that we have to square the mass ratio, thus increasing it from 2.72 to 2.72^2, or 7.4. In other words, the sled has to carry 6.4 times its own empty weight in propellant.

Similarly, for three times the exhaust speed, the mass ratio has to be cubed, giving a value of almost exactly twenty, and so on. There is no theoretical limit to the process, but clearly the practical difficulties are increasing very rapidly. Is it possible to construct a vehicle strong enough to stand the accelerations of flight whose empty weight—including payload!—is only one-twentieth of its weight when loaded with

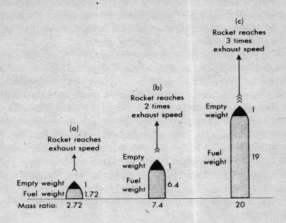

Figure 10. Rocket mass ratios.

propellants? But this is what has to be done if we are to build a rocket which can fly three times as fast as its own exhaust.

These results are shown in diagrammatic form in Figure 10. In each case the empty weight of the rocket is measured to be the same—say, one ton. That one ton, remember, must cover the weight of the propellant tanks, the rocket engine, the control system, the payload—*everything*.

The old V-2, as we have seen, is slightly better than case (a). Today's best liquid-propelled rockets can surpass (b), and there are some solid-propellant rockets that can even match case (c). The makers claim that their mass ratio of twenty beats that of nature's most efficient container, the egg. However, this figure applies to the rocket motor only, and the complete vehicle would bring us back to something poorer than case (b) again. We can conclude, therefore, that it is not practical to build a rocket with a final speed more than twice that of its exhaust. (There may be exceptions for vehicles built to operate exclusively in space, where very light structural materials and novel techniques can be employed.)

The greatest exhaust speed for conventional propellants, listed in Table 3, is 8,500 mph. Since orbital velocity is 18,000 mph, it appears impossible to build a rocket, using hydrogen and oxygen, to become a satellite of Earth.

The way out of the dilemma is the simple, effective, but expensive device of the step, or multistage, rocket. All the calculations given above refer to *single*-stage rockets, where the structure, dead weight, etc., which begin a mission are used right through to the end. But it is obvious that if we make the payload of our rocket *another* complete rocket, which starts to operate only when the first stage has exhausted its fuel and has been dropped off, we can achieve a much higher final speed. In fact, if the two rockets have the same propellants and the same mass ratio and are identical except in size, the final speed will be doubled.

How the step rocket works (and why it is expensive) is shown in Figure 11.

Let us suppose that one can design a rocket with a weight breakdown of 80 per cent propellant, 15 per cent structure, and 5 per cent payload, as shown in Figure 11 (a). (It is possible to do a good deal better than this, but these values have been

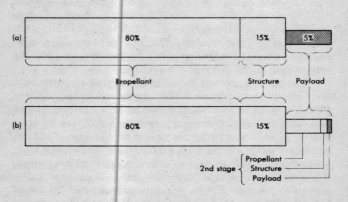

Figure 11. Weight breakdowns of one- and two-stage rockets.

chosen to give round numbers.) This being a single-stage rocket, its 5-per-cent payload might be able to attain a theoretical final speed of 10,000 mph. In practice, air resistance and gravity could reduce this to about 8,000 mph. Even if the *whole* of the payload were replaced by propellant, the mass ratio would show only a slight improvement—in this case, from 5 to 6.7. The resulting increase in speed—at the cost of zero payload!—would only be 2,000 mph.

If, however, we take the payload and make it a second rocket, with the same weight breakdown as the first [Figure 11 (b)], then this stage will have the same performance. But it would start where the first had left off, both in velocity and in altitude. It could add another 8,000 mph to the speed it already possessed, giving a grand total of 16,000 mph.

In actual practice it would do a good deal better than this. Since the second stage would not begin firing until it was scores of miles above the ground, it would lose very little velocity through air resistance, and its engine would operate at maximum efficiency. Moreover, it would no longer be ascending vertically; it would have started to curve over toward the horizontal. This means that gravity drag (which acts in the downward direction) would be less effective in reducing its speed.

For all these reasons, the second stage would approach its theoretical performance of 10,000 mph, so that its payload would achieve 18,000 mph, or orbital velocity.

The reason why a step rocket can travel so much faster than a single-stage rocket, whatever its size, is not hard to see. In a single-stage rocket, as the propellants become used up we have the situation where a now unnecessarily powerful, and therefore excessively heavy, engine is trying to accelerate a lot of useless dead weight. The big propellant tanks, for example, still have to be carried along even when they are virtually empty, so that in a sense the overall efficiency of a rocket steadily decreases as its propellants are consumed. In the last seconds of firing time the engine is wasting most of its effort imparting velocity to structural mass which is no longer serving any useful purpose. The only way to improve the situation is to throw away the empty rocket and to start again with a new, scaled-down one.

There is no limit to the number of stages that may be

employed in a step rocket or, therefore, to the speed which may be attained by the final stage when the earlier ones have been discarded. The practical disadvantage of the step principle, of course, is that after two or three stages the ultimate payload is an extremely small fraction of the initial takeoff weight. In Figure 11 the payload of the single-stage rocket is 5 per cent, but that of the two-stage rocket is only 5 per cent of 5 per cent, or a mere ¼ per cent. For multistage vehicles, such as the Saturn 5 designed for the lunar mission, the percentage of payload is even less; but that is the penalty that has to be paid for achieving high velocities.

It is sometimes asked, "Why do we need such high speeds for space flight? Could not a rocket leave the Earth at a fairly low, steady velocity, running its engines at some modest thrust level, rather than going all-out to reach the escape velocity of 25,000 mph as quickly as possible?"

Yes, it could—if it had a virtually infinite source of energy. The slower the rate of climb in the Earth's gravitational field, the more wasteful is the expenditure of fuel. This will be obvious if we look at two extreme cases.

Suppose the rocket burns all its fuel instantly, so that it acquires escape speed while it is still at ground level. (We know, of course, that air resistance, as well as engineering factors, would make this impossible in practice. But there are some anti-ballistic-missile missiles—ABM's—that do have incredible accelerations even in the lower atmosphere and will serve to illustrate the principle.)

In this theoretical case, *none* of the fuel has to be lifted against the earth's gravitational field; it therefore imparts all its energy to the rocket and wastes none lifting itself. It all stays near the ground—but the rocket escapes from the Earth. We are, virtually, dealing with the case of a gun-launched vehicle, and the propellant is used at maximum efficiency. To look at it in another way, because the whole process of reaching escape speed takes zero time, gravity—which normally reduces the speed of any vertically climbing missile by 20 mph every second—has no time to act.

Now consider the other extreme, the case of a rocket which takes off so slowly that it merely hovers at a fixed altitude. It burns its entire load of propellant merely balancing itself against gravity, and gets nowhere.*

Clearly, the nearer we can get to the first case, the most efficient the operation and the smaller the total amount of propellant needed. Escaping from Earth is difficult enough as it is, without aggravating the problem by making unnecessary concessions to gravity. We have to climb out of the gravitational crater as quickly as possible; the more time we spend lingering on its lower slopes, the more we shall slip back toward the bottom.

The above argument also throws light on a fallacy often advanced by critics of space flight in the early days; sometimes trained mathematicians, who should have known better, fell headlong into the trap. Here is a splendid specimen from a speech by one Professor Bickerton, delivered to the British Association for the Advancement of Science in 1926:

This foolish idea of shooting at the moon is an example of the absurd length to which vicious specialization will carry scientists working in thought-tight compartments. Let us critically examine the proposal. For a projectile entirely to escape the gravitation of the earth, it needs a velocity of 7 miles a second. The thermal energy of a gram at this speed is 15,180 calories. . . . The energy of our most violent explosive—nitro-glycerine—is less than 1,500 calories per gram. Consequently, even had the explosive nothing to carry, it has only one-tenth of the energy necessary to escape the earth. . . . Hence the proposition appears basically impossible. . . .

In this relatively short passage Professor Bickerton managed to compress two major errors. One would have thought it obvious that an *explosive* was the last substance suitable for a rocket propellant; in any event, nitroglycerin contains considerably less energy than equal weights of typical propellants like kerosene and liquid oxygen. This fact of elementary chemistry had been carefully pointed out years before by Tsiolkovsky and Goddard.

Bickerton's second error is the "energy fallacy" in its pur-

*General Dornberger has given a vivid eyewitness account of this happening at Peenemünde; see *The Coming of the Space Age* (Meredith Press), 1967.

est form. What does it matter if the nitroglycerin (or other propellant) contains only a fraction of the energy necessary to lift *itself* away from the Earth? It never has to do so.

What it has to do is impart that energy to a suitable payload, and (if it were not for air resistance) that could all be done at ground level. Thus even Bickerton's own argument merely proves that at least ten pounds of nitroglycerin would be required to send one pound to the Moon. For actual space vehicles, most of the propellant is burned within a hundred miles of Earth, and so lifts itself only a fraction of the way out of the Earth's gravitational field. When Luna 2 impacted on the Moon just thirty-three years after Professor Bickerton proved it was impossible, its several hundred tons of kerosene and liquid oxygen never got very far from the Soviet Union—but the half-ton payload reached the Mare Imbrium.

The passage I have quoted is also worth studying for another reason. It demonstrates how men who should be scientifically trained can let prejudices and preconceived beliefs distort their logic, so that they commit almost childish errors when attempting to prove their points. Space flight, and aviation before it, attracted a lot of this nonsense; and even today, as we shall see in Chapter 27, there are circles in which it is a popular pastime to "prove" that though interplanetary flight is perfectly feasible, we shall never, *never* be able to reach the stars.

II. AROUND
THE EARTH

8. MOONRISE IN THE WEST

The use of rockets for high-altitude research—the dream which Goddard had pursued but had never realized in his own life-time—began immediately after World War II. Many of the V-2's captured by the United States Army were launched from the White Sands Proving Ground, New Mexico, with their warheads replaced by instruments which would radio their observations back to ground stations. In addition, smaller rockets, such as the Aerobee and the Viking, were developed purely for scientific purposes.

This work was very modestly funded and would probably have led to the achievement of manned space travel around the middle of the twenty-first century. Fortunately or unfortunately, depending upon one's point of view, the main impetus for rocket development was being provided not by man's quest for knowledge but by his instinct for survival. As in the case of the V-2, the military were quietly providing the real money.

Although the United States possessed, in the Peenemünde team, the most experienced rocket designers in the world, it showed no inclination to use them. In monopoly of the atom bomb (confidently expected to last for many years) and its fleet of B-29 Superfortresses made such futuristic weapons as long-range ballistic missiles appear unnecessary. Moreover, theoretical studies showed that it would require rockets weighing several hundred tons to deliver nuclear warheads over useful distances. No competent engineer doubted that such vehicles could eventually be developed, but the cost would be enormous and there seemed no justification for a high-priority program.

The Soviet Union—and specifically Joseph Stalin— thought otherwise. From their point of view, intercontinental missiles made excellent sense. They also had a long tradition of interest in rockets, going back to Tsiolkovsky, and until the mid-1930's their engineers had probably led the world in this field—though this fact was not generally known or believed outside the Soviet Union.

In addition, they had now acquired the priceless background of German wartime research, a great deal of hardware (including Peenemünde and a complete V-2 factory), the very few top-ranking scientists and engineers who had not thrown in their lot with Dr. von Braun's team, and more than a thousand technicians. This was a prize of no small value, but to imagine that it was responsible for establishing the Soviet lead in space is absurd. The United States had the better bargain, as Stalin was quick to point out. According to one eyewitness (Tokaty), he berated General Serov as follows: "This is absolutely intolerable. . . . We occupied Peenemünde, but the Americans got the rocket engineers. . . . How and why was this allowed to happen?"

Although a carrier for their first, heavy atom bombs would have to weigh several hundred tons, the Soviet Union decided to go ahead and develop it. When perfected in the late 1950's, it was also large enough to launch heavy satellites—and to carry the first man into space. Whether this had been planned from the beginning, or whether it was a lucky bonus, is perhaps one of those questions which even the Soviets themselves cannot now answer.

When it was finally revealed to the outside world at the Paris Air Show in the spring of 1967 (ten years after its first historic flights), the giant Sputnik carrier proved to be of a highly original design, bearing scarcely any resemblance to the V-2 formula. Dr. von Braun had already forecast this when he stated that "There is every evidence to believe that [German engineers'] contribution to the Russian space program was almost negligible. They were called upon to write reports . . . they were squeezed out like lemons, so to speak. In the end they went home without even being informed about what went on in the classified Russian projects."

The American long-range rocket program remained in limbo

until about 1950, though well over one billion dollars was spent on the development of jet-propelled guided missiles such as Navaho and Snark, which were no more than robot airplanes, capable of cruising only at relatively low speeds inside the atmosphere. All were abandoned after the ICBM breakthrough.

The two events which suddenly revived American interest in long-range rockets were the outbreak of the Korean War in 1950 and the realization that thermonuclear (or fusion) weapons could soon be built. These would not only be hundreds of times more powerful than the first fission bombs, but also lighter; they could be delivered by vehicles weighing about a hundred tons, instead of several hundred. And so, after several false starts, were initiated the programs which led first to ballistic missiles of intermediate range such as Redstone, Jupiter, and Thor, and later to the true intercontinental missiles Atlas and Titan.

All this was going on during the period 1950–55, and meanwhile the scientists were also getting involved. Many of the younger ones had been using sounding rockets to explore the upper atmosphere and had pioneered new fields of research in meteorology, astronomy, and geophysics. But this work was as frustrating as it was exciting, for sounding rockets could spend only a few minutes reporting from space before they fell back into the atmosphere. The obvious answer was the artificial satellite, which could stay aloft indefinitely, behaving, as one wit put it, like a Long-playing Rocket.

There was much discussion, therefore, of scientific satellites around 1950; as early as 1951, the British Interplanetary Society sponsored a congress in London on "The Artificial Satellite." By an accident of history, all these studies (some of which went into great technical detail) appeared just at the time when the scientific community was planning the greatest global research effort ever conceived—the International Geophysical Year (1957–1958).

The United States committee of the IGY, under the chairmanship of Dr. Joseph Kaplan, recommended that a satellite be launched as part of the nation's program; the suggestion was approved by the government, and the White House made the announcement to a somewhat startled world on July 29, 1955. Little notice had been paid to the statement on April 15, 1955, in the Soviet press that an Interdepartmental Commission on Interplanetary Communications had been set up to develop satellites for meteorological purposes, so when the U.S.S.R. repeated this item the day after the American announcement, it was received with amused skepticism.

Then followed the tragicomedy which has been the subject of millions of words of excuse, apology, accusation, recrimination, and 20:20 hindsight. Having resolved to orbit a satellite, the United States next had to decide on the launch vehicle.

There were three principal candidates. The Army proposed the Redstone, being developed at Huntsville, Alabama, by the von Braun team. Using this as a first stage, and mounting clusters of solid rockets on top of it, small payloads could be launched into orbit by the beginning of 1957. This scheme had the great advantage of using hardware that already existed, and so could be ready in the shortest time.

The Air Force wanted to use the still-to-be-tested Atlas as the first-stage booster; this would put a much larger payload into orbit, as was later amply proved by Project Mercury. However, it was practically certain that Atlas would not be ready in time for the IGY, unless there was interference with its overriding military priority. (Its first successful flight did not in fact take place until December 17, 1957).

The Navy proposed to develop what was almost a new vehicle, though its first stage would be based to some extent on the successful Viking research rocket, which had now carried substantial payloads to heights of up to 158 miles. One of the arguments in favor of this approach was that the whole project could then be an unclassified, civilian one, using no military hardware—in keeping with the peaceful, scientific nature of the IGY.

To decide between these conflicting proposals, a committee was set up under the chairmanship of Dr. Homer Stewart; to the bitter disappointment of the Army, it selected the Navy's project, which was given the unhappy name Vanguard. The reasons for this decision were as much political as scientific (if not more so), and the "Stewart Committee" has since been widely criticized for its verdict. This is particularly bad luck for Dr. Stewart himself, as he submitted a minority report in favor of the Army's Redstone project.

The Office of Naval Research, given the go-ahead, started to design the complex and sophisticated Vanguard vehicle, most of which was built by the Martin Company of Baltimore. Work proceeded on an unrealistically low budget, with no priority; more important rockets had the first call on men and materials. Yet the final outcome was a highly successful launch vehicle, which made great contributions to space technology; it should not be forgotten that the longest-lived of all satellites, which would be in orbit a thousand years hence, apart from the near certainty that it will soon be collected for the Smithsonian Aerospace Museum, is the little three-pound Vanguard 1, launched March 17, 1958. And Vanguard 3 (September 18, 1959) far exceeded the originally designed payload, taking 50 pounds of instruments to a high point of more than 2,000 miles. But by *that* time no one took much notice, for a week earlier the Soviets had hit the Moon.

This was merely one episode in a national humiliation that had begun on October 4, 1957, when to the utter astonishment of the world the U.S.S.R. did exactly what it had said it was going to do, and orbited the first artificial satellite of Earth. It was at once obvious that a full-sized ICBM vehicle—not a small, purely scientific rocket—had been used as a launcher. Radar and optical observations showed that though the announced payload was 184 pounds, the empty final stage also circling the Earth must weigh several tons; when the even larger Sputnik 2 went into orbit carrying the dog Laika on November 3, 1957, photographs obtained by powerful tracking cameras proved that the combined structure of payload and final stage was more than 60 feet long.

Fortunately for the United States, the Redstone team had refused to accept permanent exclusion from space. Dr. von Braun had made repeated attempts to get authorization for his project, and though they were all turned down, he continued the struggle. On one occasion he was preparing to launch a slightly clandestine satellite with a Jupiter-C (virtually a duplicate of the vehicle which eventually orbited the first United States satellite, Explorer 1), but the Department of Defense discovered the project in time to frustrate it.

Not until the first Vanguard test vehicle had exploded spectacularly on the pad (December 6, 1957) was the Army given permission to go ahead. On January 31, 1958, the United States had its first satellite in orbit and could obtain some consolation from the fact that it had made the most important discovery of the IGY. For it was Explorer 1 that detected the wide-ranging, invisible halo of the Van Allen radiation belt.

So, in circumstances more dramatic than any novelist could have contrived or any scientist would have desired, Earth's new moons came into being. Millions of people were to see Sputnik 2, still catching the sunlight on the edge of space, gliding slowly from west to east across the ancient constellations. Few could have remained unmoved by the knowledge that they belonged to the first generation to set its sign among the stars.

The uses—scientific and otherwise—of artificial earth satellites will be discussed in the next two chapters, but before some of these can be fully appreciated it may be well to look a little more closely at the orbits they must follow. These are the expression of nature's traffic laws; we violate them at our peril.

The critical speed of 5 miles a second, necessary to establish an orbit, is quite independent of the size or mass of the satellite concerned; it applies equally to the 100-ton-payload of Saturn 5 and the barely visible wire hairs launched by the millions in the notorious "Needles" experiment. If Earth had a natural moon just outside the atmosphere, it would have to orbit at this speed; and since at 18,000 mph it takes one and a half hours to circumnavigate the globe, this would be the duration of the "month." A month that was shorter than the day sounds an odd phenomenon; but stranger things happen on other planets.

At greater distances from the Earth, less speed is necessary to counter the weakening gravitational pull, so the period of revolution steadily increases; 1,075 miles up, it is exactly two hours, or one-twelfth of a day. For many purposes, such as regular tracking from ground stations, it is convenient to have satellites "geared" to exact ratios of the Earth's rotation; the twelve-hour orbit is particularly useful. But the most valuable of all is the twenty-four-hour, or synchronous, orbit, which permits a satellite to hover apparently motionless over one spot

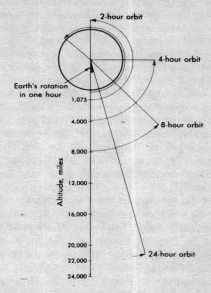

Figure 12. Angular speeds of satellites.

on the globe. The idea of a body hanging fixed in the sky seems
more than a little uncanny, but of course such a "geostationary"
satellite is not really motionless. It is merely turning through
space at the same rate as the Earth; and in order to do that at
a distance of 26,000 miles from the center of rotation, it has
to move along its orbit at almost 7,000 mph—very far from
standing still. Figure 12, which is drawn to scale, shows the
altitudes at which these various phenomena occur.

Although it is simplest to talk about circular orbits, all real
ones are elliptical, as explained in Chapter 6. In some cases,
the ellipticity—or eccentricity, to use the correct term—can
be very high, a satellite coming to within a few hundred miles
of the Earth and then rising tens of thousands of miles out into
space at its far point. Oddly enough, the eccentricity does not

affect the period of a satellite; that is determined only by the length of its longer axis. Elliptical orbits are sometimes referred to as "egg-shaped," but this is incorrect, since eggs are— usually—more pointed at one end than the other. An ellipse is perfectly symmetrical about both axes.

The dimensions of an orbit and its eccentricity are its own most important characteristics; but they do not define it completely, for it can be tilted at any angle to the Earth's axis. From the practical point of view, it is easiest to launch a satellite in the equatorial plane, because when it takes off it can get the maximum boost from the 1,000 mph of spin available there. Unfortunately, equatorial sites tend to be politically unstable, though in 1967 the Italians neatly avoided this in their San Marco project by launching from an oil-drilling rig in the Indian Ocean. (For *very* large spacecraft, ocean launches may one day be mandatory.)

At the other extreme from the equatorial orbit is the polar one, which is slightly more difficult to achieve, since it cannot take advantage of the Earth's spin. This handicap is more than offset by the fact that a polar satellite, in the course of a few revolutions, can observe the entire surface of the globe, whereas an equatorial one is limited to low latitudes.

It is also perfectly possible to launch a satellite *against* the direction of the Earth's spin, so that it has what is known as a retrograde orbit. If it were exactly retrograde—moving from east to west, as the natural celestial bodies appear to do— it would require an extra 2,000 miles an hour of launching speed to overcome the effects of the Earth's rotation, and there would be little point in such a fuel-wasting procedure. But satellites that are very slightly retrograde—a few degrees "backward" from the orbit over the poles—do have some valuable properties (see p. 80).

The ground track of a satellite—the path it traces over the surface of the Earth—may be almost as important as its orbit. It determines the regions from which the satellite can be observed by ground stations, either electronically or optically. It also determines the areas of Earth which the satellite itself can observe and the frequency with which it can view them, obviously a deciding factor for meteorological or reconnaissance satellites.

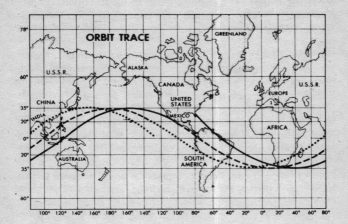

Figure 13. Ground track of low-inclination orbit.

The very simplest case is that of the equatorial satellite; it remains always above the equator and retraces the same path forever. It will go over the same spot once in every orbit, at regular intervals determined by its period of rotation. The only exception is the stationary satellite, which always stays over one spot and may thus be regarded as having an infinite period.

A satellite in a polar—90-degree—orbit, on the other hand, will weave a pattern embracing the entire Earth as it shuttles from north to south, and the planet turns beneath it. A similar kind of basketwork pattern, but spanning a narrower band of latitude, is traced out by satellites launched in inclined orbits. The typical Cape Kennedy ground track, made familiar to millions by the Mercury and Gemini flights, is that shown in Figure 13.

Satellites with unusual periods and angles of inclination can produce the most extraordinary ground tracks, forming loops, apparently going backward, and so on. All these cases can be worked out with the aid of a globe, as long as one remembers that the plane of the orbit stays fixed in space, while the Earth revolves at a uniform speed inside it. Highly instructive models can be purchased from educational stores to illustrate all these cases, so no attempt will be made to describe them here.

The stability of an orbit is obviously a matter of the greatest practical importance, especially for expensive satellites, which must operate for many years to pay for themselves—either scientifically or commercially. However, there are two kinds of stability to be considered. The first involves a satellite's lifetime—how long it will remain aloft before it re-enters the atmosphere and is burned up (or recovered). The second and more subtle point is: how long will the satellite remain in its *original* orbit?

As far as lifetime is concerned, the simple answer is that a satellite will stay up forever, as long as no part of its orbit ever enters the atmosphere. But if the lowest point of the orbit (the perigee) is close enough to Earth for there to be any appreciable air resistance, the satellite is bound to come down sooner or later. Every time it slices into the atmosphere, it loses a little of its energy, so it does not rise quite so far out into space the next time around. The far point (apogee) therefore steadily descends, coming closer and closer with each revolution—though perigee remains almost unaffected. To put it expressively though not quite accurately, the satellite spirals in toward Earth.

At last, the orbit becomes perfectly circular; apogee and perigee are identical. The orbit is now wholly inside the atmosphere; resistance is acting over the entire path, and the satellite has only a few hours of life remaining to it. Unless it is a heavily protected re-entry vehicle, designed to survive the thousands of degrees of heat produced by boring through 5 miles of gas in every second, it will burn up in a spectacular display of artificial meteors.

The period of a satellite in the closest possible orbit, just before the final catastrophe, is almost precisely 90 minutes (the very last orbit is completed in about 84 minutes). This means that, by pure coincidence, during the last few days of its life every satellite makes *exactly* 18 revolutions in every 24 hours, and so retraces the same path over the surface of the turning Earth, day after day.

So, in the spring of 1958, millions of people throughout Europe were able to watch, at almost the same time every night, and moving along the same track through the constellations, the brilliant star of Sputnik 2 carrying the corpse of the dog Laika. This nightly death-watch for a dying satellite may well be repeated, with far deeper emotions, in the years ahead, as some future space mission terminates in a celestial funeral pyre.

This fate can never befall a satellite whose perigee is more than 1,000 miles from Earth—still very close indeed, as cosmic distances go. But though an orbit may be stable, it is not necessarily permanent; there are forces at work which may slowly change it.

Among these are the gravitational attractions of the Sun, Moon, and planets, engaged in an endless tug-of-war. Their influence, however, is very small, at least for satellites close to the Earth. But one "perturbation" which is not small is that due to the Earth itself.

If our planet were a perfect sphere, with a uniform distribution of matter inside it, a satellite would always repeat the same orbit. But in the real case, the Earth has a pronounced equatorial bulge, as well as other less conspicuous dents and bumps. The polar flattening produces a most important effect known as precision, which is well demonstrated in the case of a spinning top.

When a top loses its speed and begins to fall over, the downward pull of gravity has a paradoxical effect on its behavior. The axis of the top, which until now has been fixed vertically in space, starts to trace out a conical path. Anyone who has ever played with a toy gyroscope and has noticed how it appears to move at right angles to the direction in which a force is applied has observed the phenomenon of precision in its clearest form.

A satellite whirling around the Earth is in effect an enormous gyroscope, several thousand miles in radius, and the plane of its orbit tends to remain fixed in space. This indeed happens, when the orbit is directly over the equator, and its axis coincides with the Earth's. But when the orbital plane is tilted, the attraction of the Earth's equatorial bulge can then come into play, and the orbital plane begins to twist, so that after a few thousand, or a few million, revolutions it may have precessed around a complete circle.

By selecting the right inclination, one can choose any rate of precession desired. This has been used to advantage, in the case of some meteorological and reconnaissance satellites, to produce an orbit whose plane makes one revolution every year. Such an orbit is called "sun synchronous"; it exactly cancels the Earth's annual rotation around the Sun, and a satellite moving in it passes over the same spot on the Earth at the same time every day. The United States Air Force's Samos reconnaissance satellites have this useful characteristic, so that they can re-photograph the same areas under identical illumination. To do this, they have to be launched into a slightly retrograde orbit, tilted about six degrees backward from the axis of the Earth. Who would have thought, even a decade ago, that the intricacies of celestial mechanics would one day be of military importance?

Magnetic and electrical effects in space can also produce minor effects upon satellite orbits; more surprisingly, so can the pressure of sunlight, as discussed in Chapter 24. Feeble

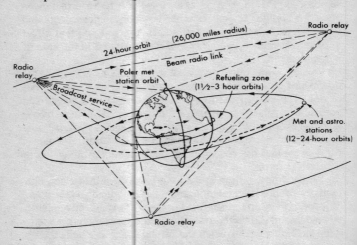

Figure 14. Applications satellites.

though it is, as it acts continuously it can produce large effects on satellites of low density, like the Echo balloons. These huge but flimsy structures have been "blown" hundreds of miles out of their original orbits by the pressure of solar radiation.

To sum up, it is possible to establish satellites in orbit around the Earth at almost any distance, eccentricity, and angle of inclination. Figure 14 shows just a few of these, with their scientific and technical applications.

This illustration was prepared in 1950 for the first edition of *The Exploration of Space*, and I see no purpose in altering it; the next two chapters will describe how all these concepts, and more, have now been realized.

However, two comments may be in order. The first is that even now we do not have *direct* links between relay satellites, and there are some slight advantages in this. The second is that the "Met and Astro Stations" are shown at an altitude which no one could have then guessed was occupied by the intense radiation of the Van Allen belt, not discovered until eight years later.

This does not invalidate the diagram. If we find these orbits useful for manned stations, that will be just too bad for the Van Allen belt. We will simply sweep it up.

9. OPENING SKIES

It is rather amusing, in the second decade of the Space Age, to look back on the hopes and predictions of those who first proposed the launching of artificial satellites—and to see how modest they were in the light of later achievement. In 1954, for example, the Space Flight Committee of the American Rocket Society prepared a report for the National Science Foundation on "The Utility of an Artificial Unmanned Earth Satellite." Some of the points it rather diffidently made were:

ASTRONOMY AND ASTROPHYSICS. A satellite could overcome some of the limitations on observations made through the atmosphere. *GEODESY (INCLUDING NAVIGATION AND MAPPING).* The size and shape of the earth, the intensity of its gravitational field, and other geodetic constants might be determined more accurately. Practical benefits to navigation at sea and mapping over large distances would ensue. *GEOPHYSICS (INCLUDING METEOROLOGY).* The study of incoming radiation and its effects upon the earth's atmosphere might lead eventually to better methods of long-range weather prediction.

Within five years of the committee's report, all these forecasts had been amply demonstrated; within ten, the sciences mentioned were undergoing something like a revolution. And this was entirely due to the fact that, for the first time, it had been possible to establish observing stations above the atmosphere.

In the first few years of the Space Age scores of "scientific" satellites were launched, carrying instruments for hundreds of experiments. Some were extremely simple; others, like the

Soviet Union's giant "Proton" satellites, nothing less than orbiting physics labs. Even to list them would take pages, and to describe the results they have obtained has already required many volumes. At the Goddard Space Flight Center, Maryland, where the instrument readings are stored for later analysis after they have been relayed to earth, hundreds of thousands of reels of magnetic tape are stacked in endless rows while the scientists try to cope with the flood of new knowledge pouring down from the stars.

Only a few typical or unusually interesting satellites will be described here, together with a sampling of the results they have obtained. But which of these results are the most important we may not know for generations. Only time will tell what secrets are now hidden away in the vaults at Goddard, waiting to demolish long-held theories or to establish new ones.

For simplicity, it would be hard to beat the "balloon" satellites, of which Echo 1 was the first and most famous. On June 24, 1966, NASA launched a singularly perfect specimen, the 100-foot-diameter Pageos, which looks exactly like a giant, highly polished ball bearing. Made of mylar film 0.0005 inch thick, Pageos weighed only 120 pounds and when inflated in orbit was half a million times larger than the canister into which it had been skillfully packed. Moving in a polar orbit at an altitude of 2,600 miles (period 181 minutes), it is easily visible to the naked eye.

Its purpose is geodesy—the mapping of the Earth to a degree of precision never before possible. Surveyors thousands of miles apart can observe it simultaneously and photograph it as it moves across the stars; when analyzed, these photographs will allow points on the Earth to be fixed to within about ten yards. Similar results have also been obtained by using satellites carrying flashing strobe lights (Anna 1-B, 1962) or mirrors reflecting back laser beams (Geos 1, 1965), but Pageos requires the minimum of ground equipment.

High-precision studies of orbits made possible by satellites of this type have already revised our knowledge of the Earth's shape. It is not a simple flattened sphere (ovoid); there are bumps and bulges which will tell us much about its evolution and the distribution of matter in its interior. Of course, these deviations from the ideal shape are very small—utterly invisible to the eye of the astronaut looking back at his home from a few thousand miles away. But they are of great importance scientifically, and it is a curious thought that knowledge of the Earth's interior can best be obtained by going far out into space.

However, most of the instrumentation aboard satellites has been designed to study the environment through which they pass, and undoubtedly the greatest discovery yet made is that due to the very first United States satellite, Explorer 1 (1958). This revealed, as someone put it expressively, that "space is radioactive," and for a while there was considerable alarm about the effects of this discovery upon orbiting astronauts.

We now know, thanks to Explorer 1 and its much more elaborate successors, that our planet is surrounded by a huge radiation belt, roughly doughnut-shaped, with the Earth in the hole. The inner part of the belt—named after its discoverer, Dr. James Van Allen—consists mostly of positively charged protons (hydrogen nuclei) and reaches its maximum intensity at a height of about 500 miles. In the outer zone, negatively charged electrons predominate, with their maximum intensity at 10,000 miles. At one time it was believed that there were two separate belts, but it is now known that they merge into each other, though they are separated by a region (about 8,000 miles high) where the intensity of radiation is a minimum. There is also very little radiation over the poles; it all lies above the equatorial and temperate zones.

The great radiation belt is produced by streams of electrons and protons from the Sun, which have become trapped in the Earth's magnetic field. As a result there is an extremely complicated interrelation between solar and terrestrial magnetic activity, both of which vary with time. For tens of thousands of miles around the Earth there is an invisible cloud of electronic and protonic "weather," with its storms and winds and calms, never suspected until our generation.

The great radiation belt is not symmetrical; the gale of charged particles "blowing" from the Sun compresses it on the daylight side of Earth and makes it trail out on the night side. The doughnut is therefore badly distorted—three or four times thicker on one side than on the other. At its outer fringes it merges imperceptibly into the (very weak) general background of radiation between the planets.

Almost every scientific satellite launched from the Earth—as well as many space probes on greater journeys—has carried instruments to measure the ever-changing phenomena in the great radiation belt. A good example is the Orbiting Geophysical Laboratory (OGO), of which the third, and first fully successful one, was launched on June 6, 1966.

OGO 3 has an orbit specifically designed to sample an enormous volume of the near-Earth environment. Its perigee is only 170 miles up, but its apogee is 75,800 miles from Earth, or one-third of the way to the Moon. Completing this very elongated path once every two days, it reports on the energy and concentration of the protons and electrons in the radiation belt, fluctuations in the Earth's magnetic field, radio propagation characteristics, cosmic rays, interplanetary dust, radio noise—to mention only some of the twenty-one separate experiments it conducts.

One of the most important—and most uncertain—characteristics of the space environment before artificial satellites became available was the frequency of meteoroids; some pessimists believed that any spacecraft would be riddled by cosmic machine-gun fire as soon as it left the protective blanket of the atmosphere. In fact, meteoroids have turned out to be so rare that it is quite difficult to accumulate reliable statistics about them, and rather heroic efforts were needed to do so. Perhaps the most impressive of these were the launchings of the three huge Pegasus satellites (February 16, May 27, July 30, 1965) by the last three of the Saturn 1 rockets. In orbit, the Pegasus satellites extended vast "wings," almost a hundred feet across, which consisted of thin aluminum panels, varying in thickness between 1.5 and 16 thousandths of an inch. These panels were connected to electrical circuits which reported any meteoroid penetrations, and signaled them back to Earth. After many months of successful operation, the three Pegasus satellites showed conclusively that, at least for flights of short duration, meteoroids were not a serious danger.*

The ionosphere—that electrified layer in the upper at-

*Note on terminology: a *meteoroid* (usually micrometeoroid) is a small solid object moving through space; a *meteor* is the streak of light it produces when it enters the atmosphere; a *meteorite* is what remains in the rare cases when it reaches the ground. The words are often used interchangeably.

mosphere which reflects radio signals back to Earth, and so makes long-distance communication possible around the curve of the globe—is one piece of near-space that has been of tremendous scientific, commercial, and military interest for half a century. It is not surprising, therefore, that dozens of satellites have been launched to investigate it. One of the first and most successful was the Canadian Alouette (lark), sent into a 600-mile-high polar orbit on September 29, 1962. It carried a radio transmitter which swept continuously across the VHF (very-high-frequency) band; after the signals from this "topside sounder" had passed through the ionosphere, they were picked up by ground stations and their intensity gave a measure of the electron density in this region. Ionospheric probing was also the main purpose of the first United Kingdom satellite, Ariel 1 (April 26, 1962). Its instruments measured and sampled the charged particles between 242 and 754 miles above the Earth.

From the scientific point of view, perhaps the most exciting satellites are those which, although they may be within a few hundred miles of the Earth, are looking outward to deep space. For by lifting our instruments through a distance which is quite trivial, even by terrestrial standards, we have been able to obtain a completely new view of the universe.

Until our age, astronomers had to make all their observations from the bottom of the atmosphere. As a result, they were rather like color-blind men straining their eyes through a fog—or, to use a well-known and not inaccurate analogy, like fish peering upward from the bottom of a muddy pool.

On a clear, moonless night, when we look up at the stars, it seems that there is nothing to obscure our view. But this is an illusion—the result of evolutionary necessity. Our eyes have, naturally enough, adapted themselves to use the light which passes through the atmosphere, and that is only a small fraction of the radiations that fall upon the Earth from space. Most of them, luckily for us, are completely blocked by the 100-mile-thick gaseous shield above our heads.

The complete range of the electromagnetic spectrum—that is, all possible types of wave that can pass through space—is shown in Figure 15, which also shows the regions in which the Earth's atmosphere is normally transparent. It will be seen that there are a number of "windows" through which radiation

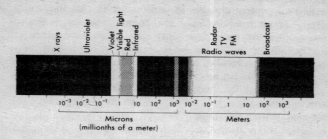

*Figure 15. The transparency of the atmosphere at varying wave
lengths.*

can penetrate; the most important is that centered around visible
light, but a second one—the radio window—has been opened
in our lifetimes and has given rise to the vast new science of
radio astronomy.

Between and beyond these windows there is partial or
complete opacity. Even a few feet of atmosphere acts like a
brick wall to the very short waves of the spectrum, such as the
X-rays and the far ultraviolet. Ground-based astronomers had
no way of telling if such waves existed in space, but they could
be certain that, if they did, they would carry priceless information about the Sun and stars.

The Orbiting Solar Observatory (OSO) and Orbiting Astronomical Observatory (OAO) were very complex satellites
designed to explore this hitherto unseen universe. OSO-1 was
launched on March 7, 1962, and observed the Sun for 2,000
hours during its operational lifetime. OSO-2 (February 3, 1965)
was also successful, but the third, OSO-C (August 25, 1965),
failed to orbit. The satellites were of unusual design, consisting
of a spinning wheel on the axis of which was mounted a semicircular "sail" carrying instruments pointing with great precision at the Sun. These instruments measured and analyzed the
solar radiation in the X-ray and the far-ultraviolet region.

There are at least two reasons why this particular radiation
is of major importance. Unlike visible sunlight, it shows great
fluctuations in intensity, as a result of gigantic eruptions, or

"flares," on the surface of the Sun. Sometimes these outbursts cause such violent changes in the ionosphere that they completely disrupt long-distance radio communications. It is also possible that they may have some effect upon the weather.

Even more serious, as we move into the Space Age, they may herald the advent of ionized gas clouds leaping from Sun to Earth, and so could give warning to astronauts of "solar storms." As manned space flight becomes more common and more widespread, it will be essential to keep a regular patrol of Sun-watching satellites.

The first Orbiting Astronomical Observatory was launched on April 8, 1966. It contained a battery of telescopes (the largest having an aperture of 16 inches), and with its 440,000 separate parts and 30 miles of wiring was, at that time, one of the most complex satellites ever developed. It was injected into a perfect orbit, but within a few hours something went wrong with its power supply and its signals slowly faded out. In its first attempt to see the unknown universe of ultraviolet stars and nebulae, the United States had gambled enough to build half a dozen Mount Palomar telescopes, and had lost.

At the other end of the spectrum, there is also unknown territory represented by the very long radio waves which are reflected back into space by the upper surface of the ionosphere and so do not normally reach ground level. The waves concerned are those longer than 30 meters (100 feet), and to study them properly it will be necessary to use very large antenna systems. The Canadian Alouette pioneered in this field by carrying antennas rolled up like steel rules, and these have been developed now to such a degree that a small drum can extrude an antenna several hundred feet long. The really advanced radio astronomy satellites, however, will probably be in the form of spinning webs; design studies show that centrifugal force would permit the automatic deployment of antenna systems which may be tens of *miles* in diameter, yet may weigh only a few hundred pounds.

The heartbreaking demise of the first multimillion-dollar Orbiting Astronomical Observatory—which might have been saved had there been a man on the spot with a screwdriver—strongly suggests that the very large and complex scientific satellites of the future will be designed for easy servicing, even if they are not permanently manned. As a step in this direction, a large number of experiments were carried out by the Mercury and Gemini astronauts. Plans for the next stage—the orbital laboratory—will be discussed in Chapter 12.

Meanwhile, the robot probes which have been leaving the atmosphere in such numbers have already started a revolution, comparable to that which began three and a half centuries ago when Galileo pointed his first crude "optic tube" at the heavens. Every breakthrough in instruments produces a corresponding breakthrough in knowledge; the satellites have given us new eyes and ears, and for a long time to come we will be dazzled and deafened by the information they bring us. But, later, we will begin to understand.

10. FIRST HARVEST

In the last chapter we glanced briefly at the new knowledge now being obtained by artificial satellites; in this one we shall look at their practical uses. It is essential to realize, however, that this is a very arbitrary distinction, and the dividing line is constantly on the move. All really great advances in technology, as opposed to mere gadgetry, arise from scientific discoveries which at the time seem to be of no relevance to everyday life. Electric power and light were made possible because men like Faraday played with magnets and coils of wire, trying to understand the workings of nature and sometimes even taking a perverse pride in the invariably mistaken belief that their discoveries would never be of use to anybody. Yet always, a generation or two later (a decade or two later, nowadays), the Edisons come along and turn their "pure" science into billion-dollar industries.

As yet, the magnetic fields in space, the great radiation belt, the harmonics of the Earth's gravitational field, the solar wind, and similar exotic phenomena have little value in the marketplace. But their time will come.

Meanwhile, there are types of satellite which have obvious and immediate practical uses, which everyone can appreciate and many millions can indeed share. These are the so-called applications satellites which do not gather scientific facts, but work for a living. (Many do both, for applications satellites usually carry instrumentation of various kinds.)

As already mentioned in Chapter 1, the first fictional project for an artificial satellite—Hale's "Brick Moon"—was an aid to navigation. Indeed, it is hard to see what other use could have been imagined in 1869, since no practical way then existed of collecting information automatically and sending it over great distances.

Probably no one would have been more surprised than Hale to know that his inspired fantasy came true in less than 90 years, though it did so with the aid of techniques of which he could scarcely have dreamed. His brick moon was to be observed visually, like any other of the celestial bodies, which meant, of course, that it would be useless in daylight and in cloudy weather. The navigational satellites of today make their presence known by radio and so can be tracked under any conditions.

The first to be launched, Transit 1 B (April 13, 1960), carried two radio beacons and utilized the Doppler effect—the change of pitch of a signal with varying speed. The operation of the system can best be imagined by this analogy: Suppose you are standing at some distance from a railroad track and that a train passes with its whistle blowing. While the train is approaching, the whistle will seem to have a higher frequency than normal; while it is receding, the frequency will be lower than normal. Only at the moment of closest approach will you hear the whistle's note as it really is; if you possessed what musicians call perfect pitch, you could pinpoint this moment and would know, even without being able to see it, when the train was nearest to you.

The Transit satellite is the train, and because its orbit is known with great precision, it runs to a more accurate timetable than any railroad. The radio beacon provides the whistle; by analyzing its rate of change of pitch, ship- or air-borne electronics systems can obtain a "fix" with an accuracy of one-tenth of a mile.

A series of Transit satellites was launched between 1960 and 1964; they included the first satellites ever to be powered by nuclear energy, and the system became operational in July, 1964. Although at first its main customers were the Polaris submarines, it is now available for use by all ships which fit the fairly simple receivers and computers required; oceanographic survey vessels have particularly benefited by it.

More advanced systems are now being developed which

will involve satellites fixed in the 24-hour stationary orbit above the equator; this arrangement will be much simpler and will permit a far wider range of users. The time will come, in the not-too-distant future, when a wristwatch-sized computer turned to the Navsat network will tell a man exactly where he is anywhere on the surface of the globe, and no one need ever again be lost, even in the remotest corner of the world.

Now that millions of TV viewers are accustomed to seeing, in their regular weather forecasts, photographs of cloud cover over whole continents it may seem surprising that anyone ever doubted the utility of meteorological satellites. Yet their value was not at first obvious even to the experts, as I can testify from personal knowledge.

When the American Museum of Natural History's Hayden Planetarium asked me to arrange its 1954 symposium on space flight, I wrote to Dr. Harry Wexler, chief of research of the U.S. Weather Bureau, suggesting that he should present a paper on the meteorological uses of satellites. I was somewhat taken aback when he replied that they would be of very little value. After brooding awhile I wrote again, challenging him to demonstrate this—if only to stop us space cadets from wasting the valuable time of the meteorological authorities. To his credit, Dr. Wexler accepted the challenge; by the time he had written his paper, he had converted himself completely. Afterward he became the United States' chief protagonist for this new research instrument and played a major role in the development of meteorological satellites until his death in 1962. Perhaps I should add that Dr. Wexler's attitude was precisely correct and demonstrates all the stages (skepticism, inquiry, enthusiasm) a scientist *should* pass through when confronted with some novel and (in this case literally) far-out idea.

The first meteorological satellite, Tiros (Television and Infrared Observation Satellite) was launched on April 1, 1960, into an almost circular orbit a little more than 400 miles above the Earth. Because its orbit was inclined to the equator at an angle of 48 degrees, during the course of every few revolutions it ranged over half the surface of the globe. As the first of its 22,500 photographs was received by the ground stations, the meteorologists realized that they had, as one of them put it, "gone from rags to riches overnight."

Seven further satellites were launched in the Tiros series between April, 1960, and December, 1963, all into similar orbits with periods of 100 minutes. Most of them equaled or exceeded their designed life, and between them they sent back to earth several hundred thousand photographs. In addition, they carried instruments that could measure the flow of heat from our planet back into space—information vital to the meteorologist but previously unobtainable.

The last of the Tiros series—9 and 10—were even more successful; they were launched into high-inclination (81–82-degree) orbits so that they passed almost over the poles and gave virtually global coverage. Similar orbits were used by the still more advanced Nimbus and ESSA (Environmental Science Services Administration) satellites, which have continued and extended the work begun by Tiros, establishing the world's first operational weather-satellite system. Today any electronic enthusiast with a few hundred dollars and a certain amount of ingenuity can build a simple ground station that can interrogate the ESSA satellites as they pass overhead, and can read off, on a cathode-ray tube or commercial facsimile receiver, the weather picture for a thousand miles around him. This Automatic Picture Transmission (APT) system was introduced with Tiros 8 in December, 1963, and has made the multimillion-dollar satellites freely available to any country or any individual who cares to use them.

The first high-definition photos of an entire hemisphere, made by a satellite sufficiently far from Earth to show it as a planet, were obtained in December, 1966, from the first of the Applications Technology Satellites. Stationed over mid-Pacific, ATS 1's special electronic camera produced superb studies of changing cloud patterns over almost half the Earth; these were later combined to give speeded-up movies so that meteorologists could watch the circulation of the atmosphere with their own eyes, thus learning in a few minutes facts which might never have been revealed in years of ground-based observations.

It is probable that the various "metsats" have already paid for themselves many times over. They have detected hurricanes far out at sea, hours before their existence could have been discovered in any other way. They have improved the quality of weather forecasting, with all that this implies to human wealth, productivity, safety, and happiness. It has been claimed that really accurate prediction of rain, snow, monsoons, and other meteorological phenomena will eventually be possible, thanks to the new knowledge from this source—with savings that have been estimated at *tens* of billions of dollars a year. Looking even further ahead, if weather control or modification ever becomes possible (or desirable, which is not at all the same thing), it can hardly be attempted without the complete understanding of atmospheric processes that only satellites can provide.

The ATS satellites, built by the Hughes Aircraft Company and exploiting the technology its engineers developed for Syncom and Early Bird (see pp. 98–101), may be regarded as a series of space buses for testing various practical applications of satellites. In addition to obtaining meteorological information by their own onboard cameras, they can serve as communications links in an elaborate data-collecting system, relaying information from dozens of ground stations. This information includes readings from rainfall gauges, oceanographic buoys, met balloons—and possibly beacons attached to large land and marine animals for zoological research.

Probably the most interesting, and doubtless the most advanced, of the applications satellites are those about which nothing has been published; in some cases, even their names are classified. I refer, of course, to the military reconnaissance satellites.

In his 1929 book Hermann Oberth had already pointed out that a manned space station could be used to watch the movements of warships. With the development of TV techniques and camera-carrying capsules that could be recovered from orbit, satellites became of intense interest to the military, particularly after the 1960 U-2 debacle had proved the vulnerability of reconnaissance aircraft in the missile age. It is true that a satellite can also be destroyed, perhaps more easily than it can be launched. But there is a very important distinction; even the people who use reconnaissance aircraft admit that they are illegal and apologize when they are caught, for they are operating in another country's airspace. Satellites, however, fly only in the no-man's-territory beyond the atmosphere and are at liberty to take as many pictures as they please. It is true that for a while the Soviet Union considered that they were provocative and unfriendly, but since it too started using them in large numbers, very little has been heard of this objection.

The United States Air Force has, naturally, been most active in this field; it orbited its first Samos reconnaissance satellite on January 31, 1961, and since then has launched dozens of anonymous payloads, mostly into polar orbits at fairly low altitudes, so that they can thoroughly scrutinize the whole Earth. The quality of the resulting photographs may perhaps be judged by some of those sent back from the Moon by the Orbiter vehicles. Where there is physical recovery of the capsules (as happens with the Discoverer satellites), the definition may well be much higher. Although haze and cloudiness set operational limits to the system, the photographs brought back by the Gemini astronauts show the astonishing amount of detail that can be observed from space when the atmosphere is clear.

There are some military satellites which do not depend on light waves and so are less affected by weather conditions. The Midas satellites were designed to spot ICBM launchings by detecting the immense amounts of infrared radiation produced by rocket exhausts.

Other space vehicles listen in to radar and communications networks; yet others are involved in precision mapping and navigation. (The Transit program, mentioned previously, was classified for some years because of its military applications.) And particular mention should be made of the VELA, or Sentry, satellites, which swing slowly along almost circular orbits 70,000 miles above the Earth, waiting to detect clandestine nuclear explosions.

The Soviet Union has its counterpart to this program, though it talks about it even less than does the United States. As long ago as December, 1965, it reached number one hundred in its rather mysterious Cosmos series, most of which return to Earth after a few days' traveling along close, high-inclination orbits. It may be doubted if their purpose is always entirely scientific.*

On balance, these satellites have probably had a stabilizing

---

*Some of these—e.g., Cosmos 57 (February, 1965)—have exploded into hundreds of fragments, to the great annoyance of the satellite-tracking networks. It has been suggested that this was to prevent them from descending on United States territory.

effect upon international affairs; they have made a reality of President Eisenhower's imaginative "Open Skies" proposal. The advance announcement of Chinese nuclear tests by the United States proves that it is now impossible for one country to conduct military preparations without the knowledge of the two super powers; nor can these hide anything from each other. It has been stated that the United States reconnaissance satellites have already paid for the *entire* space program—for by revealing that the Soviet Union's missile deployment was not as fast as had been feared, they allowed the Department of Defense to establish more modest goals for its own ICBM program. The Samos satellites have been worth many times their weight in gold to the United States taxpayer.

A few months before Sputnik 1 opened the Space Age, the following wild-eyed prophecy appeared in print: "It may seem premature, if not ludicrous, to talk about the commercial possibilities of satellites. Yet the airplane became of commercial importance within thirty years of its birth, and there are good reasons for thinking that this time scale may be shortened in the case of the satellite, because of its immense value in the field of communications" (*The Making of a Moon*, Clarke, 1957). The first $100 million of Comsat stock went on the market seven years later (June 2, 1964) and promptly disappeared into myriad safety deposit boxes.

The idea of employing satellites as radio relays, so that all possible wavelengths—including light, if desired—could be used for communications purposes, now seems a rather obvious one, and it is somewhat surprising that it did not appear until 1945. It is true that Oberth, in his 1929 classic, *The Road to Space Travel*, mentioned that manned space stations could signal to remote parts of the Earth by flashing *heliograph* mirrors, which today seems a very primitive idea. We tend to forget that the astonishing developments in electronics, miniaturization, and communications techniques which now permit us to control robots on the surface of the Moon, or in orbit around Mars, have become possible only since World War II. Willy Ley once pointed out that when Oberth wrote his book, the only long-range radio stations in existence used antenna systems acres in extent, supported by towers hundreds of feet high. The idea that this sort of equipment might one day be squeezed into a hatbox would then have seemed slightly more fantastic than space travel itself. Even as late as 1945 I still assumed that communications satellites would be large, *manned* structures. Several years of battling with balky electronics had convinced me that it was essential to have a servicing engineer on the spot; I have modified this position only slightly.

The simplest type of communications satellite is passive, an orbiting radio mirror which reflects signals back to Earth without itself modifying them in any way. Such was the giant Echo balloon, launched on August 12, 1960, into a 1,000-mile-high orbit, and for a long time one of the most conspicuous objects in the night sky. Echo 1 (and its slightly larger successor Echo 2, launched into a near-polar orbit on January 25, 1964) was used for many test transmissions of speech, teletype, and facsimile and clearly demonstrated the potential value of satellites for communications. However, passive systems (though they are simple, have nothing to go wrong, and can provide an unlimited number of circuits) are extremely inefficient; only a tiny fraction of the power beamed at the Echo balloon actually fell upon it, and an even smaller fraction of that power was picked up by ground stations. Although some of these limitations may be overcome (for example, by replacing the spherical reflector by one so shaped that it sends a much larger signal back to Earth), passive systems appear to be largely of historic interest.

Active satellites are true relays, receiving the signal from the ground station, amplifying it, and rebroadcasting it at greatly increased power (and at a different frequency, to avoid interference). Such a system, though complex, is millions of times more efficient than a passive one; it received its first public demonstration with Telstar 1 (July 10, 1962). Though the United States Army's earlier Atlas-Score (December 18, 1958) and Courier (October 4, 1960) had provided a very limited experimental service with radio signals only, Telstar heralded the age of intercontinental television when it inaugurated the first live transatlantic program on July 23, 1962.

Telstar was also the first privately owned satellite, and thereby created another precedent. It was built by the American Telephone and Telegraph Company, which the Bell Laboratories' energetic director of communications research (and occasional science-fiction author), John R. Pierce, had dragged singlehanded into the space-communications field. Dr. Pierce was not only one of the instigators of the Echo project but was also co-inventor of the special wide-band amplifier—the traveling wave tube—which is the heart of all communications satellites to date.

Because the rockets then available could not lift large payloads to very high orbits, Telstar and its Radio Corporation of America successor, Relay (two of each were ultimately launched), orbited relatively close to the Earth; they therefore moved fairly rapidly and remained in view from any given pair of ground stations for only a few minutes at a time. As a result, they could not provide the continuous type of service essential for commercial operations.

There were two ways of overcoming this difficulty. One was to use a whole series of Telstar-type low-altitude satellites, more or less equally spaced around the world so that there was always at least one above the horizon at any given point. The other was to go out to the synchronous orbit, 22,000 miles above the equator, where a satellite would appear to stand fixed in the sky, and three could provide a worldwide service.

The synchronous system was forcefully advocated by Dr. Harold Rosen of the Hughes Aircraft Company, whose Syncom 2 was launched on July 26, 1963. (Syncom 1 achieved the correct orbit on February 14, 1962, but because of an onboard mechanical failure never returned any signals.) This satellite was stationed over the Atlantic, but because its orbit was inclined to the equator, it did not remain absolutely fixed over the same spot. Instead, it described a small north-south figure eight every day, but as the ground tracking stations followed its excursions in latitude, it was available for 24-hour use.

The first satellite that was truly stationary (i.e., both in a 24-hour orbit *and* above the equator) was Syncom 3, launched August 19, 1964, with the specific intention of covering the Tokyo Olympics, which it did brilliantly. After many thousands of hours of operation, the two Syncoms were handed over to the Department of Defense to provide reliable transpacific communications; Syncom 2 was "walked" along the equator by gentle puffs from its control jets, until it had joined its companion on the other side of the world.

The operational experience provided by the first synchronous satellites provided the basis for a commercial system and also disposed of a number of bogeys. It was obvious from the beginning that a satellite which appeared to be fixed in the sky would have enormous advantages over one that must be constantly tracked; perhaps most important, it would not require movable antenna systems backed up by computers, for once the ground antennas had been aimed in the right direction, they could be left pointing that way, and simple television-type arrays could thus be used. However, there was a price to be paid for this simplicity.

In the first place, the synchronous orbit is so far from Earth that reaching it is quite expensive in terms of rocket fuel. Surprisingly, it is harder to put a payload in the 22,000-mile-high orbit than it is to send it to the moon.

Moreover, a "stationary" satellite will not stay in one place without occasional assistance. The perturbations of other heavenly bodies, and in particular irregularities in the Earth's gravitational field, make it drift slowly from its initial position, so from time to time it has to be nudged back on station by corrective thrusts. Only a very small amount of fuel is required, even for several years of operation, but this does add to the complexity of the system.

These problems, and several others of a technical nature, were triumphantly solved by the Syncom satellites, but there remained a more fundamental one which no engineering advances could remove. It takes an appreciable time—about one-fourth of a second—for a radio signal to climb 22,000 miles and to return to Earth. If you are talking to anyone over a synchronous circuit and ask a question, it is a little more than half a second before you can receive the reply, even if your listener reacts instantly. During that brief but perceptible interval, you may have changed your mind and started to say something else—so you may be speaking when the answer comes. Moreover, unless special precautions are taken, you may hear the delayed echo of your own voice, and nothing is more inhibiting to speech than this.

The echo could be dealt with by suitable circuits; the half-second delay was a law of nature and had to be lived with. For a time it was feared that it might be unacceptable to the public, but in practice it was found that few people even noticed it, though it may occasionally cause trouble to excitable, interruption-prone Celts and Latins. Low-altitude satellites, which would have had shorter time delays, could therefore be dispensed with, and the much more elegant synchronous system could be used for telephony. For radio and television relaying, of course, there had never been any problem. No listener or viewer knows or cares if his program is half a second later than it might have been, had it come from a nearer transmitter.

The United States moved swiftly to set up an operational communications-satellite system; the result was the remarkable semipublic, semiprivate, national-international Communications Satellite Corporation, established by Act of Congress in 1962. Comsat's first child, Early Bird, was launched on April 6, 1965* and placed in service on June 28; it could provide either one TV channel *or* 240 voice (telephone) circuits, but not both. Because of this limitation, the initial rates were high, and before long Comsat was receiving squawks of protest from indignant customers. Exactly the same thing had happened 99 years before, when the first successful Atlantic telegraph went into operation. It had taken just under a century to progress from cable to satellite.

In the spring of 1967 Early Bird was joined by two larger brothers—Intelsat 2 over the Pacific and Intelsat 3 over the Atlantic. With these three satellites, all the world's TV networks could be linked together, and the first global telecast was broadcast on June 27, 1967.

Meanwhile, the Soviet Union had not been idle and had launched Molniya (lightning) communications satellites of its own, into unusual, highly elliptical orbits, with a perigee only 300 miles up and an apogee 24,000 miles high. At first it was thought that Molniya 1 had failed to go into the synchronous orbit, but it was soon realized that its high inclination to the

---

*I was present at Comsat headquarters on that memorable occasion and watched the launch on closed-circuit TV. The three-stage thrust-augmented Thor Delta booster was still on the way up when Vice-President Humphrey started to give us one of his little speeches. The circuit to Cape Kennedy was switched off, and it occurred to me that if anything went wrong now, everyone in the United States would know it *except* the staff of Comsat. They were all listening to the Vice-President.

equator (65 degrees) and period (almost exactly 12 hours) permitted it to arc slowly high over Russia at the same time each day. For a country in northern latitudes, such an orbit has some advantages over the synchronous, equatorial one.

The first generation Comsats were all low-powered devices, so that their signals could be picked up only by sensitive receivers coupled to large antenna systems; the ground stations using them cost $1 million or more and were linked to the various national television or telephone networks. However, many experts believe that the *real* communications revolution will start when Comsats are large and powerful enough to broadcast directly into the home, bypassing the ground stations completely. Only in this way will it be possible to open up the undeveloped countries—Africa, South America, much of Asia—which have never had, and now may never require, surface communications networks.

Direct *radio* (voice) broadcasting from Comsats to simple ground receivers is already technically possible and could have immense social, political, and educational consequences. TV broadcasting, which requires much more power, will take a little longer, but even here the problems are not so much technical as they are economic and political—especially the latter, for direct broadcasting obliterates national and linguistic boundaries and means, among many other things, the end of censorship. It is not surprising that some countries are very worried about it.

Whole volumes and innumerable international conferences have been devoted to the social impact of space communications.* Within a lifetime, they may change our world out of recognition and alter the patterns of business and society at least as much as the telephone has done. They may give us instant "newspapers," with updated hourly editions flashed on to portable receivers no bigger than this book; they may make all telephone calls local ones, so that it will be just as quick and cheap to call a friend at the antipodes as in the next apart-

*I have combined my essays on the subject in *Voices from the Sky*, which also contains a "Short Pre-history of Comsats, or: How I Lost a Billion Dollars in my Spare Time." For the propaganda uses of Comsats, see the short story "I Remember Babylon," in *Tales of Ten Worlds*. Though this is required reading by Comsat staff, I do not wish to raise any false hopes.

ment; they may result in the swift establishment of English (or
Russian, or Mandarin . . .) as a global language; they may result
in the disintegration of the cities and a great reduction in travel,
as telecommunications plus telecontrol will allow most men at
the executive grade to live wherever they please. And there
may be even more dramatic changes, for good or bad, that no
one can foresee today—any more than Samuel Morse or Thomas
Edison could have imagined that one day a quarter of the human
race would watch the same pictures and hear the same sounds.

Whether we like it or not, the world of the communications
satellites will be one world. In the long run, the Comsat will
be mightier than the ICBM. It will put the clock back to the
moment before the building of the Tower of Babel—when,
according to *Genesis* 11: "The Lord said: Behold, they are one
people, and they have all one language, and this is only the
beginning of what they will do; and nothing that they propose
to do will now be impossible for them."

11. MAN IN ORBIT

The first serious students of astronautics had taken it for granted that men would be the most important payloads that rockets would carry into space. Tsiolkovsky and Oberth had written of little else, and though the cautious (as well as more practical-minded) Goddard had confined his few public statements to instrument-carrying vehicles, his private notebooks leave no doubt as to where his interest lay. In these, he went so far as to speculate about refueling bases on the planets—a far cry indeed from "A Method of Attaining Extreme Altitudes."

One reason for this attitude was that these pioneers saw, much more clearly than many who came later, that space travel was the next stage in man's exploration of his environment. Today's controversies between the protagonists of manned and unmanned spacecraft would have seemed to them as pointless as the theological disputes of the Middle Ages.

The conditions which men would encounter in flight beyond the atmosphere were well understood long before any rockets had entered space, and the more conscientious science-fiction writers had quite accurately described ways of coping with them. The rise of aviation medicine from the 1920's onward put these speculations on a more scientific basis, and when the Space Age dawned in 1957 there was only one serious unknown. Every condition that could be encountered in space was reproducible in the laboratory, with the single exception of weightlessness. Rocket flights with animals (especially dogs and monkeys) in the decade up to 1957 had shown that the apparent absence of weight could be endured for several minutes, so at least there was no danger, as some had feared, of the heart promptly running amok when the gravitational load was removed from it. But the effects of really prolonged weightlessness were still unknown, and there were plenty of dire predictions from the pessimists. I can well recall crossing swords at an international conference, as late as 1963, with a distinguished biologist who stated categorically that lack of weight could not be tolerated for more than a week.

The reason why an astronaut is normally weightless is perhaps more misunderstood than anything else in the whole business of space travel. It is nothing to do with being "beyond the pull of the Earth's gravity"—not that such a thing is literally possible in any case. As we saw in Chapter 5, most manned orbital flight takes place in regions where gravity has diminished by only a few per cent from its sea-level value. Yet, despite this, astronauts weigh exactly nothing once their rockets have ceased to thrust.

This confusing paradox is largely due to poor semantics. On Earth we tend to use the words "weight" and "gravity" interchangeably, because in almost all terrestrial situations the two phenomena occur together. But they are really quite separate entities and can exist independently of each other; in space they normally do so. On occasion, however, they can be separated even on Earth, as will now be demonstrated. (This is another Einsteinian "thought experiment"; carry it out at your own risk.)

If you place a set of bathroom scales on a trapdoor and stand on the platform, the pointer will indicate your weight. But if the trapdoor is opened, the reading on the scales will drop instantly to zero. Nothing has happened to the Earth's gravity—but your weight has vanished!

For weight is a *force*, normally produced by gravity, and you cannot feel a force if it has "nothing to push against," to use a familiar phrase. You do not feel any force when you push against a swinging door; you cannot feel any weight when you have no support and are falling freely. And an astronaut, except when he is firing his rockets or re-entering atmosphere, is *always* falling freely. The "fall" may be upward or downward or sideways; the direction does not matter, as long as it is free and unrestrained.

This is why one can feel weightless even in the presence of gravity. A man in free orbit around one of those dense dwarf stars whose gravitational field is a million times as great as Earth's would still feel completely weightless.

And, conversely, one can feel "weight" even if there is no gravity; acceleration can produce an identical effect. If you were standing on those bathroom scales out in deep space, billions of miles from any celestial body, they would again register zero weight. But attach a rocket motor and start it firing—then weight would return. At an acceleration of 32 feet per second per second the scales would read correctly: you would be under "1 g," and unless you had some other means of discovering the truth, there would be no way of telling that you were not standing on the surface of the Earth. The absolute equivalence of weight due to gravity and that due to accelerations is one of the cornerstones of Einstein's General Theory of Relativity. As we shall see in the next chapter, it also provides us with a means of generating weight artificially, should that be desired.

When Sputnik 2 launched the dog Laika into orbit, the experiment proved two things. It demonstrated that higher animals (presumably including man) could endure long periods of weightlessness, and it showed that the Soviet Union was intensely interested in space *travel*, not only space science. Later experiments, in which dogs were safely recovered after several days in orbit, gave the Soviet Union further valuable information, but it was generally believed that the first manned flights would be fairly brief sub-orbital or ballistic shots, like those with which the United States did in fact open its own program (Shepard, Grissom, 1961). Hence it was a great surprise to most people when the Soviets went straight for orbit on April 12, 1961, and Yuri Gagarin circled the world in 89 minutes aboard Vostok 1. There were men still alive who had been born when Jules Verne had dared to suggest that this feat might be accomplished in eighty *days*, and millions who could well recall when it was first done in as many hours.*

From the opening of the Space Age to the first man in

*In *Profiles of the Future* I have given reasons for doubting if this will ever be done in eighty seconds, though it may ultimately be achieved in about one-eighth of a second. That "ultimately" is quite a long way off.

orbit was only 3½ years—largely because the Soviets had made their very first ventures into this new ocean with boosters already large enough to carry a man, and merely had to develop the life-support systems. The United States not only had to do this but also had to stretch its existing rockets to perform a task for which they had never been designed. By brilliant improvisation, the Atlas ICBM was upgraded and "man-rated," so that less than a year after Gagarin, John Glenn was able to perform three orbits of the Earth in the Project Mercury capsule Friendship 7 (February 20, 1962).

The four Mercury orbital flights were followed by the still more successful Gemini launches, ten in all, each involving two astronauts. The Vostok was succeeded by Voshkod, carrying as many as three men. During the first five years of manned space flight (page 107) gives a good idea of the re- achievement and safety was established, neither the Americans nor the Soviets (contrary to numerous reports) suffering any casualties. By a sad coincidence, the first fatalities in both space programs occurred within a few weeks of each other during tests of the *third* generation of manned vehicles (Apollo and Soyuz). And in each case, the disasters occurred virtually at ground level, not in space—which remains the safest medium for transportation yet discovered.

A list of the outstanding events in this first half decade of manned space flight (page 107) gives a good idea of the remarkable rate of progress. The nationalities involved have been carefully omitted; if any reader finds it hard to remember who did what, it may occur to him that, perhaps, it may not be as important as he had imagined.

Since a lunar round trip takes less than two weeks, this series of flights proved that there were no outstanding physiological barriers between Earth and Moon. Although numerous minor problems and difficulties had been encountered, these had all been overcome, and it seemed that man could do anything that he wished in space. Adaptation to weightlessness had been astonishingly easy; although it caused housekeeping and, above all, sanitary* annoyances, most astronauts found it

*To the invariable question "How *do* they manage?" the answer is "Not very well." At least one American astronaut had a rather damp flight. The ultimate solution to this problem is given in the next chapter.

DATE	ACHIEVEMENT
April 12, 1961	First man orbits Earth
August 6–7, 1961	First man spends full day in Orbit
August 11–15, 1962	First launch of two spacecraft; first near-rendezvous
October 12, 1964	First multimanned (3) spacecraft; first "shirt-sleeve" (no spacesuits) environment; first nonastronaut passenger
March 18, 1965	First man to leave spacecraft in orbit
March 23, 1965	First manned orbital maneuver
June 3–7, 1965	First manned propulsion outside spacecraft
August 21–29, 1965	First men spend week in orbit
December 4–18, 1965	First men spend two weeks in orbit; first sustained space rendezvous
March 16, 1966	First docking of two spacecraft
December 24–25, 1968	First manned voyage to orbit around Moon
July 20, 1969	First men land on Moon

a delightful experience, and some were afraid that they might become addicted to it. Myriads of skindivers had known this for years.

However, it is important to realize that although *weight* is nonexistent in orbit, *mass* or inertia remains quite unaffected. It is just as difficult to set a given object in motion aboard a spaceship as it is on Earth, and it requires just as much effort to stop it again. The inherent laziness of matter—its tendency to keep on doing the same thing—is independent of gravity. Although this fact can be used to advantage, it can also cause problems.

Astronauts engaged on the early extravehicular activities found it very difficult to control their movements, because these continued even after the initial force was applied. Hampered as they were by their clumsy pressure suits, they found even the simplest tasks exhausting; they needed both hands merely to keep themselves in position. However, by the time the Gemini series of flights had terminated, suitable constraints, tethers, and handrails had been tested, and the astronauts were able to carry out all their assigned tasks without difficulty.

What is perhaps surprising is that a man can step out of a vehicle hundreds of miles above the Earth and drift along beside it for hours without any sense of vertigo or disorientation. It is true that all those who have experienced this have been highly selected, trained, and motivated; it may well be doubted that the average person would enjoy it. But once again the adaptability of the human organism may astonish us; in view of the universal fear of heights, who would have believed a century ago that flight would be possible for almost everybody?

There was never any doubt that the other problems of maintaining life in space could be solved by straightforward engineering techniques. What made the building of "Life Support Systems" very difficult in practice were the contradictory requirements of extreme reliability and minimum weight; the Mercury capsule, in particular, was a tour de force of expensive engineering. Everything, including a heavy heat shield, had to be included in the 3,000-pound payload which was the maximum that the Atlas could inject into orbit. The much more powerful Titan booster used for the Gemini flights could orbit 8,000 pounds, but even this was little enough to keep two men comfortable in space for fourteen days. By contrast, Gagarin's Vostok weighed 10,000 pounds, and the three-manned Voshkod more than 12,000, so from the very beginning the Soviet Union was operating under much less severe weight restrictions.

This reflected itself in many details of design. For example, the Soviet space capsules had sufficient braking ability to touch down softly on land, with their crews inside (though the astronauts landed separately on the earlier flights). The American spacecraft had to splash down at sea, with all the resulting complications, expense, operational restraints, and possible dangers of a mid-ocean recovery. And perhaps even more important, the cabin atmosphere in the Soviet spacecraft was normal air, whereas to save weight and reduce complexity, the American designers elected to use pure oxygen. There was nothing wrong with this decision per se, but by a series of disastrous errors and oversights it led to the loss of three lives, tens of millions of dollars, numerous reputations, and perhaps a year of time on the journey to the Moon.

The air we breathe is normally under a pressure of slightly less than 15 pounds per square inch, and one-fifth of it consists of oxygen; the remaining four-fifths is nitrogen (with a trace of other gases) and plays no part in respiration.

From the physiological point of view, therefore, a pure-oxygen atmosphere at three-pounds-per-square-inch pressure is just as good as air (one-fifth oxygen) at five times that pressure. From the engineering point of view it has several advantages: the risk of leaks is smaller, the pressure cabin need not be so strong, extravehicular activities are easier, and the whole air-purification system is simplified. The fact that in the 1967 Apollo disaster the capsule under test contained (a) pure oxygen at *full sea-level pressure* (and a little more); (b) inflammable substances that had accumulated unnoticed, and (c) electrical equipment that may have been faulty, does not mean that there was anything basically wrong with the design.

Under normal conditions a man uses about two pounds of oxygen per day—a surprisingly small quantity—which presents no storage problems for flights of a few days or even a few weeks. After the "combustion" of the food which provides the human machine with energy, the gaseous exhaust products are carbon dioxide and water vapor; these must be continuously removed, otherwise the atmosphere will quickly become un-breathable. Various types of CO_2 absorber and water separator have been available for decades, largely as a result of submarine technology, though they have had to be carefully redesigned to work in the weightless condition. In principle, oxygen can be regenerated from the carbon-dioxide absorber, but the additional complications are not worth it except for the very long-duration missions involved in planetary flights or permanent space stations.

A man requires even less food than oxygen—about 1½ pounds per day for a 3,000-calorie diet. But this is the *dry* weight, assuming that it is completely dehydrated, as is the case with the freeze-dried foods used on the Gemini and Apollo missions. An astronaut also needs 5 to 6 pounds of water for drinking and for reconstituting the food.

However, the water problem is much simpler than the oxygen one, for it is easily extracted from the atmosphere, purified, and reused. In addition, the electrical generating system of fuel cells used on both Gemini and Apollo actually produces water as the reaction proceeds, so ample supplies are available for both consumption and toilet purposes.

The temperature of a spacecraft has to be regulated very accurately, for though men can survive for limited times over an extraordinary range (from above boiling point in very dry air, down to far below freezing), for optimum working conditions the cabin temperature should not stray outside 70–80 degrees Fahrenheit. In order to keep within these limits, a manned spacecraft usually has to be *cooled*.

This will come as a great surprise to those who have heard about the "intense cold" of outer space. But temperature, like color, is a property of matter; as space is a vacuum, it can be neither hot nor cold. Only an object in space can have any temperature, and the value of this will depend in a rather complicated way on the heat falling upon it from an outside source (usually the Sun, but possibly a nearby planet), its own rate of radiation into space, and any internal sources of heat (electrical, metabolic) it may possess.

A large manned spacecraft may generate many kilowatts of heat from its equipment and the bodies of its crew. (One kilowatt is the power of the average portable electric heater.) If this were all trapped by an efficient insulating system, neither machines nor men could survive for more than a very few hours. The excess heat has therefore to be radiated away into space by suitable cooling fins or surfaces. At the same time, it is just as essential to see that too much is not radiated away. The empty universe can absorb unlimited amounts of heat, as anyone who has stood under a clear sky on a still winter's night can testify. If the spacecraft's radiating system is *too* good, the temperature inside will start heading for absolute zero (-460 degrees Fahrenheit). It won't get there, of course; whether it levels off at minus 300 or only minus 100 depends partly on the vehicle's location.

If the spacecraft is in full sunlight, every square yard facing the Sun will receive almost 1½ kilowatts of solar heat, and it may easily get too warm. If it is in shadow—on the night side of Earth, for example—it will be shielded from this intense source of heat and will tend to get too cold. It must therefore have some way of adjusting its radiation to varying conditions, and this can be done by opening and closing reflecting screens. The fact that this problem has been already solved for the worst possible case—a close satellite that swings from midnight to midday every forty-five minutes—proves that this matter is fully under control.

A much more difficult heating problem is that encountered in re-entering the atmosphere; for a long time it was not even certain if this could be solved. The energy of a body moving at orbital speed is enormous; anyone who has picked up a rifle bullet immediately after it has hit a target will know that it is uncomfortably hot, and an object traveling at 18,000 miles an hour has at least thirty times as much energy. There is, in fact, no substance which would not be completely vaporized if all its orbital energy were converted into heat. This problem had to be solved as part of the ICBM program; if missile nose cones could not be brought safely back into the atmosphere, there seemed little hope that fragile human cargoes could survive the same treatment.

The answer was found in 1952 by H. J. Allen, chief of the high-speed research division of the Ames Aeronautical Laboratory. For almost half a century aircraft had been growing slimmer and more streamlined, and it seemed logical to assume that this process would continue as even greater speeds were attained. But this was a case where intuition, and even advanced mathematics, was completely misleading. At the hypersonic velocities of re-entry, where temperatures of up to 12,000 degrees Fahrenheit were encountered, all the needle-nosed models melted down within seconds.

Allen realized that the opposite approach was needed. By using a blunt body—the very reverse of streamlined—a powerful shock wave would be produced ahead of the missile, and most of the frictional heat would be carried off in a sheath of incandescent air; only a small fraction would leak back into the capsule itself. So evolved the inelegant, approximately conical shape first made famous by the Mercury vehicles; the Soviets, presumably using similar arguments, chose a completely spherical design, so that Gagarin flew around the world in a giant cannonball that might have come straight out of Jules Verne's novels.

Curiously enough, nature had given a hint that flattened, rounded shapes would best survive re-entry. The small, glassy meteorites known as tektites often assume this form, as they are fused and molded by their passage through the upper atmosphere. The importance of this minor astronomical curiosity, which might have saved the United States a few hundred million dollars had it been realized earlier, was first noticed by the meteorite expert H. H. Nininger, at the very moment that Allen was circulating his highly secret findings to the skeptical missile makers.*

Even with the blunt-nosed configuration, enough heat would reach the forward part of the spacecraft to produce temperatures of several thousand degrees, and it was therefore necessary to provide additional protection. After experiments with various alternative systems, a saucer-shaped plastic and fiberglass "ablation shield" was developed, which slowly burned or charred away during re-entry. Millions of Americans will remember the alarm felt during John Glenn's three-orbit flight, when a faulty indicator lamp suggested that his heat shield had come adrift. If this had really been the case, nothing could have saved him from a meteoric fate.

In the decades before man went into space, there was much concern over the human body's ability to withstand the accelerations involved. However, space travel does not *necessarily* demand high acceleration; the time will come, though perhaps

---

*The problems of the needle-nosed re-entry vehicle have now been solved, and it is now used in certain applications, especially for warheads designed to frustrate antimissile missiles.

not in this century, when it will cause no more physical stress than the takeoff of a jet airliner. But for the reasons given in Chapter 7 fuel economy requires that today's rocket vehicles perform their task as quickly as structural considerations allow,* and this involves peak accelerations (at the moment before engine cutoff, when the propellant tanks are almost empty) of up to eight gravities. Even higher accelerations are encountered during the return through the atmosphere, when up to 12 g may be experienced briefly. (At 12 g, a 170-pound man weighs one ton.) But thanks to form-fitting couches and prior training, the astronauts felt little more than momentary discomfort; they were even able to continue talking while their apparent weight increased almost tenfold and their blood became as dense as molten metal.

Anyone who has ever witnessed the takeoff of a large launch vehicle will have marveled that a human being can survive even within several hundred yards of such a continuous concussion; the unimaginable volume of sheer sound produced by a multimillion-horsepower rocket engine is not even faintly conveyed by radio or TV. But this, too, has proved to be little problem to the astronauts in their double-walled, insulated capsules. Rockets, like jets, leave most of their noise behind them. Though they may disturb whole countries, they do not inconvenience their passengers.

Apart from weightlessness, the greatest unknown hazards of space in the days before men entered it were meteoroids and radiation. There had been many conflicting estimates of their possible dangers, and much of the early experimental work with space probes was devoted to resolving these.

Meteoroids come in all sizes, from barely visible specks of dust to giant boulders, or even small mountains like the object which produced the famous Arizona meteor crater. They move at velocities of anything from 7 to 40 miles per second with respect to the Earth, depending upon whether they are

---

*Ideally, a rocket should take off from the launch pad at the highest possible acceleration. The huge propellant tanks, however, would become impractically massive and heavy if they had to withstand acceleration of several gravities when full. It turns out, after all the calculations ("optimization studies") are made, that for a large liquid-propellant rocket the best compromise involves a lift-off at the surprisingly low acceleration of about one-fourth of one gravity.

overtaking it or meeting it head-on. Needless to say, there is no hope of providing protection against the larger varieties; the only safety lies in statistics. Fortunately, those statistics are quite reassuring.

A meteoroid weighing as much as one ounce is exceedingly rare: 100 square feet of spaceship would experience an impact with such a giant about once every million days, or three thousand years. The numbers rise rapidly as the size of the particles decreases; for a 1/100-ounce meteoroid, the waiting period between impacts would be only about three years, but an object as small as this presents little danger to the hull of a spacecraft. The best proof of the relative harmlessness of meteoroids is the millions of hours of successful operation that robot probes—some with extremely fragile structures—have now accumulated beyond the atmosphere.

Meteoroids may be a nuisance—not a danger—to windows and optical elements (especially telescope mirrors) in space; they may eventually produce a kind of sand-blasting effect which could degrade performance. Additional protection for critical areas may be needed on very long voyages, especially through the asteroid belt between Mars and Jupiter, where there seems to be a great deal of space junk. And they may be a slight hazard to men wearing spacesuits, which naturally cannot provide as great a safety margin as the metal hull of a spaceship.

Even on those rare occasions when one of these cosmic bullets does penetrate the wall of a spacecraft, the damage is not likely to be serious; in most cases the small hole produced would merely add to the existing inevitable air leakage and could be easily sealed. (Self-sealing materials, like those used in aircraft fuel tanks, could be employed if necessary.) Even if the hull damage were quite serious—but short of catastrophic—there would normally be ample time for the crew to put on spacesuits and then set about repair and repressurization. It takes many minutes for all the atmosphere of a space cabin to escape, even through quite a large hole.

This seems a good point to deal with one of the most persistent myths of the Space Age—the almost universally held idea that exposure to vacuum would not only be instantly fatal, but could result in the victim exploding because of internal pressure. There was never any reason for believing this, and it has now been disproved experimentally. Dogs and chimpanzees have survived vacuum for astonishing lengths of time—up to 3 minutes—with no permanent ill effects, though they normally lose consciousness after about 15 seconds. A man who was psychologically and physiologically prepared for the experience (which does not even seem painful, though it is probably uncomfortable) would have at least a quarter of a minute of useful consciousness—a great deal of time in an emergency. And even after he had lost consciousness, he would recover if he could be repressurized within one or two minutes.

The human body is a tough piece of engineering, and, as every skindiver knows, all its internal airspaces open into the surrounding medium so that pressure quickly equalizes. Swimming upward 10 feet, which takes only a few seconds, produces the same drop in pressure as opening an Apollo capsule to the vacuum of space.

The remaining hazard—radiation—has also turned out to be not so serious as was once feared, although the discovery of the Van Allen belt caused a momentary flurry of alarm. Beneath these zones of trapped radiation, astronauts can orbit for months without risk, and all long-range space missions will pass through the belts so swiftly that they can be ignored.

The real radiation danger may be the Sun—especially around its 11-year peaks of maximum activity, one of which coincided with the first Apollo flights. Several times a year, tremendous eruptions known as "flares" occur on the surface of the Sun, and these spray high-speed, charged particles (mainly the nuclei of hydrogen atoms) throughout the Solar System. It is possible to provide some shielding against these, at least for short journeys like the flight to the Moon. On longer missions, such as voyages to Venus or Mars, the situation may be more serious, and spaceships may have to be provided with a special "storm cellar" for protection against the occasional but possible lethal solar outbursts. Even this is not certain, and judging by the way in which all the other space bogeys have evaporated, no one will be surprised if solar flares also turn out to be more spectacular than dangerous.

Dr. Charles Stark Draper, president of the International Academy of Astronautics and head of the M.I.T. Instrumentation Laboratory, which developed the Apollo guidance system, once made the rather startling remark, "Space is a *benign* environment." It is beginning to appear that this is indeed the case. Certainly it is not so implacably, relentlessly hostile as the Antarctic or the ocean depths. It presents problems, as does all new territory, and we have to proceed with caution as we move into it. But it also presents tremendous opportunities which we now have the skill to exploit.

We are like seamen who have just landed on the coast of a new and—perhaps—empty continent. On our first brief forays into the interior we move in a spirit of mingled excitement and fear. But we are learning fast; and the time may come when our descendants in this new land will far outnumber our ancestors in the old.

12. ISLANDS IN THE SKY

The space station, or permanent manned orbiting structure, may be regarded as the next step beyond the brief extra-atmospheric excursions which opened the Space Age. A great deal of study and thought has been devoted to the project, which has a literature going back at least fifty years. In fact, if one stretches a point, Hale's 1869 "Brick Moon" must be classed as a true space station, since it was inhabited, albeit involuntarily.

The whole subject of space stations raises once again the question: "What can men do in space better than machines?" This is more of a philosophical than a technical problem, and we shall return to it later in this book; for the moment, let us say that the question should really be framed: "What can space stations do for men?" It is already obvious that they can do a very great deal indeed.

Many, though not all, of the applications satellites described in Chapter 10 could perform their functions better if they formed part of a manned complex. A good example is provided by the meteorological satellites. Though these have transmitted enormous quantities of information to Earth, this is only a tiny fraction of that available even to the unaided human eye. This is dramatically shown if one compares the superb, full-color photographs taken on the later Gemini flights with the best TV pictures from Nimbus or ESSA. Moreover, this is only part of the story. The robot automatic systems are unselective and often transmit virtually the same information over and over again. A human observer, especially one who was a trained meteorologist, could concentrate on areas of particular interest, focus special instruments on them, and ignore those that were not important. Although this sort of thing could, in principle, be done with robot systems, there comes a point when it is cheaper and more effective to have the decision-making computer (i.e., the man) on the spot, and not at the far end of an expensive communications link which cannot handle full-color video signals in real time.

The meteorologists are still debating this point, but the military have already decided; in 1965 the United States Air Force was given authority to proceed with a Manned Orbiting Laboratory (MOL). A veil of secrecy promptly descended (or ascended?) over the subject, but a good deal has been published about similar schemes, such as the Manned Orbiting Research Laboratory (MORL) and the Orbital Workshop—both NASA projects.

The earliest space stations, like the MOL (a 25-foot-long cylinder weighing about 15,000 pounds), would be launched into orbit as a single unit; more ambitious ones would be built up section by section, until ultimately they became virtual space cities. They would be supplied with essential materials by a shuttle service from Earth but would be largely self-sufficient as far as oxygen and water were concerned, for they would purify both in a closed-cycle system. Eventually they would be able to provide their own food (or the bulk of it), through either compact hydroponic farming systems or chemical synthesis.

Most designs for space stations envisage disk- or wheel-shaped structures, slowly revolving like giant carousels. This rotation would generate centrifugal force, and so give the station a kind of artificial gravity. "Up" would be toward the axis, "down" away from it, and the sensation of weight would slowly ebb as one moved toward the center, becoming zero at the axis. A wheel 600 feet in diameter has to make three revolutions a minute to produce a force equal to normal earth weight (1 g) at its rim. Smaller structures spinning more rapidly would give the same result but might cause vertigo and difficulties with scientific experiments. Probably a fraction of a gravity—say, one-fourth—would be quite adequate for most purposes. It would permit almost normal walking and would remove most of the housekeeping problems, especially the sanitary ones.

Service vehicles would have to approach such a station along its axis and match its spin before they docked to it; alternatively, there might be a docking section which could be given a spin exactly countering the station's, so that it was motionless with respect to any approaching vehicle. Yet another idea is that space stations might be built in two or more sections, not necessarily in physical contact. Only the part where the crew ate, relaxed, and slept might have rotational gravity. With all these possibilities, it is no wonder that many thousands of man-hours of amateur and professional engineering skill have been devoted to space-station design. The moment of truth is now approaching, when we shall learn which of these actually work.

Launch vehicles of the Titan 3 C and Saturn 1 B class can place payloads of 10 to 15 tons in close Earth orbit; the giant Saturn 5 developed for the Apollo program can orbit no less than 120 tons. What is more, the propellant tanks of the last stages will also go into orbit with the payload, and some of these have the cubic capacity of a large house. With the addition of an airlock and a life-support system, they can be fairly readily turned into shirt-sleeve environments where men can work without having to wear pressure suits. Near-space will soon be full of large, empty tanks which can be rather easily converted into desirable orbiting residences, so its population may increase rapidly.

The uses of space stations may be purely scientific, "practical" (including commercial), or military. As far as the last category is concerned, the Space Treaty approved by the UN General Assembly on December 15, 1966, has set certain limitations on what may now be legally done; in particular, "nuclear weapons or any other kinds of weapons of mass destruction" must not be placed in orbit. This would seem to restrict the use of military space stations to largely defensive roles, i.e., reconnaissance, communications, and perhaps missile interception. Looking some distance into the future, it has been suggested that the only effective missile defense will be based upon radiation weapons, probably laser heat rays or beams of charged particles. Such weapons could be employed *only* outside the atmosphere, which would absorb most of their energy and limit their range. The technical problems involved in generating and beaming the quantities of power involved are gigantic but not insoluble. However, by the time we are able to build death-ray-wielding orbital fortresses, missiles will be obsolete. The defense will be deadlier than the weapon it was designed to counter.

To turn to more cheerful and constructive subjects, manned laboratories and observatories in space open up new horizons for knowledge such as have not been glimpsed since the invention of the telescope itself. What the unmanned automatic satellites have gleaned on the other side of the atmospheric curtain is impressive enough, and they will continue to gather immense quantities of data, often from places where it would be extremely unhealthy for human beings to go. But manned activities can produce results of a wholly new order; anyone who thinks otherwise may try to imagine how fast the physical sciences would have progressed if all experimentation and observation had to be done via remote-controlled handling devices and TV screens. Even the simplest piece of scientific equipment requires innumerable adjustments, and this is particularly true of new and untried apparatus designed to extend the frontiers of knowledge. The fully automated physics laboratory or astronomical observatory is a nightmare to contemplate, as the expensive failure of the first robot OAO (Orbiting Astronomical Observatory) may remind us.

Since the early part of this century astronomers have made heroic efforts to improve seeing by building their observatories on mountaintops, but even here the problem is merely reduced, not abolished. Only on very rare occasions, for a few seconds at a time, can the world's great telescopes be used at even one-tenth their theoretical magnifying power. For many purposes (such as photographing faint galaxies), this is not a very serious limitation; but for observing fine detail on planets or resolving crowded star fields, it is a crippling one. The images are smeared and scrambled by their passage through the last few miles of atmosphere, and increasing the magnifying power of the instrument only makes matters worse—like looking at a newspaper block under a magnifying glass. Some ground-based astronomers of the past who have spent their entire working lives studying the Moon and planets probably saw them with

real clarity for a total time that could be measured in minutes—
spread over half a century.

Yet, above the atmosphere, not only are seeing conditions
always perfect, but the completely blocked X-ray, ultraviolet,
and infrared bands of the spectrum, crammed with undiscovered secrets, are waiting to be explored. Because it spans an
enormously greater range of frequencies (see Figure 15), the
far-ultraviolet band may contain hundreds of times as much
information as visible light.

The word "information" is used in the perfectly general
sense; it does not imply intelligent signals (though it certainly
does not exclude them). In the astronomical field it usually
means spectral lines, which to the skilled interpreter speak
whole volumes about stellar compositions, velocities, temperatures, and the types of nuclear reaction that power the stars.
No wonder, therefore, that astronomers have long felt frustrated
because the atmospheric window slams shut on the spectrum,
just when it starts to become most informative. Nor is it surprising that one enthusiast for space observatories, Professor
Kopal of Manchester University, has stated that manned telescopes in orbit may "cause our more fortunate descendants to
relegate most of what we have learned about the universe from
observations at the surface of the Earth into a crude pre-
history."

There is still a friendly disagreement as to whether the
best location for future space telescopes is in Earth orbit or on
the airless Moon. Both sites have great advantages, and both
will ultimately be used, but the lunar observatory is still several
decades in the future. Orbital telescopes, on the other hand,
could be operating in the early 1970's, using the hardware
developed for the Apollo project. As part of the "Apollo applications program," detailed engineering studies have already
been made to see how the lunar landing vehicle (Chapter 15)
could be adapted as a mount for a telescope, so that instead of
descending to the Moon it could remain in orbit as a first-
generation astronomical observatory, able to outperform Mount
Palomar.

Though it is quite impossible to evaluate the cost-effec-
tiveness of pure research, Dr. William Tifft, director of the

Manned Space Astronomy Branch (*that* title is a sign of the times) of the University of Arizona's Steward Observatory, has calculated that a 200-inch telescope in space could collect information *one thousand times* as efficiently as a ground-based one. To put it in terms of hard cash: even if it cost $2 billion to build an orbital 200-incher, it would do the work of a hundred such instruments at ground level costing $20 million each. This argument must be taken with a large grain of salt; for one thing, there would be no way at present of handling such an avalanche of information. But the main thesis is valid, and the important thing to remember is that the space telescope could do work utterly beyond the power of any number of instruments at the bottom of our muddy wavering atmosphere.

It could, for example, vastly multiply our knowledge of the other planets, which would suddenly appear at least ten times closer and a hundred times sharper. Such increased knowledge is essential before we embark on expensive planetary missions, either manned or unmanned. It would allow us, for the first time, to search for planets of other suns with the hope of detecting at least Jupiter-sized companions of the nearer stars. And by peering many times further into extragalactic space, it would throw new light—or, rather, much *older* light—on the origin of the universe and the great questions of cosmology.

If this sort of knowledge seems somewhat theoretical, and perhaps not worth the billions of dollars it will undoubtedly cost, it should be remembered that astronomy has always been one of the cutting edges of scientific progress. The universe is the great physics laboratory where we have been able to study matter under conditions where it does not exist on Earth; and from those studies have emerged not only new insights but also new industries.

The stars can conduct experiments on a scale which we will not be able to match for centuries; and the research possibilities of orbiting space stations may keep us busy for most of those centuries. For the first time, we will have access to vacuum of unlimited extent, with all that this implies to physics and electronics. Our civilization is now practically founded on electronics, and this in turn depends entirely on vacuum technology. The very low and very high temperatures that are readily available in space will also make possible experiments that cannot, or should not, be conducted on Earth. Perhaps the final breakthrough in thermonuclear power will be achieved a few hundred miles out in space, where any unfortunate accidents will result in nothing worse than a very temporary second sun.

But it is, of course, the unique zero-weight environment which makes the orbital laboratory so attractive. We will be able to study the behavior of atomic and molecular, living and nonliving systems, under conditions that can never be reproduced on Earth. As a result, there may be fundamental advances in our knowledge of those two most intractable of all phenomena—gravity and time. Anyone who bets on this as a certainty would be foolish, but not as foolish as anyone who thinks it unlikely.

No scientists have been more interested in weightlessness than the biologists and doctors, and not only because of their natural concern with astronaut safety. The way in which living matter, at the cell level and above, reacts to the apparent absence of gravity is certain to give new insights into the nature of life. On Earth the size of most organisms is gravity-limited, or at least gravity-controlled; what will happen when this factor is removed? Will there be an explosion of growth, so that we can produce giant amoebas, guinea pigs, or other entertaining science-fiction monsters? One form of uncontrolled cell growth is cancer; anything we can learn about such a phenomenon is obviously of the highest medical importance. This should give pause to those who are fond of suggesting cancer research as an alternative to space exploration—as if money cut from one program is *ever* switched to another.

The knowledge, instrumentation, and technology derived from space have in fact already contributed to medicine, but the greatest advances may come from a project which may still seem like fantasy—the orbital hospital. Anyone who has ever suffered from bedsores will know what a boon a low- or zero-gravity environment could be; and for serious burns or postoperative therapy, it might make the difference between life and death. The last letter I ever received from one of the finest minds of our century, Professor J. B. S. Haldane, was written in severe discomfort after he had been operated on for cancer;

in it he remarked what a blessing a space hospital would be to "millions of patients like myself."

There is also a possibility—wildly speculative, but this is a field where the stakes are indeed high—that the expectation of life may be increased when the wear and tear of gravity is removed. Whether this discovery would be beneficial or otherwise is a good subject for debate, but it is one that could hardly be ignored.

These last conjectures may seem absurd to those who still look on manned space flight in terms of today's multimillion-dollar productions. But, as will be shown later, the cost and difficulty of space travel will be reduced by orders of magnitude in the decades to come, until it is eventually little more unusual—or more expensive—than jet transportation. Anyone who finds this hard to believe should consider the fact that, just forty years after Lindbergh, twenty thousand people were flying the Atlantic *every day*.

The development of efficient and reliable space transporters, which can be used over and over again like conventional aircraft, not dropped into the ocean after every mission, will make space travel an economically as well as scientifically sound proposition. The orbital hospital will be one of the first beneficiaries; so will the orbital hotel, with its variable-gravity suites and its cylindrical swimming pool. In the spring of 1967 such a project was seriously presented at the Dallas Symposium on the Commercial Uses of Space; the speaker was one Barron Hilton, whose name is not unknown to those seeking accommodation in the far places of this planet.

Orbital hotels will be good fun, but orbital industries may be a much more serious matter. It is virtually certain that many types of manufacturing will become simpler and cheaper in space, when advantage is taken of the low pressures and, possibly, high radiation levels available there. And there may be many chemical and metallurgical processes which will be possible *only* under weightless conditions. What they are, of course, we will not know until our orbital laboratories discover them; this is one of the best reasons for their construction.

One of the most important functions of manned space stations will be the maintenance of the numerous scientific and applications satellites in orbit around the Earth. As more and more services—environmental surveying, meteorology, navigation, communications—are lifted into the sky, so we will depend to an ever-increasing extent upon satellite facilities. Troubleshooting, replacing expendables like the propellants required for station keeping, repair, and the installation of large and complex antenna systems—all these will be done by service crews based upon orbital depots, flying to their jobs in low-powered shuttle vehicles. Since most of the applications satellites will probably be in the synchronous orbit, 22,000 miles above the Earth, we may expect the largest of the service stations to be there. Luckily, the problem of shielding from Van Allen radiation is not too serious at this altitude.

Finally, let us look a little further into the future. The large space station is the ideal starting point both for robot probes and for manned expeditions. All equipment can be checked out, and even assembled, in space, and when everything is ready the propulsion can be switched on and escape velocity built up gradually. (In orbit, a body already has 70 per cent of escape speed, so only an additional 30 per cent is required.) There are none of the dangers posed by a takeoff from Earth—bad weather, an abort near ground level, the possibility of falling onto an inhabited area. A failure to depart from orbit would mean delay but not disaster.

The great ports of the centuries to come will be in orbit, hundreds or thousands of miles above the Earth; here we will see the full flowering of the rendezvous techniques pioneered by the Gemini and Apollo flights. Today's missions will lead ultimately to fuel depots, repair and maintenance facilities, traffic-control systems, navigation and quarantine authorities—everything that has evolved for the needs of terrestrial transportation, with a few extras appropriate to space.

Every age has its dreams, its symbols of romance. Past generations were moved by the graceful power of the great windjammers, by the distant whistle of locomotives pounding through the night, by the caravans leaving on the Golden Road to Samarkand, by quinqueremes of Nineveh from distant Ophir.... Our grandchildren wil! likewise have their inspiration—among the equatorial stars.

They will be able to look up at the night sky and watch the stately procession of the Ports of Earth—the strange new harbors where the ships of space make their planetfalls and their departures. Often, one of these brightly orbiting stars will suddenly explode in a silent concussion of light, and a fierce, tiny sun will draw slowly away from it. And they will know that some nuclear-powered mariner has set forth once more, on the ocean whose farther shore he can never reach.

III. AROUND
THE MOON

13. VOYAGERS TO THE MOON

We are very fortunate to have, so close at hand, such a large and fascinating world as the Moon for our first target in space. For terrestrials, the nearest land is only a quarter of a million miles away. The inhabitants of Venus, in the unlikely event that they exist, have to travel a hundred times that distance.

As we saw in Chapter 5, the problem of getting from the Earth to the Moon is essentially that of climbing out of one gravitational crater and descending into another. Figure 6 shows this in a qualitative manner; the table on page 130 gives the numerical values for the mission.

If Figure 6 was modeled out of some smooth material, such as glass, a ball bearing dropped into it could reproduce all the movements of a space vehicle in the Earth–Moon system. For example, a rocket which left Earth at escape velocity would lose speed—at first rapidly, later very slowly—as it receded from Earth. If it were aimed toward the Moon, it would be barely moving as it "went over the hump"; thereafter, however, it would gain speed as it fell into the Moon's gravitational crater, and in the absence of any corrective action it would crash against the lunar surface at the escape velocity of 5,300 mph.

It is clear that the precise path to (or around) the Moon would depend very critically upon the initial velocity and speed of projection. A direct hit is quite unlikely; what is much more probable is that any unpowered space probe would gain speed, make a hairpin bend around the Moon, and head off again in some other direction. It could even do a figure eight and return

TABLE 4
THE EARTH-MOON MISSION

DEPTH OF GRAVITATIONAL CRATER, MILES		ESCAPE VELOCITY	
		MPH	MILES/SEC.
Earth	4,000	24,800	7
Moon	180	5,300	1.5

to the vicinity of Earth, perhaps to repeat the performance many times, unless it came close enough to re-enter the atmosphere.

One thing that it could *not* do would be to become a satellite of the Moon; it would always gain too much speed in its fall toward it to be captured. Only if, by rocket braking, its speed were reduced in the neighborhood of the Moon could it become a lunar satellite.

It will also be seen that the duration of the journey will depend, in an equally critical manner, on the initial speed. A rocket that can just make it—that can barely climb over the hump—will take about five days for the trip.* But a very slight excess speed cuts the time down rapidly, though this may not be a good idea if the extra velocity has to be neutralized for a landing. The very first object to make the journey (Luna 2, September 12–13, 1959) took only 35 hours.

There is one respect in which Figure 6 does not reproduce the real situation. It is a static model, and the Moon is of course moving around the Earth in a period of about 29 days. This does not affect the general argument given above, but the actual shape or trajectory of the paths between Earth and Moon will be affected. Even this could be taken care of by a more complicated model made out of sheet rubber, in which the little

*As might be gathered from Figure 6, the velocity of a rocket that can *just* reach the Moon is only about 200 mph short of the velocity of escape. From the energy viewpoint, the Moon's orbit is already 99 per cent of the way to "infinity."

crater representing the Moon's field could be set creeping around its orbit at an appropriate speed.

With this theoretical background, we are now in a better position to understand the lunar explorations of the Early Space Age. The first attempt to launch a payload to the Moon was made by the United States Air Force on August 17, 1958, using a Thor-Able-1 booster, which exploded soon after takeoff. Another launch on October 11 was *almost* successful; the 84-pound Pioneer 1 payload failed to reach escape velocity by the maddeningly small margin of 2 per cent (570 mph). The launch vehicle still had ample fuel for the mission when the onboard computer prematurely cut the engine.

At 98 per cent of escape velocity, Pioneer 1 was able to rise 70,000 miles before it crashed back to Earth, and it gathered valuable information about the great radiation belt. Though it did not reach the Moon, it was the first scientific probe into deep space. It may not be easy to recall that, in 1958, 70,000 miles still seemed an enormous altitude.

A month later, Pioneer 2's last stage failed to ignite; on December 6 Pioneer 3—the United States Army's entry to the race—just failed to reach escape velocity and almost matched Pioneer 1's performance, rising 64,000 miles and again sending back valuable data on the radiation belt.

So, by a few hundred miles an hour, the United States lost the opportunity of being first into the Solar System,* for on January 2, 1959, the Soviet Union launched Luna 1, or "Mechta" ("dream"), on a trajectory that took it within 5,000 miles of the Moon. Its payload of no less than 795 pounds included instruments for analyzing cosmic rays, recording meteoroids, and measuring the lunar magnetic field.

After swinging past the Moon (apparently it was not intended to make an impact), Mechta had sufficient velocity to escape from both the terrestrial and the lunar gravitational field. But it was still a captive of the Sun, which it now circles in an orbit a little larger than the Earth's. It thus achieved not

---

*The first manmade objects ever to leave the Earth were small metal pellets launched by an explosive charge on an Aerobee rocket 50 miles above New Mexico on October 16, 1957. One of these artificial meteors attained a speed of 33,000 mph—far in excess of escape velocity. The experiment was conceived by Professor Fritz Zwicky of the California Institute of Technology.

only the first lunar fly-by, but became the first artificial planet, with a "year" of 443 days.

A similar feat was achieved only two months later by the United States Army's Pioneer 4 (March 3, 1959). This, the first American space probe to escape from the Earth, passed within 37,000 miles of the Moon and then went into a 407-day orbit around the Sun.

None of these feats, however, was as dramatic as the first physical contact with the Moon, achieved by Luna 2 on September 13, 1959, at 21:02:23 Universal Time. After its 35-hour flight, the 860-pound instrument package (and the empty 3,330-pound final-stage rocket) landed on the great plain of the Mare Imbrium. Like thousands of other amateur astronomers, I was watching for the moment of impact, with my Questar aimed out over the Indian Ocean at the setting Moon. However, there is no conclusive evidence that the event was observed—except by the radio telescopes which recorded the change in pitch of the transmitter as it accelerated in the Moon's gravity field, and the exact moment when its sudden silence announced that the first manmade object had reached another world.

Less than a month later, on October 4, 1959, Luna 3 revealed something that had been hidden from the human race since the beginning of history—the far side of the Moon. Although the photographs radioed back from its automatic darkroom were crude by later standards, they showed hundreds of craters and hinted at subtle and still unexplained differences between the two lunar hemispheres.

Luna 3, after looping around the Moon, shuttled back and forth between the two gravitational fields for about six months, then re-entered the Earth's atmosphere. It had opened up a new era in astronomy, proving that the time was coming when the smallest details of the most distant planets would no longer be hidden. Yet after this dramatic opening, there was a pause of almost five years before the next advance in lunar reconnaissance, and this only after a series of heartbreaking failures.

This delay was partly due to concentration of efforts into other and more rewarding missions—manned space flight, probes to Mars and Venus (see Chapter 21), and many other scientific and applications satellites. Moreover, the rather poor quality of the Luna 3 pictures—which had even provoked cries of "Fake!" from irresponsible or ignorant journalists—showed that considerable improvements in technique were still needed.

Luna 3 had taken photographs with a conventional camera system, automatically processed them onboard, then scanned them at leisure and radioed the images back to Earth. This system has a number of advantages; the United States orbiter vehicles also used essentially the same process when they completed the mapping of "Farside" seven years later. It permits working at low radio-power levels—the main consideration in the design of any space probe—because the picture transmission can be spread over as long a time as is necessary.

The Jet Propulsion Laboratory's Ranger spacecraft, however, were designed to use a real television system, though one limited to a transmission rate of one frame every 2½ seconds instead of the 25 or 30 frames per second of domestic television. In this case there was no alternative; the spacecraft were going to fly straight into the Moon and would be destroyed on impact, so the pictures had to be sent back as quickly as they were taken.

The first five Ranger shots (August, 1961–October, 1962) failed for a variety of reasons, not all connected with the spacecraft itself. However, Ranger 4 did reach the Moon on April 26, 1962, being the first American spacecraft to do so.

Between Rangers 5 and 6 there was a pause of fifteen months, while numerous scientific subcommittees tried to find what had gone wrong. During this hiatus, the Soviet Union launched its fourth Luna, on April 2, 1963, but it too failed to achieve its objectives.

On January 30, 1964, the Jet Propulsion Laboratory tried again with Ranger 6. Everything went perfectly all the way to the Moon, until the last fifteen minutes. Then, when the TV cameras were switched on, nothing happened. Later it was decided that a power supply had shorted, perhaps owing to the failure of an insulator costing a few cents. This was probably the lowest point in the history of the United States space program since the explosion of Vanguard TV3 on December 6, 1957.

Six months later, after more agonizing reappraisals, JPL launched Ranger 7; it is probably not too much to say that the future of the entire laboratory was riding with this payload's six TV cameras. This time the years of effort and heartbreak were rewarded; the Atlas-Agena launch vehicle worked perfectly, the trajectory was exactly as planned, and when, seventeen minutes before the calculated moment of impact, the cameras were switched on, signals started coming back at once. Within the next quarter of an hour the Moon was brought a thousand times nearer to Earth than ever before. The closest of the 4,316 high-quality photographs obtained showed craterlets on the lunar surface only a few feet in diameter. Until then the best telescopes had been unable to resolve objects less than half a mile across. Ranger 7 had beaten the telescope by a greater factor than that instrument had surpassed the unaided human eye.

Ranger 8 (launched February 17, 1965) performed even better than its precursor, sending back 7,000 photographs during the final 23 minutes of its flight. It seemed impossible that Ranger 9, the last of the series, could top this; but it did so, little more than a month later, on March 24, 1965. This time the JPL scientists had devised an image converter so that, as quickly as the pictures came back from the Moon, they could be displayed on a TV screen. These images were carried by the national networks. and so, for the first time, millions of people watched the Moon racing toward them, as it was actually happening. Moreover, the impact point chosen was in dramatic, mountainous terrain, not the rather flat and uninteresting "seas" which the previous missions had reconnoitered as possible landing sites. The target now was the 70-mile-diameter crater Alphonsus, chosen because slight volcanic activity had been reported near its central peak.

No one who watched the mountain walls of Alphonsus expanding second by second and saw more and more details never before witnessed by human eyes swimming into view is likely to forget that transmission, or the sign that then appeared on the television screen for the first time in history—LIVE FROM THE MOON.

Almost as impressive as the photographic coverage obtained was the amazing accuracy of these last Ranger shots. When you next look at the Moon, notice what a small object it appears to be, and remember that it is actually over 2,000 miles in diameter. Then consider that the last four Rangers missed their nominal aiming points by these margins:

	ACCURACY, MILES
Ranger 6	20
Ranger 7	10
Ranger 8	20
Ranger 9	3

Such remarkable performances are made possible by mid-course corrections; when a spacecraft has been launched on its initial trajectory, it is tracked for many hours by radio equipment which can measure its position to within a few feet in range, even at the distance of the Moon. Velocity can be measured to a similar degree of accuracy, and given this information, computers can predict the future position of the spacecraft as it moves under the influence of gravity. Sometimes the injection into orbit is so precise that no correction is necessary, but normally a change of a few miles an hour is needed. The amount and direction of this impulse is calculated, the spacecraft is reoriented and a brief burst of power applied from its control jets, and tracking continues until the effectiveness of the correction can be determined. Naturally, a trifling alteration in velocity at mid-course can produce a huge change at the end of a quarter-million-mile journey, and the correction therefore has to be made with great care. Sometimes things can go badly wrong during this operation, as the Soviet scientists found on June 11, 1965.

They were now going through much the same ordeal, though without the glare of publicity, that JPL had endured between Rangers 1 and 7. Less than two months after the last of the Rangers had made its TV spectacular, the Soviet Union began a new series of experiments, designed to achieve the most difficult yet most significant of all space feats to date— a landing on the Moon. All earlier probes had crashed, unretarded, into the lunar surface at over 5,000 mph.

Such was the fate of Luna 5 on May 12, 1965; its braking rockets failed to operate properly, and it crashed into the Sea of Clouds. A month later—June 10—Luna 6 disgraced itself;

when a course correction was applied, the rocket engine refused to stop thrusting after the desired impulse had been given. It continued firing until it had exhausted its fuel, and so Luna 6 missed the Moon by a little matter of 100,000 miles.

On October 8 Luna 7 did somewhat better; it reached the Moon, but its retrorockets canceled only part of its speed, and it was destroyed on impact. Exactly the same thing happened to Luna 8 on December 7; as some consolation, however, the Soviet Union achieved its second photograph reconnaissance of the lunar Farside in 1965 from Zond 3, a deep-space probe that then continued in orbit around the Sun.

By this time no one could doubt the determination of the Soviet space scientists to achieve their goal of a lunar landing. Sir Bernard Lovell, who had tracked all the Luna flights with the giant 250-foot radio-telescope at Jodrell Bank, remarked after analyzing the maneuvers of Luna 8 that they "narrowly missed complete success. . . . They have probably obtained a great deal of new information which will enable them to correct the remaining minor faults."

However, some pessimists were beginning to fear that the trouble might not be with the Lunas, but with the Moon itself. They revived the old theory—only slightly shaken by the Ranger photographs—that the Moon might be covered by a deep layer of dust which could swallow any descending spacecraft. The persistent Soviets put this fear to rest on February 2, 1966, when Luna 9 made a successful touchdown in the Ocean of Storms.

The small, egg-shaped camera capsule was attached to a larger rocket-propulsion unit, and the whole assembly, after it had been aimed toward the Moon, was allowed to coast until it was within 50 miles of the surface. By this time it had been falling for hours through the lunar gravitational field and had acquired a speed of more than 5,000 miles an hour. In less than a minute it would impact on the Moon's surface; it actually took the retrorockets 48 seconds to reduce its speed to about 100 miles an hour at a very low altitude. Just before landing, the camera capsule was detached from the propulsion unit and fell separately some distance away.

It was not what a human astronaut would have called a good landing ("one you can walk away from"), but the instruments had been designed to withstand the expected shock. A few minutes later the capsule opened up like a flower, unfolding four petals. Its periscopic camera lens started to survey the scene, and the first ground-eye view of the Moon was radioed back to Earth.*

Since the camera was only two feet above the surface, the horizon was very close—less than a mile away. The view, in fact, was that which a sitting man would have, and was limited by the steeply curving lunar surface. (From a given elevation, one can see only half as far on the Moon as on Earth.) But the pictures were excellent; Luna 9 had a full 360 degrees of vision, and objects in the foreground only one-tenth of an inch across could be resolved.

Luna 9 settled the question still left open by the Ranger series: the Moon's surface, at least in one region, was made of some porous, crunchy material and was firm enough to support a considerable weight. The designers of the Apollo landing vehicle breathed a sigh of relief.

On April 3, 1966, Luna 10 achieved a much easier, but still very important feat by becoming the first satellite of the Moon. At the appropriate point, its retrorockets reduced its speed from 4,700 to 2,800 mph, so that it could no longer escape from the Moon's gravitational field. Accordingly, it went into a 3-hour orbit, ranging in height between 220 and 630 miles from the lunar surface. During several days of operation, before its batteries were exhausted, it radioed back a vast amount of information concerning the environment close to the Moon, information which cannot be gathered by impact probes which pass through this region in a few minutes.

While all this had been going on, the United States was preparing for similar exploits. Its lunar-landing vehicles, the Surveyor series (built by the Hughes Aircraft Company), had been delayed several years owing to problems, and downright disasters, with the Centaur-Atlas launch vehicle. When the

---

*To be released, not by the Soviets, but by Jodrell Bank, via the London *Daily Express*. When the radio signals from Luna 9 were received by the 250-foot telescope, it was realized that they were in standard picture-telegraphy code. The *Express*, which may not be the best newspaper in the world but is undoubtedly the most enterprising, rushed a facsimile receiver to Jodrell Bank and thus made one of the most remarkable scoops of the Space Age.

incredibly complex Surveyor 1 lifted from Cape Kennedy on May 30, 1966, it was the first flight of the space probe *and* the first operational use of the liquid-hydrogen-fueled booster. No one would have given odds of better than one in ten for a successful mission.

In the event, everything worked with textbook precision. The new booster launched the spacecraft on an excellent trajectory; a small course correction was made in flight, and Surveyor headed straight toward the Moon. About 1,000 miles up, the vehicle was oriented so that its solid-propellant retrorocket pointed exactly along the flight path. Its gyros kept it locked in this direction as it continued to gain speed, and 200 miles above the Moon its radar was switched on by a signal from Earth.

Thereafter it was controlled by its own electronic brain. It continued to fall until about 60 miles from the surface, at which point it had reached a speed of 6,000 miles an hour. The big retrorocket was then fired; by the time it had burned out, 40 seconds later, Surveyor was only 6 miles up and traveling at 250 miles an hour.

Now it was very much on its own, for it was impossible to provide effective guidance from Earth. Radio signals take 1¼ seconds to make the journey from the Moon, so by the time any error had been noted and a correcting signal sent from the JPL control room at Pasadena, there would have been a delay of not less than 2½ seconds. Yet the critical landing manueuvers had to be made instantly, during the final stages of the descent.

For the last 6 miles, therefore, Surveyor eased itself down toward the Moon on gentle blasts from three small liquid-fueled vernier (fine-adjustment) rockets, under the control of a computer which was kept informed of height and velocity by the onboard radar. So well did this work that the vehicle came to rest only 13 feet above the lunar surface; it fell freely for this distance, equivalent to only 2 feet in the Earth's gravitational field, and the shock-absorbing undercarriage easily neutralized the slight impact.

Unlike Luna 9, Surveyor did not rely on batteries but carried solar cells, generating electricity from sunlight; so it was able to transmit thousands of superb photographs (some in color) before the Sun set and the long lunar night began. Even then, to everyone's surprise, it survived the low temperatures and revived at dawn, giving the experimenters an additional bonus. The moonscape it viewed was similar to that seen by Luna 9, 500 miles away; we will discuss the interpretation of these remarkable photographs in Chapter 17.

On August 10, 1966, the United States began its third series of Moon-orientated experiments, with the launching of Lunar Orbiter 1. Unlike the Soviet Union's Luna 10, which carried only instruments, Orbiter 1's mission was primarily photographic. Its Kodak-designed automatic darkroom could process a 200-foot roll of 70-mm film; after the images had been fixed, they were scanned by a flying spot of light and the resulting electrical impulses radioed back to the stations of NASA's Deep Space Network in Australia, Spain, and California.

Despite minor technical troubles, Orbiter 1 functioned superbly, producing the first high-definition pictures of the lunar Farside. Its most memorable achievement, however, was a wonderful study of the crescent Earth hanging low above the edge of the Moon. For many millions of terrestrials, their first glimpse of this photograph must have been the moment when the Earth really became a planet.

Later Orbiters did even better, producing a portfolio of lunar photographs that would have been beyond the wildest dreams of astronomers only a few years before. These studies included the stunning low-angle shot of the crater Copernicus, which almost every newspaper in the world carried on its front page and which was widely heralded as the "Picture of the Century." (Ironically enough, this was an unplanned test shot made by Orbiter 2.) These photographs were of great psychological as well as scientific importance, for the Rangers, Lunas, and Surveyors had begun to give the impression that the Moon was a somewhat dull, flat, and uninteresting place. But now the image was beginning to emerge of a world with landscapes as dramatic as any on Earth—where, moreoever, there might still be a considerable amount of volcanic or other activity taking place.

When Luna 13 landed on the Moon on Christmas Eve, 1966, and Surveyor 3 made a slightly bouncy but safe touchdown on April 19, 1967, robots had been installed on the Moon that could dig and pry into its surface, which, rather surprisingly, turned out to be more like good honest dirt than any substance that the theoreticians had predicted. There was no longer any question that men could walk safely there; and it was becoming more and more certain that it would also be an interesting and scientifically rewarding place to visit.

Which was indeed good news—since that visit was scheduled to take place within less than five years.

14. THE BIRTH OF APOLLO

By the mid-1960's there were a number of rockets in existence which could, if everything went well, land a man safely on the Moon. But this was all they could do; they could not possibly carry the additional fuel for the return journey, even though it is very much easier to escape from the Moon than from the Earth.

Indeed, for a long time it seemed unlikely that *any* rocket, no matter how large, could make the round trip if it were powered by chemical propellants. The calculations gave absurd answers—million-ton vehicles to bring payloads of one pound back from the Moon, for example.* On such a basis, manned expeditions were obviously quite impracticable.

Yet there was a way of avoiding these enormous ratios, and the theoreticians of the 1920's and 1930's had clearly indicated it. There was no need to use a single rocket to go to the Moon and back; by employing orbital techniques, the journey could be broken down into a number of relatively easy stages, flown by vehicles of moderate size.

A favorite scheme was that of refueling in space. A rocket would be launched into a close orbit around the Earth, exhausting its supply of propellants in the process. Then "tanker" vehicles could rendezvous with it and pump fuel aboard. When

*I am quoting an actual figure, worked out by a distinguished Canadian astronomer and published in a lengthy mathematical paper in the *Philosophical Magazine* for January, 1941.

this operation had been completed—which might take weeks, if desired, since the orbit chosen would be a stable one—the spaceship would then be refueled, above the atmosphere, and already moving at 70 per cent of the speed necessary to escape from the Earth. At the appropriate time it could turn on its engines and inject itself into the mission trajectory.

The first operation of this type was carried out, though in a slightly different manner, during the Gemini 11 flight of September, 1966. The spacecraft docked with its Agena target vehicle at an altitude of 180 miles, and the Agena was then commanded to fire its unexpended fuel. This extra kick boosted the Gemini to the then record-breaking altitude of 850 miles.

Even without refueling, however, a rendezvous in space could much improve the logistics of a mission. For example, the spacecraft which has to make the final landing back on Earth requires a heavy heat shield and parachutes; why waste hundreds of tons of fuel carrying this equipment all the way down to the surface of the Moon, only to lift it back into space again? The sensible thing to do would be to leave it in orbit around the Earth, to be picked up on the homeward journey.

When these ideas are taken to their logical conclusion, it seems that a lunar voyage could best be carried out using not one spacecraft, but three. Type A would be a short-range vehicle, possibly winged, which would carry equipment from Earth to orbit, and return by atmospheric braking. Type B would be similar, but without wings or streamlining, and more lightly constructed; it would be designed to land on the Moon by rocket braking alone. It might be carried up from Earth in a Type A ship or assembled in space.

Type C would be a true spaceship; it would never land on Moon or Earth, but would shuttle payloads between them, making a rendezvous with Type A or Type B at destination— like an ocean liner being met by tugboats. Since each vehicle would be designed for its specific mission, it could be highly efficient. Thus only the Type A, which has to climb up to Earth orbit, need have powerful motors and rugged construction. The others could be very lightly built and relatively low-powered.

The importance of orbital rendezvous and refueling techniques in avoiding enormous takeoff weights was first realized by the Austrian engineer Baron Guido von Pirquet in 1928 and further developed by many other writers on astronautics. In January, 1949, H. E. Ross published a paper ("Orbital Bases") in the *Journal of the British Interplanetary Society*, pointing out the great value of a rendezvous in orbit around the Moon; he suggested that a lunar-bound spaceship, before landing, should leave the propellants for the return journey circling the Moon, ready to be picked up on the way home. A few years later, when discussing these ideas in *The Exploration of Space*, I wrote this description, which is interesting to compare with the lunar modules of today: "When the ship is on the Moon, the undercarriage would play the role of a launching rack, holding the rocket in the required position for takeoff. It could, therefore, be left behind . . . and so might be made detachable. However, this would be bad economics, because it would be cheaper to bring it back than to carry a new set of landing gear from the Earth . . . when the ship was preparing for its next voyage." It will be noted that reusability was taken for granted; it never occurred to us that multimillion-dollar vehicles would be used for a single mission and then abandoned in space. We were not that imaginative.

If human beings were logical entities, controlled by reason instead of emotion, these or similar ideas would probably have been developed in an orderly manner, rendezvous techniques would have been perfected, and we would have been ready to land on the Moon sometime around the end of the century. But once again politics and astronautics combined, with results that no historian could ever have predicted. On May 25, 1961, President Kennedy announced that a manned lunar landing "in this decade" was a prime national objective of the United States.

The previous month Yuri Gagarin had been the first man to go into orbit; that, as well as earlier Soviet space achievements, was still rankling. So was a debacle only one week later, and much nearer to home, the ill-fated Bay of Pigs adventure, America's answer to the Anglo-French Suez shambles. Only a person of extreme political naïveté would imagine that there was no connection between these events and the challenging goal which the United States had set itself. Yet only cynics or fools could fail to be moved by the eloquence of President Kennedy's message to Congress:

We have examined where we are strong and where we are not, where we may succeed and where we may not. . . . Now is the time to take longer strides—time for a great new American enterprise—time for this nation to take a clearly leading role in space achievement, which in many ways may hold the key to our future on Earth. . . . We have never made the national decision or marshaled the national resources required for such leadership. We have never specified long-range goals on an urgent time schedule, or managed our resources and our time so as to insure their fulfillment. . . . For while we cannot guarantee that we shall one day be first, we can guarantee that any failure to make this effort will make us last. . . . I believe this nation should commit itself to achieving the goal, before this decade is out, of landing a man on the moon and returning him safely to the earth. No single space project in this period will be more impressive to mankind, or more important for the long-range exploration of space; and none will be so difficult or expensive to accomplish.

For some years NASA and its subcontractors had been conducting design studies of a manned lunar landing, which it was thought might take place in the 1970's at the earliest. Now these theoretical exercises suddenly became of the utmost practical importance; they would be the foundation of the greatest scientific and industrial effort in the history of mankind. The $2 billion Manhattan Project which produced the atomic bomb was only a tenth-scale model of the Apollo Project. Although the arguments for and against it would begin at once and would slowly heat up during the coming decade, the die had been cast. The verdict of history may well be that the United States made the correct decision, even if from dubious motives.

The political decisions having been made, some equally difficult technical ones were now necessary. There were three basic ways of achieving the lunar flight, and each had its advantages and disadvantages.

First there was the direct, or brute-force, method. Thanks to improvements in propulsion systems and remarkable reductions in structural weight, it now appeared that even the early space enthusiasts had been too pessimistic. It was, after all, possible to build a single vehicle which could make the round trip to the Moon, using conventional chemical fuels. However, at takeoff from Earth it would have to weigh about 5,000 tons— forty times the size of any rocket then possessed by the United States.

The second approach was to use some kind of rendezvous, in orbit *around the Earth*. For example, the lunar spacecraft might be launched, and unfueled by one booster, and a later flight could carry the propellants for the mission—perhaps in a complete propulsion unit that could be coupled to the orbiting lunar ship. This would permit the use of very much smaller boosters than the direct approach; instead of a single 5,000-ton rocket, two or more 1,000-tonners would be used.

For a number of reasons, and despite bitter protests from some advisers, this apparently attractive approach was turned down. At that time no space rendezvous had been achieved and no one knew what the difficulties would be in practice. It is possible that the decision might have been different, had the knowledge and experience of the Gemini program been available, but that was still five years in the future.

A compromise was therefore adopted, which would allow the mission to be carried out by a single launch from Earth. This could be done using a vehicle in the 3,000-ton class, with one rendezvous *in lunar orbit*. The main spacecraft would not descend to the Moon but would remain circling it while two of its three-man crew visited the surface in a small landing vehicle, which would be abandoned when it had completed its mission.*

This scheme appeared to have a number of advantages, though there were many who thought that if a rendezvous in space *had* to be made, it should be done a couple of hundred miles above the Earth, rather than a quarter of a million miles away in lunar orbit. Against this, the LOR protagonists argued that their scheme involved landing the minimum amount of equipment on the Moon—probably the most difficult and cer-

*Credit for originating the concept of Lunar Orbit Rendezvous (LOR) is often given to Dr. John C. Houbolt, then (1962) head of the Theoretical Mechanics Division of NASA's Langley Research Center. The first thorough analysis of the technique is certainly due to Dr. Houbolt and his colleagues.

tainly the most expensive part of the operation. Even if there were a disaster during the landing or takeoff, the surviving astronaut could bring the orbiting mother ship back to Earth. And, finally, there was no other way in which the feat could be achieved with a single launch vehicle of reasonable size by the deadline set by the President. These arguments were accepted, and the Apollo Project was committed to using Lunar Orbit Rendezvous.

15. THE VEHICLE

At the foot of the artificial mountain known as the Vehicle Assembly Building there is a briefing room, one large wall of which is completely covered with an immensely elaborate chart. It must be the most complex specimen of scientific graffiti in the world, and it details all the thousands of separate operations that must be carried out, in the correct order, and at the correct time, so that three men may make the round trip to the Moon. The planning behind that chart represents an investment of some millions of man-years and some tens of billions of dollars. We are a long way indeed from the backyard spaceships built, with a little help from their beautiful daughters, by the eccentric professors of early science fiction.

Yet there is no need to go into this overwhelming degree of complexity to understand the Apollo mission, which breaks down into a series of consecutive, logical steps. Most of the complication arises from the need to anticipate, and to overcome, problems and emergencies that may occur during the two-week, half-million-mile voyage. The whole operation has been planned so that, at any time, the mission may be called off (aborted) and the men brought safely back to Earth. The road to the Moon is like a highway from which many side turnings branch off at intervals, most of them leading back to the starting point. We will ignore all these detours (a few are, literally, dead ends) and concentrate only on the main highway—the Nominal (i.e., desired) Mission.

Let us start by looking at the payload which has to be

dispatched toward the Moon. It consists of two separate vehicles, each a complete little spaceship in itself—the Command Module (CM) and the Lunar Module (LM). The Command Module is conical in shape, bearing a family resemblance to the Gemini and Mercury capsules; and like them, it is fitted with a saucer-shaped heat shield for protection as it re-enters the atmosphere—at 25,000 mph—on its return from the Moon. For most of the mission it is the home of the three-man crew, and it is the only part of the huge Apollo-Saturn 5 vehicle which survives the round voyage.

The Command Module has no propulsion system of its own, though it is fitted with small control jets so that it can position itself at the correct angle when it begins re-entry. The rocket engine that will send it homeward from the Moon, with its propellants, is housed in a separate Service Module (SM)—a large cylinder upon which the Command Module sits snugly, like the nosecap on an artillery shell. The Service Module also contains electrical-power supplies and part of the life-support system; its task is completed when it has brought the Command Module back to the edge of the Earth's atmosphere, and it is then jettisoned.

If only a lunar circumnavigation were intended—without landing—these two modules would suffice for the whole mission. (In fact, if it were not for food and air requirements, this combination would allow even a trip around Mars or Venus.) For the landing, the Lunar Module is carried, tucked away in an adapter section immediately beneath the Service Module. One may liken its function, and indeed its initial location, to a dinghy towed behind a cabin crusier. Thus the complete Apollo spacecraft consists of the three units: Command Module, Service Module, Lunar Module. Their combined weight comes to almost fifty tons.

To launch fifty tons on an escape trajectory toward the Moon requires a truly enormous rocket. (It is worth remembering how huge the Atlas once seemed—when it boosted the 1½ tons of the Mercury capsule to only 70 per cent of escape velocity.) The vehicle designed for the task is the Saturn 5, latest of the evolutionary line V-2 (Redstone, Jupiter, Saturn 1). Standing 280 feet high (without its Apollo spacecraft payload, which adds another 80, to give a total of 360 feet), the Saturn vehicle weighs 3,000 tons. This is almost all fuel and oxidizer; the empty weight of the huge structure is little more than 200 tons.

It is all too easy to become numbed by statistics when contemplating Saturn 5, but here is a modest figure that is nevertheless highly impressive. The vehicle carries more than thirteen times its empty weight in propellants, despite the fact that two of these—liquid oxygen and liquid hydrogen—require special insulation because of their extremely low temperatures. And to make matters worse, hydrogen also demands very large storage tanks in proportion to its weight; it is the lightest liquid known, with only one-fourteenth of the density of water.

To lift this 3,000 tons of dead weight off the pad, the first stage uses five rocket engines (hence the designation 5), each of a million and a half pounds' thrust, giving a total thrust of 7,500,000 pounds, or 3,750 tons. The margin to produce lift is thus rather small, and the vehicle will therefore rise quite slowly until it has lightened itself by burning fuel.

It does this at the unbelievable rate of fifteen tons *per second*, and this introduces another awesome statistic. The pumps necessary to drive such quantities of fuel and oxidizer into the giant combustion chambers require turbines generating a total of 300,000 hp to drive *them*; this is twice the engine power of the largest ocean liner. There are few other facts which demonstrate so conclusively the new order of magnitudes involved in space transportation. The giant engines that propel the floating cities of the North Atlantic could not run even the *fuel pumps* of the Saturn 5.

The nomenclature of the Apollo booster is somewhat confusing, as it is derived from earlier vehicles in the Saturn program. There are three stages, and it would be convenient if they were labeled S-1, S-2, and S-3, or even A, B, and C. But for once the well-known Germanic sense of order has been defeated (the whole Saturn program is managed by NASA's Marshall Space Flight Center, directed by Dr. von Braun), and the final configuration has turned out to be: S-IC, S-II, and S-IVB. We shall just have to live with it.

The first (lowest) stage is the S-IC, with its five enormous

TABLE 5
APOLLO—SATURN 5

	CODE	NAME	LENGTH, FEET	DIAMETER FEET	EMPTY WEIGHT, POUNDS	PROPELLANT WEIGHT, POUNDS
1	LES	Launch Escape System	34	2	—	—
2	CM	Command Module	12	13	—	—
3	SM	Service Module	24	13	10,000	23,000
4	LM	Lunar Module	20	22		
5	IU	Instrument Unit	3	22	3,500	—
6	S-IVB	Saturn Third Stage	60	22	22,000	230,000
7	S-11	Saturn Second Stage	82	33	80,000	930,000
8	S-IC	Saturn First Stage	139	33	300,000	4,400,000

APOLLO SPACE-CRAFT (rows 1–4)

SATURN 5 VEHICLE (rows 5–8)

FULL WEIGHT, POUNDS	THRUST, POUNDS	PROPELLANT	FUNCTION	MAIN CONTRACTOR
6,600	150,000	Solid	Removal of CM at launch emergency	Lockheed
11,000	—	—	Transporting 3 men to lunar orbit; return to Earth	North American
33,000	22,000	Self-Igniting Storage Liquids	Inserting CM into lunar orbit; returning to Earth	North American
—	10,500 (descent) 3,500 (ascent)	Self-Igniting Storage Liquids	Lunar landing and return to CM with 2 men	Grumman
—	—	—	Guidance and control of launch vehicle	I.B.M.
252,000	200,000	LH$_2$ lox	Injection into lunar trajectory at 25,000 mph; one J-2 engine (rocketdyne)	Douglas
1,100,000	1,000,000	LH$_2$ lox	Boost from 5 to 15,000 mph at 115 miles altitude; five J-2 engines (rocketdyne)	North American
4,700,000	7,500,000	Kerosene lox	Lift-off to 5,000 mph at 40 miles altitude; five F-1 engines (rocketdyne)	Boeing

1,500,000-pound-thrust engines.* It is by far the largest element of the whole assembly, containing 2,200 tons of propellants—a brand of kerosene known as RP-I, specially processed for rockets—and liquid oxygen (lox). This is not the most powerful combination known, by a wide margin, but it is much the cheapest—three cents per pound—so it is economic good sense to use it for the first and largest stage of a launch vehicle.

The second (S-II) stage burns high-energy liquid hydrogen and lox and has a total propellant capacity of 460 tons, but because liquid hydrogen is a dozen times as bulky as kerosene, it is not very much smaller than the S-IC stage. Like that stage, it has five engines, though much smaller ones, giving a total thrust of 500 tons. Thus it would be unable to lift itself off the ground under its own power, and can function only under orbital conditions.

The third (S-IVB) stage is also liquid hydrogen–lox fueled; it carries 115 tons of propellants and is powered by a single 100-ton-thrust engine. It is topped by a section carrying the electronics for guiding and controlling the whole launch vehicle; and on top of *that* is the final payload—the Apollo spacecraft itself, which is the only thing left when the spent components of the gigantic Saturn 5 have dropped back into the sea or joined the rest of the debris now orbiting Earth.

At this point it may be as well to take an inventory and to list the vital statistics of the complete vehicle and payload. It must be realized that Table 5 could easily be expanded into a whole shelf of thick volumes, since it summarizes the activities of more than 20,000 companies (including many of the largest in the world) and hundreds of thousands of individuals.

Table 5 gives the cold facts of the Saturn 5 vehicle; no one would have believed most of them a few years ago. For when those five F-1 engines ignite, the mass of a fully loaded destroyer will climb straight up into the sky.

---

*Anyone who drives into New York from Kennedy or La Guardia airports can judge the size of this power plant for himself. There is a full-scale mockup, easily visible from the road, in the "Space Park" just opposite the 1964–65 World's Fair site.

16. THE MISSION

An Apollo mission begins many months before the dramatic moment when the first stage is ignited, and a hundred million horsepower of manmade thunder rolls along the Florida coast. It begins in a thousand factories, where giant fuel tanks are fabricated, rare metals are machined into strange shapes, and electronics systems are assembled into sealed boxes worth many times their weight in gold.

It continues while all these myriads of components—some weighing many tons, some barely visible to the eye—converge on Cape Kennedy. Whole books could be written about this fantastic place, making no more than a brief mention of the missiles and vehicles it exists to serve. The ground support equipment, communications and radar, control centers, fuel-storage tanks, gantries—and not least the enormous quantities of real-estate involved—represent an investment that must now total several billion dollars. And "investment" is the correct word; unlike the present generation of one-shot launch vehicles, the facilities at the Cape can be used over and over again. They will be ready and waiting when the time comes to go to Mars.

The monuments of the new age of exploration stand for miles along the cape the Spaniards called Canaveral when they left their bones and their treasure here four centuries ago. The largest of all these structures is the Vehicle Assembly Building, designed to hold, service, and check out four Saturn 5's simultaneously. It is more than 500 feet high; through its door the entire United Nations Building could be pushed, with room to spare.

Yet when you see it first, the V.A.B. does not look particularly impressive. Because it is a plain, cubical box, there is no sense of scale; it is just another building on the flat Florida skyline. It is a little while before you realize that it is still 5 miles away.

And when you are standing in front of it, it still doesn't seem unusually large. For, by that time, your mind has simply rejected it in self-defense.

After it has been assembled inside the V.A.B., a Saturn 5 is enclosed by movable floors and working platforms, so that all one can see of it at any level is what looks like a section of 33-foot-diameter storage tank, coming up through the floor and going on through the ceiling. Here it stays for several weeks while all its systems are checked out, largely by automatic equipment conducting computer-controlled test programs.

When everything is ready, the doors of the V.A.B. slide upward and the Saturn 5 slowly emerges, riding on the largest vehicle ever built. The 3,000-ton "Crawler" is really a land-going ship; each of its eight sets of caterpillar tracks is higher than a man, and they support a platform half the size of a football field. On this stands not only the Saturn 5 but also the 400-foot-high umbilical tower, with the numerous access platforms, propellant supply lines, electric-power and control connectors, and so forth needed to fuel and service the rocket. The Crawler can carry a load of 6,000 tons, and its driver's cabin and controls seem absurdly small—until one stops to think that the driver is just the same size as usual. A series of hydraulic jacks keeps the load vertical as it rolls along the 3 miles of special highway to the launching pad; flat out, the Crawler can hit 1½ miles an hour. I once noticed Representative George Miller, chairman of the House Committee on Astronautics, toying thoughtfully with the controls—and warned him not to try breaking the local speed limits, because Chief Justice Warren was standing right behind him.

In the past, space vehicles have been erected and checked out on the pad from which they were to be launched, but this is impracticable for boosters of the Saturn 5 class. The launch pads, which have to absorb volcanic heats and earthquake impacts from the rocket blasts, are so massive and so expensive that it is uneconomical to monopolize one for weeks, or even months, while a single vehicle goes through its elaborate test procedures. Separating the launch and assembly operations results in much greater efficiency; moreover, inside the V.A.B. the great rockets can be fully protected from the weather, including, it is hoped, the hurricanes that occasionally lash the Florida coast.

When all systems were in readiness for the first Apollo flight to the Moon and the immense vehicle was fully loaded with its propellants, the three astronauts crossed the catwalk—more than 300 feet from the ground—into the Command Module, which was to be their home for many days and half a million miles. All the time, automatic checking equipment was probing and testing every vital component, while the last seconds before the moment of departure ticked away.

The "launch window"—the interval during which the mission is possible—opened; the five F-1 engines thundered into life. Watched by more people than any previous event in the history of the world, the rocket started to climb toward the sky.

At first it moved very slowly; the full thrust of four of its giant engines is required merely to balance its weight, so only the fifth can provide acceleration. It took almost ten seconds—and they seemed very long seconds indeed—for the rocket to lift through its own length and to clear the umbilical tower. But as it lost weight it gained speed more and more rapidly, curving away from the vertical and heading out over the sea along its preprogrammed trajectory. Any deviations from the desired course would be corrected by signals from the onboard electronic brain in the instrument unit, housed immediately beneath the Apollo spacecraft compartment. Four of the S-IC stage engines are gimbaled—the central one is fixed—and their barely perceptible movements would keep the vehicle on its course.

In two minutes the first stage had burned its 2,200 tons of propellants; it was jettisoned and driven backward from the remainder of the vehicle by retrorockets. The second stage—the S-II—ignited.

At this point the solid-fueled emergency escape system, mounted on the top of the Command Module, was also discarded. It was no longer needed to jerk the spacecraft to safety in the event of an abort near ground level; the vehicle was now 30 miles up, and if anything went wrong the CM could return by its own parachutes.

The booster was still climbing when the second stage exhausted its liquid hydrogen and was dropped. The third—S-IVB—stage ignited, and it continued to thrust until it had driven the spacecraft into a circular "parking" orbit, at an altitude of 115 miles. Then it was cut off, but with most of its propellant still unburned.

Now the whole spacecraft assembly was orbiting the Earth, only 115 miles up, at 17,500 mph. It could remain there for weeks, if necessary while the crew carried out further checks. If for any reason it was decided to abandon the mission at this stage, it would be easy enough to deorbit and re-enter the atmosphere.

But the flight was going perfectly, and so the spacecraft used its still attached, partly fueled S-IVB stage to break out of the parking orbit, at the correct moment, to head for the Moon. The S-IVB's remaining propellant was just sufficient to give the extra 7,000 mph needed to reach escape velocity; at burnout, the Apollo spacecraft and the now empty stage were receding from Earth at 25,000 mph. In 70 hours of free coasting, they would reach the Moon.

Now followed, at the beginning of the outward leg, some complicated maneuvering—in fact, a kind of mini-rendezvous. It will be remembered that the Lunar Module—"Not Needed On Voyage," as the baggage labels have it—is stowed away *below* the Service Module. But this means that the SM's propulsion systems, required for entry into lunar orbit, cannot be used; the LM is sitting right beneath the rocket exhaust. So it has to be moved around to the front.

To make this possible, the Apollo astronauts cut their spacecraft neatly in two with explosive charges, so that it separated into the Command and Service modules on one side, the LM and the empty S-IVB stage on the other. Under very gentle bursts of power from its control jets, the Command/Service-module assembly—now a small, self-contained spaceship—was turned around through 180 degrees and docked with the LM, so that the CM and LM met head-to-head. The maneuver is exactly like a shunting operation in a railroad marshaling yard, when a coach is switched from behind to in front of an engine and its tender.

It should be realized that if for any reason this turn-around and docking maneuver had failed, the result would not have been a disaster, though it would certainly have been an expensive disappointment. The Command and Service modules could have continued to the Moon and circumnavigated it; but of course the LM would have had to be abandoned in space, and no landing would have been possible.

The empty S-IVB third stage, and its attached instrument unit, were now jettisoned. All that was left, coasting toward the Moon, was the odd-looking head-to-head LM and CM combination, plus the Service Module, attached to the base of the CM.

These operations had all taken place quite close to the Earth, right at the beginning of the translunar trajectory. Perhaps this is of psychological rather than practical importance, but at least if anything had gone wrong all this maneuvering would have been clearly visible, weather permitting, in ground-based telescopes. And, of course, at this range radio and TV communication would be excellent.

The voyage now had begun; nothing (except a collision with a really large meteoroid) could stop the spacecraft from reaching the neighborhood of the Moon in approximately three days. Astronomical and radio observations would be made continually to check the orbit; if needed, there would be a mid-course correction.

At last the spacecraft started to accelerate, increasing its speed as it fell into the Moon's gravitational field. Only a few hundred miles from the surface, at a carefully calculated moment, the Service Module's engine started to fire for the first time in the voyage, slowing the spacecraft to about 3,500 mph. This put it in a circular, two-hour orbit about 70 miles above the surface of the Moon.

To orbit the Moon was the triumphant achievement of the Apollo 8 astronauts—Colonel Frank Borman, Captain James A. Lovell, Jr., and Major William A. Anders—in their historic flight of December, 1968. These lunar circumnavigators left

Cape Kennedy atop their Saturn 5 rocket on December 21, entering an orbit around the Moon 69 hours later, and relaying to Earth breathtaking television pictures of the Moon's desolate, crater-scarred face from a distance of 70 miles. After orbiting the Moon 10 times in 20 hours they returned safely to Earth, having begun a new chapter in the story of human exploration. But their voyage around the Moon was only a preliminary to the lunar landings ahead.

Another necessary preliminary came in March, 1969, when the Apollo 9 trio—James A. McDivitt, David R. Scott, and Russel L. Schweikart—successfully tested the LM docking techniques in an Earth orbit. Two months later, the men of Apollo 10—Thomas R. Stafford, Eugene A. Cernan, and John W. Young—repeated the Apollo 8 lunar orbital flight, but this time took the LM on a practice descent to within nine miles of the Moon's surface. Now, at last, all was ready for the full-scale Apollo mission that began on July 16, 1969, and culminated in the lunar landing of Neil A. Armstrong and Edwin E. Aldrin, Jr., with Michael Collins orbiting in the Command Module above them.

The landing maneuver required the spacecraft to make several revolutions in its parking orbit while the crew prepared for the descent. Then Armstrong and Aldrin transferred to the LM; well may they have wondered, in that tense moment, "When shall we three meet again?"

After a pre-descent checkout, the LM separated from the Command Module. Using the larger of its two engines as a retrorocket, it reduced speed and dropped toward the Moon, while Collins and the Command Module remained overhead in orbit. The two vehicles were in sight of each other, as well as in direct radio contract, during this phase, so Collins was able to monitor the whole landing operation.

As it approached the chosen landing place in the Sea of Tranquillity, Armstrong had to take manual command of the LM, steering it past some troublesome-looking boulders and bringing it safely to rest in a level, rock-strewn plain. "Tranquillity Base here," Armstrong radioed at 4:17:40 P.M. Eastern Standard Time on Sunday, July 20, 1969. "The Eagle has landed."

The Eagle—code name for Apollo 11's LM—remained

on the Moon for less than 24 hours. First Armstrong and then Aldrin went outside, wearing protective spacesuits, to collect rock and soil samples, make observations, and install scientific equipment, which was left on the Moon to radio information back to Earth. In man's first eye-witness description of another heavenly body, Armstrong reported, "The surface is fine and powdery. I can pick it up loosely with my toe.... I can see the footprints of my boots in the treads in the fine sandy particles." The entire Moon walk, beginning with the moment of Armstrong's "one small step," was watched by much of the human race over television. This was not merely a publicity gimmick (though the American taxpayers certainly deserve their money's worth), but a sensible precaution. Pictures can convey more than thousands of words, especially if some emergency should arise. In that event, the TV camera might be the only reporter.

The day after they had written their astonishing new page in human history, the men in the LM took off from the Moon, using their module's landing gear as a launch pad and leaving the empty fuel tanks, the descent engine, the shock-absorbing legs, and an assortment of other equipment as souvenirs for future explorers. Under the power of a small ascent engine, they climbed back to orbit and made a rendezvous with the Command Module. The vehicles docked together, and with two men aboard the LM—or what was now left of it, the Lunar Launch Stage—rejoined their companion. The LM then was jettisoned, remaining in lunar orbit.

Once more there was an orbital checkout, the final one, to prepare for the return journey. At the right moment, the Service Module's engine was fired, and almost all its remaining fuel used to achieve escape from the Moon. Only an extra 1,500 mph was needed to do this; then the two modules were on their way back to Earth.

The homeward journey took about 2½ days. Precise calculation of the course was essential, for the returning spacecraft, building up to a speed of 25,000 mph as it fell back through the Earth's gravitational field, had to enter a corridor only 60 miles deep in order for the atmospheric braking to be carried out properly. If it came in too low, it would burn up; too high, and it would shoot on out into space once more.

A few hours before re-entry, the faithful Service Module was jettisoned; now, of the 360 feet of towering rocket that started from Cape Kennedy, only the squat 11-foot cone of the Command Module was left. Using small attitude-control jets, the CM flipped itself around so that its base—the heat shield—was pointing in the direction of motion. The atmosphere thickened around it; resistance built up rapidly, and the energy acquired in a fall all the way from the Moon was dissipated in a meteoric trail arcing high across the Pacific.

The Command Module was not quite unguided even during the last minutes of its blazing descent. The pilot could fly it, to some extent, by altering its angle of tilt and could thus vary his landing point by several thousand miles.

Twenty-five thousand feet above the ocean, the Command Module, its heat shield still glowing redly, had spent its energy. Three giant parachutes deployed and lowered it to the sea,

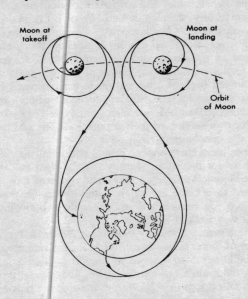

Figure 16. The Apollo mission.

where the recovery ships were waiting. And then the returning lunar voyagers were hustled off into a three-week period of quarantine, lest it turn out—and it did not—that they had carried some infectious microorganism back with them from the Moon.

Jules Verne described the scene, exactly a century earlier, when his three astronauts returned from *their* voyage from Florida to the Moon and back, and were found bobbing on the waves by the United States Navy's corvette *Susquehanna*. The imperturbable Barbicane, Michel Ardan, and Nicholl were playing dominoes when the boats reached them. Perhaps NASA should have included a set in the Apollo Command Module, as a tribute to the great master, who inspired, without exception, all the pioneers of astronautics.

17. THE MOON

Until a few years ago—say, up to 1964—astronomers thought they knew a great deal about the Moon. They had been studying it, with telescopes of ever-increasing power, for three and a half centuries, and many had spent their entire lives making beautiful maps of the details visible on its surface. Those maps—and the splendid photographs taken by such instruments as the 100- and 200-inch reflectors—gave an illusion of knowledge which was abruptly shattered by the Ranger, Luna, Surveyor, and Orbiter spacecraft of the mid-1960's.

Looking at an Earth-based photograph of the Moon, it is easy to forget that the smallest object that can be seen is about half a mile across and that what is visible is no better than a *naked-eye* view from 1,000 miles away. What would we really know of our own planet—its surface texture, its small-scale topography, everything that goes to make up the environment which controls our lives—if we could perceive no details smaller than a super tanker or the Pentagon building?

Telescopic photos were also misleading for another reason; they were almost always made under slanting sunlight, so that shadows stood out dramatically and all slopes, valleys, or hills were greatly exaggerated. Though all serious students of the Moon were perfectly well aware of this, it was difficult even for them to avoid the mental picture of a rugged world of sharp peaks and steep-sided canyons; and popular artists, who naturally wanted their illustrations to be as exciting as possible, made little effort to put the record straight.

Of course, there was a large body of facts which were not

in dispute and which have remained unaffected by the discoveries of the Space Age. The Moon's diameter—2,160 miles—is one quarter of Earth's, so its surface area is one-sixteenth. This may seem rather small, but since three-quarters of our planet is under water and has until recently played no part in Man's explorations, it would be less misleading to say that the Moon has one-fifth of the land area of Earth. This is 14 million square miles of new territory, slightly larger than Africa.

The Moon has no atmosphere and no water—at least in the free state. Whether it possessed either in the past is uncertain; its gravity—only one-sixth of Earth's—is too feeble for it to have retained any gaseous envelope over astronomical periods of time. Any primitive atmosphere must have leaked away into space, ages ago.

The absence of an atmosphere has profound effects upon the lunar environment. Some are obvious; others are more subtle; and there will be many (perhaps the most important) which we will not discover until we get there.

Among the obvious ones are the total silence; there can be no sound on the Moon, though there can be ground-transmitted vibrations. (Signaling systems may be developed using these.) There can be no large, active life forms of the type that exist on Earth, for these are all burners of gaseous oxygen. The sky will be black, and because there is no scattered light, the stars will be visible even in the daytime, but only if the viewer shields his eyes completely from the surrounding glare and waits until he is dark-adapted. Above all, there will be tremendous temperature changes between day and night, and even between sunlight and shadow. In a few hours, or over a distance of a few feet, the temperature can range between plus *and* minus 200 degrees Fahrenheit.

The subtler effects of the vacuum environment will concern the nature of the lunar surface—its physical structure and its behavior when disturbed. Volcanic rocks (if they exist) may be very light and porous, perhaps a kind of froth or foam. There will undoubtedly be minerals and types of rock which do not occur on Earth. And there will be none of that sense of distance which gives scale and perspective to terrestrial landscapes by reducing the contrast and definition of remote objects. A boulder 10 feet away will appear as sharp as a mountain 10 miles away; that is why lunar photographs have a slightly unreal, model-like appearance. There is no atmospheric haze to tell the eye that it is looking across 50 miles of moonscape and that the mountains in the foreground are thousands of feet high.

When the full Moon rides in the night sky, it looks a dazzling object, and the adjective "silvery" seems appropriate enough, but this is another illusion. It appears brilliant only by contrast against the utter blackness of space, and it is in fact a very poor reflector indeed. At close quarters, it has about the optical qualities of dirt. Careful studies of the way in which sunlight is scattered back to Earth during the course of the lunar day had convinced most astronomers, even prior to the Luna 9 and Surveyor 1 landings, that the Moon's surface must be extremely porous, full of minute holes that trapped most of the sunlight falling upon it. Green cheese definitely would not fit the specifications, but stale black bread might.

Even a casual glance at the Moon with the naked eye shows that its brightness varies over its surface, producing patterns which have been the raw material of myths and legends since time immemorial. The telescope confirmed these, and when it was found that the bright areas were mountainous, whereas the dark ones were much flatter and at a lower level, they were given the names of seas (in Latin, *mare*, plural, *maria*) or oceans. Although it soon became obvious that there was not even a single small lake on the Moon, the Sea of Crises, Ocean of Storms, Bay of Rainbows, etc., remain as charming reminders of the first age of lunar exploration.

The lighter areas of the Moon are peppered with hundreds of thousands of circular rings, or craters, ranging in size from 150 miles in diameter down to a fraction of a mile across. (As we now know from the Apollo flights, they continue on down to diameters that must be measured in inches.) The origin of these craters has been the subject of a bitter controversy for more than a hundred years; apart from those entertaining crackpots who thought that they were coral atolls, phenomena in a lunar atmosphere, or the results of thermonuclear brinksmanship, the serious students of the Moon divided themselves into two classes—those who believed that the craters were due to the impact of enormous meteoroids, and those who considered that they were volcanic, or at least produced by internal, igneous forces.

It now appears that the controversy will be settled in the usual way; both sides are probably right. It seems indisputable that the most extensive of the lunar formations, including many of the great seas—which are almost perfectly circular—are due to impact phenomena on a gigantic scale. This would probably have been accepted long ago if the extraordinary formation known as the Mare Orientale had been on the visible face of the Moon. But, as luck would have it, this 600-mile-diameter example of cosmic target practice lies almost entirely in the lunar Farside, so that only its outermost ring of mountains can be seen from Earth. Orbiter 4 (1967) was the first to reveal its true structure.

Yet there are many other features on the Moon that cannot possibly be due to such sudden, catastrophic events. There are clear traces of lava flow, channels that look almost like dried-up riverbeds, and suspicious stains that may be deposits from volcanic outgassing. The dark "seas" themselves appear to be composed of some material which has flowed over, and perhaps melted down, many ancient craters; some have been only partly obliterated, while others appear merely as buried ghosts, like the foundations of lost cities in aerial photographs.

Perhaps the remarkable formation known as Tsiolkovsky is the most striking example of this. This giant crater—or small sea—was first detected by Luna 3; it is the most conspicuous formation on the far side of the Moon, and few would grudge the Russian astronomers the name they gave to it. But it took the United States' Orbiter 3 to show that it is full of some intensely black material that seems to have congealed in the very act of melting down the surrounding, brighter walls of the mountains that contain it.

A great deal has been happening on the Moon; it is a much more complicated and interesting place than we imagined a few years ago. There is also increasing evidence that it is by no means dead, geologically (or selenologically) speaking. Physical changes, obscuration of features by temporary clouds or gas emissions, and even minor volcanic activity have been reported by amateur astronomers for years. No one took them seriously, partly because, until quite recently, the professional astronomers had no interest in the Moon at all. Now the situation has radically changed, and there are teams on the alert, with special instruments, for any sign of lunar activity. Apart from its scientific interest, this may reveal sources of power or valuable minerals for future explorers.

It is also possible, though unlikely, that it may indicate the existence of microclimates—locally favorable regions—where life may exist. The first telescopic observers were quite sure that the Moon must be inhabited—it was almost blasphemy to suggest that the Creator would waste a world—but as understanding of lunar conditions grew, this belief was reluctantly abandoned. It seemed quite impossible that any form of life could survive on a world with no atmosphere and no free water, although it was not out of the question that the Moon might have had a brief evolutionary episode in its youth. In that case, there was the faint chance that fossils might be discovered, but nothing more.

The pendulum has now swung again, not back to the naïve optimism of the seventeenth century, but at least to a less pessimistic viewpoint than that of the early twentieth. We now know very much more about the adaptability of life, especially at the microscopic level, and have discovered that there are plenty of organisms that can thrive in a vaccum, and even some that are killed by air. If life ever got started on the Moon—perhaps in some long-vanished lunar sea—it may still be there. Any biologist worth his salt could design a whole menagerie of plausible Selenites, granted the existence of a few common chemicals on or below the lunar surface.

Anyone who finds this hard to believe should look at the deserts of the American Southwest. From the air they appear to be utterly barren and empty; but as Walt Disney showed in one of his nature films, the desert is really seething with life. So let us reserve judgment on the Moon, at least until we have explored a great many of its 14 million square miles, and not merely the areas around a few landing sites.

This exploration is a task which will occupy us for decades, if not for centuries. Although the Moon will be mapped and photographed and probed by innumerable low-level satellites, the fine details must be filled in by the geologists with hammers and microscopes and Geiger counters and neutron activation analyzers. It may turn out that large areas of the Moon are so similar that there is no point in making more than a few limited surveys; but it may also turn out that it has almost as much variety as Earth, though of very different kinds.

Nature is always far richer and more complex than we can imagine. When the first scientific satellites were being planned, there were those who could see little point in them, because, after all, there was "nothing" in space. Now we have discovered that it is teeming with strange radiations, swept with tenuous gales of solar gas, drenched with signals—and perhaps messages—from distant galaxies, permeated by magnetic fields which may control the destiny of the stars. What had appeared empty has turned out to be inexhaustible.

So it may be with the Moon. A generation ago, it seemed a dusty slag heap in the sky. Now, thanks to the impact of the voyages of the Apollo astronauts, it has suddenly become a real and tangible country, full of wonder and mystery and the only wealth that time can never destroy—knowledge.

18. THE USES OF THE MOON

What the human race will do with the Moon during the centuries to come may be as far beyond imagination as the future of the American continent would have been to Columbus. Nevertheless, it is possible to foresee certain lines of development, culminating not only in large permanent lunar bases but also, ultimately, in self-sufficient colonies and even projects to make the whole Moon habitable. Such a suggestion should no longer seem fantastic; if we have learned one thing from the history of invention and discovery, it is that in the long run—and often in the short one—the most daring prophecies turn out to be laughably conservative.

The first lunar explorers will be concerned chiefly with survival and with collecting as much scientific information as possible from a restricted area and in a limited time. They will have very little mobility; a spacesuit can provide oxygen and life support for only a few hours, and is not the most comfortable garb for long-distance hiking, even where everything has only one-sixth of its terrestrial weight.

Walking, in fact, may be quite difficult on the Moon; weight is barely sufficient to provide traction. Explorers may have to develop a new mode of locomotion, perhaps a sort of buoyant stride. They would be well advised to avoid the spectacular leaps popular in space fiction; loss of balance and a head-first landing could easily be fatal.

Spacesuit design involves complexities that can only be hinted at here; in some ways it is easier to design a spaceship than a spacesuit. They must both contain the same life-support system, but the suit must also be flexible and form-fitting. The men who wore the first models felt as if they were living inside inflated tires; the pressure made the suits so rigid that it was almost impossible to move. One way of avoiding this problem may be the constant-volume suit, a semirigid structure very much like medieval armor.

Temperature control is of prime importance, especially on the Moon during the daytime, when the exposed rocks will be hotter than boiling water and the Sun will be dumping almost two horsepower of pure heat on every square yard. However, this problem should not be exaggerated; thanks to the lunar vacuum, it is easier to handle heat loads on the Moon than in the dry, tropical deserts of Earth. The almost ludicrously simple expedient of an adjustable sunshade will suffice; we may have to get used to the spectacle of lunar explorers carrying Robinson Crusoesque umbrellas.

It will be extremely frustrating to come all the way to the Moon, and then be limited to ranges of a couple of miles around the spacecraft. (From the LM window the horizon is about 2½ miles away, and though radio contact could be established over a greater distance, it would be wisest for the astronauts always to keep in sight of each other.) As soon as possible, therefore, some kind of lunar transport vehicle must be provided, preferably one which will allow the explorers to work in a shirt-sleeve environment, so that it will serve as a mobile base and laboratory.

On a one-way trip, the Saturn 5 could land several tons of supplies on the Moon, and there have been many NASA and industry studies of ways in which this capability could be used to support lunar operations. For example, the Apollo Logistic Support System (ALSS) envisages the use of a modified Lunar Module—a "LEM Truck"—to put 7,000 pounds of cargo on the Moon. Most of this might consist of a surface vehicle, weighing two or three tons, which could carry two astronauts on a 14-day exploration mission covering several hundred miles. It would be able to unload itself automatically from the descent stage which landed it on the Moon, and would await the arrival of its passengers in a later LM.

Numerous odd vehicles have been designed—and some built—to test these concepts. Uncertainty about the nature of the lunar surface, and particularly its bearing strength, resulted in moon rovers which traveled on wheels, caterpillar tracks, legs—and even some that hopped or drilled their way through the thick layer of dust which some theorists had confidently predicted.

It is quite possible that *every* sensible theory of the lunar surface is true, somewhere, and that all these vehicles may eventually be needed. But when Surveyor 1 photographed its own footprint, a collective sigh of relief went up from the engineers who had to design transportation and landing systems. It almost seems as if the Moon's surface—or much of it—is the ideal compromise. Unlike rock, it yields, and so absorbs the shock of impact; but it also has considerable bearing strength, and most types of vehicle could make good progress over it. So could a walking man, once he was accustomed to the gravity.

A lunar supply operation based on the Apollo-Saturn 5 system or modest extensions of it could maintain a scientific base on the Moon at a cost of about fifty million dollars per man-year. (Some people in the business have been quick to point out that one can afford to pay a pretty good salary to a man whose upkeep costs fifty million a year.) Long-term programs of lunar exploration, therefore, will have to be justified on the grounds of scientific value or practical applications; national prestige, after the first landings, will not be enough.

On the purely scientific side, we can still make no more than educated guesses; it has been truly remarked that, if we knew what we'd find on the Moon, there would be no need to go there. But the geologists and the astronomers are already convinced that the Moon is a treasure house of knowledge that can be found nowhere else; as one has put it, "a virtual Rosetta Stone that, if properly read, may permit us to learn how the solar system, the earth, and the continents on which we live were formed."

Until now we have had only one planet for study; we do not know in which ways our Earth is typical (if this word means anything), and in which it is unique. Almost all its surface features have been shaped and reshaped by wind and rain, until practically nothing has been left of its primordial crust. The "eternal" mountains are jerry-built structures which were thrown up yesterday and will be torn down tomorrow. On the very rim of the Grand Canyon—already hundreds of millions of years back in time—may be found the sponges and corals of recent seas; in the miles of rock below lie the records of far more ancient oceans, interleaved with the ruins of continents that have come and gone and come again in the four billion years since the crust of our planet congealed.

There are still greater canyons on the Moon; what story do they tell? A very different one, it is certain. Despite the evidence of massive bombardment in the remote past, the Moon may furnish a much more complete and undisturbed geological record than the Earth can ever provide. Not only the scientific, but also the practical—and even commercial—importance of this can hardly be overestimated. We do not know, for example, why metallic ores are distributed and concentrated as they are in the Earth's crust. The Moon may help us to answer this question, with economic consequences that could pay for any lunar exploration program a hundred times over.

Even from Earth-based photographs it has been possible to identify twenty different types of lunar features, indicating a complex geological history. They include craters of at least five different ages, rills, domes, rays, crater chains, central peaks, wrinkles, maria, highlands. Now, closeup photos have produced many more; for example, there are curious, shallow depressions that appear to indicate some type of subsidence, as if surface material has drained away into underground cavities. And there is, surprisingly, much evidence of erosion; even to a casual glance, some craters look worn and smoothed down, whereas others are still sharp and new, meaning, perhaps, no more than a few million years old.

Drilling rigs, seismometers to detect artificial moonquakes—or natural ones, if they exist—gravimetric, electrical, gamma-ray, and magnetic surveying instruments, will be just a few of the devices used to probe the Moon's interior. When one considers how long it has taken to unravel the past history of our own world, and how much still remains to be done, it is obvious that the Moon will keep us very busy for centuries to come.

Every question that is answered will pose a dozen more,

and we must not assume that even the apparently straightforward questions will be easily settled. A classic example of this is given by the odd case of the American geologist G. K. Gilbert, who first put the meteoric theory of lunar craters on a sound scientific footing. Gilbert also devoted much time to the famous Barringer Crater in Arizona and eventually decided that it was *not* meteoric, but volcanic. Today we are quite certain that it was indeed caused by the impact of a large body from space, and it is regarded as one of the best proofs of Gilbert's theory—though his own verdict prevented this fact from being recognized for about thirty years. This instructive episode once led me to predict that as soon as we land the first two geologists on the Moon, in ten minutes they will be throwing rocks at each other in defense of their rival theories.

The Moon will also be of the utmost importance, not only as an object of study but also as a base for an enormous variety of experiments. Everything that has been said about the value of space stations for physical, biological, and astronomical research also applies to the Moon. It also gives us an observation platform beyond the obscuring effects of the atmosphere, but one of virtually infinite mass, upon which instruments of any size could be mounted. We will not be able to take full advantage of this until we can obtain at least basic construction materials from lunar resources, so that they do not have to be carried from Earth; but even now there are a great many experiments which may be performed more conveniently on the Moon than in space.

One example lies in the exciting and brand-new field of X-ray astronomy. Since these rays cannot penetrate the atmosphere, the first celestial X-ray sources were not discovered until rockets carried instruments into space; and it is very difficult by this means to pinpoint the fainter objects (some of which have been identified with the baffling "quasars"). Dr. Herbert Friedman of the United States Naval Research Laboratory, a pioneer in this work, considers that the Moon is an ideal site for a big X-ray telescope. It could be based on the floor of a crater and sighted at the surrounding rim; then, as an X-ray "star" rose above the mountain wall, the moment it appeared could be noted with great accuracy, and hence the location of this invisible object could be found. In such an experiment, the knife edge formed by the solid body of the slowly rotating Moon would act as part of the telescope system.

The Moon turns on its axis, with respect to the stars, once in every 27.3 days, and this very low rate of rotation makes it ideal as a base for an astronomical observatory. A celestial body can remain in continuous view for two weeks at a time, and, of course, visibility is always perfect. Even the presence of the Sun would be little handicap, as long as the telescope was shielded from its direct rays.

Two other crippling limitations of Earth-based instruments would also be removed or greatly alleviated. One is gravity; a large telescope mirror weighs many tons, and its surface has to be shaped to an accuracy measured in millionths of an inch. But because no material is rigid, it changes its shape and therefore loses its focus as it is moved in the Earth's gravitational field. Extraordinary measures have to be taken to avoid this deformation.

On the Moon this problem would be vastly reduced. Moreover, the whole telescope structure, which has to be just as rigid as the mirror, could be very much lighter. Because it has to contend with our gravity, the 200-inch reflector on Mount Palomar weighs 500 tons. A lunar 200-incher might have a mass of only 60 tons, and hence a lunar *weight* of only 10 tons.

The second terrestrial limitation, or problem, is simple bad weather, and there is no weather on the Moon, though perhaps some protection from micrometeorites may prove necessary. So no expensive domes will be needed; the spidery telescope structure could be erected in the open.

The radio telescopes even more than the optical telescopes will benefit from this state of affairs. The giant parabolic dishes which are now one of the characteristic symbols of the Space Age have to be designed to withstand the maximum wind forces they are ever likely to encounter—as well as gravity. They also have to keep their shape and alignment with great precision; it is not surprising, therefore, that they are among the most massive and expensive structures yet built by man. On the windless, low-gravity Moon, the design problems would be simplified to an unbelievable extent.

And as if that were not enough, the Moon has yet another—possibly overwhelming—advantage for the radio astronomer. Already, here on Earth, he is harassed by electrical interference from myriad motors, automobiles, television stations and thunderstorms; a single electric shaver can put a $10 million radio telescope out of business during a crucial observation. (All radio astronomers have horror stories of such incidents.) But the very center of the far side of the Moon is the only place *in the whole Solar System* that is permanently shielded from our noisy planet—by 2,000 miles of solid rock.

This, of course, is a consequence of the fact that the Moon keeps the same face always turned toward us; it revolves on its own axis in precisely the same time that it takes to go around the Earth. Needless to say, this "synchronous" rotation is not a coincidence; the braking action of the Earth's gravitational field has robbed the Moon of its initial spin and slowed it down until it has entered its present stable state. (The Moon is returning the compliment; in some billions of years it will have slowed the Earth down, so that one hemisphere always faces it; and then moonrise and moonset will be no more.)

For centuries astronomers have been tantalized by the fact that almost half the Moon is permanently hidden from them. Now the time is coming when they may be thankful that the Earth is permanently hidden from half the Moon.

In the 1930's a science-fiction magazine published a story called "The World Behind the Moon," based on the idea that there might be a second moon of Earth, forever hidden from us by the one we know. It is just the sort of idea that would appeal to mystics; the old concept of a "counterearth" on the other side of the Sun is a similar one.

A little knowledge of astronomy (see the discussion of orbits in Chapter 6) appears to show that this idea is nonsense. A body behind the Moon, and therefore more distant from the Earth, would move more slowly in its orbit. Thus it would quickly lag behind and become visible from Earth.

However, this is a case where a little knowledge is, if not dangerous, at least misleading. When the effect of the Moon's own gravity field is added to the Earth's, it can be shown that there is a point, L_2 35,000 miles behind the Moon, where a satellite could hover. This result was first obtained by the eighteenth-century French mathematician Lagrange; he also found that there were five positions in all where a body could remain fixed with respect to both Earth and Moon (Figure 17). These are known as Libration points, and L_1, and L_2, on the Earth-Moon line, may one day be of great importance for lunar communications. (L_3 is on the same line, but on the other side of the Earth.) Incidentally, the position L_1, between Earth and Moon, has nothing to do with the so-called neutral point, where the gravity fields of the two bodies balance; that is a mathematical abstraction with no physical significance.

L_2 and L_1 (which is 36,000 miles from the Moon) are regions of instability, so objects placed here would eventually wander away. This would be no problem for space stations, as the amount of thrust needed to correct deviations would be very small. L_4 and L_5, known as the equilateral, or Trojan, points, are more stable; in 1961 the Polish astronomer Kordylewski claimed to have detected patches of light here which may be due to accumulations of cosmic dust. It may be worth investigating these regions with space probes to see what kind of celestial junk has accumulated on these moving ledges in the Earth-Moon gravitational crater.

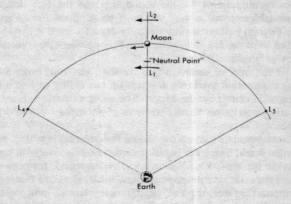

Figure 17. Libration points in the Earth-Moon system.

19. THE LUNAR COLONY

In the last chapter it was mentioned that the cost of maintaining one man on the Moon might be of the order of $50 million a year. In the face of such horrendous statistics, it may seem ridiculous to talk of establishing large bases—and even colonies—on the Moon.

But this is looking at the problem through the wrong end of the telescope. It would be more accurate to say that the huge cost makes it mandatory to set up a lunar base, so that it becomes self-supporting in the shortest possible time. The present vast expense of lunar exploration is largely due to the need to carry propellants for the round trip and the fact that all expendables (food, water, air) must be supplied from Earth. The Pilgrim Fathers would not have done too well if they had had to send the *Mayflower* back to Europe when they became short of breath.

The future of lunar (and, as we shall see later, Solar System) exploration therefore depends on our ability to find supplies of all kinds on the Moon. The most valuable substance of all—as it is on Earth, when in short supply—would be water.

It certainly exists on the Moon; the question is where, and in what form. The free, liquid state can be ruled out—at least near the surface—but ice may occur underground, for in caves where the solar heat never penetrates, the temperature is always far below the freezing point. (Radio measurements indicate that only a few feet below the surface the temperature is constant at perhaps −30 degrees F.) There are certain lunar formations—low domes—which may indicate the presence of permafrost. At the other extreme, if there are local hotspots, or not quite extinct volcanoes, steam may be available, as well as power and useful chemicals.

These are the optimistic assumptions, which may be wrong. If worse comes to worst, it will be necessary to extract water from the minerals in which it occurs; straightforward heating would be sufficient in most cases. During daytime, unlimited quantities of heat can be collected by concave mirrors; however, the physical problem of handling the amounts of rock involved would be formidable.

Since water is 90 per cent oxygen, the two major necessities of life would be provided. But the hydrogen would be almost equally important, since this is the best of all rocket fuels. Once it could be liquefied and stored, the economics of Earth-Moon space transportation would be revolutionized.

Beyond water and oxygen lies the much more complex problem of food. Perhaps by the time (around the turn of the century?) we are planning extensive lunar colonization, the chemists may be able to synthesize any desired food from such basics as lime, phosphates, carbon dioxide, ammonia, water. In fact, this could be done now if expense was no object; it will *have* to be done *economically*, within the next few decades, to feed Earth's exploding population.

An obvious alternative is soilless, or hydroponic, farming, already widely used in locations where land is at a premium; it has also been tried experimentally in the Antarctic and aboard nuclear submarines. Yet another is algae culture; both systems of food production would be ideally suited for the Moon, where there is fourteen days of unbroken sunlight—and no bad weather. The plants would not only provide food but also would be an essential part of the life-support system, regenerating oxygen and recycling waste products, just as they do on Earth.

Another idea is more speculative, and I have yet to see it given serious scientific study. If it works, I am prepared to claim it as original; otherwise I shall hastily disown it.

We may be able to develop plants which can grow *unprotected* on the lunar surface; some desert-adapted forms on Earth give hints as to how this may be done. There is a small African cactus, popularly known as a "window plant," which is entirely enclosed in a tough spacesuit of skin, difficult to cut even with a razor blade. Having solved the problem of conserving water, this admirable and ingenious organism then admits the equally essential sunlight through a transparent windowpane. (Perhaps in a few more million years, it may be the first plant to evolve an eye.)

With a little help from terrestrial geneticists, a lunar flora could be designed; indeed, we may find one already there, which would save us a great deal of trouble. I am sure that I am not the only farmer's boy who felt his fingers itch when he saw the good earth pushed up by Surveyor 1.

Though such speculations may seem premature at the moment, the rate of buildup of the lunar bridgehead may depend upon concepts which today appear no less fantastic. Until we know just what is possible on the Moon and what its natural resources may be, we cannot tell whether its maximum future population will be a few score scientists occupying temporary, inflatable igloos or millions of men living comfortable and, to them, quite normal lives in huge, totally enclosed cities. The greatest technical achievements of the next few centuries may well be in the field of planetary engineering, the reshaping of other worlds to suit human needs. We shall return to this theme in Chapter 25, but it will already be apparent that the conquest of the Moon will be the necessary and inevitable prelude to remoter and still more ambitious projects. Upon our own satellite, with Earth close at hand to help, we will learn the skills and techniques which may one day bring life to worlds as far apart as Pluto and Mercury.

The Moon will not only be a training ground for the other planets; it may be an essential stepping stone toward them. Look again at the energy diagram in Figure 6, showing the work necessary to climb from the Moon, and from the Earth, up to the flat plateau of interplanetary space. Compared with the Earth, the Moon's surface is already 95 per cent of the way to Mars and Venus. If rocket propellants can ever be manufactured there—and this could be done simply by electrolyzing lunar water—it could become the key to the Solar System.

Spaceships making any interplanetary journey would, on departure or arrival, refuel there. They would probably not land, but would orbit the Moon while specially developed, short-haul tankers brought fuel (and other locally produced supplies) up to them.

It would even be good economics to refuel, *from the Moon*, spaceships that had just reached orbital velocity *around the Earth* and were circling it outside the atmosphere. Sending rocket fuel the quarter-million miles from the Moon might well be cheaper than lifting it the few hundred miles up from Earth.

This would be especially true if it could be dispatched to the point where it was needed, *without* the combustion of vast amounts of propellants. Because the Moon has no atmosphere, the old Vernian concept of the spacegun is no longer a fantasy; the low escape speed (5,000 mph, as against the Earth's 25,000 mph) also makes such schemes much more attractive.

One would not use a gun, of course, but a horizontal or gently rising launching track, probably operated electrically. It might be impracticable to launch manned spacecraft by this means, because the acceleration would be too high, unless the track was about a hundred miles long. But containers full of rocket propellant could be shot off into space by a track only two or three miles long and intercepted near the Moon, the Earth, or even some other planet after a journey of a few months. Perhaps one day the specialized products of the Moon's high-vaccum industries will be dispatched to Earth by some such launching system.*

It is possible that major improvements in propulsion, especially the development of nuclear rockets, will make such schemes unnecessary. Just how much room for improvement there is may be judged by one rather striking fact that even scientists find it hard to credit.

As had been repeatedly stated, the problem of leaving the Earth and traveling to another celestial body is one of energy, or work. The amount of energy needed to lift the average man all the way to the Moon is about 1,000 kilowatt-hours—which, if purchased from an electric utility company, may cost only

---

*I developed this concept in a paper entitled "Electromagnetic Launching as a Major Contribution to Space Flight" (*Journal of the British Interplanetary Society*, November, 1950) and gave it rather wide circulation in the short story "Maelstrom II" (*Playboy Magazine*, November, 1962.) In 1962 the idea was revived by William Escher of the Marshall Space Flight Center, who coined the term "lunatron" for such a launcher.

$10. This should be compared with the price of the first ticket to the Moon, which is approximately $10 billion, though in later Apollo flights, as development costs are written off, it should come down to something like $1 billion.

This billion-to-one inflationary factor is a perhaps exaggerated yet not wholly unfair measure of our present ignorance and of the backward state of the astronautical art. I do not suggest that a ticket to the Moon will ever cost $10 (after all, there will be a few expensive but rather essential extras like lifesupport systems and navigational equipment to be provided), but I *do* suggest that many of those depressing zeroes will be slashed off as our technology improves.

It is generally considered that reusable boosters, which can be flown (or parachuted) back to their launching site for further missions, are an essential step in this direction. Certainly space travel can never be much more than an expensive, though worthwhile, scientific venture if something like a Saturn 5 has to be thrown away on every flight. An Atlantic liner that delivered three passengers and sank after its maiden voyage would not be an engineering achievement of which one could be very proud.

Improvements in technology never merely add together; they *multiply*, as the history of commercial aviation has shown. That story will be repeated in space; some of the advances which will make this possible may be: reusable launch vehicles ("aerospaceplanes"); orbital rendezvous with specialized spacecraft tailored for each stage of the mission; refueling in orbit; refueling on the Moon; refueling *from* the Moon; nuclear propulsion. The last, and perhaps most important of all, will be discussed in Chapter 24.

These are all things that can be anticipated, therefore, in accordance with past lessons; we can be sure that the really revolutionary factors are not on this list. (Gravity control? Matter transmission?? At this stage, one guess is as good as another.) Nevertheless, the exploitation of the foreseeable techniques to their limit could result in truly commercial space transport being in sight by the end of this century. And perhaps fifty years from now, anyone should be able to afford a visit to the Moon at least once in his lifetime—perhaps to see grandchildren who, having been born under lunar gravity, can never come to Earth and have no particular desire to do so. To them it may seem a noisy, crowded, dangerous, and, about all, *dirty* place.

It is strange to think that in a few more years any amateur astronomer with a good telescope will be able to see the lights of the first expeditions, shining where no stars could ever be, within the arms of the crescent Moon. Those lights will spread out over the world, as they have covered the old; and in a few generations more, they will sometimes be a little hazy. The features near the edge of the lunar disk will no longer appear so crystal sharp in the telescopes of Earth; over the bitter protests of the astronomers and physicists, who must now look for a new home, the Moon will be acquiring an atmosphere.

And two hundred years from now there will be committees of earnest citizens fighting tooth and nail to save the last unspoiled vestiges of the lunar wilderness.

IV. AROUND
THE SUN

20. THE TRILLION-MILE WHIRLPOOL

There are two ways of looking at the Solar System. The first is purely descriptive; it is the way that most astronomy books begin—the family of planets, asteroids, satellites, comets, and meteoroids of which the Earth is a small but hardly negligible member. The second is dynamic; it is concerned with energies and velocities and gravitational fields—things which cannot be seen but which are as much the concern of the new navigators as winds and currents and soundings were of the old.

Even the descriptive approach presents difficulties, because the Solar System is built on such a scale that to most people the figures are quite meaningless. Moreover, it involves an acute disparity in size. If we concentrate on the distances and try to reduce them to manageable proportions, even the largest of the planets becomes a mere point.

Nevertheless, the effort should be made, for no man can call himself educated if he has no conception of the universe in which he lives. There are still primitive peoples to whom a hundred miles is an inconceivably great distance; yet there are also men who think nothing of traveling ten thousand miles in a day. As speeds of transport have increased, so our sense of distance has altered. Australia can never be as remote to us as it was to our grandfathers. In the same way, one's mental attitude can adapt itself to deal with interplanetary distances, even if the mind can never really envisage them. (And, after all, can the mind really envisage a thousand miles?)

The first step in this "familiarization procedure" is the scale model. To begin with, let us concentrate on Earth and Moon

185

alone, ignoring the other planets. We will take a scale on which a man would still be visible to the naked eye, our reduction factor being 1,000 to 1. The Earth is now a sphere 8 miles in diameter, and 240 miles away is another sphere, the Moon, 2 miles across. On this scale a human being would be a little less than one-twelfth of an inch high, the speed of a subsonic airliner would be half a mile an hour and that of an orbiting spacecraft about 18 miles an hour. The twelfth-of-an-inch-high man contemplating the gulf between Earth and Moon is thus in much the same position as an intelligent ant trying to picture the size of England or Pennsylvania.

To bring in the planets, we must alter the scale again, making the man sink far below visibility. With a reduction of a millionfold, the Earth is now 40 feet in diameter, the Moon 10 feet across and a quarter of a mile away. The Sun is 93 miles away and almost a mile across; 36 and 67 miles from it, respectively, circle Mercury and Venus. Mercury is 15 feet across, Venus 38—a little smaller than the Earth. Beyond the Earth's orbit is Mars, 20 feet in diameter and 140 miles from the Sun. It is accompanied by two tiny satellites, only about half an inch across

Outward from Mars is a great gulf, empty save for thousands of minor planets, or "asteroids," few of which on this scale are much larger than grains of sand. We have to travel 483 miles from the Sun—340 beyond Mars—before we meet Jupiter, the largest of all the planets. In our model it would be over 400 feet in diameter, with twelve satellites ranging in size from 15 feet to a few inches across.

You may feel that our model is getting somewhat unwieldy despite our drastic reduction of a million-to-one; but we are still nowhere near the limits of the Sun's empire. There are four more planets to come—Saturn (diameter 350 feet), Uranus (150 feet), Neptune (160 feet), and Pluto (20 feet). And Pluto is 3,700 miles from the Sun.

This model of our Solar System shows very clearly the emptiness of space and the difficulty of representing on the same scale both the sizes of the planets and the distances between them. If we reduced the Earth to the size of a table-tennis ball, its orbit would still be half a mile across, and Pluto would be 10 miles from the Sun.

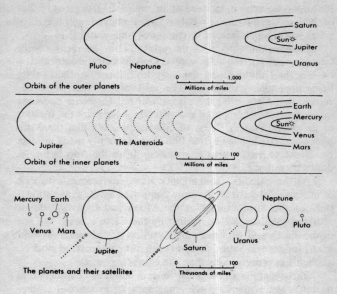

Figure 18. The Solar System.

A pictorial attempt to show the planets, their satellites, and their orbits to the correct scale is given in Figure 18. Even in the most "magnified" of the diagrams, however, it is not possible to represent the smaller satellites accurately.

Three other points remain to be mentioned before our picture of the Solar System is complete. In the first place, it is not a stationary affair. All the planets are moving, and in the same direction around the sun. The innermost planet, Mercury, takes only 88 days to complete one revolution, while Pluto takes 248 years so that astronomers will have to wait until A.D. 2178 before it returns to the part of the sky where it was discovered in 1930.

The second important point is that almost all the planets lie in or very near the same plane, so that the Solar System is fairly flat. There are exceptions to this rule, the worst being

Pluto, whose orbit is inclined at an angle of 17 degrees to that of the Earth's; but on the whole it is well obeyed, and it greatly simplifies the problem of interplanetary navigation.

Finally, the shapes of the orbits. They are very nearly circular, with the Sun at the center. Only Mercury, Mars, and— once again—Pluto depart seriously from this rule, their orbits being appreciably elliptical. That of Pluto, in fact, is so eccentric that after 1980 the planet will be, for some decades, inside the orbit of Neptune and will no longer mark the frontier of the Solar System. It is, of course, possible that there are undiscovered planets beyond Pluto, and certainly many comets travel out to vastly greater distances from the Sun before it draws them back.

All these bodies, from gigantic Jupiter to the smallest speck of meteoroidal dust, are entirely controlled by the gravitational field of the Sun, exactly as the Moon and today's halo of artificial satellites are controlled by the Earth's field. We see in the Earth and Moon a small version of the Solar System itself; Jupiter and Saturn provide even more impressive models, as each has more moons than the Sun has planets.

The dynamics of the Solar System can thus be understood by once again invoking the imaginary "gravitational crater" used to explain the movement of the Earth satellites (Chapter 6). It will be remembered that the Earth's field could be represented by a crater 4,000 miles deep, around whose upper slopes circles the Moon with its own much smaller—180 miles deep—craterlet (Figure 6). All possible orbits in the Earth-Moon field can be reproduced by the movements of a smooth object rolling along the inside of this surface.

Because the Sun's gravitational field is so much more powerful that the Earth's, the corresponding model is also far bigger; using the same scale as before (the work done to leave Earth being equivalent to a 4,000-mile climb), the Sun's field must be represented by a crater about 12 million miles deep! In other words, it is *3,000 times harder* to escape from the Sun than from the Earth.

Luckily this is not our problem; we do not have to climb all the way out of the Sun's gravitational crater, as well as the Earth's. But in moving across the planetary orbits, we do have to travel up and down the far-ranging solar field; so the location of the Earth and planets on its outer slopes is of vital importance.

When we look into this matter, we discover something that could never have been guessed from the purely descriptive map of the Solar System which has just been given (Figure 18). This shows the inner planets crowded around the Sun, with the outer worlds at progressively increasing distances, out to almost 4 billion miles.

The "energy diagram" of the Solar System, however, presents a completely different picture. Far from being near the Sun in the gravitational sense, even the innermost planet, Mercury, is very remote from it. Whereas the full depth of the imaginary crater is 12 million miles, all the planets are crowded together on its uppermost slopes, within 150,000 miles of the rim. This is indeed fortunate for the future of astronautics; the planets are 99 per cent free of the Sun's gravitational field, and moving between their orbits requires only a small fraction of the energy that it might well have done. It is easy to imagine solar systems in which the planets are much more tightly gripped by gravity, and the energies of chemical fuels would be utterly inadequate for transfer from orbit to orbit. But in our case it takes less energy to cross the immense spaces between Earth and Mars than the relatively trivial distance between Earth and Moon.

In other words, the Sun's gravitational field, though of enormous extent, is very "flat" in the region of the planets, and the climb up its slope requires relatively little energy. But superimposed on this field are the much smaller fields of the individual planets; they are effective only over very short distances, astronomically speaking, but their slopes are very steep. Hence the paradox that the first thousand miles of an interplanetary journey usually requires more energy than the next hundred million.

To give some idea of the values involved, Table 6 lists the depths of the gravitational craters for the Sun and major planets, as well as the velocities needed to escape from them and to orbit them.

It will be seen that the energy values vary so enormously that it is impossible to show them on a single diagram, but in any case the figures that are of most direct interest are the

TABLE 6
PLANETARY GRAVITATIONAL FIELDS

BODY	DEPTH OF GRAVITATIONAL CRATER AT 1 G, MILES	ORBITAL VELOCITY, MPH	ESCAPE VELOCITY, MPH
Sun	12,000,000	980,000	1,380,000
Mercury	560	6,600	9,300
Venus	3,700	17,000	24,000
Earth	4,000	17,500	24,800
Moon	180	3,700	5,300
Mars	850	8,000	11,400
Jupiter	120,000	95,000	135,000
Saturn	42,000	57,000	81,000
Uranus	16,000	35,000	50,000
Neptune	20,000	40,000	56,000
Pluto	3,000?	15,000	20,000?

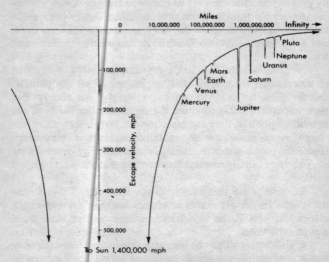

Figure 19. The gravitational field of the Sun.

respective velocities of escape. These also cover a smaller and more easily handled numerical range, so they have been used to construct Figure 19.

This map of the Solar System bears little resemblance to the conventional representation in the astronomy books, but it is much more useful to astronauts. It shows how difficult it is to land on the giant planets and how relatively easy it is to move between the inner ones. Of course, this diagram is only static and must be used with caution; the planets are all moving around the rim of the solar crater at velocities ranging from over 100,000 mph for Mercury to a mere 10,000 mph for Pluto. All these velocities must be taken into account when actual voyages are planned; as we shall see later, they can be used to good advantage.

So let us now try to animate this static model by an act of imagination.

Picture an immense whirlpool—12 million miles deep— whose funnel is almost vertical for millions of miles, but at last flares out toward the horizontal, where it merges into an infinite ocean. On the upper slopes of this great maelstrom, at distances below the surface ranging from 2,000 to 150,000 miles, are much smaller whirlpools, circling independently at almost constant levels; their own depths vary from a few hundred (Mercury) to more than a hundred thousand miles (Jupiter). Naturally, the lowest one has to move swiftly to avoid being sucked down into the greater abyss; the outermost one can maintain itself by moving at a much more leisurely pace, far out on the slowly circling rim. There is, of course, no definite limit to the extent of this gravitational vortex; its influence reaches out to at least a trillion miles from the Sun, and at still greater distances it merges imperceptibly into the combined field of all the other stars in the universe.

Our Earth is at the bottom of the third little whirlpool from the center; a smaller vortex, the Moon, circles very close to it. Scattered up and down the greater slope are the moving whirlpools of all the other planets, passing and repassing each other at their different levels. Until our time, nothing, so far as we know, has ever traveled from one to another.

The whole immense system is perfectly stable. It was set spinning billions of years ago, and there is every reason to suppose that its future may be far longer than its past.

On completing the above paragraphs, I was suddenly smitten with the familiar sense of *déjà vu*. For once, it did not take long to identify the cause:

And now, concentric circles seized the lone boat itself, and all its crew, and each floating oar, and every lance-pole, and spinning, animate and inanimate, all round and round in one vortex, carried the smallest chip of the *Pequod* out of sight.

Our "lone boats" should fare somewhat better when they venture forth into the vortex of the Sun, for it does not seem likely that Captain Ahab would ever have survived a NASA selection board.

21. PATHS TO THE PLANETS

If our spacecraft possessed unlimited sources of energy, we could fly to any planet in a straight line whenever we pleased. But as this is far from the case, and indeed it taxes our skill to the utmost merely to escape from the Earth, it is clear that for a very long time to come all planetary voyages will follow the most economical paths.

The approximate shapes of those paths should be intuitively obvious to anyone who has grasped the analogy of the great solar whirlpool, sweeping the planets around it at their various levels and speeds. The easiest "transfer orbit" from one level to another will be one that grazes both; this was proved in the late 1920's by Dr. Walter Hohmann, and these paths are now known as Hohmann orbits.*

Figure 20 shows the situation for the two cases of most immediate interest—the journeys to Mars and Venus. (The orbit of Mars is quite elliptical, but for simplicity it is shown as circular, and average values are given.) The Earth is moving at 66,000 mph along its orbit, Mars at only 54,000 mph at its considerably greater distance from the Sun. If a rocket had *just* sufficient energy to escape from the Earth, it could continue to move along an orbit identical with Earth's; but if it were given an additional boost, it would start to drift outward from the Sun. Calculation shows that an extra 7,000 mph would be

*Hohmann published his results in a book entitled *The Attainability of the Heavenly Bodies* (1925). He was the chief architect of the city of Essen, and died with it in 1945. Now Essen has been rebuilt, and Hohmann has at least a specialized immortality.

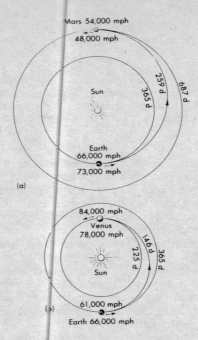

Figure 20. Hohmann orbits to Mars and Venus.

just sufficient to take it out to the orbit of Mars, which it would graze on the other side of the Sun—exactly opposite the point where it received its original impulse.

However, when it reached this point it would not be moving swiftly enough to sustain itself there. Its velocity would now have dropped, as a result of climbing up the Sun's field, to only 48,000 mph, and it would need another 6,000 mph to keep pace with Mars. So a second impulse would be necessary; otherwise it would fall back to the Earth's orbit along the other half of its transfer ellipse.

For a voyage to Venus, just the opposite procedure is

necessary. A rocket already moving in the Earth's orbit has to lose speed to drop Sunward—and it has to lose still more to remain in the orbit of Venus. This does not necessarily mean that it is easier to get to Venus than to Mars; in space, it is just as difficult to lose velocity as to gain it. The *change* of speed is all that matters, as far as fuel consumption is concerned. The only exception to this rule is when there is a convenient atmosphere where excess velocity can be disposed of by air braking.

Of course, if only a "fly-by" is needed, as in the case of a Mariner reconnoitering Mars, it is unnecessary to match velocities at the destination; once its job is done, the probe can race on past the planet and continue along its elliptical orbit around the Sun. But if it is desired to drop a landing vehicle, conduct an orbital survey, or set human explorers down onto the surface, then a rendezvous with the planet has to be made by the use of rocket propellants, atmospheric braking, or both.

When we look more closely into the problem of launching a rocket away from Earth and injecting it into a transfer orbit to another planet—say, Mars—a rather subtle point in energy conservation arises. At first sight it would seem that the velocity the rocket must achieve for the mission can be obtained by simple arithmetic: 25,000 mph is needed to escape from the Earth; 7,000 mph is needed to enter the voyage orbit—therefore, a total of 32,000 mph is required.

Luckily, it is much easier than this; 32,000 mph *would* be needed if the mission were carried out in two separate stages—if the rocket first escaped from Earth, drifted away a few million miles until it was effectively outside its gravitational attraction, and then reignited its engines to leave Earth's orbit and head for Mars. But this would be a ridiculously wasteful procedure; it would mean lifting all the fuel for the Mars transfer out of the Earth's gravitational field before it was burned. It makes far more sense to burn all the fuel that is necessary in a single impulse, as close to the Earth as possible, and then to let the spacecraft coast to its destination, apart from any minor navigational changes that may prove necessary.

When the mission is recalculated on this basis, the initial velocity needed turns out to be not 32,000 mph but a mere 26,000 mph—only 1,000 mph more than the velocity of escape itself. At first sight we seem to have got something for nothing, but this, needless to say, is an illusion. The single impulse, applied as close to the Earth as possible, is so much more efficient that it produces the same final result as the two separate ones.

Exactly the same argument applies at the other end. We *could* speed up to match the orbital velocity of Mars, which requires an extra 6,000 mph. Then, in a separate maneuver, we could fall into the gravitational field of Mars, acquiring another 11,400 mph (the Martian escape velocity) in the process, which would have to be neutralized before we approached the surface. Total velocity bill: 17,400 mph.

But doing everything in a single maneuver, as close to Mars as possible, cuts the bill to about 12,000 mph—another substantial saving. Table 7 sums up the situation by recapitulating the two ways of achieving the same result.

These figures assume the Mars landing is made entirely by rocket braking and are therefore unrealistically high. It appears certain that, thin though it is, the Martian atmosphere is admirably suitable for re-entry purposes (though in this case, the word *re*-entry is hardly appropriate). The final touchdown

TABLE 7
EARTH-MARS MISSIONS (WITH LANDING)

FOUR-IMPULSE MISSION		MPH
1. Escape from Earth		24,800
2. Transfer to voyage orbit		7,000
3. Matching Mars Orbit		6,000
4. Mars landing		11,400
	Total	49,200

TWO-IMPULSE MISSION		MPH
1. Earth escape and transfer to voyage orbit		26,000
2. Transfer to Mars orbit and landing		12,000
	Total	38,000

may require a small amount of rocket braking, but almost all the 11,400 mph of approach speed can be destroyed by air resistance. This would reduce the total impulses needed for the two missions to about 38,000 and 27,000 mph respectively, leading to the remarkable result that it is much easier to make a one-way trip from Earth to the surface of Mars than from Earth to the surface of the Moon.

The Hohmann, or minimum-energy, orbits have two serious disadvantages, at least as far as manned space travel is concerned. Like the easiest road up a mountain, they take the longest way around, and therefore the saving in fuel has to be paid for in time. The Venus journey lasts about 145 days; that to Mars is rather longer, about 260 days.

It is also obvious that such voyages can take place only at rather infrequent intervals, when the planets are in the correct positions with respect to each other. The moment of departure of the spacecraft has to be calculated so that when it has completed its semiellipse around the Sun, it makes its appointment with its target planet. Although a certain amount of latitude is possible, the fuel penalty involved in missing a launch date increases rapidly with time.

The situation is even more complicated when return journeys are considered, since it is then necessary to wait for a second suitable planetary configuration. For this reason a voyage to Mars *and back* along Hohmann orbits would last approximately 970 days. The journey time would be twice 260, 520 days; the remaining 450 days would be spent on Mars, waiting for the planets to get into the right position for the return trip. So the "cheapest" orbits may not be the most practical ones in reality, especially for manned expeditions.

When journeys to the outer planets are considered, the voyage times along Hohmann orbits become even more intolerable; one way to Jupiter would be 2 years, 9 months, and the round trip to Pluto would take just under a century! It will therefore be necessary to use much more direct and far more expensive trajectories when such journeys are seriously planned; only the use of nuclear power for propulsion will make them possible.

Some typical high-speed (and high-cost) orbits are shown in Figure 21. If a body is moving around the Sun at a moderate speed, like a planet or a comet, it travels along an ellipse. If

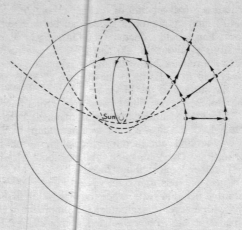

Figure 21. High-speed orbits around the Sun.

it is moving so fast that it will eventually escape from the Solar
System, its path is the open-ended curve known as the hyperbola; both types are shown in Figure 21. Given unlimited propulsive ability, a spaceship could choose whichever of these
orbits was the most convenient and travel from planet to planet
at any time, without waiting for a suitable configuration.

In this way transit times could be cut down to a few weeks
or even a few days. Unfortunately, the energies needed for
such missions would be enormous (hundreds of times greater
than for Hohmann trips), since the orbits do not utilize the
existing planetary velocities but instead partly cancel them out.

These problems are well illustrated by the case—not as
theoretical as it seems—of a rocket launched to the Sun. The
distance is relatively small, but the fuel requirements are very
great, for it is necessary to cancel the *whole* of the Earth's
66,000 mph of orbital speed. Only then can the probe drop
directly toward the Sun; if it has any sideways (orbital) velocity
at all it will miss the Sun, go around it in a tight hairpin bend,
and continually retrace a very thin ellipse stretching back to

the orbit of Earth (Figure 21). Getting to the Sun is therefore very difficult indeed,* though it will certainly be attempted with instrumented probes, which could be designed to withstand entry into the solar corona. The time of free fall from Earth to Sun is only 65 days.

After these theoretical discussions, let us now look at some actual achievements. The first object of any size to escape from the Earth was the Soviet Union's Luna 1 ("Mechta," or "dream"), aimed toward the Moon on January 2, 1959. It passed within 5,000 miles of the Moon, whose gravitational pull changed its direction of motion slightly but made very little difference to its speed. Then, having lost almost all its initial launch velocity escaping from Earth, it continued to drift slowly on into space.

But that "slowly" is a relative term. There is no such thing as absolute speed in space, as was realized long before the time of Einstein. Some convenient marker, or reference system, is always assumed, though not always explicitly mentioned. In the initial stages of an interplanetary voyage, the reference point is the Earth; later it is the Sun; and, finally, it is the planet of destination.

When it was a million or so miles out, Mechta had lost through gravity drag almost all the 25,000 mph its rockets had given it relative to its launch pad. But that launch pad was moving around the Sun at the respectable speed of 66,000 mph, and Mechta still had the whole of this velocity, plus the small change of a few hundred miles an hour left over after it had achieved escape. Thus the laws of celestial mechanics constrained it to move in an orbit very similar to the Earth's, but because of its slight speed excess, it swings out almost halfway to Mars at its far point. The actual figures for Mechta's orbit are: perihelion 91 million miles; aphelion 123 million miles. And because its orbit is larger than Earth's, it takes longer to complete one revolution, 443 days.

After fifteen months, therefore, Mechta came back to its original launch point at the orbit of Earth, but, of course, Earth was no longer there, having pulled a good many million miles ahead on its quicker, twelve-month orbit. However, after a sufficient number of revolutions, the natural planet and the

*There is, however, a way of doing it even today; see pages 205-206.

artificial one can get together again. The ratio of the two periods—443 and 365 days—is almost exactly 11 to 9; in other words, 11 Earth years equal 9 Mechta "years." So about 1970, 1981, and so on, Mechta should be in the vicinity of Earth, but since its radio is long since dead, it is most unlikely to be detected.

This simple calculation ignores some essential facts, which must be taken into account when planning any space voyage. The Solar System is not really flat, and the planetary orbits are inclined to each other at small angles. Mechta's orbit is tilted to Earth's at about one degree, which may not seem a great deal, but is enough to ensure missing an appointment by a good many hundred thousand miles. These orbital inclinations have to be allowed for by a suitable mid-course correction when a planetary encounter is attempted.

The first such encounter took place on May 19, 1961, when a space probe launched three months earlier from the Soviet Union's Earth-orbiting Sputnik 8 passed within 62,000 miles of Venus. However, radio contact was lost immediately after departure from Earth orbit, so the mission was a failure—as had been the case with two earlier and unannounced attempts to reach Mars in October, 1960.

Several further Russian launches, to Mars and Venus, were no more successful, though the elaborately instrumented Mars 1 passed within 120,000 miles of its intended goal on June 19, 1963. Unfortunately, radio contact was lost at about 66 million miles from Earth.

By that time the United States had already scored its first major scientific success in deep space, with Mariner 2, which passed within 22,000 miles of Venus on December 14, 1962, after a voyage lasting 149 days.* The first *physical* contact with Venus, or with any other planet, was made by the Russian Venus 3 on March 1, 1966, when a capsule of instruments was dropped into the atmosphere. But once again the scientists were unlucky, as radio communication with the probe had been lost some time before impact.

The first Mariner launch to Mars (Mariner 3, November

---

*Mariner 1, launched on July 22, 1962, was wrecked by the most expensive hyphen in history. Omission of a single "-" from the program fed to its guidance computer sent it off course, and the Atlas-Agena booster had to be deliberately destroyed.

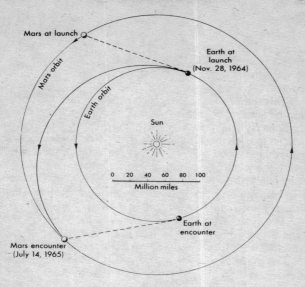

Figure 22. Orbit of Mariner 4.

5, 1964) met with a fate not quite as ignominious as that of Mariner 1. Its protective shroud collapsed under the aerodynamic forces acting on it during the ascent, and Mariner 3 was pinned captive inside, unable to extend the solar panels upon which it depended for energy. It died of electrical starvation within a few hours.

For the Jet Propulsion Laboratory's engineers, it was literally a case of "Back to the old drawing board," and by prodigious efforts a new shroud was designed, fabricated, and tested before the Mars "launch window" closed again. Mariner 4 was ready within three weeks and took off for Mars on November 28, 1964. (The indefatigable Soviets followed two days later with Zond 2, but once again they lost contact in mid-mission.)

The path of Mariner 4 (Figure 22) was a fairly close approximation to a Hohmann orbit. The space probe had some-

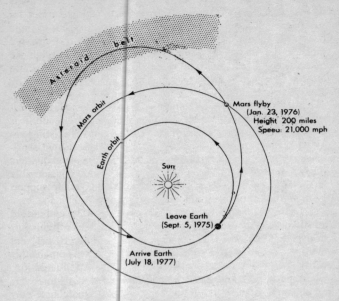

Figure 23. Mars fly-by mission.

what more than the minimum speed requirement and got to Mars in only 227 days instead of the optimum 260. This involved no great penalty, as what was desired was an *encounter*, not a rendezvous. After a mid-course correction, Mariner 4 passed within 6,000 miles of Mars on July 14, 1965, exactly as intended. It radioed back nineteen photographs, as well as a great deal of scientific information, which changed many existing ideas about the nature of Mars (Chapter 22).

An example of a more advanced Mars mission, of a type which might be flown by manned spacecraft in the 1970's, is shown in Figure 23.*

This would allow for an encounter with Mars, during which

*From E. Z. Gray and Franklin P. Dixon, *Manned Expeditions to Mars and Venus*. Fifth Godard Memorial Symposium, Washington, D.C., March, 1967.

time the planet could be studied from close range for many weeks, and from a distance of only a few hundred miles for several hours. Landing probes could also be dropped, to radio back information to the passing ship, or directly to Earth at a much lower rate. The flight would continue on through the inner asteroid belt, and the spacecraft would return to Earth after a voyage of a little less than two years, re-entering by atmospheric braking.

As far as propulsion requirements are concerned, this mission is much easier than the Moon landing; operationally it is also simpler. It could therefore be carried out by existing vehicles, except for the fact that even the most dedicated astronauts could hardly be expected to endure Apollo-sized quarters for two years. So it will be necessary to develop considerably larger spacecraft, as well as much more reliable life-support systems, before such flights are attempted.

Exactly similar missions to Venus are possible, and indeed a little easier; the initial speed needed for all these flights lies in the range 27,000–28,000 mph, which is only 10 per cent more than that needed to escape from Earth. (Compare this with the more than 35,000 mph needed for the Apollo mission, when the lunar landing and takeoff are added in.) Moreover, by choosing times carefully and using a little midcourse correction, it is possible to plan flights which include encounters with both Mars *and* Venus in a single mission.

The most favorable dates for some possible "fly-bys" are given in Table 8. The one to aim for is obviously December, 1978; let us hope that we are ready for it. There are a great many scientists who would very willingly give two years of their lives for a trip to both of our nearest neighbors in space, even though they would spend only a few hours in their vicinity.

Beyond Venus and Mars, the next targets in order of distance are Mercury, the Sun, and the giant planet Jupiter. The last is the easiest and perhaps most exciting target, demanding a launch velocity of about 32,000 mph. In this case the problem is not getting to Jupiter, but transmitting useful information back across a distance of half a billion miles.

It was difficult enough to receive Mariner 4's Martian photographs; the transmission of each frame took eight hours, over a distance of 134 million miles. An Earth-Jupiter link

TABLE 8
MARS AND VENUS FLY-BYS

| | | VOYAGE DURATION, DAYS | | |
	LAUNCH DATE	OUTWARD	RETURN	TOTAL
Mars	Sep., 1975	130	537	667
	Oct., 1977	145	533	678
	Nov., 1979	132	554	686
Venus	Jun., 1975	117	250	367
	Jan., 1977	117	257	374
	Aug., 1978	116	249	365
	Apr., 1980	109	250	359
Venus-Mars	Dec., 1978	142;230	253	625

would be three to five times longer, and since radio-power requirements increase with the square of the distance, a Mariner might require a week to send a single picture back from Jupiter. Obviously, much more powerful transmitters are needed, and they will have to operate from nuclear sources, as the rapidly weakening solar rays cannot provide useful energy beyond the orbit of Mars.

NASA's Office of Space Science and Applications has prepared an interesting study of a 500-pound space probe which could be launched to Jupiter by a vehicle based on the now relatively modest Atlas-Centaur. The flight would last about 600 days, going across the orbit of Mars and through the asteroid belt.

After the fly-by, the trajectory of the probe would be greatly modified by the enormous gravitational field of Jupiter. We could use this to good effect in at least three ways (Figure 24).

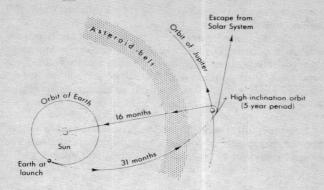

Figure 24. Orbit of Jupiter probe.

In case (a), the probe passes over one of the Jovian poles, and so its orbit is deflected right out of the plane of the Solar System; in the diagram it must be thought of as rising out of the paper, or plunging into it. In each case, a wholly unfamiliar region of space would be explored.

In case (b) the probe would sweep on past Jupiter and in doing so would acquire some of the planet's orbital velocity, as explained in Chapter 24. As a result of this "hyperbolic encounter," it could, in fact, gain so much speed that *it would escape from the Solar System completely* and head on out into galactic space, continuing to send back information until it was perhaps a billion miles from Earth, or beyond the orbit of Saturn. The limiting distance would be set purely by the power of the onboard transmitter and the size of the receiving antennas on Earth.

Case (c) is perhaps even more interesting and useful. This time Jupiter's gravity would be used to *cancel* the probe's orbital speed, so that it fell directly toward the Sun, which it would reach about sixteen months later. Its instruments could thus give a cross-section of the Solar System all the way from Jupiter into the Sun, and at a high rate of data transmission, since the ranges involved would be relatively short (only 100 million miles).

Thus, by using Jupiter we can perform missions which are otherwise quite impossible. The *direct* route to the Sun takes only two months, but even the 3,000-ton Saturn 5 could not send a useful payload along it. Yet, if we are content to take four years on the trip—which is itself an advantage for a data-collecting space probe—a launch vehicle in the 200-ton class will suffice.

Space is full of subtleties and surprises. It is hard to believe that the rocket that put John Glenn into orbit could also serve to send a payload to the Sun—or to Proxima Centauri.

22. CHILDREN OF THE SUN

For a long time to come it is going to be very risky to write anything about the planets. After decades in the doldrums, planetary astronomy is undergoing a total revolution; more has been learned about Earth's neighbors in the last few years than in all previous history. But this is merely a modest beginning, the prelude to the *real* breakthrough, which will be brought about by orbiters, landers, and, ultimately, manned expeditions.

It must not be thought that space probes are responsible for all the great advances of the last few decades; except in a few dramatic instances, they have not yet contributed a great deal. Most of our new knowledge has come from ground-based techniques—interplanetary radar, electronic devices to amplify and analyze the images seen through telescopes, or improvements in spectroscopy. Far from being obsolete, giant telescopes are being built in greater numbers than ever before, and they still have several generations of work ahead of them before they become training aids for young graduate astronomers on their way to the lunar observatory.

For reasons which are still unknown, the planets appear to form two quite distinct classes. On the one hand are the relatively small solid bodies like the Earth, Mercury, Mars, Venus, and Pluto. These range in size from 8,000 miles in diameter downward, and all have a density several times that of water. They can probably be called "terrestrial-type" planets, and they probably consist of much the same materials as does the Earth (though it may be unsafe to generalize about Pluto,

207

concerning which practically nothing is known except its diameter).

Forming a complete contrast are the giant planets—Jupiter, Saturn, Uranus, and Neptune. The smallest of these has four times the diameter of Earth, but their densities are extremely low (in the case of Saturn, being actually less than that of water). We are forced to conclude from this that the four giant planets are partly gaseous or liquid, perhaps possessing solid cores only at great depths below immensely thick atmospheres.

The two types of planets are divided by a kind of no-man's-land thinly populated by thousands of asteroids, or minor planets, whose diameters range from 480 miles down to a few yards. Most of the asteroids—an unfortunate word, as it means literally small star, and nothing could be less starlike—occupy a broad, diffuse belt between Mars and Jupiter, but some wander as far afield as Saturn, while others plunge even nearer the Sun than Mercury. At one time it was thought that they were fragments of an exploded planet; now it seems more likely that they are some of the general debris left over from the formation of the Solar System.

To complete the picture, mention should be made of the comets, those huge, tenuous clouds of gas which for thousands of years have terrified mankind by their portents in the sky. They travel around the Sun in orbits which are often very eccentric and highly inclined to that of the Earth. Many seem to have a small, solid core, or nucleus, generally believed to be made of frozen gases which expand in spectacular eruptions as they near the Sun. Though very little is known about the physical nature of comets, it is only a matter of a few years before a probe is launched through one as it comes near the orbit of Earth.

Two or three times in every century a comet is bright enough to be seen in broad daylight (as happened with Ikeya-Seki in 1965). But *every* year, for months on end, one of the planets is brilliant enough to be seen in the daytime if one knows exactly where to look for it. This is Earth's enigmatic sister-world, Venus.

At her closest, she is only 25 million miles away, or five months as the space probe flies. Through the telescope she appears as a dazzling, featureless crescent, with no trace of the surface detail that makes the Moon and Mars so endlessly interesting.

In size Venus is almost a twin of Earth; her diameter is about 4 per cent smaller, and as a result her surface gravity is 10 per cent weaker—a reduction that would hardly be noticed. But here the resemblance between Earth and Venus virtually begins and ends, though astronomers have been reluctant to accept this fact, until it was forced upon them by the overwhelming weight of evidence.

The cause of the planet's brilliance has also been responsible for our almost total ignorance about Venus. She is covered with an impenetrable layer of clouds, the composition of which has long been another major mystery. The obvious explanation is that they are composed of water; but for a long time ground-based spectroscopes failed to reveal any trace of it. So alternative theories were proposed; according to one, the clouds were huge dust storms, stirred up by continual gales raging between the hot and the cold sides of the planet; according to another, they were composed of formaldehyde, which led to the comment that Venus was not merely dead, but pickled. At various times astronomers also advocated lakes of petroleum and seas of soda water—the latter theory inspired by the one certain fact about the planet's atmosphere, that it contains vast quantities of carbon dioxide.

What made progress difficult was that even the length of the Cytherean* day was totally unknown; since no surface features (or even persistent clouds) could be detected, there was no way of measuring the planet's rotation. Guesses ranged all the way from 24 hours up to the full length of the year— 225 days. Ironically, no one even dreamed of the truth, and it was a great surprise when, in 1965, radar observations showed that Venus rotated once in every 243 Earth days—and in a *reverse* direction to the usual planetary spins. Venus's day is therefore longer than its year—a situation unique in the Solar System.

*The adjective for the planet Venus presents grave linguistic problems. "Venusian" is unacceptable to purists; "Venerean" raises false expectations; "Cytherean" is correct but no one except classical scholars understands what it means. Take your choice.

Analysis of the returning radar signals has also hinted at the existence of mountain ranges, and attempts have been made to construct the first crude maps of the hidden surface. However, this task can be carried out properly only by radar equipment just above the cloud layer, in orbiting spacecraft. This will be one of the next orders of business for Venus.

Because it receives about twice as much sunlight as the Earth, it is obvious that Venus must be hot; just *how* hot has come as another (and unpleasant) surprise. In the 1950's measurement of the faint radio waves emitted by the body of the planet indicated a surface temperature of several hundred degrees, but many astronomers found it hard to believe this. They were forced to accept the verdict when the instruments aboard Mariner 2, detecting the very short radio waves from below the cloud level, showed that the surface temperature must average about 800 degrees Fahrenheit. The maximum value at the long, hot noon must be well over 1,000 degrees. It is difficult to imagine a more forbidding place; and to make matters worse, the pressure at the bottom of the dense atmosphere must also be very high, perhaps equal to that a quarter of a mile down in our oceans.*

It is, perhaps, a relief to abandon this exasperating planet and turn to Mars, where we are not confronted with impenetrable clouds; we can see the actual surface of the planet and can make maps of its main features. Moreover, when it is nearest to us, Mars turns its illuminated face full toward the Earth, unlike Venus, who passes between us and the Sun on such occasions and is thus completely invisible.

Despite these advantages, our knowledge of the planet is full of gaps, and there are rival interpretations even of the admitted facts. Because of its distance, an observer of Mars, using a large telescope under conditions of good seeing, is in much the same position as someone looking at the Moon with the naked eye or, at the best, with a pair of weak opera glasses. Though we have telescopes that could bring Mars to within one-tenth of the Moon's distance, it is impracticable to use

---

*The Russian space probe that landed on Venus on October 18, 1967, reported a temperature of 536°F. at ground level and an atmospheric pressure at that point 15 to 22 times that at sea level on the Earth. These findings were supported by the U.S. Mariner 5 fly-by on the following day.

such magnifications, because our atmosphere is not steady enough. As was pointed out previously, simply increasing the power of a telescope very soon ceases to show any finer detail and in fact soon shows less: it is like looking at the reproduction of a photograph in a newspaper through a magnifying glass— the greater power only reveals the "graininess" of the image. To aggravate matters, as the orbit of Mars is notably eccentric, really close approaches of the planet occur at rather rare intervals, the best approaches of all being fifteen or seventeen years apart (1971, 1988).

Let us first consider the undisputed facts about our little neighbor. It is just over half the size of the Earth (4,200 miles in diameter), and thus its surface area is 25 per cent of Earth's. But three-quarters of our world is covered with water, and since there are no oceans on Mars, it follows that its land area is just about equal to Earth's.

The Martian day is very nearly the same length as the terrestrial one, being only half an hour longer, and the axial tilt of the planet is also almost the same as Earth's. Mars therefore has seasons just as our planet has, but since the year lasts 687 days, they are nearly twice as long. The changing seasons, as we shall see later, produce important effects which can be observed even across the millions of miles of space that separate us from the planet.

In the telescope Mars shows three main types of surface marking. Most prominent are the brilliant polar caps, which wax and wane alternately in the two hemispheres, almost disappearing in summer and coming halfway down to the equator in winter. Not so bright, but still very prominent, are the red or orange areas which cover most of the planet. Finally, there are the irregular, dark regions that form a belt around Mars, roughly parallel to the equator.

These are the permanent markings. In addition, temporary clouds and haziness can sometimes be observed, proving that the planet has an extensive atmosphere.

The behavior of the polar caps immediately suggests that they are composed of ice, and this explanation is now universally accepted. The Martian ice caps, however, must be far thinner than the enormously thick and permanent crusts that lie at our poles. This is obvious from the fact that even the mild summers of Mars are warm enough to make them shrink so much that on occasion the southern cap vanishes completely. They may therefore be only a few inches thick, the equivalent of a very light fall of snow.

The orange regions, which give the planet its characteristic color, show no seasonal changes and are generally considered to be deserts. This word need not, however, conjure up a picture of a drab, sand-covered waste. According to some astronomers, the Martian deserts show extremely brilliant coloring—brick-red and ocher being among the terms used to describe them. If this is true, they may resemble some of the incredibly spectacular and garish deserts of Arizona. However, it is now generally believed that the brighter colors reported may be due to telescopic or visual defects; they may, literally, be in the eyes of the beholders, not on Mars itself. But there is no doubt about the planet's general redness, and it has been suggested that this is due to the presence of metallic oxides, particularly iron oxide. If this is the case, Mars is a world which has, literally, rusted away.

The Martian deserts are probably fairly flat, for we should be able to detect any high mountains by the irregularities they would cause on the line between night and day. There is, however, no reason why hills or plateaus a mile or two in height should not exist, and indeed there is some evidence for mountains near the South Pole. The ice cap occasionally splits into two sections as it shrinks, leaving an isolated white patch which is always at the same location, as might be expected to happen if there were high ground there.

Undoubtedly the most interesting areas of Mars are the dark regions, which show seasonal changes linked with the melting of the polar caps. The early observers made the fairly natural assumption that these regions were seas and christened them "maria." The history of lunar nomenclature was thus repeated, and though we now know that Mars is as bereft of seas as is the Moon, the names are still used, Mare Cimmerium, Mare Serpentis, and Mare Sirenium being among the more fanciful inventions.

With the melting of the polar caps in the spring and early summer, a belt of darkness spreads slowly down toward the equator across the "seas." This change is so obviously produced by the release of water from the caps that the evidence for the growth of vegetation is impressive. (It is, of course, conceivable that the change might be due to chemical reactions among mineral deposits of some kind, but there seems little point in advancing this complicated explanation in place of the obvious and simpler one.) The color changes that occur are strikingly similar to those that we should witness if we observed our own Earth from space. During most of the Martian year, the "maria" are blue-green or blue, but in the late winter and early spring they become chocolate brown.

Before we jump to any conclusions regarding life on Mars, we must consider what is known about its atmosphere. The facts revealed by the spectroscope are rather disconcerting: there is no sign of oxygen, and we have tests which could detect the presence of this gas even if it were only one-thousandth as common as in our atmosphere. Carbon dioxide has been observed; it is about twice as abundant on Mars as on Earth. Water vapor has not been detected in the atmosphere, but infrared bands due to ice have been observed in the polar caps.

The air pressure at the surface of Mars is very low, perhaps one-hundredth of its sea-level value here. We would have to ascend twenty miles to encounter so low a pressure on Earth, and even if the Martian atmosphere consisted entirely of pure oxygen, we could not survive in it. It is probable that the bulk of the atmosphere consists of inert gases such as nitrogen or argon.

Although the pressure is so low, the Martian atmosphere is very deep; the weak gravity (one-third of Earth's) means a much slower falling-off of density with height than on Earth. This is supported by the fact that clouds have been observed as much as 20 miles above the surface of Mars.

Despite the tenuous nature of the Martian atmosphere, it is surprisingly hazy and normally blocks out the light toward the blue end of the spectrum. The reason for this is unknown; although one is tempted to explain it by the presence of fine dust in the atmosphere, it is difficult to see how so thin a gas could support much solid material.

This particular mystery is less important than the undoubted fact that the Martian atmosphere is very tenuous and contains no oxygen. Perhaps the Martian plants, if any exist, can obtain the oxygen they need from the soil rather than from the atmosphere. It should be remembered that the other basic raw materials for plant life are carbon dioxide, water, and sunlight, all of which are present on Mars, though water must be extremely scarce. So conditions on the planet are not too unfavorable, and it has been found that a great many terrestrial micro-organisms can thrive and even reproduce in a simulated Martian environment.

Nor is the temperature of Mars so low, despite its greater distance from the Sun, that life would be severely handicapped. At noon during the summer, temperatures of 80 degrees Fahrenheit have been recorded by the thermocouple, and the equatorial regions of the planet must be not much colder, on the average, than the temperate zones of Earth. However, the range of variation is much greater, the Martian nights and winters being extremely cold. Even on the equator, the night temperature is −120 degrees Fahrenheit.

It is worth remarking that the seasonal variations would not be a great hardship to animal or mobile forms of life. Owing to the smallness of the planet, the length of the year, and the absence of geographical barriers, it would be quite easy to migrate from one hemisphere to another with the changing seasons. The average speed required would be only 5 or 10 miles a day. Presumably nonmobile forms of life would go into hibernation during the winter, as do the plants of our Antarctic.

The shortage of water is probably one of the greatest handicaps to Martian life, and the yearly melting of the polar ice is clearly of extreme importance. It is possible that the water is carried away from the poles in the form of vapor; the atmospheric pressure is too low for it to exist in the liquid state.

This is, perhaps, the moment to say something about the much-discussed "canals," the network of fine, narrow lines reported by Schiaparelli and Lowell toward the end of the last century. Lowell was convinced that the canals formed a vast irrigation system built by an intelligent race to conserve its dwindling water supplies. Few astronomers today accept this interpretation, and most do not believe in the existence of the canals at all. Yet there can be little doubt that large numbers of curious linear markings do exist on the planet. Even if they do not actually form unbroken lines, many of them seem to be arranged in a rectilinear fashion; but this does not mean that they must be artificial. They could quite possibly be old riverbeds, canyons, or similar formations, and it is probably safe to say that nowadays few, if any, astronomers could be found who believe that there is the slightest evidence for intelligent life on Mars. If anyone finds this discouraging, we might point out that the Martians could hardly have detected intelligent life on Earth if their telescopes were no better than ours.*

Mars has two tiny satellites, only 5 or 10 miles in diameter. Phobos, the closer of the two, is so near the planet that it is invisible from the polar regions, being hidden by the curvature of the globe. As it moves around Mars more quickly than Mars revolves on its axis, it rises in the west and sets in the east. Much of the time it must be eclipsed by the shadow of the planet, and as it would be about a quarter the apparent size of the Moon, it would provide only a small percentage of its light. Deimos, the outer satellite, is still less conspicuous and may not even show a visible disk to an observer on the planet, seeming perhaps merely a bright star.

These tiny moons may well be the first extraterrestrial bodies, next to our own satellite, on which human beings will ever land. Since their gravitational fields are negligible, it would take very little power for a spaceship to make contact with them once it had entered an orbit around Mars. The gravity of Deimos must be so low that a man could jump clear away from it, reaching escape velocity with his unaided muscles.

The Mariner 4 fly-by of July, 1965, gave the first tantalizing glimpse of another Mars, proving, to the general surprise, that the planet was almost as cratered as the Moon. Some of the craters showed considerable erosion, though whether by rain, sandstorms, or some other cause has yet to be determined. On the photograph—the famous Number 11, showing a crater some 70 miles across—there appeared a barely perceptible straight line which at once started up echoes of the canal controversy. Though it is probably a natural feature, perhaps like the lunar canyons, it is remarkably straight and narrow for at least 150 miles.

The Mariner photographs proved nothing, one way or the

*This is perhaps debatable. They might be able to see the lights of our great cities shining on the dark side of the planet.

other, about the existence of Martian life, nor could they have been expected to do so. The smallest details they showed were at least two miles across; photographs taken of the Earth from meteorological satellites with similar resolution give no hint of life, still less of human civilization.

Through the 1970's, more advanced types of robot spacecraft will be launched toward Mars, and our knowledge of the planet will advance in quantum jumps, though there will be much that we shall never know until the first men walk upon its surface. The planned Voyager spacecraft will be the Martian equivalent of the Lunas and Surveyors, though they will have a far more difficult task, as the communications range is at least 150 times greater and the power requirements, owing to the operation of the square law, accordingly increased more than 20,000-fold. Clearly, the rate of flow of information back from the Martian surface will be very slow.

For this reason it is essential to devise robot instruments that can do as much thinking as possible for themselves and radio back their conclusions—not masses of raw, undigested data. Among these, now being developed, are ingenious life-detecting devices—essentially, microbe traps that can look for the various biochemical reactions that characterize life as we know it on Earth.

Of the three possible outcomes of this search, they will be able to report back only two, "Yes" or "Don't Know." We may find Martian life immediately, but to prove that it does not exist may take a hundred years. And to prove that it never *did* exist may take very much longer.

After Mars and Venus have been reached (or at least orbited), the next goal will be Mercury, nearest of all planets to the Sun. It is a small, airless world, not very much larger than the Moon, and perhaps physically similar to it. Until quite recently it was believed that it kept one face always turned toward the Sun, so a whole astronomical (not to mention science-fictional) mythology was built up of a world divided between eternal day and eternal night. If this were true—and the smudgy maps made by visual observers for almost a century confirmed it—then the same planet held both the hottest and the coldest places in the Solar System. The center of the daylight side, forever directly beneath a sun twice as large (and therefore four times as hot) as Earth's, would be at a temperature of at least 800 degrees, so that such metals as lead or tin would be molten. On the night side, shielded from any source of heat and with no blanket of atmosphere to protect it, the temperature would be about −450 degrees Fahrenheit, or not far above absolute zero.

This description will be found in all astronomy books published before 1965; in that year it was discovered that the one fact we were certain of about Mercury was untrue. Radar echoes from the planet showed that, after all, its "day" was not synchronized with its brief year (88 Earth days); instead, it rotates on its axis once in 59 days.

This 59 does not seem to be a random number; it is exactly two-thirds of the Mercurian year. Some kind of resonance or tuning effect appears to have been operating; though the tidal drag of the Sun has not locked Mercury completely into step, it has at least partly succeeded in doing so.

The orbit of Mercury is quite eccentric, the planet's distance from the Sun varying between 28,500,000 and 43,350,000 miles. As a result, its orbital speed also changes considerably during the course of its 88-day year, and this, combined with its slow rotation, can produce some most extraordinary effects. The interval between sunrises averages about 170 days, but Mercury is the only planet where the sun can rise, hover uncertainly on the horizon for a few days, change its mind, set again, and then reappear and creep slowly across the sky, perhaps repeating its performance at sunset. In the excessively unlikely event that there are intelligent beings on Mercury, their knowledge of astronomy would be either nonexistent or highly advanced. It took the human race several thousand years to unravel the movements of the heavenly bodies on a much better-regulated planet.

These new discoveries do not change our picture of Mercury as a barren, inhospitable planet with very great temperature extremes. Nevertheless, it seems likely that it will be much easier to explore than Venus, and it may serve as an excellent site for a solar research station.

Mercury will be a very interesting place to visit, but it seems unlikely that anyone will really want to live there.

23. THE OUTER GIANTS

Beyond Mars the scale of the Solar System widens rapidly. Between Mars and Jupiter there is what seemed, for a long time, to be a disproportionately great gulf, as if a planet had been overlooked.

At the end of the eighteenth century an attempt was made to locate this missing world. The result of the search was unexpected; not one planet was found, but hundreds, and we are still nowhere near the end of them. The total number of asteroids, of all sizes, must run into at least five figures. Until recently astronomers were unable to keep track of even the two thousand or so already detected; the work involved in calculating their orbits was too great. With the modern development of electronic computers, this difficulty has been overcome, and almanacs for minor planets can be calculated and printed quite automatically. With this tedious work taken off their hands, astronomers no longer regard the asteroids with quite such a jaundiced eye.

Even the largest of these little worlds, Ceres (480 miles in diameter), is far too small to possess an atmosphere—its gravitational field is so weak that any gas would escape into space immediately. Nothing whatsoever is known about their physical composition or surface features, since the vast majority appear simply as dimensionless points of light in the telescope. The smaller asteroids are probably not even spherical, but are simply jagged lumps of rock, mountains wandering through space. Although so many thousands of them exist, they cannot constitute a "menace to navigation," as has sometimes been suggested. The gulf between Mars and Jupiter is too enormous for a few thousand, or even a few million, asteroids to go very far toward filling it.

Unfortunately one cannot, as some naïve enthusiasts have suggested, use these bodies to get a free ride around the Solar System. In the first place, suitable approaches would occur only at intervals of decades or even centuries, and for one way only. But much more important, "riding on an asteroid" would confer no benefit at all. The spaceship would have to make a rendezvous with the body, and once it had matched velocities, it would continue to travel along the asteroid's orbit, whether the asteroid was there or not. The presence of a few million tons of rock would merely result in a little propellant being wasted, to overcome its minute gravitational attraction. Of course, asteroids will be visited in their own right as interesting (and perhaps exploitable) objects; they may one day represent a very valuable source of metals and minerals for deep-space operations. But they are not of the slightest use to hitchhikers.

It is convenient to treat the four giant planets, Jupiter, Saturn, Uranus, and Neptune, together, for they differ in degree rather than in kind. All have these points in common: they have a very low density; have atmospheres composed of the light gases hydrogen, helium, methane, and ammonia; and turn very rapidly on their axes. Jupiter, being the nearest and also the largest, is the most easily observed of the four; much of the information gained about it probably applies to Saturn, Uranus, and Neptune.

We can see no permanent surface markings on these planets; what we observe is the top of an immensely deep and turbulent atmosphere, perhaps thousands of miles thick. They may indeed possess no stable surfaces; the compressed gases may go on getting denser and denser until the center of the planet is reached, with no definite transition from gas to liquid, or liquid to solid.

Because they are so far from the Sun, one would naturally expect these planets to be extremely cold, and indeed thermocouple measurements give values of −190 degrees F. for Jupiter and −270 degrees F. for Saturn. But these values, it must be remembered, apply only to the top of the visible cloud layer; conditions far below will be very different.

Even in a small telescope Jupiter is a fascinating and beautiful sight, with its bands of cloud and the four bright sparks of its larger moons changing their positions every night. But we now know that there is much more happening on and around Jupiter than meets the eye, for in 1955 intense radio emissions were discovered coming from the planet. This was a great surprise; no one had expected such a large, cold body to be a generator of radio waves. One might have imagined this to be true of the incandescent Sun, as has turned out to be the case, but on occasion Jupiter is an even more powerful source of radio noise than the Sun itself.

Most of these hissings and fryings and cracklings come from a region outside the planet, high above its equator. This was the first indication that Jupiter, like Earth, is surrounded by radiation belts; in Jupiter's case they appear to be of great intensity, and they may be a major hazard to astronauts. In addition, there are occasional radio outbursts—lasting for a few seconds up to more than an hour—which are at much longer wavelengths (in the 10-meter band) and which are of incredible power. They sound very much like thunderstorm "static" and appear to originate in the Jovian atmosphere; there is also some evidence that they are linked with definite regions of the planet's hidden surface. If these radio emissions are indeed due to thunderstorms, they must be of a violence that we cannot begin to imagine. A single second of Jovian 10-meter-band noise contains the power of *a hundred billion* terrestrial lightning strokes.

Jupiter has twelve known satellites, more than any other planet. One of them (Jupiter V, so-called because it was the fifth moon to be discovered) is a close approximation to a natural synchronous satellite. It takes 12 hours to revolve around Jupiter, and as the planet rotates in 10, Jupiter V takes six Jovian "days" to drift slowly around the sky.

Beyond Jupiter V, which is only about 75 miles in diameter, are the four much larger satellites discovered by Galileo in 1609. They are all about as large as Earth's Moon, ranging in diameter from 2,000 to 3,000 miles.

Although the four large satellites all lie within little more than a million miles of Jupiter, travel between them requires almost as much energy as a journey from Earth to Mars or

Venus. This, of course, is a consequence of Jupiter's extremely powerful gravitational field (Figure 20).

The remaining satellites are at much greater distance from the planet—out to 14 million miles—and move on eccentric and highly inclined orbits. They are all less than 100 miles in diameter, and the outermost ones may well be asteroids that Jupiter has, perhaps temporarily, captured as they strayed into its neighborhood.

Far beyond Jupiter—indeed, at almost twice its distance from the Sun—the slightly smaller but much lighter planet Saturn moves on its leisurely, 29-year orbit. With ten moons, and the same type of hydrogen-helium-methane-ammonia atmosphere, Saturn would probably be regarded as a not very exciting carbon copy of Jupiter were it not for one astonishing feature—its unique system of rings. Through the telescope, they look so obviously artificial that it is hard to believe that they do not form part of some intricate and beautiful machine.

The rings, which span a total diameter of 170,000 miles, consist of myriads of particles traveling around the planet in almost perfectly circular orbits. They also lie in a plane so flat and thin that when, as happens every fifteen years (1966, 1981), the rings are edge-on, they appear to vanish completely. Although they appear solid, when a star passes behind them it can still be seen shining; at close quarters, the rings would probably look like a sheet of hail or snow, perhaps only a few yards in thickness—a kind of eternal blizzard, forever sweeping around Saturn.

Although ten moons of Saturn have been discovered, there can be little doubt that others still remain undetected. The latest to be found, Janus, practically rolls along the very edge of the rings, and was spotted during their disappearance in 1966. All have been dignified with names, not merely, as in Jupiter's case, with numbers. The muster is so poetic that I cannot resist giving it in full; working outward from the planet, it runs Janus, Mimas, Enceladus, Tethys, Dione, Rhea, Titan, Hyperion, Iapetus, and Phoebe.

Most of these little worlds are only a few hundred miles across, but the largest, appropriately named Titan, is a giant among satellites. Being 3,500 miles in diameter, it is larger than Mercury and not much smaller than Mars. As a result of its size, it has sufficient gravity to retain an atmosphere, a thin, cold envelope of methane. As this could be a good propellant for nuclear rockets (see Chapter 24), Titan may play a vital role in the opening up of the outer planets. It may provide us with a refueling point halfway to Pluto.

There appears to be something rather odd about the smaller of these moons, for their densities are abnormally low—in at least two cases, less than that of water. Although this is also true of Saturn, its deep atmosphere easily accounts for its low density, but worlds only three or four hundred miles in diameter cannot possibly have an atmosphere. Perhaps, as Fred Hoyle has suggested, they are extremely porous, "gigantic snow-balls."

The strangest of all the satellites, however, is the ninth from the planet—Iapetus, 700 miles in diameter. On one side of its orbit Iapetus is at least five times brighter than on the other. This means that it is either a very peculiar shape or that it has some surface feature of exceptional brilliance on one hemisphere. Iapetus is only one of the intriguing bits of unfinished, indeed, barely started, business represented by Saturn—its glorious icy halo and its 16-million-mile-wide family of moons.

We know very little about Uranus and Neptune because their immense distances make it impossible to observe them successfully except in the very largest telescopes. Once again, they are giants with tremendously deep hydrogen-methane atmospheres, but possibly because of their extreme coldness they do not show the disturbances that can be seen on Jupiter and, to a lesser extent, on Saturn.

Uranus has five satellites—Ariel, Umbriel, Titania, Oberon, and Miranda. (Presumably the next to be detected is doomed to be christened Caliban.) Titania is about half the size of our Moon, but the others are much smaller. Neptune has only two moons—Nereid and Triton; the latter is one of the largest known satellites, about 3,000 miles in diameter.

Until 1930 Neptune's orbit marked the frontier of the Solar System. In that year Pluto was discovered, as a result of a long search by the Lowell Observatory. The discovery was based on mathematical calculations by Dr. Lowell, but it has now been found that Pluto cannot be the planet whose existence he predicted. It is far too small, having a diameter of less than 4,000 miles, so we can only assume that its discovery was fortuitous and that the planet for which Lowell was looking still remains to be found. Although nothing is known about Pluto except its size and its orbit, it probably resembles the inner planets in composition and so will have nothing in common with its giant neighbors. It must be exceedingly cold, the temperature never rising above −350 degrees F. Almost all gases except hydrogen and helium would be liquefied at this temperature, so it is not likely that Pluto has an atmosphere. It has an unusually long "day" for an outer planet—6.4 days. This fact, and its peculiar orbit, has led some astronomers to suggest that it may be a "lost" satellite of Neptune.

Planets, satellites, asteroids, comets—this completes our survey of the Solar System. In Chapter 26 we will discuss the probable existence of other planetary systems around other stars, but as far as our present definite knowledge goes, the only possible abodes of life in the universe are the worlds we have been describing. Most people will probably feel that the resulting picture is not exactly an encouraging one. They may be right; there may well be no advanced form of life in our Solar System beyond the atmosphere of the Earth, and no life of any kind except a few lichens on the Moon and Mars. Yet there is a danger that this assumption, plausible though it may seem, is based on a hopelessly anthropomorphic viewpoint. We consider that our planet is "normal" simply because we are used to it, and judge all other worlds accordingly. Yet it is we who are the freaks, living as we do in the narrow zone around the Sun where it is not too hot for water to boil and not too cold for it to be permanently frozen. The "normal" worlds, if one takes the detached viewpoint of statistics, are the Jupiter-type planets with their methane and ammonia atmospheres.

We do not know the limits to the adaptability of life. On our planet life has learned to function over a temperature range of almost 200 degrees Fahrenheit. It is based on oxygen, carbon, and water, which are among the most abundant substances in the crust of the planet. Yet these basic materials are utilized in very varied fashions. Some organisms (e.g., jellyfish) consist almost wholly of water; others, such as cacti, use very little and survive in environments too dry for any other form of life.

Certain bacteria have even performed the astonishing feat of partly replacing carbon by sulfur and can live happily in boiling sulfuric acid.

The importance of water arises from the fact that it dissolves such an enormous variety of substances, and so acts as a medium in which countless chemical reactions can take place. In this respect, however, it has a number of rivals, liquid ammonia among them. On a planet whose temperature was less than −28 degrees F. but above −108 degrees F., ammonia might take the place of water for many purposes. On even colder worlds methane, which remains liquid down to the extraordinarily low temperature of −300 degrees F., might take over. It is true that most chemical reactions proceed very slowly, if at all, at low temperatures. However, fluorine, the most reactive of all elements, could conceivably replace oxygen under these conditions.

In the direction of increasing temperatures, it is again difficult to set a limit to nature's ingenuity. The discovery of silicon-carbon compounds has opened up new vistas in organic chemistry, and a life form based partly on silicon is by no means beyond the bounds of possibility. The silicon compounds retain their identity at temperatures high enough to destroy their carbon analogues, and they might make life possible on worlds a few hundred degrees hotter than Earth—for example, on parts of Mercury.

Faced with an unpromising environment, life has the choice of two alternatives—adaptation or insulation. Examples of both can be seen on our world. In the polar regions the seals and penguins adapt; the Eskimos insulate. One of the most remarkable examples of the latter technique is provided by the humble water spider, a wholly air-breathing creature which nevertheless spends much of its time submerged. By carrying its appropriate living conditions with it, it manages to survive in a completely alien environment. In the same manner, carbon life based upon water could conceivably exist even on the frozen outer worlds. One can imagine beings with tough, insulating skins through which the heat loss would be very small. As long as they had some source of energy—chemical, solar, perhaps even nuclear—and the necessary food, they could still survive though their surroundings were not far above absolute zero.

It may be objected that though such life forms might be able to exist on very cold worlds, they could hardly have originated there. The indigenous life would probably be based on low-temperature reactions and would not be much hotter than the surroundings. Yet from this type of organism higher forms of life might be able to evolve, just as the warm-blooded mammals evolved from the cold-blooded reptiles.

We know, of course, very little about the laws that govern the appearance and the evolution of life on any planet. The above speculations may help to show the danger of generalizing from the solitary example of our own Earth and trying to produce laws applicable to totally alien planets. It is illogical to conclude that because the other worlds of the Sun are so different from our own, we cannot hope to find familiar forms of life there.

It is the very strangeness of the planets that provides one of the greatest incentives for visiting them. If they were all like Earth, we might just as well stay at home.

24. THE COMMERCE OF THE HEAVENS

For I dipt into the Future, far as human eye could see
Saw the Vision of the world, and all the wonder that would
be;
Saw the heavens fill with commerce, argosies of magic
sails,
Pilots of the purple twilight, dropping down with costly
bales.

When Alfred, Lord Tennyson, wrote those words more than a
century ago, he was certainly not looking beyond the atmosphere, and his vision must have seemed the wildest fantasy
to his readers. But now it is the everyday reality of our age,
and perhaps the real wonder, which would have astonished
Tennyson most of all, is that our pilots are not only dropping
down with costly bales; they are dropping down with *cheap*
ones.

This is the pattern that must be repeated in space if the
exploration of the planets is to be more than a long-term scientific project that only a prosperous world state can afford.
Even on this basis it would certainly be possible and worthwhile; but all the lessons of the past and everything we can
foresee in the way of technological progress suggest that this
is taking a very pessimistic and shortsighted view.

The pace and ultimate extent of what we may call the
exploitation of the Solar System depends upon two factors. The
first is a vast unknown, though there are small patches where
our ignorance is slowly lightening. It involves the resources

226

and surface conditions of the planets and the technologies that may be devised to use, control, or combat them. The second is even less predictable, the motivation of future societies. We have already seen, in the early history of the Space Age, how politics and technology react upon each other, in both directions, and it would be naïve to assume that this process will not continue.

We will discuss these now unanswerable, but not unarguable, questions in later chapters. Their ultimate importance, however, depends upon something that can be defined a little more precisely, even at this early stage—the cost of space flight. If travel to the other planets can be made little more expensive than today's intercontinental jet transportation or an around-the-world ocean voyage, the heavens will indeed fill with commerce. But if the cost is a thousandfold higher, all we can look forward to is the occasional scientific expedition.

This would certainly be the case if we were always restricted to chemical propellants, such as the kerosene-oxygen and hydrogen-oxygen combinations which power most of today's large rockets. Even here, however, there is great room for improvement—certainly by a factor of ten, perhaps by one of a hundred when all possible techniques have been developed. That might not be sufficient for true commercial space operations, but it would allow for a good deal of planetary travel without bankrupting the human race.

The most powerful chemical propellant combination used today—the liquid-hydrogen, liquid-oxygen mixture burned in the two upper stages of the Saturn 5—gives an exhaust speed (in vacuum) of about 10,000 mph, or more than half the velocity needed to go into orbit around the Earth. There are a few theoretically more powerful combinations; for example, oxygen can be replaced by the still more reactive element fluorine, producing an improvement of about 5 per cent. Another 5 or 10 per cent can be obtained by adding light metals such as beryllium or lithium, but the most we can hope for is an advance of 10 to 15 per cent over present values, and this at great difficulty and expense.

It is just possible that the chemists may produce weird, meta-stable substances, not occurring in nature, which can provide more energy than existing propellants, but it would be foolish to count on it. There are more promising lines of development.

One, already mentioned in Chapter 19, is the reusable booster or aero-space plane, which flies or parachutes back to its base, to be refueled and used again. Such a vehicle becomes even more attractive if it can use the surrounding atmosphere for propulsion during its ascent. Although the rocket has the freedom of space, because it carries its own oxygen, it has won this freedom at an enormous cost in extra weight and size. One can imagine a system in which, for the first stage at least, only the liquid hydrogen was carried aboard the vehicle and the oxygen was obtained from the surrounding air. Such a reusable space transporter might take off and land like a conventional aircraft, carrying on its back the pure-rocket stage which made the final leap into orbit. There can be no doubt that *something* like this has to be developed; we cannot continue indefinitely to carpet the Atlantic seabed with Saturn 5's.

Refueling in space, at orbital filling stations kept supplied by tankers from Earth, may play an important role in interplanetary operations. But it does not necessarily result in great savings; in fact, it *increases* the total amount of propellant required for a mission. The great advantage of orbital refueling is that it allows the use of much smaller spacecraft, though they have to carry out many more flights than a single giant vehicle.

It becomes much more attractive and may result in major savings if the propellants can be obtained from low-gravity sources such as the Moon, as suggested in Chapter 19. And refueling, *on* the Moon or on bodies with known sources of hydrogen such as Titan, could also result in great economies. When all these things are added up, one can imagine a day when a twenty-first-century millionaire (should any still exist) might be able to afford a ticket to Mars. For commercial operations, we must do a good deal better than this.

It is important to realize that the difficulty of space travel does *not* lie in the great amount of energy needed. As was pointed out in Chapter 19, to lift one man away from the Earth requires only 1,000 kilowatt-hours of energy, costing only about $10. It is indeed tantalizing to realize that if we could build an elevator to the Moon, it would cost $10 a passenger to get there!

It costs billions today because our portable energy sources are too heavy. Ninety-nine per cent of the fuel in a big rocket is expended in merely lifting other fuel; the remaining one per cent could do all the work that is really required. If we had a virtually weightless energy source, the problem would be solved.

We have such a source, at least in theory. Nuclear reactions release about a million times as much energy, weight for weight, as chemical reactions. The 2,350 tons of propellant in a Saturn 5 could be replaced by a few pounds of fissionable material if energy were the only criterion. Unfortunately, it is not as simple as this. Pure energy can provide heat or radiation, but it cannot provide thrust unless it has something to react against. So even with nuclear power, we are still forced to use the rocket principle. An exhaust jet of some material—a "working fluid"— has to be expelled; the only difference is that its energy of motion will now be derived from nuclear, and not from chemical, reactions.

Although the basic principles of the "atomic rocket" were published within a few years of the first release of nuclear power, the development of practical, flyable units has been an extremely difficult and lengthy task, covering two decades of time and costing hundreds of millions of dollars. On paper, all that one has to do to build an atomic rocket is to construct a high-temperature reactor and blow hydrogen through it (Figure 25). The heated gas can then be allowed to expand through a nozzle, to give a propulsive jet. However, unless temperatures of 4,000–5,000 degrees F. can be attained, nuclear rockets have no advantage over chemical ones—and many grave disadvantages, such as the need for heavy radiation shielding.

Despite these problems, nuclear rockets have now been successfully built and tested in the United States as part of the Atomic Energy Commission's Project Rover. Exhaust velocities about double those of chemical rockets have been achieved at quite high thrust levels—more than a hundred tons—together with remarkably long running times. Although nuclear engines are not likely to be used for takeoff from Earth, they will prove very valuable for the final stages of deep-space craft,

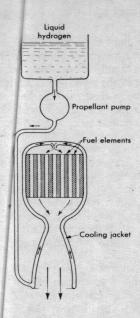

Figure 25. Solid-core nuclear rocket.

doubling or tripling their payloads.

But this improvement, worthwhile though it is, uses only a minute fraction of the energy available from nuclear sources. This is already so enormous that it makes the demands of even the most ambitious interplanetary expeditions look quite trivial. A 25-megaton H-bomb (like the one lost by the United States Air Force off the coast of Spain in 1966) liberates enough energy to carry 2 million tons to Mars. This astonishing statistic shows that we already have enough sheer power to do anything we wish in the Solar System; unfortunately, we are not yet clever enough to control it.

Some most ingenious (and occasionally hair-raising) schemes have been suggested for very high-performance nuclear-propulsion systems. In some, the fissionable material

(U_{235} or plutonium) would be in the gaseous state, and so the temperature limitations of today's atomic rockets would be removed. If the slightly fantastic engineering problems involved in building "gaseous-fission reactors" can be solved, the economics of space flight would be totally transformed. The whole of the Solar System would be thrown open to mankind.

Maxwell Hunter, general manager of research and development for the Lockheed Missile and Space Company, has outlined a hypothetical gaseous-fission ship in his stimulating book *Thrust into Space*.* It sounds far too good to be true, and perhaps it is, but it is based entirely on theoretically sound engineering principles. Hunter's spaceship would weigh 500 tons, of which no less than 100 would be payload. And its propellant fluid would be *ordinary water*, with all that this implies for ease of storage and refueling, not to mention cost. Perhaps even more remarkable, after one has grown used to the multistage rockets of today, the propellant tank is only a small part of the total volume. As Max Hunter writes, "The design looks more like a Buck Rogers spaceship than a conventional ballistic missile—the cargo compartment takes up more space than the propellant tank. That is the way a good spaceship should be."

Running on a weekly schedule, such a ship could carry 5,000 tons of payload to the Moon every year, and ten of them could provide the tonnage of supplies now delivered to the United States bases in the Antarctic. It could even compete commercially with existing jet transports, delivering cargo more cheaply between any two points *on Earth*—in less than an hour.

Once again, it should be stressed that such a spacecraft is very much in the realm of theory and that its construction involves enormously difficult engineering problems. It may take the remainder of this century before we know if they can be solved.

Yet beyond the fission-powered (uranium or plutonium) systems is an even more glamorous possibility, the use of fusion (i.e., hydrogen) power. So far, this has been liberated only

*Holt, Rinehart and Winston, 1965.

explosively, and vast efforts have been made to achieve sustained fusion, or thermonuclear, reactions. The task has proved more difficult than earlier optimistic forecasts suggested, but few doubt its ultimate realization. When that comes about, we shall have all the power we need to do anything on Earth, in space, or on the planets. And we shall be able to think seriously about going to the stars (Chapter 29).

To come back from this intoxicating dream world to the more immediate future, nuclear energy may also be used to provide thrust by electrical rather than thermal processes. Various types of electric rockets have already been tested, some on actual space flights. They operate by accelerating charged particles or ionized gases in electric fields. Extremely high jet velocities can be achieved in this way, but the thrust levels are microscopic—mere fractions of a pound. Obviously, such devices are useless for the escape from Earth, but once in orbit they could continue to provide acceleration for days or weeks, until very high speeds were finally achieved. So the nuclear-energized, electrical-propulsion systems may be developed for use in deep space, while chemical rockets are still used for takeoff and landing.

Mention should also be made of Project Orion, the most startling of all the ideas put forward for space propulsion by nuclear energy. This involves nothing less than a series of atom-bomb explosions—one every few seconds—which would kick a spaceship into orbit. The ship would carry a large number of small bombs (perhaps a thousand), and these would be detonated a short distance from a massive pusher plate, which would take up the shock. The impact would be smoothed out through powerful springs, so that the spacecraft received a fairly uniform acceleration.

Design studies and a few tests with conventional explosives showed that this nuclear-pulse technique would certainly work, but it would become economical only for very large spacecraft carrying payloads of thousands of tons, and it will be quite a few years before there is a pressing need for these. Meanwhile, of course, the nuclear-test ban has put a stop to further development along these lines—permanently, many will hope. A-bombs going off at the rate of one a second for twenty minutes at a time just outside the atmosphere may be too high a price to pay for the conquest of the Solar System.

Finally, it is necessary to ask the question: Is the rocket the only way of crossing space? May we not one day discover better forms of propulsion, for example, the "space drives" and "antigravity" devices beloved of the science-fiction writers?

Perhaps; but at the moment there is not the faintest sign of such a breakthrough. The reaction principle—throwing mass in one direction to obtain a thrust in the other—still remains the only means of driving a space vehicle. Not even in theory is any alternative known.

It can be shown that all the mechanical devices that have been proposed from time to time (see Chapter 1) are based on ignorance of simple dynamics. In the final analysis, which may be so difficult for a complicated gadget that no engineer would waste his time attempting it, they are all schemes for lifting oneself by one's own bootstraps.

It is not so obvious that gravity screens of the type used by Wells in *The First Men in the Moon*, and by countless other writers, also involve a fundamental fallacy. If such a substance as Wells' "Cavorite" existed, which cut off gravity as a roller blind cuts off the sunlight, it could be used to produce an unlimited amount of energy—from nowhere. It would be necessary only to put the screen under a heavy object, let it soar upward, remove the screen, and collect free energy from the falling body by a rope-and-pulley system. The cycle could be repeated indefinitely, giving a classic perpetual-motion machine.

But the energy to lift an object out of the Earth's gravitational field has to come from *somewhere*; it is equivalent, remember, to an ascent of no less than 4,000 miles against a force equal to gravity at sea level. So an antigravity system, even if it is possible, may not be as useful as it might seem. It will require an enormous amount of energy to run it; and if that has to come from electrical generators and conventional fuel supplies, we might be better off using rockets, after all.

The late Roger Babson, statistician and business analyst, endowed a "gravity research foundation" in the hope that one day we would be able to do *something* about gravity. Most scientists would agree that this is a vain expectation. Probably all would agree that if there is any advance in this field, it will result from discoveries in a totally different area of science. Perhaps when we can experiment with matter and energy under the weightless (though not gravityless, remember) conditions in an orbital laboratory, there may be some hope of progress. If antigravity is ever found, it will be by someone who isn't looking for it.

Surprisingly enough, there is one way in which a form of gravity propulsion can be used to considerable advantage in space flight. A rocket falling into the gravity field of a planet from a great distance—say, a million miles—gains speed on the approach; then, if it merely loops around the planet without making contact, it loses all this speed on the outward climb. When it is once more a million miles away, it is moving at exactly the same speed with respect to the planet as before, having neither lost nor gained even a fraction of a mile an hour.

However, it will be moving in a completely different direction; it may well have been deflected by ninety degrees or more by the encounter. It is precisely as if it has bounded off the planet, like a ball thrown against a perfectly elastic wall. In this case, too, there is no change of speed, only of direction.

So how can anything be gained? It cannot—*if the wall is stationary*. But if the wall itself is moving, the ball will acquire some of its velocity during the impact. And this is what happens in the astronomical case, for the planets are all moving in orbit around the Sun. After a spacecraft has "bounced" out of a planetary field, its speed with respect to the planet will not have changed; but its speed *with respect to the Sun*, which is the important factor, will have done so, perhaps by a very large amount. So it may have gained, or lost, a considerable amount of energy.

In the over-all picture, of course, there is no change of energy. What the rocket gains, the planet loses, so that its velocity is reduced by an infinitesimal amount.

By skillful navigation, therefore, and practically no expenditure of rocket fuel, we can play a kind of "interplanetary billiards," perhaps using the gravity fields of several planets in succession—gaining or losing speed at strategic points. The operational advantages could be enormous; for example, in 1978 it would be theoretically possible to launch a rocket from Earth to the outer planets, Saturn, Uranus, and Neptune, bouncing from one to the next. The tour would take 9 years—though normally it would take 30 years to go merely to Neptune at the same departure speed from Earth. The Jupiter probe described in Chapter 21 would employ the same principle.

This is an interesting example of the way in which we can take advantage of the laws of nature; a more obvious and even more important example is the use of atmospheric braking, though that can be employed only to lose speed. But this is just as vital as gaining speed; manned space flight would be out of the question for decades to come if the enormous velocities developed in the return to Earth or a landing on Mars had to be neutralized entirely by retrorockets.

Naturally, scientists have looked for other cosmic energy sources that may be exploited for space propulsion, and so far they have found only one—the Sun. Solar panels, turning the Sun's rays into electrical energy, are of course used in almost all space probes as a source of power for the electronic equipment and the radio transmitters. But they could also be utilized in place of nuclear reactors, to power low-thrust electric-propulsion systems. An alternative idea is to use the Sun's rays directly to heat a gas (probably hydrogen) and to let it expand through a nozzle. The solar-powered rocket bears a somewhat uncanny resemblance to the device which the ingenious Cyrano de Bergerac used in his *Voyage to the Sun*. This was a large box surmounted by burning glasses so that "the sun's rays uniting by way of the concave glasses would attract a furious abundance of air to fill it, which would lift up my box, and in proportion as I rose up the horrible wind which rushed through the hole could not reach the roof except by passing furiously through the machine and lifting it up."* The solar rocket would also use concave reflectors and would be driven by a "horrible wind" of hot hydrogen.

Yet another possibility, which seems even more fantastic but is scientifically completely sound, is to use sunlight itself for propulsion. Although nothing could appear more imponderable than a sunbeam, even light has weight and can exert a definite pressure when it falls upon a surface. That pressure is, of course, almost unimaginably small; yet it has been meas-

*Richard Aldington translation (New York: Orion Press, 1962).

ured, and comes to about one-ten-millionth of a pound on every square foot of surface directly facing the Sun. If the surface is a good reflector, the force is doubled.

So imagine a sail made of the thinnest possible plastic sheet, mirror-coated on one side by a layer of aluminum only a few atoms thick. Even if it were a mile on a side, it might weigh less than ten tons; and the total pressure of sunlight acting on it would come to about five pounds. So it would slowly start to move, "blown" by the Sun at an acceleration of about one-four-thousandth of a gravity.

This rate of increase of speed may sound utterly negligible, but it is maintained indefinitely in the vacuum of space. After one day the sail will have gained 500 mph, after ten days 5,000 mph, which begins to look interesting, especially since it costs nothing, because the "fuel" is free. If one could devise sufficiently lightweight rigging and methods of controlling the angle of the sail, then small cargoes or robot space probes might be towed around by this means.

At first sight it might appear that solar sailers could travel only away from the Sun, since radiation pressure is like a wind blowing forever outward from the center of the Solar System. But just as a conventional sailboat can tack against the wind, so a "sunjammer" could move toward an inner planet. By tilting its sail so that it lost part of its orbital speed, it would necessarily fall in toward the Sun.

Whether solar sailboats are practical or not, they are certainly a delightful idea. Perhaps one day they may be developed for sporting purposes, and "rounding the Sun" may have something of the glamour that rounding the Horn did in the seafaring annals of the past. If so, another line of Tennyson's verse will come strikingly true: the heavens will indeed see "argosies of magic sails."

25. TOMORROW'S WORLDS

That stay in Britain made me envisage a hypothetical empire governed from the West, an Atlantic world. Such imaginary perspectives have no practical value; they cease, however, to be absurd as soon as the calculator extends his computations sufficiently far into the future.

M. YOURCENAR—*Memoirs of Hadrian*

We will now take as proved the argument, developed in the last chapter, that one day the large-scale transportation of men and materials to the planets will be relatively cheap and simple. If by 1966 a 5-ton hydrogen bomb could send 2 million tons to Mars, though admittedly in rather small pieces, it is not particularly optimistic to hope that by 2066 a few hundred tons of advanced nuclear engineering would deliver several thousand tons of payload anywhere in the Solar System. Indeed, when one considers the past history of technology, any other assumption appears totally unrealistic, a refusal to face high-order probabilities, if not indisputable facts. So let us be realistic and consider the colonization of the planets.

Much that has been said about exploring and exploiting the Moon in Chapter 19 can be applied to similar airless bodies— Mercury, the larger asteroids, the satellites of the giant planets, perhaps even Pluto. All these worlds, many of no mean size, are essentially in a space environment. Though their surface temperatures vary wildly—from at least 1,000 degrees F. in the case of Mercury, to −450 degrees F. for Pluto—these figures do not have anything like the meaning they would in a terrestrial context. In a vacuum it is relatively easy to arrange almost complete protection against extremes of heat or cold; the familiar thermos flask is proof of that.

On Mercury and the Moon, reflecting surfaces turned toward the slowly moving Sun would take the heat load off buildings and equipment, and the diverted energy could be usefully employed. It is known that the surface material of the Moon is an excellent thermal insulator, so that the temperature is constant a few feet underground. This is probably true of all the other planets and satellites which have solid, stable surfaces.

Even on very cold worlds the problem is more likely to be one of losing heat at a controlled rate rather than conserving it. Electrical equipment, nuclear reactors, the explorers themselves, all generate vast numbers of calories, which must be dissipated. One could die of heatstroke in a too well-insulated base on Pluto, even though the temperature a few inches away was not far above absolute zero.

The investigation of all these airless worlds will be greatly simplified by a factor that it is very hard for us to appreciate, because it is as unfamiliar as weightlessness. *They will have no weather*. There will be wholly predictable climatic (for want of a better word) variations due to their periods of rotation, but these will affect only the temperature of the surface layers. Storms, rain, fog, cloud, wind, dew, snow—the innumerable meteorological phenomena which control our lives, and often our deaths, on Earth will all be absent. At one sweep this will remove most of the hazards of exploration.

But, of course, there will be others. On some of the larger, cold satellites there may possibly be lakes of liquefied gas, or "snow" fields of frozen ammonia. Temperature changes of only a few degrees could have spectacular consequences in such places. This may be particularly true of some of Saturn's low-density moons; even apparently dead and changeless worlds may produce some unpleasant surprises and should be inspected carefully from space before a landing is made.

After the Moon, it now appears fairly certain that Mars will be the chief target for exploration, and a permanent base may be established there before the end of the century. In many ways it will be a less difficult challenge, and perhaps a much more rewarding one. No one really expects to find life on the Moon; everyone hopes to find it on Mars.

The presence of an atmosphere, tenuous though it may be, has a considerable effect on Martian surface conditions. It moderates the temperature extremes (though they are bad enough) and is a better shield against meteoroids than is the Earth's atmosphere. With this danger to surface structures eliminated, it would be possible to erect large, pressurized domes, big enough to enclose whole settlements or even small towns.

Air-supported flexible shelters, like grounded balloons, are already in wide use for military and other applications. They would be even more practical on a world where gravity has only one-third of its terrestrial value; on Mars, domes a thousand feet or more in diameter could easily be constructed. Inside these great bubbles of air the explorers, or colonists, would live in a shirt-sleeve environment; only when they went outside would they have to wear pressure suits or travel in closed vehicles. If desired, the domes might be made of some transparent, flexible plastic to let through the sunlight, though this is by no means essential and might result in too great a heat loss during the night. The best arrangement would be a dome which was transparent during the day (when the temperature can rise to the 80's), so that it collected heat on the greenhouse principle, and which could be made opaque at night.*

So as not to have too many eggs in one basket, it would be better to use several small domes, interconnected by airlocks, instead of a single large one; the major buildings could also be pressurized in an emergency. It should be realized that even if the dome were badly ripped or punctured, it would take many minutes to collapse, and there would be ample time for anyone out of doors to reach safety.

It will be very convenient if aircraft can be used on Mars, as they would be invaluable for exploration and travel. At the moment it is not certain if this will be the case; the low gravity assists aircraft, but the excessively thin atmosphere means that they will require very large wings and high cruising speeds. (Of course, self-contained power systems will also be neces-

---

*I have described such a colony in the novel *The Sands of Mars* (New York: Harcourt, Brace & World, Inc., 1967).

sary, because of the absence of oxygen.) Perhaps we may see the revival of blimps on Mars, as we may see that of railroads on the Moon.

A few years ago it seemed that most of these ideas might also be applicable to Venus; now the discovery of 1,000-pound-per-square-inch surface pressures and furnace-hot temperatures makes this planet one of the Solar System's less desirable building sites. Any vehicle that can land on Venus will have to be a combination of spaceship and submarine; unless there is some extraordinary incentive, all our explorations will be done by robots for a long time to come. One may speculate about the existence of very high mountains (which radar does indeed suggest), where the temperature and pressure are both low enough to make manned operations feasible. Even if this turns out to be the case, it seems unlikely that permanent bases will be established there in the immediate future.

Yet, a century or two ahead, Venus represents opportunities which surely will not be neglected. It is inconceivable that a planet as large as Earth, drenched with solar energy, and only a few light-minutes away, will have nothing to offer our descendants, who will have at their command forces and technologies that we can scarcely imagine. The Harvard astronomer Dr. Carl Sagan has suggested that, even if Venus has never been able to develop life of its own, it might be seeded from Earth. At some level in the atmosphere, between the −40-degree cloud top and the +1,000-degree surface, water may exist in the liquid state, and small aerial life forms—probably bacteria, which have an extraordinary adaptability—might be able to flourish. The biologists of the future may be able to devise cultures which could break down the vast quantities of carbon dioxide, release oxygen, and eventually change the whole climate of Venus by reducing the present greenhouse effect which now makes the surface so hostile. Then, without any further intervention a biological chain reaction might be started; after all, something quite similar once took place on Earth, to give it an atmosphere in which oxygen-breathing creatures could exist.

This is certainly a grandiose idea, but it differs only in scale from the projects that have brought life to the barren places of this planet. That we of the twentieth century can think of plausible ways in which it might be achieved suggests that our descendants will know far better ones.

The giant planets, Jupiter, Saturn, Uranus, and Neptune, present even greater problems than Venus, yet at the same time they may present even greater opportunities, though in a still more distant future. Since we know practically nothing about the outer three, except that they are basically similar to Jupiter, we will take that planet as characteristic of all the "gas giants." That is certainly quite wrong in detail, but our ignorance leaves us little alternative.

The overwhelming fact about Jupiter is its sheer size; it contains more material than all the other planets added together. (Dr. Isaac Asimov once remarked that the Solar System consists of Jupiter plus debris.) Even if it possessed a solid and readily accessible surface, the task of exploring a planet with 120 times the area—350 times the *land* area—of Earth would be awe-inspiring.

In fact, it is possible that Jupiter has no stable, solid surface. Its hydrogen-methane-ammonia atmosphere may grow steadily denser with increasing depth, until, at some enormous pressure, it turns liquid and then finally solid. However, the existence of such a semipermanent feature as the Great Red Spot, which has now been under observation for three centuries, suggests that there must be some degree of stability beneath the whirling cloud belts which are all that we can see from our distant viewpoint.

What makes Jupiter of such extraordinary interest, despite the difficulties of approaching it, is the fact that it may be a primitive world, a protoplanet or even a protosun. It may show us how our own Earth came into being, and, what is even more exciting, may provide us with working models of the origin of life.

Until quite recently any consideration of life on the outer planets was dismissed as not worthy of serious thought. "Obviously" it was ridiculous to talk about living creatures on worlds where the temperatures never rose to − 100 Fahrenheit, and the atmosphere contained no oxygen, but consisted of suffocating or even poisonous gases.

This conclusion is probably correct, but it may be completely and dramatically wrong, for the argument itself is certainly fallacious. Far from being uninhabitable, it now appears that Jupiter may be even *more* suitable for life than our own planet, at least according to some optimistic biologists.

In the first place, the indicated temperature of Jupiter, as read by instruments on our telescopes, is only that of the upper cloud layer. The clouds of Venus are at −50 degrees F., but the surface beneath is 1,000 degrees hotter. As we go down into the Jovian atmosphere, the temperature will steadily rise; even that observed at the cloud layer is higher than it should be, suggesting that the planet has some internal source of heat and is not warmed only by the Sun.

So at some level water will be able to exist in the liquid state. There may be seas on Jupiter that dwarf our oceans into puddles.

As for the atmosphere, it is now believed that life on Earth evolved in precisely such an oxygenless environment of methane (CH_4) and ammonia (NH_3), plus carbon dioxide and water. (There was probably little free hydrogen, as that would have escaped into space.) In a famous series of experiments begun by Stanley Miller at the University of Chicago in 1953, it has been shown that such mixtures, in the presence of sunlight or electrical discharges, inevitably and automatically produce a whole range of very complex organic substances—the immediate precursors of life itself. It is now generally accepted that the first simple cells arose in this warm, dilute soup and then evolved into plant forms. At this point a new situation arose, for plants liberate gaseous oxygen as a byproduct of the manufacture of starch:

$$\text{Water } + \text{ carbon dioxide } + \text{ sunlight } = \text{ starch } + \text{ oxygen}$$

So, over millions of years, the composition of Earth's atmosphere began to change from its original, "natural" state, until today it contains about 21 per cent oxygen. That this is really a very peculiar fact was not realized until quite recently, owing to the human race's understandable habit of taking the normal for granted.

An oxygen-bearing atmosphere is *not* normal. Oxygen is so reactive—as its use in rockets demonstrates—that one would not expect to find it in the free state; it should have combined, by burning and rusting, with the other elements. Indeed, most of it has done so; over half the crust of the Earth, by weight, is oxygen.

The coming of plant life reversed this process, liberating the free element. And because evolution always takes advantage of a changing situation, the parasitic creatures we call animals duly arrived—breathing the oxygen and eating the plants. Evidence of this is given by the fact that some primitive organisms not only do not need oxygen, but are actually poisoned by it. (Hence the treatment of gangrene cases in oxygen chambers: the bacteria which produce this condition are anerobic.) Even human beings are poisoned by pure oxygen at pressures of more than two atmospheres, as divers with oxygen-rebreathing gear have often found to their cost.

It is not true, therefore, that life requires oxygen. *Oxygen requires life.* So all the conditions for the evolution of life may very well exist in the gigantic, thoroughly stirred caldron of chemicals that is the Jovian atmosphere. It is true that the intensity of sunlight is low, as compared with Earth, but this is not a fatal objection. The far higher level of electrical activity, as indicated by lightning flashes which can sometimes be detected on simple transistor radios half a billion miles away, may more than compensate for the lack of sunlight.

Jovian life forms, if they exist, could be of any size from the microscopic upward. The high gravity would seem to favor small creatures, but this limitation would apply only to land-dwellers. Organisms that lived in the sea or floated in an atmosphere which might be compressed to densities greater than that of most liquids could be of any size. And pressure itself, of course, is no handicap to life, as is proved by the fragile sponges and starfish going about their business in the Pacific trenches, under seven tons to every square inch.

Perhaps the only useful generalization one can make about Jovian life forms is that they would probably be very sluggish—more akin to the vegetable than the animal kingdom. They would have no choice, not having access to the high-energy propellants that power the creatures that run and jump and swim and fly on our planet. The rocketlike performances of our bodies are possible only because we can squander, in a few minutes, the energy that plants have patiently accumulated over many hours.

It would seem that the evolutionary road to high-energy or animal-type organisms on Jupiter has been blocked by gravity, though in a rather indirect manner. The Jovian atmosphere consists largely of hydrogen, which has been unable to escape from the planet's gravitational clutch. So even if free oxygen were liberated by any process, it would quickly recombine with the excess hydrogen to form water. There would be no possibility of large amounts accumulating in the presence of so much methane and hydrogen; at the very first lightning flash, the whole atmosphere would explode. Our planet bypassed this dilemma; any hydrogen quickly leaked away into space, and the presence of large amounts of inert nitrogen may also have prevented the formation of unstable, explosive mixtures. On such apparently random factors—the difference between 1 g and 2½ g—do the destinies of worlds depend.

This argument against higher life forms must not be taken too seriously. The ingenuity of Nature appears unlimited; she may have found other answers to the problem. Certainly there are ample supplies of energy on Jupiter, and biological systems may have found other ways of tapping them besides oxidation. Nor does it necessarily follow that life must be fast-moving to be intelligent.

So Jupiter's twenty-five *billion* square miles of surface, plus almost the same for the combined areas of Saturn, Uranus, and Neptune, may be full of the most astonishing surprises. Asimov's description of the Solar System as Jupiter plus debris may apply not only to its material but also to its biological resources. Our world may be a sparsely populated desert compared to the seething fecundity that lies beyond the orbit of Mars.

If the manned explorations of the giant planets is ever attempted, it will require vehicles combining the attributes of spaceships and bathyscaphes—not merely, as in the case of Venus, spaceships and submarines. Jupiter also presents a special, though not insoluble, problem because of its high gravity. A 160-pound man would weigh 400 pounds on Jupiter and would have to spend most of his time immersed in water; the three other giants have gravities that are slightly higher than Earth's but that can probably be tolerated.

Even if the surfaces of these planets are inaccessible because of the pressure, purely aerial expeditions might be worthwhile, as has also been suggested for Venus. One can imagine balloon-borne observatories drifting with the Jovian tradewinds; judging by the disturbances that are visible from Earth, they would have quite an exciting time.

Also, what does one put in a balloon that is to operate in an atmosphere of hydrogen—the lightest gas that can possibly exist. To this there can be only one answer—*heated* hydrogen. It will indeed be a strange twist of fate if the recently revived sport of hot-air ballooning sees its fulfillment, a hundred years from now, in the exploration of the outer planets.

What we do with the Solar System, in the centuries and the millennia that lie ahead, will be the main theme of future history. We may merely explore it; we may colonize it; we may even rebuild it. The time may come when all the inner planets have rings like Saturn, but they will be rings of artificial moonlets, the space cities of a civilization that has regained the freedom from gravity that we lost when we emerged from the sea. Perhaps the drive into space is no more than an unconscious, lemminglike effort to regain that freedom. If this is true, the planets will merely provide the raw materials for a largely space-borne culture.

Half a century ago Tsiolkovsky dreamed that mankind would move out from the Earth, tap the illimitable energies of the Sun (of which only one part in two billion is now intercepted by our planet), and build new worlds in the empty gulfs between the old ones. But perhaps it has all been done before; how disconcerting, if the asteroids turn out to be an abandoned low-gravity housing project.

Here, in the table on pages 246–47, is the inventory of the future—the immense but not infinite treasure of the Solar System, waiting for us to use or to squander in the ages that lie ahead.

TABLE 9
THE SOLAR SYSTEM

BODY	DISTANCE FROM SUN, MILLIONS OF MILES	DIAMETER, MILES	AREA, EARTH = 1	MASS, EARTH = 1	GRAVITY, EARTH = 1	ESCAPE VELOCITY, MILES/SEC.	DAY*	YEAR*	ATMOSPHERE
Sun	—	865,000	1,200,000	332,000	28	385	24d	—	H, He, etc.
Mercury	36	3,000	0.15	0.05	0.37	2.5	59d	88	Trace?
Venus	67	7,600	0.9	0.81	0.89	6.2	243d	225d	CO_2 + N_2 + ?
Earth	93	7,900	1	1	1	7.0	24h	365d	N_2 + O_2
Moon		2,160	0.07	0.012	0.16	1.5	27d	—	None
Mars	142	4,200	0.3	0.11	0.39	3.1	24½h	1.88y	N_2 + CO_2
Phobos		10							None
Deimos		5							None
Asteroids									
Ceres	256	480	0.004	0.0002	0.1	0.4	?	4.6y	None
Pallas	257	300	0.001	0.00005	0.05	0.2	?	4.6y	None
+ 50,000 (?) others	90-500	1-100							

							Rotation*	Orbital period	Atmosphere
Jupiter	484	86,000	120	318	2.65	38.0	10h	11.86y	H_2, He, NH_3, CH_4
Io		2,000	0.06	0.01	0.15	1.5			None
Europa		1,900	0.06	0.006	0.1	1.2			None
Ganymede		3,000	0.14	0.02	0.2	2.0			Trace?
Callisto		2,700	0.12	0.01	0.2	1.5			None
+ 8 others									
Saturn	895	74,000	85	95	1.15	23	10½h	29.5y	H_2, He, CH_4
Titan		3,000	0.15	0.02	0.2	1.7			CH_4
+ 9 others									
Uranus	1,780	30,000	14	15	1.0	14	11h	84y	H_2, He, CH_4
+ 5									
Neptune	2,790	28,000	12	17	1.5	15	16h	164.8y	H_2, He, CH_4
Triton		2,600	0.1	0.02	0.02	2			H_2, He, CH_4
+ 1 other									
Pluto	3,680	4,000 ?	0.2	?	?	?	6½d	247.7y	None

*h = Earth hours; d = Earth days; y = years.

V. AROUND
THE UNIVERSE

26. OTHER SUNS THAN OURS

The Solar System, with its handful of planets scattered at immense distances from the Sun, seems to consist almost entirely of empty space. Yet looked at from the cosmic viewpoint, it is a tiny, closely packed affair. Although interplanetary distances are a millionfold greater than terrestrial ones, *interstellar* distances are a million times greater still. Even light, which can pass from the Sun to Pluto in a few hours, takes more than four years to reach the nearest of the stars. It is not surprising, therefore, that it was quite late in astronomical history before it was proved that the stars were actually other suns, made pinpoints of light purely because of their enormous distance.

Our Sun is a quite typical star, although it is a good deal brighter and hotter than the average. (Only three of the twenty nearest stars exceed it in brilliance, and the vast majority are much fainter.) It is one of a very large number—at least 100 billion—of stars forming a roughly disk-shaped system known as the Galaxy. If we could see our Galaxy from outside, it would probably look not unlike the famous Andromeda Nebula.

The stars vary in size and brightness over a truly enormous range. (Here we are referring, of course, to real variations, and not to those caused merely by the effect of distance.) If, as is customary and convenient, we take our Sun as a standard, then the biggest known stars have a diameter a thousand times as great, so that they could enclose the orbits of all the planets right out to Saturn. On the other hand, the smallest stars have less than one-hundredth of the Sun's diameter, being thus smaller than the Earth.

The range of luminosity among the stars is even greater. Stars a million times as bright as the Sun are known, as well as stars 10,000 times fainter. With these variations of brilliance go variations of color. Our Sun, whose light we regard as normal, is actually a somewhat yellow star. The hottest stars of all shine with a brilliant bluish-white light, and indeed the greater part of their radiation would be quite invisible to us since it would lie in the ultraviolet, perhaps even in the X-ray, region. In descending temperatures the colors of the stars run: white, yellow-white, yellow, orange-yellow, orange, deep orange-red. There are also suns of almost every possible intermediate color—gold, blue, green, topaz, emerald—so that in the telescope some of the great star clusters look like collections of jewels glittering against the blackness of space.

As shown by Table 10, there are eight stars (two of them double) within ten light-years of the Sun. (This unit, the distance light travels in a year, is a convenient one for measuring stellar distances. It equals 5,880,000,000,000, miles.) Only one of our nearest eight neighbors is visible without a telescope in the northern hemisphere; this is Sirius, the brightest star in the sky, about nine light-years away. (The closest of all stars is the very faint Proxima Centauri, quite invisible to the naked eye despite its distance of "only" 4.3 light-years.)

Our Sun is in a moderately well-populated region of the Galaxy, though nowhere near its center. On a clear moonless night the sky seems full of stars more or less equally distributed around the heavens, with the pale band of the Milky Way wandering through them. This faint arch of light, which continues around the southern hemisphere and so divides the sky into almost equal parts, was a mystery to mankind until the invention of the telescope revealed that it was composed of millions of faint stars. We now know that their faintness is due only to distance, and the reason why they form a continuous band around the Earth arises purely from our location in space. When we look toward the Milky Way, we are looking along the major axis of the Galaxy, so that we see the stars packed in endless ranks as far as the eye, or even the telescope, can

TABLE 10
THE TWENTY NEAREST STARS

NAME	DISTANCE, LIGHT-YEARS	BRIGHTNESS (SUN = 1)	COLOR
1. Sun	0	1.0	Yellow
2. α Centauri A	4.3	1.0	Yellow
3. α Centauri B	4.3	0.28	Orange
4. α Centauri C (Proxima)	4.3	0.00005	Red
5. Barnard's star	6.0	0.0004	Red
6. Wolf 359	7.7	0.000017	Red
7. Luyten 726-8A	7.9	0.00004	Red
8. Luyten 726-8B	7.9	0.00003	Red
9. Lalande 21185	8.2	0.0048	Red
10. Sirius A	8.7	23.0	White
11. Sirius B	8.7	0.008	White
12. Ross 154	9.3	0.00036	Red
13. Ross 248	10.3	0.0001	Red
14. ε Eridani	10.8	0.25	Orange
15. Ross 128	10.9	0.0003	Red
16. 61 Cygni A	11.1	0.052	Orange
17. 61 Cygni B	11.1	0.028	Orange
18. Luyten 789-6	11.2	0.00012	Red
19. Procyon A	11.3	5.8	White
20. Procyon B	11.3	0.00044	Red

see. When we look in other directions, however, our gaze quickly passes out through the Galaxy's relatively thin disk and we can see only a few stars—and beyond those the great emptiness in which the other island universes float. Anyone living on a planet in the outskirts of the Andromeda Nebula would see a very similar band of stars around the sky.

The heart of our own Galaxy, where the stars are clustered

together more thickly than they are in the neighborhood of the Sun, lies toward the constellation Sagittarius. Here, in the densest regions of the Milky Way, lie great star clouds, which in addition to suns contain immense clouds of luminous gas—perhaps the raw material from which the stars are made.

Although the study of the stars themselves is a fascinating and never-ending pursuit, from the viewpoint of astronauts we are interested only in planets. Unfortunately, the greatest of planets would be totally invisible at a distance of a few light-years, so we do not know if even Proxima Centauri has worlds revolving around it. Our views on the existence of planets in the universe are likely, for the time being, to be determined by whether we think the Solar System to be something usual, or an astronomical freak.

Until quite recently the latter opinion was generally held, because the only conditions under which anyone could imagine the Solar System forming seemed to demand very unusual circumstances, such as the near-collision of two stars. Today quite a different outlook prevails. We are still by no means sure *how* planets are formed, but it is felt that many, if not most, stars may possess them. Certainly among the 100 billion stars of this Galaxy alone, there must be myriads with solar systems. But as to which are the stars with planetary companions and which are alone, there is as yet no reliable way of discovering. This is a problem which may be solved when we can build observatories in space.

In a very few exceptional cases there is some evidence of bodies of planetary size revolving around other stars. The first to be discovered was in the system of the double star 61 Cygni, about eleven light-years away. This pair of faint stars has been carefully studied for more than a century, and from the movements of one component the existence of a third body has been deduced. This object has about 15 times the mass of Jupiter, or 5,000 times that of Earth. It seems too small to be a sun and may therefore be a very large planet.

In 1960 a slightly larger companion was discovered circling another nearby star, Lalande 21185, and in 1963 came perhaps the most remarkable discovery of all—an object only 50 per cent heavier than Jupiter, and thus almost certainly a planet, orbiting around the faint red dwarf known as Barnard's star.

Barnard's star, six light years away, is the second-closest star; Lalande 21185 the fifth, 61 Cygni the eleventh. It is important to realize that only the very largest planets can possibly be discovered by this means; a world as small as Earth would be a thousand times too light to be detected. Yet despite this limitation, three such bodies have been found among the eleven nearest stars, so it can hardly be doubted that there must be many others. Solar systems may be almost as common as suns.

Another line of evidence also suggests that this is the case. When the total "spin" (or angular momentum) of the Solar System is added up, it is found that most of it resides in the planets—not in the Sun itself, despite its far greater mass. The Sun, in fact, appears to be rotating with abnormal slowness, as though it has exhausted itself with the effort of throwing off the planets.

It is possible, by means of the spectroscope, to measure the spin, or rotational velocity, of the stars, even though they appear as dimensionless points of light. When they are classified in what is believed to be increasing order of age, it appears that there is an abrupt loss of spin in early youth, and the simplest explanation is that planets are born at this stage.

Our Sun is, apart from its planets, a solitary wanderer through space. Many stars, however, occur in pairs, revolving around each other under their mutual gravitation. The variety of these partnerships is immense; sometimes the two stars are of identical types, but sometimes they are so disproportionate in size that an elephant waltzing with a gnat would not be an inaccurate comparison.

Systems of three, four, five, six, or even more suns occur, often with fantastic and beautiful combinations of color. (The nearest star is one of a triplet—Alpha Centauri A, B, and C; the latter is sometimes known as Proxima, since on occasion it is slightly closer to us than its larger companions.) Although planets may occur in such systems, in many cases they would undergo such violent changes in temperature that they would be uninhabitable. Their orbits would be exceedingly complex, sometimes even weaving from one star to another, so that our concept of a "year" would be utterly meaningless. The problem of contriving a calendar for such worlds would be an appalling one—even worse than for Mercury (see Chapter 22)—but in compensation, any inhabitants would have skies whose splendor we can scarcely imagine.

Even more incredible would be the view of the heavens from a planet near the heart of a globular cluster. These are great spherical swarms of stars, so closely packed toward the center that the separate suns must be only light-weeks apart, as against the light-years that normally lie between stars. There could be no such things as night and darkness on any worlds at the core of a globular cluster: the sky would be a continuous blaze of multicolored light. The dwellers of such worlds would have a very limited knowledge of astronomy, for they would be unable to observe the structure of the universe through the screen of stars which hid them from the rest of space.

Stars vary greatly among themselves in physical structure, as well as in size and brilliance. Some of the giants are so rarefied that they are a million times less dense than our atmosphere: they have been picturesquely christened "red-hot vacuums." At the other extreme are stars whose density is thousands of times greater than any substance on Earth. The best-known example of these "White Dwarfs" is the Companion of Sirius (Sirius B), with a density six thousand times that of lead. A matchbox of this star's material would weigh a couple of tons—but it should be pointed out that if one *did*, by some miraculous means, obtain a matchboxful, it would not stay that size for even a millionth of a second. Its density is produced by the enormous temperatures and pressures inside the star, and if these were removed it would explode with a violence probably eclipsing that of an atomic bomb.

Something of this kind may indeed happen occasionally, for detonating stars (novae) are frequently observed. At rare intervals they are conspicuous enough to be really prominent objects, and one (Tycho's nova, 1572) was so brilliant that for some weeks it was visible *in broad daylight*.

The cause of this gigantic stellar explosion is unknown; in its most spectacular form, a star will, within a few hours, increase its brilliance a hundred-million-fold and may even, for a short while, outshine all the other suns in its universe added together. These supernovae are relatively infrequent, but ordinary novae are quite common, and one cheerful theory suggests that *all* suns may become novae at some time or other during the course of their evolution. As far as the inhabitants of any planets were concerned, the final result would be much the same whether their sun became a nova or a supernova. The difference would be, roughly speaking, that between being slowly melted or swiftly vaporized.

There are also large numbers of stars (variables) whose brilliance fluctuates over a more modest range. Some of these stars appear to be pulsating, and they go through their cycle of brightness with clockwork precision. Others show no regularity in their variations; they behave like great, flickering bonfires, sometimes quiescent, sometimes flaring up for days or years, then relapsing again.

Such changes, as long as they were not too great, would not rule out the possibility of life on any planets of these stars. They would simply have complicated seasons—predictable in the case of the regular variables but quite erratic for the irregulars.

It would always be possible, as far as the stars which shine with a steady light are concerned, for planets with temperatures between the boiling and melting points of water to exist. They might have to be very close to some of the cooler stars and a long way from the brilliant blue-white suns. This would mean that their "year" might be, in the one case, only a few terrestrial days, and in the other, perhaps thousands of our years.

All the stars, including of course our Sun, are in motion through space. Their movements are not entirely random, for the great disk of the Galaxy is rotating, sweeping the stars around with it and completing one revolution in about 200 million years. Since our planet was formed, therefore, the Sun has made only about twenty circuits of the Milky Way.

This slowly turning disk of stars is about 100,000 light-years in diameter, and its greatest thickness is perhaps one-fifth of this. In the neighborhood of the Sun (about two-thirds of the way toward the rim) the thickness of the great lens-shaped system of stars is about 10,000 light-years—though it has, of course, no definite boundaries.

As we look out past the thinly scattered stars away from the plane of the Milky Way, we can see, at immense distances, the other galaxies. Some we observe turned full toward us, like great catherine wheels of stars, showing intricate and still unexplained spiral structures. Others are edge-on; still others, like the Andromeda Nebula are tilted at an angle. As we look at Andromeda, the stars scattered closest to us are the relatively close suns of our local system. We can look past them, and across the immensity of intergalactic space, as a town-dweller might look past the streetlamps of his suburb to the lights of another city, many miles away.

The Andromeda Galaxy is the nearest of the other universes,* and it is about 2 million light-years away. In whatever direction we look (except those in which clouds of obscuring matter block our view), we see other galaxies, extending to the limits of telescopic vision. They appear to be roughly the same size as our own system, and on the average their distances apart are of the order of a million light-years (though local clusterings occur). It will be seen that there is a breakdown here of a law which has applied so far in the architecture of the cosmos. The distances between stars and planets were hundreds of thousands of times greater than the dimensions of these bodies themselves. Yet the distances between the galaxies are only about ten times as great as their diameters.

The limit which we can reach with the most powerful telescope (the 200-inch reflector on Mount Palomar) is perhaps ten billion light-years. So far, the galaxies show no signs of thinning out or of forming more complex structures. It is possible that we have come to the end of the hierarchy, but this is a matter concerning which we can only speculate at the moment. In the next few decades—thanks to quasars, orbiting telescopes, and other developments still unforeseen—we shall have a great deal of fresh information, and the pattern of the cosmos as a whole may be taking clearer shape. We may have discovered that space is infinite, and the galaxies extend onward forever, or we may have proved that it is curved and of limited

---

*The word "universe" is employed here in the restricted sense of a single galaxy. Thus "our universe" is merely the Milky Way system. Astronomers usually employ the word "cosmos" to describe the whole of creation, i.e., *all* the galaxies.

volume, so that although the total number of galaxies will be immense, it will nevertheless be finite. These questions of cosmology are, however, outside the scope of this book; let us return to our own galactic system, the Milky Way.

If we assume that only one sun in a thousand has planets—and this may well be a gross underestimate—that would give a total of perhaps a hundred million solar systems in our Galaxy alone. Among all these, it can hardly be doubted that there would be many worlds on which life of some kind would be possible; there would even be a large number which would have physical conditions similar to those of Earth.

A few decades ago, such speculations, fascinating and irresistible though they might be, seemed of no practical value. Almost any scientist in the world before the 1950's would have stated that there was no possibility that we could ever learn anything about the existence of life in other planetary systems.

In 1835 the philosopher Auguste Comte came to an even more forthright conclusion. In his *Cours de Philosophie Positive*, he attempted to define the limits within which scientific knowledge must always lie, and he made this statement regarding the heavenly bodies:

We see how we may determine their forms, their distances, their bulk, their motions, but we can never know anything of their chemical or mineralogical structure; and much less, that of organized beings living on their surface. . . .

Within a generation the spectroscope had utterly refuted the first part of this dictum, and the "chemical structure" of the stars became the dominant theme of astrophysics. Soon the mineralogy of the Moon and planets will be of prime scientific, and practical, importance.

And now there is every reason to believe that the last part of M. Comte's pronouncement will be equally untrue.

27. ACROSS THE ABYSS

The subject of interstellar communication—if not transportation—became suddenly respectable soon after the first artificial satellites were launched. This is certainly no coincidence; the intellectual climate now allowed scientists to discuss such ideas without risking their reputations. A striking example of the change that had taken place in little over twenty years will be found in the pages of the famous scientific journal *Nature*. In the 1936–39 period it printed several highly critical reviews of books and articles on such modest projects as the journey to the Moon; but in 1959 it published the first of an already classical series of papers on interstellar communication and superior cosmic societies.

These papers pointed out that developments in radar and its direct scientific offspring, radio astronomy, have now given us the technology with which we can signal to the stars. This has happened in a very short time, historically speaking, so it seems reasonable to assume that, *if* there are other technically advanced societies much older than ours, interstellar signaling should be child's play to them. But as it is much easier, cheaper, and perhaps safer to receive than to transmit signals, we should start to listen to the universe before we attempt to talk to it ourselves. (It would be too bad, of course, if everybody has come to the same conclusion, and the Galaxy is full of patient listeners and no talkers.)

The problem of sending a radio signal over interstellar distances is one that can be precisely defined in terms of a relatively few variables. Basically, they are the distance, the power available, the narrowness of the beam, the size of the receiving antenna, the sensitivity of the receiver, and the rate at which information is transmitted.

As far as the first is concerned, we have now established contact with space probes more than a hundred million miles from Earth. Only a few of the closer stars are within a million times this distance, and as signal strength weakens with the square of the range, this means that the problem of sending a signal to, say, Altair (sixteen light-years away) is about a million *million* times more difficult than contacting a Mariner spacecraft when it is halfway around the Sun.

One can compensate for distance with increased power, but an increase of a million million times is out of the question; it would mean putting more than the entire electrical output of the Earth into the transmitter. However, the situation is not quite as bad as this, for Mariner had a very small antenna—only about 4 feet across—and we can assume that one of at least 100 times that diameter, and hence 10,000 times the area, would be used by any interstellar receiver. In fact, even this may be unduly modest, as radio telescopes up to 1,000 feet in diameter have already been built.

Using shorter waves also improves the situation by giving narrower beams, so that less energy is wasted. So does reducing the rate of signaling to a low level; it takes thousands of times more energy to transmit a television picture than a few dots and dashes, which are all that would be required for the first attempts at interstellar contact.

When all these points are taken into account, it appears that, with a slight extension of existing technology, we could send detectable signals to a distance of at least a hundred light-years—that is, over a volume of space containing many thousands of stars. And when we can establish transmitters in space, or on the Moon, clear of the Earth's absorbing atmosphere, we will be able to do very much better; for then we will be able to use the fantastically narrow beams made possible by the laser.

But this argument assumes that there is a fully cooperative party at the receiving end, listening in at the right frequency, with the appropriate equipment, and with an antenna system aimed at the correct, microscopically small portion of the sky.

The odds against this are, of course, so enormous that they might seem to be infinite.

In a famous letter to *Nature*, published in 1959 ("Searching for Interstellar Communications"), the physicists Giuseppe Cocconi and Philip Morrison pointed out a way of improving the odds. They argued that there is one specific radio frequency which would be familiar to every science-orientated civilization in the universe and on which one might therefore expect to find listeners. The magic frequency is 1420 megacycles/ second, corresponding to the rather short wavelength of 21 centimeters. It is unique, characteristic, unmistakable—standing out against the general radio din of the universe as a pure and very intense musical note might be audible in the cacophony of a boiler factory. On this planet we have already spent millions of dollars building equipment to trap waves of this frequency, for reasons that have nothing to do with interstellar communication. Other cultures, if they are remotely like ours, might be expected to do the same.

This unique radiation is that emitted by hydrogen atoms in space; it is their natural call sign, or station identification. Most of the universe consists of hydrogen, and by studying these waves radio astronomers have been able to work out details of galactic structure that could not be obtained in any other manner. If there are any radio astronomers on other planets, not only will they be doing exactly the same thing, but they too may have concluded that they are not alone in doing it. So if any wish to announce their presence, they might be expected to signal at this frequency—or, possibly, at exactly half, or exactly twice, its value, to avoid interference with the natural 21-centimeter omission.

Cocconi and Morrison therefore suggested that it might be worthwhile to aim our largest radio telescopes at some of the nearer stars, and to listen out at 1420 megacycles/second. Although a successful outcome would be very unlikely, the matter was of such importance that it was worth a considerable effort. And, if we *never* searched, the chance of success would certainly be zero.

With this encouragement, a number of radio astronomers (probably more than have confessed to it) have made tentative searches with limited equipment; as far as is known, none of the really big telescopes has been used for this purpose. Probably thousands of hours of radio listening, to hundreds of selected areas of the sky, will have to be carried out before any verdict can be obtained. This would cost millions of dollars—and, of course, a negative result would prove nothing. It is a sobering thought that not one of the cultures which produced Akhenaton, Confucius, Buddha, Plato, Christ, Dante, Shakespeare, Leonardo, Newton, Beethoven, Darwin, Einstein, could have made its presence known even as far away as the Moon. Not until the development of the first high-powered radars in the mid-1940's was there any possibility that intelligent life on Earth could be detected at interstellar distances, and then only by the wildest chance.

It is conceivable, though unlikely, that the use of radio for long-distance communication may be only a brief, passing phase in the development of a technological culture—a stepping-stone between smoke signals and something that we cannot imagine today. In this case, only a minute percentage of interstellar civilizations—those occupying our century-wide slot on a million- or even billion-year band—would be in a position to communicate with us. However, if more advanced races are interested in announcing their presence to undeveloped planets, presumably they would set up a few primitive mega-megawatt radios for this very purpose. It is the sort of project that might keep the children amused.

Other far more ambitious schemes for attracting attention over interstellar distances have been proposed. A large thermonuclear explosion, for example, has unique characteristics that enable it to be distinguished from natural phenomena; a series of explosions at precisely timed intervals would be proof positive of an advanced technology. However, it would be difficult, and certainly expensive, to send useful information in this manner.

A very advanced civilization might "label" its sun by dumping into its atmosphere vast quantities of artificial elements which did not occur in nature, so that their spectral lines would convey an unmistakable message to other astronomers; in some cases, the amounts of matter needed would be a few hundred thousand tons—not an unreasonable figure. Or a series of occulting screens might be put in orbit, so that a star became a celestial lighthouse, blinking across the ocean of space.

Soviet scientists have shown particular enthusiasm for this type of speculation and have taken it to daring lengths. The astrophysicist N. S. Kardashev, for example, has suggested that after a technical civilization has endured for a sufficiently long period, it should be able to control energy resources equal to the output of its sun—say, 500,000,000,000,000,000,000 hp (*our* civilization's current resources are only about 50,000,000,000 hp). And there may even be civilizations able to control the energy output of an entire galaxy; expressed in horsepower, this is a number with 34 zeros.

If such societies exist, we should be able to detect their activities over most of the observable universe. Not merely their deliberate attempts at signaling, but what might be called their civil-engineering projects, would be apparent over cosmic distances. We should, therefore, be on the watch for astronomical phenomena, and perhaps even stellar configurations, which do not appear to have a natural explanation.

These ideas have been taken perhaps to their limit by Dr. Freeman Dyson of the Institute for Advanced Studies, Princeton. Dyson points out that as our Galaxy appears to be at least 10 billion years old, any really ancient civilization with a history of continuous technological development will have had ample time to take it over and reconstruct it, should it feel so inclined. However, as far as we can see, the Galaxy is still in what Dyson calls the "wild" state. It has not yet been turned into a well-kept cosmic park.

So perhaps there are no *really* advanced civilizations— only ones a few thousand years ahead of us. Yet, when we look back at the changes that have taken place on our planet in a mere moment of historic time (it has been only 400 years since men were burned for saying that the Earth is not the center of the universe), we may well wonder if we will find anyone near enough our level of development to talk to us in language we can understand.

What that language might be is another problem that has engaged a good deal of attention. Even if we established radio contact with another species, we would be rather like two prisoners in adjacent cells, trying to exchange messages by tapping on the walls—and neither knowing a word of the other's language.

In such a situation, is any meaningful communication even theoretically possible? The answer is yes—if the two parties are sufficiently intelligent and sufficiently patient. Philologically minded scientists have already had a good deal of fun working out possible codes, which might lead from "1 + 1 = 2" up to the highest levels of abstract thought. (I have even seen one attempt to explain modern poetry to an extraterrestrial. I did not understand it.)

The problem would be much simplified if pictorial information could be transmitted, and there are many ways of doing this. Radio astronomers are fond of constructing "messages" out of strings of ones and zeros—the equivalents, say, of radioed dots and dashes—and sending them to their friends to see if they can decipher them. For example, Dr. Frank Drake once mailed his colleagues a series which began: 111100001010010000 ... and so on for a total of 551 digits.

If we received such a mesage from space, repeated several times, undoubtedly our first reaction would be to look at the curious number 551. It does not take much effort to discover that it is the product of two prime numbers, 19 and 29. The obvious step then—or so it seems to us of the TV age, though perhaps a medieval monk or a Greek philosopher might not think of it—is to arrange the ones and zeros as black and white squares in a 19-by-29 grid, to see if any kind of pattern emerges.

This can be done in only two possible ways, with either 19 or 29 squares horizontal. In Dr. Drake's example, one arrangement gave a meaningless jumble, but the other resulted in an obvious and clearcut picture of a biped surrounded by geometrical symbols.

It is clear that by such methods a great deal of information could be transmitted, though to what extent full communication at all intellectual and emotional levels could be attained is a question that completely transcends technology. (We are still trying to decide if the dolphins are saying anything to us, and we can *touch* them.) In the cosmic case, we are also limited by the fact that no true conversation would be possible; there would be none of the quick feedback—the process of question and answer—which is so essential for understanding between different individuals here on Earth.

This is an inevitable result of the distances between the stars. If we sent a radio signal to Proxima Centauri, it would be almost nine years before we could possibly get a reply. A more probable time lag would be decades or centuries. If the nearest radio-using civilization is at the center of the Galaxy, any message we received from it today would be coming from ten times farther back in the past than the siege of Troy.

Interstellar radio communication, therefore, will be a very tedious business—a search project for the centuries. This would not be a great disadvantage for a long-lived, scientifically oriented civilization, which might be conversing with dozens of other cultures; eventually, even at the limiting speed of light, there would be time for any amount of back-and-forth discussion. But the scholars who asked the questions would never live to hear the answers.

Even so, they would be much better off than the archaeologists, who can never ask questions at all. How much more we should know of history if Gibbon had been able to interrogate the Caesars and Toynbee had received their replies. This is a rough analogy of the situation that may arise in interstellar dialogues.

There are many scientists who profess themselves quite satisfied with this state of affairs; there is no need, they say, to go traveling around the universe if we can send messages which are far cheaper, quicker, and safer in every way. Some, making a virtue of a necessity, have even argued that the effective quarantine of the interstellar distances is a good thing. The various races in the Galaxy can exchange information, but they can never do each other any harm through physical contact.

This is really a very naïve attitude, rather like that of Auguste Comte quoted in the last chapter. It assumes that the limits of technological progress are already in sight; one would have thought that by this time no scientist with the slightest knowledge of history would fall into such a trap.

In a celebrated lecture at Brookhaven ("Radioastronomy and Communication Through Space") Dr. Edward Purcell once remarked that "all this stuff about traveling around the universe . . . belongs back where it came from, on the cereal box."

Dr. Purcell should have remembered that this is just where most talk of travel to the Moon was only a generation ago.

28. TO THE STARS

Travel to the stars is not difficult, if one is in no particular hurry. As we have seen in Chapter 24, today's vehicles could send substantial payloads to Proxima Centauri, especially if they went by way of Jupiter. Unfortunately, the voyage would take the better part of a million years.

However, no one doubts that there will be enormous increases in spacecraft velocities, especially when we have discovered really efficient ways of harnessing nuclear energy for propulsion. Theoretically, a rocket operating on the *total* annihilation of matter should be able to approach the speed of light—670 million mph. At the moment, we can reach about 1/20,000 of this figure; clearly, there is plenty of room for improvement.

Let us be very pessimistic and assume that rocket speeds increase tenfold every century. By the year 2000 we will certainly have vehicles which could reach the nearer stars in 100,000 years, carrying really useful payloads of automatic surveying equipment.

But there would be no point in building them, for we could be sure that they would be quickly overtaken by the ten-times-faster vehicles we would be building a hundred years later. And so on.

The situation, in round figures, might look something like this:

LAUNCH DATE	TIME TO PROXIMA CENTAURI (YEARS)
2000	100,000
2100	10,000
2200	1,000
2300	100
2400	10

Clearly, there is no point in making anything but paper studies until about the year 2300; but after *that*, it is time to start thinking about action. A wealthy, stable, scientifically advanced society would be accustomed to making hundred-year plans, and it might well consider building space probes to survey the nearer stars, as our Mariners have surveyed Mars and Venus. They would report back along tight laser beams to gigantic reflecting telescopes orbiting the Earth; or they might even come back themselves, loaded with quantities of information too enormous to be transmitted across the light-years in a period less than their own transit time.

This proxy exploration of the universe is certainly one way in which it would be possible to gain knowledge of star systems which lacked garrulous, radio-equipped inhabitants; it might be the only way. For if men, and not merely their machines, are ever to reach the planets of other stars, much more difficult problems will have to be overcome. Yet, they do not appear to be insoluble, even in terms of the primitive technology we possess today.

We will first of all assume—and the evidence is over-whelmingly in favor of this—that it is impossible for any material object to attain the velocity of light. This is not something that can be explained; it is the way that the universe is built. The velocity of light represents a limit which can be more and more closely approached but never reached. Even if all the matter in the cosmos were turned into energy and that energy were all given to a single electron, it would not reach the speed of light, but only 99.99999999999—and so on, for about 160 digits—per cent of it.

We may eventually be able to build rockets driven by the *total* annihilation of matter, not the mere fraction of a per cent that is all we can convert into energy at present. No one has the faintest idea how this may be done, but it does not involve any fundamental impossibilities. Another idea that had been put forward is that, at very high speeds, it may be possible to use the thin hydrogen gas of interstellar space as fuel for a kind of cosmic, fusion-powered ramjet. This is a particularly interesting scheme, as it would give virtually unlimited range, and remove the restrictions imposed by an on-board propellant supply. If we are optimistic, we may guess (and guessing is all that we can do at this stage) that ultimately speeds of one-tenth of that of light may be attained. Remember that to make even a one-way voyage, this would have to be done *twice*—once to build up velocity, the second time to discard it, which is just as difficult and expensive. (Atmospheric braking is not going to work very well at 70 million mph. Even at 1 g it would take many times the width of the Solar System to slow down from such a speed.)

On this assumption, we will be able to reach the nearer stars in a few decades, but any worthwhile explorations would still have to last thousands of years. This has led some scientists to make the striking pronouncement: Interstellar flight is not an engineering problem, but a medical one.

Suspended animation may be one answer. It requires no great stretch of the imagination to suppose that, with the aid of drugs or low temperatures, men may be able to hibernate for virtually unlimited periods. We can picture an automatic ship with its oblivious crew making the long journey across the interstellar night until, when a new sun was looming up, the signal was sent out to trigger the mechanism that would revive the sleepers. When their survey was completed, they would head back to Earth and slumber again until the time came to awaken once more and greet a world which would regard them as survivors from a distant past.

Another solution was first suggested, to the best of my knowledge, in the 1920's by Professor J. D. Bernal in a long-out-of-print essay, *The World, the Flesh, and the Devil*, which must rank as one of the most outstanding feats of scientific imagination in literature. Even today many of the ideas propounded in this little book have never been fully developed, either in or out of science fiction.

Bernal imagined entire societies launched across space, in gigantic arks which would be closed, ecologically balanced systems. They would, in fact, be miniature planets upon which generations of men would live and die so that one day their remote descendants would return to Earth with the record of their celestial Odyssey.

The engineering, biological, and sociological problems involved in such an enterprise would be of fascinating complexity. The artificial planets (at least several miles in diameter) would have to be completely self-contained and self-supporting, and no material of any kind could be wasted. Commenting on the implications of such closed systems, *Time* magazine's science editor, Jonathan Leonard, once hinted that cannibalism would be compulsory among interstellar travelers. This would be a matter of definition; we crew members of the three-billion-man spaceship Earth do not consider ourselves cannibals, despite the fact that every one of us must have absorbed atoms which once formed part of Caesar and Socrates, Shakespeare, and Solomon.

One cannot help feeling that the interstellar ark on its 1,000-year voyages would be a cumbersome way of solving the problem, even if all the social and psychological difficulties could be overcome. (Would the fiftieth generation still share the aspirations of their Pilgrim Fathers, who set out from Earth so long ago?) There are, however, more sophisticated ways of getting men to the stars than the crude, brute-force methods outlined above.

The ark, with its generations of travelers doomed to spend their entire lives in space, was merely a device to carry germ cells, knowledge, and culture from one sun to another. How much more efficient to send only the cells, to fertilize them automatically some twenty years before the voyage was due to end, to carry the embryos through to birth by techniques already foreshadowed in today's biology labs—and to bring up the babies under the tutelage of cybernetic nurses who would teach them their inheritance and their destiny when they were capable of understanding it.

These children, knowing no parents, or indeed anyone of a different age from themselves, would grow up in the strange artificial world of their speeding ship, reaching maturity in time to explore the planets ahead of them—perhaps to be the ambassadors of humanity among alien races, or perhaps to find, too late, that there was no home for them there. If their mission succeeded, it would be their duty (or that of their descendants, if the first generation could not complete the task) to see that the knowledge they had gained was someday carried back to Earth.

Would any society be morally justified, we may well ask, in planning so onerous and uncertain a future for its unborn—indeed, unconceived—children? That is a question which different ages may answer in different ways. What to one era would seem a coldblooded sacrifice might to another appear a great and glorious adventure. There are complex problems here which cannot be settled by instinctive, emotional answers.

At the moment, our whole attitude to the problem of interstellar travel is conditioned by the span of human life. There is no reason whatsoever to suppose that this will always be less than a century, and no one has ever discovered just what it is that makes men die. It is certainly not a question of the body "wearing out" in the sense that an inanimate piece of machinery does, for in the course of a single year almost the entire fabric of the body is replaced by new material. When we have discovered the details of this process, it may be possible to extend the life span indefinitely if so desired—and this would drastically reduce the size of the universe from the psychological point of view.

Whether a crew of immortals, however well balanced and carefully chosen they might be, could tolerate each other's company for several centuries is an interesting subject for speculation. But the mobile worldlet in which they would travel might be larger—and would have incomparably greater facilities in every respect—than the city of Athens, in which small area, it may be recalled, a surprising number of men once led remarkably fruitful lives.

If medical science does not provide the key to the universe, there still remains a possibility that the answer may lie with the engineers. We have suggested that one-tenth of the speed of light may be the best we can ever hope to attain, even when our spacecraft have reached the limit of their development. A number of studies* suggest that this is wildly optimistic, but these are based on the assumption that the vehicles have to carry their own energy sources, like all existing rockets. It is at least conceivable that the interstellar ramjet may work, or that it is possible to supply power from an external device, such as a planet-based laser, or that the universe contains still unknown sources of energy which spacecraft may be able to tap. In this case, we may be able to approach much more closely to the speed of light, and the whole situation then undergoes a radical change. We become involved in the so-called time-dilation effect predicted by the Theory of Relativity.

It is impossible to explain *why* this effect occurs without delving into very elementary yet subtle mathematics. (There is nothing at all hard about basic relativity mathematics; most of it is simple algebra. The difficulty is all in the underlying concepts.) Nevertheless, even if the explanation must be by-passed, the results of the time-dilation effect can be stated easily enough in nontechnical language.

Time itself is a variable quantity; the rate at which it flows depends upon the speed of the observer. The difference is infinitesimal at the velocities of everyday life, and even at the velocities of normal astronomical bodies. It is all-important as we approach to within a few per cent of the speed of light. To put it crudely, the faster one travels, the more slowly time will pass. At the speed of light, time would cease to exist; the moment "now" would last forever. Let us take an extreme example to show what this implies. If a spaceship left Earth for Proxima Centauri at the speed of light and came back at

---

*See the papers by Sebastian von Hoerner and Edmund Purcell in the volume *Interstellar Communication*, ed., A. G. W. Cameron (1963).

once at the same velocity, it would have been gone for some
eight and a half years according to all the clocks and calendars
of Earth. *But the people in the ship, and all their clocks or
other time-measuring devices, would have detected no interval
at all.* The voyage would have been instantaneous.

This case is not possible, even in theory. But the one that
follows does not involve any physical impossibility, though its
achievement is so far beyond the bounds of today's—or tomorrow's—technology that it may never be realized in practice. Nevertheless, since it illustrates the working of the universe,
it is worth careful study.

Imagine a spaceship that leaves the Earth at a comfortable
1-g acceleration, so that the occupants have normal weight.
Today's rockets could maintain this rate for about twenty minutes, but we will assume that our X-powered supership can
keep it up indefinitely. Its velocity and its distance from Earth
would increase as follows:

TABLE 11
1-G VOYAGES

DURATION	VELOCITY, MPH	DISTANCE, MILES
1 hour	80,000	40,000
1 day	1,900,000	2,300,000
1 week	13,000,000	1,100,000,000
1 month	57,000,000	22,000,000,000
(1 year)	(675,000,000)	(3,000,000,000,000)

The last line of the table is in parentheses, as after one
year at 1-g acceleration the ship would have exceeded the
velocity of light (670 million mph) according to this straightforward, nonrelativistic calculation, and this is impossible. Professor J. B. S. Haldane once remarked to me, half seriously,
that perhaps nature intended us to be interstellar voyagers, since
one year at 1-g was a reasonable price to pay, even for organisms living only 70 years, to attain almost the speed of light.

But, of course, one has to slow down again to complete any desired journey, and decleration requires exactly as much time—and distance—as acceleration. It would require one year of each, plus three years of coasting at peak velocity, to make the four-light-year trip to the nearest star, Proxima Centauri.

Even if we could exceed the speed of light, the journey could not be made much more quickly, at a comfortable 1-g acceleration and deceleration. If the coasting period was eliminated, and the ship went on gaining speed until mid-voyage (when it would be moving at twice the velocity of light), the total transit time would be reduced only by one year, from five years to four.

Higher accelerations could be endured—if the passengers spent the whole journey floating in liquid or frozen in blocks of ice. Or we might assume the invention of the famous "space-drive" that acts upon every atom of matter in its domain, so that it could produce acceleration without any apparent force. (As gravity does precisely this, the idea does not violate any known laws.) So with artificial gravity plus an infinite power source—plus the repeal of relativity—we could get to any place in the universe just as quickly as we pleased.

But asking for three miracles is a little greedy; let us stick to one and see what would really happen if we could continue a modest 1-g acceleration indefinitely.

What *does* happen now depends on the point of view of the observer. To the people in the ship, the thrust is constant and their instruments tell them that they are gaining 80,000 mph every hour. Everything is perfectly normal.

But an observer back on Earth, if he could look into the ship,* would see that something very strange was happening. It would be like watching a film that was slowing down.

When the ship had reached 87 percent of the speed of light (580 million mph), everything inside it would seem to be taking twice as long as it should from the point of view of the outside observer; two hours of ship time would be only one hour of Earth time. At 98 per cent of the speed of light the time rate would be slowed fivefold, at 99.5 per cent tenfold, at 99.99

*I am fudging some philosophical points here and hope that relativistic purists will forgive me for describing observations which, even in principle, cannot be performed.

per cent a hundredfold. Thus the effect increases very rapidly as one nears the velocity of light; but once again it must be emphasized that to the crew of the ship, not only does everything appear normal—everything *is* normal. They are not responsible for the peculiar behavior of the rest of the universe; their clocks and tape measures are just as good as anybody else's.

Only when they had slowed down, turned around, and come home again would they discover any discrepancy, and then they would be confronted with the most famous paradox of the Theory of Relativity. For centuries might have passed on Earth, while they had aged only a few years aboard their speeding ship.

It is not really a paradox, of course; it is the way the universe is built, and we had better accept it. (A tiny minority of mathematicians—Professor Herbert Dingle is their most vehement spokesman—still refuses to accept a universe in which this sort of thing can happen. But the weight of the evidence is against them.)

In 1522 the Western world was suddenly confronted by a paradox which must have seemed equally baffling to many people at the time. Eighteen sailors landed at Seville on a Thursday, whereas by their own careful reckoning it was only Wednesday aboard their ship. Thus they were, in their view, a day younger than the friends they had left behind.

They were the survivors of Magellan's crew—the first men to circumnavigate the world—and they presented the Church with the frightful problem of deciding just when they should have kept the various Saints' days on the latter half of their voyage. Four and a half centuries later, we have learned to get along with the International Date Line, though it is going to cause us more and more trouble with the advent of global television. Perhaps four and a half centuries from now, time dilation will present no greater intellectual difficulties—though it may certainly cause grave social ones, when young astronauts return home to greet their senile great-grandchildren.

The effects that time dilation will produce have been calculated by Dr. von Hoerner for various 1-g round trips, with the fascinating results shown in the table on page 277. It will

TABLE 12
INTERSTELLAR ROUND TRIPS AT CONSTANT 1 G

DURATION (OUT AND BACK), YEARS		DISTANCE REACHED, LIGHT-YEARS
ON BOARD SHIP	ON EARTH	
1	1.0	0.06
2	2.1	0.25
5	6.5	1.7
10	24	10
15	80	37
20	270	137
25	910	455
30	3,100	1,560
40	36,000	17,500
50	420,000	208,000
60	5,000,000	2,470,000

(Adapted from Sebastian von Hoerner. "The General Limits of Space Travel," in INTERSTELLAR COMMUNICATION, *ed. A. G. W. Cameron, N.Y., 1063.)*

be seen how spectacularly the time-stretching increases with speed; the power consumption and engineering difficulties, unfortunately, increase even more rapidly. In the opinion of most scientists, Table 12 begins at a level of mere absurdity and swiftly mounts to the utterly preposterous; yet it is (*pace* Professor Dingle) mathematically sound.

Similar results have been calculated by Dr. Carl Sagan in a paper with the forthright and uncompromising title, "Direct Contact Among Galactic Civilizations by Relativistic Interstellar Spaceflight," the gist of which will be found in his book (with I. S. Shklovskii) *Intelligent Life in the Universe*. Dr. Sagan takes these ideas quite seriously and concludes that as far as energy requirements are concerned, there are no fundamental objections to high-speed (near-light-velocity) travel to the stars.

As a final example of the time-dilation effect, which also gives some idea of the energy requirements, it would be rather difficult to surpass a calculation made some years ago by the late Dr. Eugen Sänger. He considered a spaceship *circumnavigating the cosmos*—assuming that this represents a distance of ten billion light-years. If the ship could achieve 99.999,999,999,999,999,996 per cent of the velocity of light, the crew would imagine that the journey had lasted thirty-three years—yet ten billion years would have elapsed before they returned to Earth (if it still existed, and they could find it). Since this feat would require the complete conversion into energy of a mass approaching that of the Moon, Sänger decided that this far surpassed the limits of the technically feasible.

Of course, he may be right. But because now we know that there are energy sources in the universe which appear to be turning Moon-sized masses into radiation every ten seconds, it might be best to reserve judgment even on this point.

Everything that has been said in this chapter is based on one assumption, that the Theory of Relativity is correct. However, we have seen how Newton's theory of gravitation, after being unchallenged for three hundred years, was itself modified by Einstein. How can we be sure that this process will not be repeated and that the "light barrier" may not be shattered, as the once formidable "sound barrier" was a generation ago?

This analogy is often drawn, but it is quite invalid. There was never any doubt that one could travel faster than sound, given sufficient energy: rifle bullets and artillery shells had been doing it for years. (In fact, manmade objects first broke the sound barrier at least 10,000 years ago, though very few people would guess how. Think it over before you look at the footnote.*)

During the last half century, however, the equations of relativity have stood up to every test that can be applied, and billions of dollars' worth of engineering have been based upon them. The giant accelerators that speed atomic particles up to almost the velocity of light simply would not work unless

---

*The crack of a whip is a sonic bang.

Einstein's formulas were obeyed to as many decimal places as can be measured.

Nevertheless, there is a faint possibility that even this apparently insuperable barrier may be breached and that we may be able to signal—conceivably, even travel—faster than light, with all that this implies. And we might do it *without* violating the Theory of Relativity.

I am indebted to Professor Gerald Feinberg of Columbia University for these ideas, which are taken (I hope accurately) from his stimulating paper "On the Possibility of Faster Than Light Particles." Professor Feinberg makes a point which is usually overlooked: the Theory of Relativity does *not* say that nothing can travel faster than light. It says that nothing can travel *at the speed of light*; there is a big difference, and it may be an important one. As Professor Feinberg puts it, the speed of light is a limiting velocity, but a limit has two sides. One can imagine particles or other entities which can travel *only* faster than light; there might even be a whole universe on the other side of the light barrier, though please do not ask me to explain precisely what is meant by this phrase.

It may be argued that even if this were true, it could never be proved and would be of no practical importance. Since we cannot travel *at* the speed of light, it seems obvious that we can never travel any faster.

But this is taking an old-fashioned, pre-twentieth-century view of the universe. Modern physics is full of jumps from one condition of energy or velocity (quantum state) to another *without* passing through the intermediate values. There are electronic devices on the market now which depend on this effect— the tunnel diode, for example, in which electrons "tunnel" from one side of an electrical barrier to the other without going through it. Maybe we can do the same sort of thing at the velocity of light.

I am well aware that this is metaphysics rather than physics; so are even more *outré* ideas like shortcuts through higher dimensions—the "space-warps" so useful to science-fiction writers. But we have been wrong so many times in the past when attempting to set limits to technology that it would be well to keep an open mind, even about surpassing the speed of light.

J. B. S. Haldane once remarked: "The universe is not only queerer than we imagine—it is queerer than we *can* imagine." Certainly no one could have imagined the time-dilation effect; who can guess what strange roads there may yet be on which we may travel to the stars?

29. WHERE'S EVERYBODY?

Any reader who has followed the argument of the last few chapters will note how skillfully I have managed to paint myself into a corner. If it is true that the universe is full of intelligent races and that physical travel between the stars is possible, why are we still alone?

This question has been asked many times and has received many answers. It may well be that the sheer extent of the universe—in time as well as in space—is sufficient explanation.

Even in the densest star clouds at the heart of the Milky Way, each of the stars in those closely packed fields is separated from its neighbors by distances of several light-years. To travel from one side of even one group of stars to the other, even at the speed of light, would take centuries; the examination of every star and planetary system shown here might occupy fleets of spaceships for millennia. It seems probable that even if the Galaxy is full of advanced civilizations, we could not expect our own Solar System to be visited except at very rare intervals.

The situation would hardly be affected even if the speed of light were not a limiting factor. A man may walk the length of a beach in a few minutes, but how long would it take him to examine every grain of sand upon it? The problem of surveying the universe is of a similar magnitude, and this is only considering its extension in *space*.

To look at its duration in time, imagine that the height of the Empire State Building represents the age of the Galaxy; on this scale, an inch is about a million years, and each of the 102 floors represents 150 million years.

The Earth was formed somewhere about the seventieth floor; the first traces of life appear around the eightieth. Yet almost all the familiar evolutionary sequence—the rise and fall of the great reptiles, the triumph of the mammals, the discovery of tools—takes place on the very topmost floor.

And man? His entire history, back to the building of the pyramids, spans the thickness of the paint on the ceiling of the 102nd floor.

How many civilizations may have arisen, flourished for millions of years (several inches) on the 102 floors that lie below us, and then vanished before the onslaught of time? And how unlikely that there is, at this moment, even *one* society in the entire universe poised just where we are, at the beginning of our atomic age, and dreaming of the conquest of space! It is far more probable that any cultures now existing are so many millions of years ahead of us that our activities would not be of the slightest interest to them. We flatter ourselves if we expect visitors.

But perhaps we are being flattered. Reluctant though I am to get involved in the subject, it would be arrant cowardice on my part not to say something about UFO's, or flying saucers; whether their explanation is psychological or physical, they constitute one of the most remarkable phenomena of modern times. Unfortunately, it has become extraordinarily difficult to arrive at the truth in this matter; seldom has any subject been so invested with fraud, hysteria, credulity, religious mania, incompetence, and most of the other unflattering human characteristics.

Much of the trouble arises from the fact that the sky presents an almost endless variety of peculiar sights and objects, only a few of which are likely to be encountered by one person in a lifetime. And when this does happen, he may be misled into thinking that he has seen something extraordinary—instead of merely unfamiliar.

Let me give an example that may seem a little farfetched but that illustrates my point perfectly. Suppose you are completely ignorant of meteorological phenomena and live in a desert country where it never rains. Then one day you step out of doors—to see a huge, semicircular arch spanning half the sky. It is so geometrically perfect that it *must* be artificial— yet it is obviously miles across and is beautifully colored in red, orange, yellow, green, blue....

To most of us a rainbow is so familiar that it no longer causes the least surprise, and unlike our ancestors, we do not need supernatural explanations for it. Reason has told us what it is; there would be many fewer UFO's around today if reason, or even elementary common sense, were in better supply.

For a long time my own answer to questioners on this agitated subject was: "If you've never seen a UFO, you're not very observant. And if you've seen as many as *I* have, you won't believe in them." Over the last thirty years, in fact, I have encountered at least ten aerial phenomena that would have fooled almost anybody, and would have left believers in a state of rapturous euphoria.

In all but one case I was able to dispose of them without difficulty. The tenth was much more stubborn; several discussions with the Air Force and some hard work by the Hayden Planetarium computer were needed to exorcise it. But it taught me more than all the others: I learned the hard way that any witness, no matter how skeptical and scientific he considers himself to be, can misinterpret the evidence of his own eyes.

The night sky, in particular, is now so crowded with optical apparitions—meteors, satellites, mirages, met balloons, jet exhausts, high-flying birds (unbelievably, perhaps the most convincing of all)—that I no longer take seriously anything I see there myself, still less anything reported by someone else. The most genuine of UFO's from outer space could never be unambiguously identified among all the visual junk now wandering overhead.

What completely killed my interest in *nighttime* UFO's was the discovery of this report by a British astronomer, Walter Maunder, published in the May, 1916, issue of the Royal Astronomical Society's journal *The Observatory*, thirty years before the phrase "flying saucer" was invented. And Maunder was describing something that he had witnessed thirty-four years earlier still, in November, 1882, when he was standing on the roof of the Greenwich Observatory, looking across London. Soon after sunset:

A great circular disc of greenish light suddenly appeared low down in the East-North-East, as though it had just risen, and moved across the sky, as smoothly and steadily as the sun, Moon, stars and planets move, but nearly a thousand times more quickly. The circularity of its shape was merely the effect of foreshortening, for as it moved it lengthened out . . . when it passed just above the Moon its form was almost that of a very elongated ellipse, and various observers spoke of it as "cigar-shaped" "like a torpedo" . . . had the incident occurred a third of a century later, beyond doubt everyone would have selected the same simile—it would have been "just like a Zeppelin."

And today, of course, it would be "just like a rocket."

The thing that Maunder and thousands of other witnesses all over Europe saw on that night was part of a great auroral display. Of that explanation there is no possible doubt; the apparently solid object disintegrated later, its glow was analyzed by the spectroscope and gave the characteristic auroral lines, and triangulation showed that it was at least 50 miles long and at an altitude of over 100 miles. Some freak of the Earth's magnetic field had briefly focused beams of solar electrons into this strange shape. I find this much more incredible than any mere visiting spaceship, but the evidence is beyond dispute.

Auroral displays are a form of electrical discharge in the upper atmosphere, and their theory is now fairly well understood. This is not true of the extraordinary phenomenon known as ball lightning, and in 1959 I suggested that this (or something analogous to it) may be responsible for some UFO sightings.* This theory has recently been revived, but it can account for only a few cases.

There is evidence that ball lightning is more common at high altitudes than at sea level, and Professor J. S. Haldane is said to have encountered it when he was studying low-pressure physiology. So I once asked his much more famous son: "Is it true, Professor, that your father did some work on ball lightning when he was experimenting at the top of Pike's Peak?" "No," said J. B. S., "ball lightning did some work on my

*See the essay "Things in the Sky," reprinted in *The Challenge of the Spaceship*, which also gives an account of my own UFO sightings up to 1959.

father." That was all the information I could get.

But when all possible conceivable and even unlikely explanations are taken into account, there remains a hard core of UFO sightings in which either some solid artifact of a very advanced technology has been observed, or there has been some downright lying and/or massive hallucinating. In most of these cases there can be very little doubt that fraud or self-delusion is the answer; for a hilarious example, see Carl Sagan's account of the criminal trial of "Helmut Winckler" (Shklovskii and Sagan: *Intelligent Life in the Universe*, Chapter 2). Herr Winckler has encountered some Saturnians who happened to be speaking Hochdeutsch (as Saturnians will) and used the information they gave him to extract money from those ladies of an all-too-certain age who seem peculiarly addicted to sauceritis. Yet even in the case of this blatant fraud, Dr. Sagan could not decide to what extent Winckler believed his own concoctions; how much more difficult it is, therefore, to deal with those reports where apparently sincere and educated people, who have nothing to gain and a good deal to lose, tell of their meetings with extraterrestrials. In many cases there are obvious psychological explanations which account both for the incidents themselves and for the avidity with which thousands of frustrated, worried, or unstable believers accept their truth.

Nevertheless, when all this sad rubbish has been rejected, there still remains a tiny residue of reports, some of them backed by photographs, which are very difficult to explain. This is why many people were relieved when, in 1966, the United States Air Force called in an independent scientific team, headed by Dr. Edward Condon, to investigate the better-authenticated sightings. Perhaps this should have been done a long time ago.

The theory that the "genuine" UFO's are visitors from space, though it must be taken quite seriously, involves difficulties that make it very hard to accept. If this explanation is correct, one would have thought that it would have been established beyond any doubt, years ago. The skies are now scanned night and day by radar and optical networks that can detect a beachball as far away as the Moon. (It is literally true that some radars can track orbiting nuts and bolts.) Tens of thousands of amateur astronomers search the heavens for comets and novae, yet it is rare indeed for these skilled observers to report an unknown. They *see* plenty of strange things, but their scientific background quickly leads to an identification; they don't go rushing off to the local paper at the first glimpse of a fuzzy light in the sky.

It would be a rash man who would predict the eventual outcome of the UFO furor. Later generations may look upon it much as we now regard the various religious manias of the Middle Ages or the "miracles" which even today crop up in backward communities (*vide* Fellini's *La Dolce Vita*). My own feeling—it is nothing so definite as a belief—is that the spaceship explanation is a little too obvious and simpleminded. It is just possible that UFO's may turn out to be something *really* surprising, not merely humdrum visitors from other planets.

And having already said much more than I intended to, let me make one other point. After twenty years of the wretched things, I am bored to death with UFO's. Any letters on the subject will not be forwarded by my publishers. If forwarded, they will not be read. And if read, they will not be answered.

The laws of mathematical probability suggest that for evidence of extraterrestrials we must look much more deeply into space and time than at our own age and our own planet. In addition to the search for interstellar signals, there are two other possibilities.

First there is the record of the past. Visitors from space may have landed on our planet dozens—hundreds—of times during the long, empty ages while Man was still a dream of the distant future. Indeed, they could have landed on 90 per cent of the Earth as little as two or three hundred years ago, and we would never have heard of it. If one searches through old newspapers, one can find large numbers of curious incidents that could easily be interpreted as visitations from space. That stimulating and eccentric writer Charles Fort made a collection of such occurrences in his book *LO!*, and one is inclined to give them more weight than any comparable modern reports, for the simple reason that they long predate current interest in space travel.

Going further back in time, it has been suggested that some of the legends and myths of prehistory, perhaps even the weird entities of many religions—look at the marvelous pantheon of Hindu gods—may have been inspired by glimpses of beings from other worlds. Shklovskii and Sagan give several striking examples in *Intelligent Life in the Universe* and reproduce some Babylonian seals that are, to say the least, stimulating material for such discussions.

Unfortunately, indirect evidence can never be conclusive; the myth-making abilities of the human mind appear to be virtually limitless. Only some artifact—a derelict spaceship, a fossilized radio—would be good enough to establish a case; and even then it might be difficult to eliminate the possibility that some advanced terrestrial culture was not responsible, though of course this would be almost as exciting and important.

The chances of such a discovery on this planet are remote indeed. Weather, war, the ravages of time—these would combine to destroy all but the most adamant of relics. Anything made of metal would certainly be broken up for tools or weapons; perhaps the only hope of such a find lies in the vast new realm of underwater archaeology. What secrets may be lying in the seas that cover two-thirds of the world! Were it not for the Antikythera wreck salvaged in 1900, we should never have known that the Greeks had constructed highly sophisticated astronomical computers in the first century B.C.* On land the valuable bronze of this mechanism would have been melted down and reshaped over and over again during the last two thousand years. The ocean bed is a time capsule whose treasures we have only just begun to recover.

The Moon and planets, when we reach them, may provide even better opportunities. On airless satellites, particularly in caves protected from meteoric bombardment, even the most fragile objects would be preserved unchanged for millions of years. The abandoned debris of interstellar expeditions, perhaps even scientific instruments deliberately left behind to monitor and report the progress of events in the Solar System—these are some of the things we may find when our own explorations begin. Remember the shock that Robinson Crusoe received

---

*See D. J. de S. Price, "An Ancient Greek Computer," *Scientific American*, June, 1959.

when he walked along his lonely beach. We may yet discover that ours are not the first footprints on the Moon.

In the long run, the prospect of meeting other forms of intelligence is perhaps the most exciting of all the possibilities revealed by astronautics. Whether or not man is alone in the universe is one of the supreme questions of philosophy. It is difficult to imagine that anyone could fail to be interested in knowing the answer—and only through space travel can we be sure of obtaining it.

We have seen that there is little likelihood of encountering intelligence elsewhere in the Solar System. That contact may have to wait for the day, perhaps ages hence, when we can reach the stars. But sooner or later it must come.

There have been many portrayals in literature of these fateful meetings. Most science-fiction writers, with sad lack of imagination, have used them as an excuse for stories of conflict and violence indistinguishable from those which stain the pages of our own history. Such an attitude shows a complete misunderstanding of the factors involved.

It has already been pointed out that ours must be one of the youngest cultures in the universe. If ships from Earth ever set out to conquer other worlds, they may find themselves, at the end of their journeys, in the position of painted war canoes drawing slowly into New York harbor.

What, then, if we ever encounter races which are scientifically advanced yet malevolent—the stock villains, in fact, of that type of fiction neatly categorized as "space opera"? In that event, astronautics might well open a Pandora's Box which could destroy humanity.

This prospect, though it cannot be ruled out, appears highly improbable. It seems unlikely that any culture can advance, for more than a few centuries at a time, on a technological front alone. Morals and ethics must not lag behind science; otherwise (as our own recent history has shown) the social system will breed poisons which will cause its certain destruction. With superhuman knowledge there must go equally great compassion and tolerance. When we meet our superiors among the stars, we need have nothing to fear save our own shortcomings.

Just how great these are is something we seldom stop to

consider. Our impressions of reality are determined, far more than we imagine, by the senses through which we make contact with the external world. How utterly different our philosophies would have been had Nature economized with us, as she has done with other creatures, and given us eyes incapable of seeing the stars. Yet how pitiably limited are the eyes we do possess, turned as they are to but a single octave in the spectrum. The world in which we live is drenched with invisible radiations, from the radio waves which we have so recently discovered coming from Sun and stars to the cosmic rays whose origin is still one of the prime mysteries of modern physics. These things we have discovered within the last generation, and we cannot guess what still lies beneath the threshold of the senses, though recent discoveries in paranormal psychology hint that the search may be only beginning.

The races of other worlds will have senses and philosophies very different from our own. To recall Plato's famous analogy, we are prisoners in a cave, gathering our impressions of the outside world from shadows thrown upon the walls. We may never escape to reach that outer reality, but one day we may hope to reach other prisoners in adjoining caves, where we may learn far more than we could ever do by our own unaided efforts.

Somewhere on that journey we may at last learn what purpose, if any, life plays in the universe of matter; certainly we can never learn it on this Earth alone. Among the stars lies the proper study of mankind; Pope's aphorism gave only part of the truth, for the proper study of mankind is not merely Man, but Intelligence.

30. CONCERNING MEANS AND ENDS

Ah who shall soothe these feverish children?
Who justify these restless explorations?
WALT WHITMAN—*Passage to India*

Having ranged, in imagination at least, throughout the universe, let us now come back to Earth for final summing-up of the position of astronautics today. Hitherto we have been concerned with purely scientific questions; now it is time to take the wider view.

Even its most enthusiastic supporters do not deny that the exploration of the Solar System is going to be a very difficult, dangerous, and expensive task. The difficulties must not, however, be exaggerated, for the steadily rising tide of technical knowledge has a way of obliterating obstacles so effectively that what seemed impossible to one generation becomes elementary to the next. Once again the history of aeronautics provides a useful parallel. If the Wright brothers had ever sat down and considered just what would be needed to run a world air-transport system, they would have been appalled at the total requirements, despite the fact that these could not have included all the radio and radar aids which were undreamed of sixty years ago. Yet all these things, and the vast new industries and the armies of technicians that lie behind them, have now become so much a part of our lives that we scarcely ever realize their presence.

The enterprise and skill and resolution that have made our

modern world will be sufficient to achieve all that has been described in this book, as well as much that still lies beyond the reach of any imagination today. Given a sufficiently powerful motive, there seems no limit to what the human race can do; history is full of examples, from the pyramids to the Manhattan Project, of achievements whose difficulty and magnitude were so great that very few people would have considered them possible.

The important factor is, of course, the motive. The pyramids were built through the power of religion, the Manhattan Project under the pressure of war. What will be the motives which will drive men out into space and send them to worlds most of which are so fiercely hostile to human life?

So far, those motives have been largely political—or ideological—arising from conditions which one hopes will not be permanent. Spacefaring, if it is to continue, needs a more stable basis than national pride.

The suggestion has sometimes been made that the increasing pressure of population may also bring about the conquest of the planets. There might be something in this argument if the other planets could be colonized as they stand, but we have seen that the reverse is the case. For a long time to come, it is obvious that, if sheer *lebensraum* is what is needed, it would be much simpler and more profitable to exploit the undeveloped regions of this Earth. It would be far easier to make the Antarctic bloom like the rose than to establish large, self-supporting colonies on such worlds as Mars, Ganymede, or Titan. Yet one day the waste places of our world will be brought to life, and when this happens, astronautics will have played a major role in the achievement through the orbital weather stations and, perhaps, direct climatic control by the use of orbiting space mirrors. When this has happened—indeed, long before—men will be looking hungrily at the planets, and their large-scale development will have begun.

Whether the population of the rest of the Solar System becomes 10 million or 10,000 million is not, fundamentally, what is important. There are already far too many people on *this* planet, by whatever standards one judges the matter. It would be no cause for boasting if, after some centuries of prodigious technical achievement, we enable ten times the present human population to exist on a dozen worlds.

Only little minds are impressed by size and number. The importance of planetary colonization will lie in the variety and diversity of cultures which it will make possible—cultures as different in some respects as those of the Eskimo and the Pacific islanders. They will, of course, have one thing in common, for they will all be based on a very advanced technology. Yet, though the interior of a colony on Pluto might be just like that of one on Mercury, the different external environments would inevitably shape the minds and outlooks of the inhabitants. It will be fascinating to see what effects this will have on human character, thought, and artistic creativeness.

These things are the great imponderables of astronautics; in the long run they may be of far more importance than its purely material benefits, considerable though these will undoubtedly be. This has proved true in the past with many great scientific achievements. Copernican astronomy, Darwin's theory of evolution, Freudian psychology—the effect of these on human thought far outweighed their immediate practical results.

We may expect the same of astronautics. With the expansion of the world's mental horizons may come one of the greatest outbursts of creative activity ever known. The parallel with the Renaissance, with its great flowering of the arts and sciences, is very suggestive. "In human records," wrote the anthropologist J. D. Unwin, "there is no trace of any display of productive energy which has not been preceded by a display of expansive energy. Although the two kinds of energy must be carefully distinguished, in the past they have been . . . united in the sense that one has developed out of the other." Unwin continues with this quotation from Sir James Frazer: "Intellectual progress, which reveals itself in the growth of art and science . . . receives an immense impetus from conquest and empire." Interplanetary travel is now the only form of "conquest and empire" compatible with civilization.

It has often been said—and though it is becoming platitudinous, it is nonetheless true—that only through space flight can mankind find a permanent outlet for its aggressive and pioneering instincts. The desire to reach the planets is only an extension of the desire to see what is over the next hill, or

Beyond that last blue mountain barred with snow
Across that angry or that glittering sea.

Perhaps one day men will no longer be interested in the unknown, no longer tantalized by mystery. This is possible, but when man loses his curiosity, one feels he will have lost most of the other things that make him human. The long literary tradition of the space-travel story shows how deeply this idea is rooted in man's nature; even if not a single good "scientific" reason existed for going to the planets, he would still want to go there, just the same.

In fact, as we have seen, the advent of space travel will produce an expansion of scientific knowledge perhaps unparalleled in history. Now, there are a good many people who think that we have already learned more than enough about the universe in which we live. There are others (including perhaps most scientists) who adopt the noncommittal viewpoint that knowledge is neither good nor bad and that these adjectives are only applicable to its uses.

Yet, knowledge surely is always desirable, and in that sense good; only insufficient knowledge or ignorance can be bad. And worst of all is to be ignorant of one's ignorance. We all know the narrow, limited type of mind which is interested in nothing beyond its town or village and bases its judgments on these parochial standards. We are slowly—perhaps too slowly—evolving from that mentality toward a world outlook. Few things will do more to accelerate that evolution than the conquest of space. It is not easy to see how the more extreme forms of nationalism can long survive when men have seen the Earth as a pale crescent dwindling against the stars, until at last they look for it in vain.

Although man has occupied the greater part of the habitable globe for thousands of years, until only five centuries ago he lived—psychologically—not in one world but in many. Each of the great cultures in the belt from Britain to Japan was insulated from its neighbors by geography or deliberate choice; each was convinced that it alone represented the flower of civilization and that all else was barbarism.

The "unification of the world," to use Toynbee's somewhat

optimistic phrase, became possible only when the sailing ship and the arts of navigation were developed sufficiently to replace the difficult overland routes by the easier sea passages. The result was the great age of exploration, whose physical climax was the discovery of the Americas and whose supreme intellectual achievement was the liberation of the human spirit. Perhaps no better symbol of the questing mind of Renaissance man could be found than the lonely ship sailing steadfastly toward new horizons, until east and west had merged at last and the circumnavigation of the globe had been achieved.

First by land, then by sea, man grew to know his planet; but its final conquest was to lie in a third element, and by means beyond the imagination of almost all men who had ever lived before the twentieth century. The swiftness with which mankind has lifted its commerce and its wars into the air has surpassed the wildest dreams. Through this mastery the last unknown lands have been opened up; over the road along which Alexander burnt out his life, the businessmen and civil servants now pass in comfort in a matter of hours.

The victory has been complete, yet in the winning it has turned to ashes. Every age but ours has had its El Dorado, its Happy Isles, or its Northwest Passage to lure the adventurous into the unknown. A lifetime ago men could still dream of what might lie at the poles, but now the North Pole is the crossroads of the world. We may try to console ourselves with the thought that even if Earth has no new horizons, there are no bounds to the endless frontier of science. Yet it may be doubted if this is enough, for only very sophisticated minds are satisfied with purely intellectual adventures.

The importance of exploration does not lie merely in the opportunities it gives to the adolescent (but not-to-be-despised) desires for excitement and variety. It is no mere accident that the age of Columbus was also the age of Leonardo, or that Sir Walter Raleigh was a contemporary of Shakespeare and Galileo. Some of these men combined in themselves the "productive and expansive energies" of which Unwin spoke. But today all possibility of expansion on Earth itself has practically ceased.

The thought is a somber one. Even if it survives the hazards of war, our culture is proceeding under a momentum which must be exhausted in the foreseeable future. Fabre once described how he linked the two ends of a chain of marching caterpillars so that they circled endlessly in a closed loop. Even if we avoid all other disasters, this could typify humanity's eventual fate when the impetus of the last few centuries has reached its peak and died away. For a closed culture, though it may endure for centuries, is inherently unstable. It may decay quietly and crumble into ruin, or it may be disrupted violently by internal conflicts. Space travel is a necessary, though not in itself a sufficient, way of escape from this predicament.

It is now 400 years since Copernicus destroyed medieval cosmology and dethroned the Earth from the center of creation. Shattering though the repercussions of that fall were in the fields of science and philosophy, they scarcely touched the ordinary man. To him this planet is still the whole of the universe; he knows that other worlds exist, but the knowledge does not affect his life and therefore has little real meaning to him.

All this will be changed before the next century is far advanced. Into a few decades may be compressed more profound alterations in our world picture than occurred during the whole of the Renaissance and the age of discovery that followed. To our children the Moon may become what the Americas were 400 years ago—a world of unknown danger, promise, and opportunity. No longer will Mars and Venus be merely the names of wandering lights seldom glimpsed by the dwellers in cities. They will be more familiar than ever they were to those eastern watchers who first marked their movements, for they will be the new frontiers of the human mind.

Those new frontiers are urgently needed. The crossing of space—even though only a handful of men take part in it— may do much to reduce the tensions of our age by turning men's minds outward and away from their tribal conflicts. It may well be that only by acquiring this new sense of boundless frontiers will the world break free from the ancient cycle of war and peace.

No doubt there are many who, while agreeing that these things are possible, will shrink from them in horror, hoping that they will never come to pass. They remember Pascal's terror of the silent spaces between the stars and are overwhelmed by the nightmare immensities which Victorian as-

tronomers were so fond of evoking. Such an outlook is somewhat
naïve, for the meaningless millions of miles between the Sun
and its outermost planets are no more, and no less, impressive
than the vertiginous gulf lying between the electron and the
atomic nucleus. Mere distance is nothing; only the time that is
needed to span it has any meaning. Our spacecraft now reach
the Moon in less time than a stagecoach once took to travel
the length of England. When the atomic drive is reasonably
efficient, the nearer planets would be only a few weeks from
Earth, and so will seem scarcely more remote than are the
antipodes today.

It is fascinating, however premature, to try to imagine the
pattern of events when the Solar System is opened up to mankind. In the footsteps of the first explorers will follow the
scientists and engineers, shaping strange environments with
technologies as yet unborn. Later will come the colonists, lay-
ing the foundations of cultures which in time may surpass those
of the mother world. The torch of civilization has dropped from
failing fingers too often before for us to imagine that it will
never be handed on again.

We must not let our pride in our achievements blind us to
the lessons of history. Over the first cities of mankind, the
desert sands now lie centuries deep. Could the builders of Ur
and Babylon—once the wonders of the world—have pictured
London or New York? Nor can we imagine the citadels that
our descendants may one day build beneath the blistering sun
of Mercury or under the stars of the cold Plutonian wastes.
And beyond the planets, though ages still ahead of us in time,
lies the unknown and infinite promise of the stellar universe.

There will, it is true, be danger in space, as there has
always been on the oceans or in the air. Some of these dangers
we may guess; others we shall not know until we meet them.
Nature is no friend of man's, and the most that he can hope
for is her neutrality. But if he meets destruction, it will be at
his own hands and according to a familiar pattern.

The dream of flight was one of the noblest and one of the
most disinterested of all man's aspirations. Yet it led in the
end to that B-29 driving in passionless beauty through August
skies toward the city whose name it was to sear into the conscience of the world. Already there has been half-serious talk

concerning the use of the Moon for military bases and launching sites. The crossing of space may thus bring, not a new Renaissance, but the final catastrophe that haunts our generation.

That is the danger, the dark thundercloud that threatens the promise of the dawn. The rocket has already been the instrument of evil, and may be so again. But there is no way back into the past; the choice, as Wells once said, is the universe—or nothing. Though men and civilizations may yearn for rest, for the dream of the lotus-eaters, that is a desire that merges imperceptibly into death. The challenge of the great spaces between the worlds is a stupendous one; but if we fail to meet it, the story of our race will be drawing to its close. Humanity will have turned its back upon the still untrodden heights and will be descending the long slope that stretches, across a billion years of time, down to the shores of the primeval sea.

BIBLIOGRAPHY

The literature of astronautics is now enormous, and only a few of the most recent or most readily available works are listed here.

The standard history and general introduction is Willy Ley's *Rockets, Missiles, and Space Travel* (New York: Viking, 1961). Also authoritative and lavishly illustrated is *History of Rocketry and Space Travel*, by Wernher von Braun and Frederick I. Ordway (New York: Crowell, 1967). *The Coming of the Space Age*, edited by Arthur C. Clarke (Des Moines: Meredith, 1967), contains a good deal of historical material, along with autobiographies of Tsiolkovsky, Goddard, and Oberth.

The annual NASA volumes, *Astronautics and Aeronautics*, are a valuable listing of each year's activities in space. The NASA Historical Series (Washington, D.C.: Government Printing Office) will provide a detailed record of the United States space program as it proceeds. See, for example, *This New Ocean: A History of Project Mercury*, by Loyd S. Swenson, James M. Grimwood, and Charles C. Alexander (1966).

On the popular level are *Careers in Astronautics and Rocketry*, by Carsbie C. Adams, Wernher von Braun, and Frederick I. Ordway (New York: McGraw-Hill, 1962); *Man and Space*, by Arthur C. Clarke (New York: LIFE Science Library, 1964); *Beyond the Solar System*, by Willy Ley and Chesley Bonestell (New York: Viking, 1964); *We Are Not Alone*, by Walter Sullivan (New York: McGraw-Hill, 1964).

More technical but entirely understandable to the nonspecialist and great fun to read is *Intelligent Life in the Universe*, by I. S. Shklovskii and Carl Sagan (San Francisco: Holden-Day, 1966). Easily understood by anyone with high-school mathematics is the stimulating *Thrust into Space*, by Maxwell W. Hunter (New York: Holt, Rinehart and Winston, 1965). This is one of a series of excellent, authoritative, and inexpensive books on astronautics in the Holt Library of Science. Other titles are *Manned Space Flight*, by Max Faget; *A History of Space Flight*, by Eugene M. Emme (the NASA historian) and *Communications in Space*, by Leonard Jaffe (all four published in 1965). A specialized and quite technical but very useful book is *Interstellar Communication*, edited by A. G. W. Cameron (New York: W. A. Benjamin, 1963). Perhaps the most valuable single reference book for the serious student is Samuel Glasstone's *Sourcebook of the Space Sciences* (Princeton: Van Nostrand, 1965), which contains in compact form all the basic scientific information about astronautics *and* astronomy.

To keep in touch with current activities in more detail than is reported by the press, the various specialized periodicals are essential. These include *Aviation Week*, *Aerospace Technology* (formerly *Missiles and Rockets*), and *Space World*. *Sky and Telescope*, though astronomically oriented, contains a great deal of material on space. In the United Kingdom the magazine *Spaceflight* is published by the British Interplanetary Society (12, Bessborough Gardens, London, S.W. 1).

INDEX

FRANK HERBERT's
11 MILLION-COPY BESTSELLING

DUNE

MASTERWORKS

____ 08002-1	DUNE	$3.95
____ 07498-6	DUNE MESSIAH	$3.95
____ 07499-4	CHILDREN OF DUNE	$3.95
____ 08003-X	GOD EMPEROR OF DUNE	$3.95

Prices may be slightly higher in Canada.

- -

Available at your local bookstore or return this form to:

 BERKLEY
Book Mailing Service
P.O. Box 690, Rockville Centre, NY 11571

Please send me the titles checked above. I enclose _____. Include 75¢ for postage
and handling if one book is ordered; 25¢ per book for two or more not to exceed
$1.75. California, Illinois, New York and Tennessee residents please add sales tax.

NAME_____

ADDRESS_____

CITY_____STATE/ZIP_____

(allow six weeks for delivery)   178

Bestselling Books

☐ 21889-X	**EXPANDED UNIVERSE,** Robert A. Heinlein	$3.95
☐ 47809-3	**THE LEFT HAND OF DARKNESS,** Ursula K. Le Guin	$2.95
☐ 48519-7	**LIVE LONGER NOW,** Jon N. Leonard, J. L. Hofer and N. Pritikin	$3.50
☐ 80583-3	**THIEVES' WORLD,** Robert Lynn Asprin, Ed.	$2.95
☐ 02884-5	**ARCHANGEL,** Gerald Seymour	$3.50
☐ 08953-4	**THE BUTCHER'S BOY,** Thomas Perry	$3.50
☐ 78036-9	**STAR COLONY,** Keith Laumer	$2.95
☐ 11503-9	**A COLD BLUE LIGHT,** Marvin Kay and Parke Godwin	$3.50
☐ 24098-4	**THE FLOATING ADMIRAL,** Agatha Christie, Dorothy Sayers, G.K. Chesterton & others	$2.95
☐ 21601-3	**ESCAPE VELOCITY,** Christopher Stasheff	$2.95
☐ 37155-8	**INVASION: EARTH,** Harry Harrison	$2.75

Prices may be slightly higher in Canada.

Available at your local bookstore or return this form to:

 CHARTER BOOKS
Book Mailing Service
P.O. Box 690, Rockville Centre, NY 11571

Please send me the titles checked above. I enclose _____. Include 75¢ for postage and handling if one book is ordered; 25¢ per book for two or more not to exceed $1.75. California, Illinois, New York and Tennessee residents please add sales tax.

NAME _____

ADDRESS _____

CITY _____ STATE/ZIP _____

(allow six weeks for delivery)   A-9